ELENA DOLGOPYAT

SOMEONE ELSE'S LIFE

SOMEONE ELSE'S LIFE

by Elena Dolgopyat

First published in Russian as *Чужая жизнь* in 2019

Translated from the Russian by Richard Coombes

Proofreading by Stephen Dalziel

Russian text © Elena Dolgopyat, 2019

Cover image © Max Mendor, 2023

Translation © Richard Coombes, 2023

Introduction © Leonid Yuzefovich, 2019

© 2023, Glagoslav Publications

Book cover and interior book design by Max Mendor

www.glagoslav.com

ISBN: 978-1-80484-018-4
ISBN: 978-1-80484-019-1

First published in English by Glagoslav Publications in May 2023

A catalogue record for this book is available from the British Library.

ELENA DOLGOPYAT

SOMEONE ELSE'S LIFE

TRANSLATED FROM THE RUSSIAN BY RICHARD COOMBES

GLAGOSLAV PUBLICATIONS

CONTENTS

INTRODUCTION

This is intelligent writing. Its simplicity is deceptive, and its apparent artlessness is the product of experience and skill. The author's restraint resonates in us with an unexpected strength of feeling.

Each of Elena Dolgopyat's stories is unique, and could only have been written by her. Each painfully stirs the soul with a sense of the fragility, the evanescence, even, of human existence, in a world that is far from illusory: it is our world, very real, recognisable. Even those stories which contain an element of phantasmagoria reach us not as fantasy, but are somehow elevated to the level of our everyday lives. I cannot tell you about the techniques by which this effect is achieved; I do not know what they are. I suspect that the mystery of the impact of these texts on the reader is contained in something not taught on any writing course.

As someone with long years of schoolteaching experience, I know that if the children start to make a racket while you are talking in class, it is useless to force your voice. There is one of you and many of them; you will not out-shout them. The best way to make them listen to you is to lower your voice. In my view, something similar is happening today in literature. Desperate to be heard, we try to shout more loudly, to out-shout the noise of the world. For most of us, this simply does not work.

Elena Dolgopyat never tries to raise her voice. Her stories have long been appearing in literary journals, and have come out as books; but only in the last few years, it seems, have we begun to understand that in her quiet voice, she is telling us of 'the multicoloured underside of life'. She is telling us of things that matter to us all.

Leonid Yuzefovich

SOMEONE ELSE'S LIFE

LYOSHA

It happened involuntarily, without effort.

The queue was not moving. Lyosha's mother was keeping him close to her, holding him by the co°llar like a tiny tot. People were coming up and asking what was available.

Sausages.

They said not to join the queue.

A kilo, no more.

The shoppers stood patiently, close together. Every so often, someone tried to push in and was met with a hail of foul language.

The queue would stand stock still for a time and then take one small step forward. How many more shuffling steps to the saleswoman in her white bonnet? A thousand? A hundred thousand? Lyosha would have hopped out and measured, but his mother would not let him go; she kept tight hold of him.

'I'm hot,' complained Lyosha.

His mother let go of his collar, and bent down.

In that instant, at the very moment when Lyosha's mother's face came close to his, time stopped. His mother, all the people, all creatures and all objects froze, like in the fairy tale about an enchanted castle that Lyosha had read many times in a slim children's book. The book had a picture of the castle's inhabitants, frozen in a dance. Mind you, any picture shows the world with all its inhabitants frozen.

Lyosha stirred, and realised that for him, time had not stopped. Everyone was in suspension, while Lyosha remained free. He showed no particular surprise. He took what had happened calmly. He stepped away from the queue. Walked along it. Noted that no sounds were audible; even his own footsteps made no sound. No squelching from the black gunge on the floor. He was walking as if in a void.

Lyosha stepped carefully, frightened of startling slumbering time. Frightened of waking it up. The way it might be best to sneak past a dozing lion.

A shiny new coin hung suspended in the air. A five ko-peck piece. Lyosha made out the year: 1972. 1972 had just begun. The shop door was ajar; it had evidently not managed to slam shut behind a chap who had gone purple with cold. The gap was wide enough for Lyosha.

The boy went out into the winter street. Diamond dust glittered in the air. There was a child skating along the icy path, arms flung wide. Lyosha glanced at his face, into his bright, clear eyes, then went on his way. Lyosha knew that the street should lead him to the river. He wanted to have a look at the ice, perhaps even walk across it to the far bank. The other kids said that the wind in the middle of the river was awful, howling, enough to blow you off your feet and drag you all the way to the plywood factory. The factory always smelled of sawn wood–though in this world on pause, Lyosha could not smell anything.

Walking turned out to be easy, weightless. Lyosha observed clouds of steam and cigarette smoke that looked as if they had been captured on photographic plates. The street running down to the river was lined with small one-storey houses. Smoke stood motionless above the chimneys. A stream of ice like sparkling jewels was beating from a standpipe into a bucket. A lady was using a hook to hold the bucket, her feet planted firmly. Felt boots with sleek black galoshes, and a grey woollen jacket from under which a long dark skirt peeped out. Lyosha walked round the lady looking at her from all sides, like a statue in a museum. He marvelled at her ample rear, at her legs as strong as concrete piles, at the hairy black mole on her upper lip.

She had screwed up her face; it looked as if she had been about to sneeze, but had not had time to do so.

Here I am, thought Lyosha suddenly, *walking around and not the slightest bit cold, and not hungry, either.* Yet in the queue he had felt very hungry, especially as the shop had smelled not only of cold and people; there was also the waft of fresh bread, and of the sausages brought in from Moscow to sell.

Now he did not want to do anything else; just look.

Lyosha left the lady and went on his way, lingering now in front of a fluttering sparrow, now in front of a passer-by. He walked out onto the carriageway, stepping out without fear of cars; their snarling was silent, and gone too was the animal smell of petrol, which Lyosha adored.

At the river, behind the sheds, an alleyway opened up, and in it Lyosha saw a small, crooked figure. It was a boy, lying on the snow, his legs tucked up and his hands covering his head, towards which a foot inside a boot as heavy as a stone was flying. Flying, but not reaching its destination; it had stopped in mid-air. The assailant's face was twisted, and his grey army cap with a dent from a cockade had fallen off and was hovering just above the ground.

Lyosha knew both boys. The one lying down was Valya, a fellow fourth year of Lyosha's. His executioner, nicknamed Bull, was an eighth year. He was not so much studying as serving time, as Lyosha's mother would say. Valya did little to draw attention to himself, except that he had a quiet, clear voice. The teacher always had to go right up to him to make out what he was saying. Frozen nearby in the pose of an observer was another acquaintance and classmate of Lyosha's, Petya. And not just an acquaintance and classmate, but his best friend. He was standing with his hands shoved into the pockets of his short coat, observing the beating with a smile.

Lyosha looked in horror at his friend's face. This was Petya! Cheerful, clever, deft, adored Petya! To whom (and no-one else) Lyosha had told his dream about death. Who had taught him to swim that summer. Petya, who knew how to make a blood pact. The best fellow on earth was watching the beating without turning a hair and with visible pleasure.

Lyosha knelt down and looked into poor Valya's face.

Valya's eyes were squeezed shut, his nose bashed and bleeding.

Lyosha thought, *I'll grab the stone boot and give it a yank. The back of Bull's head'll come smacking down onto the ice, and Valya and I'll take off. To the plywood factory, across the ice.*

Lyosha grabbed hold of the boot, and in that very instant came to in the queue. Sounds clattered around him, deafening him. Voices, footsteps, coughing, the door slamming. His mother said, 'Chin up, son. Nearly there.'

She straightened, something distracted her, and Lyosha made a dash for the door.

The alley behind the sheds was already empty. Lyosha could see drops of blood on the trampled snow. He looked around and hesitated, waiting, though he was not sure what for. Then he trudged back towards the shop. His breathing gradually returned to normal.

Back home, his mother said there were no sausages for him. 'I stood there for as long as it took to get my allowance, but you obviously didn't want yours.'

After that, she didn't say another word to him the whole evening. She didn't even look in his direction, as if Lyosha was just an empty space. She cooked a sausage and ate it. Lyosha chomped his way through potatoes and sauerkraut, and sat down to do his homework. Lyubasha, as they called their class mistress, had promised they would have a test the following day. Lyosha felt old, one of life's veterans.

The next day, Valya did not appear at school. Petya arrived with his eye all puffy and told Lyosha about how he had been walking along the alley by the river, thinking his own thoughts, and suddenly seen Bull laying into Valya.

'Obviously I went rushing in to pull him off, and caught a swinging fist. Good thing my uncle had done his army service. One chop on the neck and bam! Bull down. Uncle's promised to teach me some moves. Fighting. You want to join in?'

Realisation dawned on Lyosha, something like: you can't judge an event by an instant, by a thin slice. You can't judge with absolute precision. With certainty. You don't know why someone's face is frozen in a smile. He's looking at you, but maybe not seeing you; he's smiling at a thought of his own, something you know nothing about.

After the fight, Petya had walked Valya home, and Valya had told him that he'd been on his way to get bread, minding his own business, when he'd seen Bull standing by the shed, crying. Valya had quickened his pace but sensed Bull catching up with him. Bull caught up, shoved him in the back, and Valya had fallen.

The bell rang. Lyubasha came in.

The class stood quietly. Lyubasha looked at them with the kind of sadness with which Lyosha's mother sometimes looked at him, as if pitying him in advance for the rest of his life.

Lyubasha lowered herself onto the chair at her teacher's desk, covered her young, round face with her small hands, and sat motionless.

The class, too, stopped. No-one moved a muscle. There was a chalk mark on the sleeve of Lyubasha's cardigan. Lyosha wanted the white streak to disappear; looking at it was uncomfortable. It was all very like the way time had suddenly stopped yesterday. Except that on this occasion Lyosha was frozen in it as well.

No-one could move a muscle; no-one, until Lyubasha took her hands away from her flushed face, and sighed. And then everyone sighed.

The girls clucked, 'Miss, Miss, what's wrong, Miss?'

Lyubasha waved a hand to silence the clucking. She took a delicate white handkerchief from her cardigan pocket and dabbed her eyes and nose.

'You're going to find out anyway. Boris Yevdokimov was found murdered this morning. You can sit down now.'

Boris Yevdokimov was Bull. Was.

The following day, Petya intercepted Lyosha outside school, before lessons started. He said the year eights were going to Bull's funeral. A clapped out old bus was already waiting by the front entrance.

'While they're getting ready, let's walk.'

Lyosha did not ask why. He felt he had to go. Petya likewise, probably. To say farewell, perhaps; or perhaps to clear something up.

Bull lived (once upon a time) on the outskirts, in a village adjoining the town. The boys walked through a neglected park by the Dzerzhinsky factory. They walked along the side of a narrow, ice-covered road, went over, crossed a little frozen stream, and there was the village, already in sight. They walked the whole way in silence.

A white field lay under a violet sky. Lyubasha had brought them here in December. They had cut through the snow with a shovel and looked at the layers. Light, dark, an impregnation of soot and a hard crust of ice meant it had thawed and re-frozen. They'd spotted a yellow trail of urine and giggled. Lyubasha said that by spring this whole snow book that she was teaching them to read would have melted away without a trace.

The clean white field under the dusky sky dazzled their eyes. The boys were approaching the village along a beaten path, and everything seemed age-old: the snow, the path, the wooden houses, the smoke from the stoves, and they themselves, the little people.

'The Krysenkov brothers from Alexandrovka are in our class.'

'Yes, that's right.'

People were loitering outside Bull's house. A red coffin lid leaned against the fence beside a wide-open wicket gate. The boys walked through. The path was broad and swept smooth. The snow glinted. Men were smoking on the steps.

The room was cold, unheated.

Meagre light from a modest window. A mirror hung with a black shawl. On a bare table in the middle of the room, an open coffin, upholstered in red. On a chair beside it, a woman, all in black. Lips pressed together, dry eyes.

The boys timidly approached the coffin from the other side of the table. The body lying in it looked nothing like its old, living self. Bull was dressed in a black ceremonial suit and a white pressed shirt. His heavy black boots gleamed, and smelled of shoe polish. A clock stood on the sideboard. His face was frozen in the cold. Petya touched Lyosha's hand, and the boys quietly backed away from the coffin.

They went outside and stood with the men on the steps, breathing in the bitter smoke.

The old bus pulled up, and its door opened. The year eights got out in silence.

'Let's go home,' Petya decided.

'I'll stay a bit longer,' said Lyosha.

Petya looked at him in surprise, but did not ask why. He shook Lyosha's hand goodbye.

Lyosha stepped down from the porch and loitered nearby. God only knew what he was staying for, what else he wanted to see. Or understand, maybe.

Lyosha waited for the coffin to be carried out of the house, and followed the black, silent crowd.

In the graveyard, men were digging the earth and singing verses Lyosha had never heard before.

'Holy God, Holy and Mighty, Holy and Immortal, have mercy on us.'

There were no priests in the graveyard. A few old women were crossing themselves and crying (Bull's mother was neither crying nor crossing herself), and the men were digging the earth and singing, singing, *'Holy God, Holy and Mighty, Holy and Immortal, have mercy on us.'*

It struck Lyosha as both scary and necessary.

He stayed on for the wake in the now-heated house, listened to the conversations, ate, and even took a sip of vodka.

Bull had been stabbed in the chest on the railway tracks, behind the depot. Snow had covered him during the night.

Bull's mother sat in silence, then suddenly, in a voice low but audible to all, said, 'He departed at the right time, without sin. He was killed. He didn't kill anyone. It is God's mercy.'

'How do you know?' asked one of the women, her voice young. 'How do you know whether he has that sin on his soul or not?'

Bull's mother was silent, thinking.

'I don't know. But I don't know the opposite either.'

She filled a shot to the brim, and drank it down.

Lyosha arrived back home at nightfall. His mother did not reproach him. She offered him something to eat, but he said he was full. He brushed his teeth, had a wash, looked at his wet face in the mirror, and thought that he did not want to die, ever.

SOMEONE ELSE'S LIFE

When his hair grew out, it started to curl and show streaks of red. His wife liked it, but he tried not to let it get that long, and had it cut neatly every fortnight. The thing was that with his hair longer he looked like a particular actor from a TV serial, which had people staring at him in affection, astonishment, adoration. All looks that had nothing to do with him.

He was a polite man, but cold, not especially interested in other people. He looked older or younger than his thirty-five years, depending on the state he was in. He went to work in white, smartly-pressed shirts beneath dark jackets. He was taciturn. He especially disliked talking about politics, religion, the physical make-up of the world and the meaning of life, foreign countries (even if he had visited them), and films (even if he had seen them). He could talk about cars. Or rather, not so much talk as prevent a conversation from completely drying up.

In the summer, his wife was offered a lucrative long-term contract abroad. She arrived home that evening with a mysteriously happy face, and looked at him with darkened, apprehensive eyes, as if she had just fallen in love for the first time in her life. Mikhail could find nothing to say to her except, yes, that's great.

She studied pictures of the country she was going to as if she were off to a fairy tale. She listened to songs; she and Mikhail listened together. She understood what they meant, but he did not, and he felt uncomfortable.

'You'll easily find a job,' his wife tried to reassure him, sensing his anxiety. 'Trust me, specialists like you are needed everywhere. You'll pick up the language, get on top of it, you're clever and musical. A musical ear is important for language. Every language has its own music. I adore the music of this language. I must have lived there in a past life and been happy. I want to breathe its air again. I couldn't have dreamed this would happen.'

Well, what can I tell you. Mikhail held his peace until the time came and he needed to get his paperwork done. Whereupon he confessed that for him going away was like dying, that he was a man of habit; he made a joke about the 'Turkish coast'.

She went away in the autumn.

They let out the flat, and Mikhail went back to his mother, to his old room. His mother still slept on the sofa in the living room, and his sister also had her own room, so they were not tormented by the prospect of a housing crisis. He corresponded with his wife by e-mail. Mikhail noted with surprise that he did not miss her. He did not immediately recognise her in the photos she sent.

He was forgetting her. It was as if a current were carrying her away from him.

Some law–of storytelling, perhaps, or of fate–prescribed that Mikhail could not avoid the fatal resemblance, however hard he tried.

In February he fell seriously ill with the flu, and was in bed for almost a month. When he got up, he saw in the mirror that his curls had grown long, or rather, he saw the actor instead of himself; the actor had brazenly taken his place. Mikhail was still coughing and his legs felt weak, but he shaved, put on warm clothes, and went out. No-one was in a position to stop him; his sister and mother were at work.

Mikhail usually went to the same hairdressing salon, to the same hairdresser. He was used to the man's hands and his manner; he really was a man of habit. Appointments had to be made in advance, but on this occasion Mikhail had not called before setting off. He didn't care who he went to as long as the hated curls were sheared off as soon as possible. They even changed the colour of his eyes. He was already on the bus when his brain nudged him to the realisation that there was a hairdresser's near his home, a stone's throw away.

He was sitting by the window, opposite a young woman. He was looking out of the window and could see her distorted reflection in the glass, above floating lights. He pulled his hat over his eyes, as if he were hiding the actor, pushing him under his hat. He was in a black anorak and old jeans, and in his laddish clothes, and pale and weak from his illness, he seemed younger than his years. He seemed softer.

He rested his head against the glass, and shifted his gaze to the young woman. He studied her slender neck, her dark cheek, the shadow cast by her eyelashes. The thought struck him suddenly that the face would soon be gone. He sensed–how should one put it–the fleetingness of the face. Of this whole being. This existence. The hazel eyes would fade, wrinkles would form at the corners of the lips, the face would age and begin to crumple. There was nothing special in that; nothing lasts forever, but for some reason this face awakened in him more pity than any other. He wanted to reach out his hand to protect it, shelter it, hold it. If he could just find a room, a particular type of room, just one, one single room with a glass wall, where time, by some miracle, had stopped, Mikhail would shut the girl in it and stand the other side of the glass wall and look at her. And he would be calm, and there would be none of this sudden pity, which had him almost in tears.

ELENA DOLGOPYAT

It was his illness speaking, his weakness.

The young woman's hand was resting on a black handbag. He could see a cut on her finger. He tried to imagine her cutting something while she was cooking. Suddenly he met her brown eyes.

'What?' she asked sharply.

Her voice sounded as if it was not hers. She ought to have a different voice, not so icy.

He pulled away from the window, still not lowering his eyes from hers, and pulled off his hat. He wanted the woman to recognise the actor in him. He wanted her to be surprised, confused. He wanted to see embarrassment and timidity in those hazel eyes.

His hair came free and flopped onto his forehead. And she recognised him. But what showed in her eyes was not embarrassment or timidity. Surprise.

She turned back to the window. They were just passing the hairdresser's. Behind the wide display window, a cleaning lady was sweeping up hair of all colours.

The girl could not contain her curiosity, and looked at him again.

He smiled.

She looked at him, her expression serious.

'What happened?' he asked, glancing at her finger. 'You cut yourself?'

She raised her finger and let it fall back.

'Ages ago,' she said.

And smiled. She smiled.

It did not matter to Mikhail that she was not smiling at him.

'I had flu,' he said, 'and lost my voice.'

'That's obvious.'

They looked at each other, silent, smiling. The bus jolted on the tram tracks.

'This is mine,' she said.

He leaped up first and held out his hand. He imagined her saying that she had met a famous actor and that he was, like, wow.

She set off, apparently not noticing that he was trotting along behind her. She stopped suddenly, and looked at him.

'I thought you'd be taller.'

'The screen effect.'

'My house.' She pointed to the prefabricated nine-storey building in front of which they were standing.

'Really good house.'

'Not particularly.'

'It's yours. That makes it really good.'

Her lip curled.

'It's odd that you know my name but I don't know yours. You probably even know where I was born. So you were born ... where ...?'

She burst out laughing, and offered him her hand.

'Goodbye.'

He took her hand in his. He wanted to hold on to it, but her hand slipped out, slipped away. She headed towards the front door. He watched her go.

She punched in the code. He hoped she would look back, smile. But she did not.

The door closed behind her. Mikhail came to, and realised that it was cold. He went into his pocket for his hat, but could not find it. He must have dropped it on the bus.

A young lad was standing by the stall across the street, fixing Mikhail with a hostile stare. Mikhail crossed over to the same side, paying no attention to the lad and straightaway forgetting the way he'd stared.

He headed for the bus stop. He had already forgotten the girl. He wanted to hurry home, back to his own room. Of a sudden, he felt someone's breath right beside him.

The young lad had joined him. Was walking with him, silent. Not dropping back. Mikhail picked up his pace, and the lad matched his stride. When Mikhail stopped a few paces from the glass box where people were waiting for the bus, the lad stopped too.

He turned to Mikhail and asked, 'So what were you talking to her about?'

His eyes were white with hatred.

Mikhail kept quiet. Better not to mess with people like this. Better not to answer, and not to look them in the eye. Under no circumstances.

The bus was approaching.

'Stop. Stop.' The lad blocked Mikhail's way.

'This is my bus.'

The lad grabbed his shoulder.

'Get your hand off.'

'I asked you a question.'

'Piss off.'

'What were you talking about, asshole? To my girlfriend. Uh?'

'Nothing.'

'Shitbag.'

Mikhail tried to wrench the hand off his shoulder.

The bus had already picked up its passengers and was pulling away.

Several passers-by stopped and watched them as they jostled each other, snarling.

The stranger's hand suddenly released Mikhail, and the next thing Mikhail knew he had been punched in the face. Blood gushed from his nose. Mikhail lunged at the lad. The lad was bigger, and grabbed Mikhail by his anorak collar, hauling on it so that Mikhail started choking and wheezing.

'Think you can, eh? Just cos you're on TV you can do what you like, right?'

Mikhail's anorak tugged at his throat, and he wheezed, squirming, trying to break free, to escape. The lad jerked

Mikhail's face close to his own. He reeked of the previous night's booze.

Mikhail lashed out, kicking the lad sharply on the knee. The lad let out a howl, and loosened his grip. Mikhail kicked out again, channelling all his anger. Something crunched, and the lad slumped. Mikhail lunged at him, knocking him down. He fell on top of him, grabbing him by the hair, and started to beat his head against the asphalt, the back of his head against the asphalt. He suddenly noticed that the lad's eyes had gone dim. Lifeless. Lifeless. That's what Mikhail was thinking. Though not when he was running. When he was running, he was not thinking anything.

He ran through the courtyards. Stood, doubled over, in a dark alleyway, choking from running. Wandered quietly, slowly, touching his swollen nose.

He found his key. Dropped it. Crawled around on the tiles looking for it. Pushed it into the keyhole. The key was trembling slightly. Alive in a lifeless hand. Dry heat in his mouth, pain in his temples.

He dragged everything off and threw it all in a heap: trainers, jeans, anorak, sweater, underpants. He turned out his bedside table drawer, sending a pair of scissors jingling to the floor. He shoved his face into the mirror, grabbed his forelock, and cropped it. His big forehead peeked out. His face became strange. He didn't look like anyone else. Not Mikhail, not the actor, no-one. A stranger. With a broken nose. Gingerly, Mikhail touched his nose. It hurt so much he almost cried.

He crawled under the blanket. Hid. Took refuge in sleep. Oblivion.

He woke up to what was either morning or a dark, grey day. A sewing machine was tap-tap-tapping, chattering. It was as if he had woken up in the beautiful past, twenty years previously, when they had still had a machine and his mother sewed. He nodded off to the sound of the sewing.

At dinner, when the three of them were sitting together and he had shaved and Dasha had evened up his hair, Dasha studied him and said he looked like an alien, and but for the broken nose, he would even be handsome. He had made up a story: he had wanted a trim, gone out, and fallen in the street. He'd slipped, hit himself, smashed his nose, and come home with his head spinning. He said he'd woken up once and heard the tap-tap-tap of a sewing machine.

'You didn't wake up,' said his mother. 'You dreamed it.'

'I don't have dreams.'

'Put raspberries in your tea instead of sugar.'

After dinner he went to his room, shut the door, and finally brought himself to turn on his computer. He opened his mail. Deleted the spam. Read his emails carefully. Answered his wife.

Outside, it was snowing quietly. Mikhail looked out at the snow and typed the actor's name into the search engine.

He had been arrested, and charged with murder.

The actor was denying nothing. But he had nothing to say about the fight either. He could not remember. Witnesses to the fight had called an ambulance and the police but were too afraid to chase after him. When he was detained, he was extremely drunk and had a broken nose. The concierge said he often came back drunk, drunk and beaten up, so no surprise there. The actor insisted that he had no idea who the lad was, and could not remember, and that he usually remembered next to nothing when he had sobered up. He said all his drunken days were black days, total washouts. He was planning to get treatment, he said. He needed to finish filming and then book himself into rehab.

The young woman, the unwitting instigator of the tragedy, asserted that the actor was absolutely sober. Her testimony was completely at odds with the general picture. People on the internet thought she was lying for some reason of her own. She wanted to ruin the actor or, conversely, to save him. Suggestions were made that there was something going on between them.

Mikhail read through everything he could lay his hands on, then turned off his computer.

The room was dark. Snow was falling beyond the window, like in a Christmas film. The following day he would have to go to work.

He was hoping witnesses would turn up and testify incontrovertibly that they had seen the actor elsewhere. He was hoping the case would fall apart. But it solidified. The actor made no effort to deny anything. Everyone lamented his talent; they talked about the psychological subtlety that showed through in any role he played, of the gentleness and submissiveness of his character, traits that had caused him to fall under the influence of bad people.

The confrontation aroused no doubt in anyone except the young woman. But everyone considered her testimony to be dubious. Especially as passengers were found from the same bus who insisted that of course the actor was drunk, and the girl could not have failed to notice it. They insisted firmly, with complete certainty.

In some surprising way, the case dovetailed with the actor's fate, with the trajectory of his life. As if it had been predestined. Mikhail comforted himself by deciding that everything would have worked out just like that, that everything had been leading to that point and would have come to it anyway. With or without him. If not this day then the next. He persuaded himself that he had nothing to do with it.

What else was an actor but a ghost, only pretending to be a real person? Such was the notion that came into Mikhail's head, and he found comfort in it.

By mid-spring, new material about the actor had stopped appearing on the internet. The search engine produced everything Mikhail had already read and re-read. Still, every day after dinner he typed in the actor's name and pressed 'enter'. Sometimes the TV ran repeats of serials featuring him, but Mikhail did not watch serials. He did not watch TV at all, not even the news.

He had always dropped off instantly and slept without dreaming. At least, he did not remember any dreams when he woke up. He would wake up, look at his alarm clock, and realise that he had been gone for seven hours, as if those seven hours had been cut out of his life. More precisely, he had been cut out of life for seven hours. Sleep to him had always been non-existence.

After the murder, which he had not committed (as he convinced himself), his night life was turned upside down. Still no dreams. But no sleep either.

He still fell asleep instantly. But after a couple of hours he would suddenly wake up.

Night. A car was going past outside the window; the racket it was making was what had awakened him, he thought. His neighbour was smoking on the balcony, and the smoke from his cigarette was wafting into the room. His head remained clear. An eerie clarity, like an obsession from which there was no escape, no wriggling away.

He lay, eyes open and staring into the darkness. He thought of his past life. Not the past with his wife. That past seemed like a mistake. His whole life now seemed to Mikhail to have been a mistake. One episode alone he remembered as real.

Dark corners in the hallway. Water streaming from a black umbrella. He does not know where to put it. A woman takes the umbrella from him.

Mikhail washes his hands and sees the umbrella folded up and hanging on a hook. Water is dripping from it into the bathtub. Mikhail dries his hands on a towel handed to him, a clean one, freshly taken from the cupboard, it would seem. The woman offers him tea. The computer is working again; he has 'cured' it. Jokingly, she says, 'Come in, doctor, don't be shy.'

And strange though it might seem to him, he is not shy. He drinks the proffered tea with jam. It's not so much that he likes jam as that here, in this kitchen, it seems an excellent supplement to his tea, his mood, his state.

He has no desire at all to leave. Outside the window, in the dark, the rain is lashing down. It seems to Mikhail that he has always been here, in this house, in her life. Always. He had known it before he was properly over the threshold.

They sit in the kitchen and drink tea. A child, most likely a boy, picks up a glass of milk. Of course they have a child. He is seven years old.

The doorbell rings. She goes to answer it, and he hears her saying, 'Hi darling, what rain, still, the computer's fixed, the repair man's in the kitchen, tea with raspberries, Vitya called, he's missing us, still, what do you think?'

So he was a stranger in this kitchen, a guest. But it was a mistake that he was a stranger here. Not right.

Mikhail lay awake staring into the darkness, hearing a car going by downstairs. He imagined the right version: the same flat, the same woman, her warmth, their eternity.

In the dark, the sound of the sewing machine from his childhood also seemed something true, the one right thing, something to return to.

Come daybreak, he was dozing off.

Fancies and fantasies of the life he might have had with the woman began to appear to him not only at night instead of dreams. Even during the day, with his eyes open, he daydreamed of that unfulfilled life in which he could be happy, which was his destiny. The right version of his life. But he was living in the wrong one. The right one was the stuff of daydreams, no more.

One day Mikhail woke up from his daydreaming in a remote park in the late afternoon.

He was sitting on an icy bench.

A deserted avenue. He could not remember how he had got there. He looked at his watch, as if time was now his only reference point in a confused world.

Mikhail was frightened that he was going crazy, with his fantasies of his other, right life. The things that happened in it, the experiences he went through: his imaginary life felt so much more real, more material, more substantial. That time, in the avenue, he had even thought of going to the woman's house; he could remember the way. He pictured himself arriving, and her opening the door to him and saying, 'Darling, you're frozen. Dinner's just ready.'

He did more than picture it; he went there. Stood for a while outside the house. Looked at her windows. Could not bring himself to go in.

That same evening–night, near enough–he went to a twenty-four hour pharmacy and asked for a good sleeping draught. When it came down to it, he wanted to live, not daydream. He retained some sense of the value of his real life. Or perhaps he just wanted to get to the crux, the denouement.

The sleeping draught worked: he dropped off each night and did not dream. By sheer force of will, he weaned himself off his daydreaming. His mother noted that he was finally starting to look better. It had worried her that he had not gone with his wife. She had been looking for some other reason for his not going. She was afraid that her son had been wronged, cheated, betrayed.

His mother prepared aspic, baked a walnut and prune roll, made stewed beef and vegetables, pressed out a chunk of liver pâté. Still it all seemed too little to her, insufficient, prosaic. She regarded New Year as a poetic, magical holiday.

Mikhail and his mother celebrated New Year just the two of them. Dasha had gone to her friends out of town. Mikhail stayed in his room all evening, working. He was an in-house technical translator, and repaired computers through connections; he was well versed in both hardware and software. Two hours before midnight, his mother fell to setting the table in the big room. She laid a traditional white tablecloth, and fetched out and rinsed the Czech New Year service and crystal wine glasses. Set out the cognac. Made sure the champagne was in the fridge. Turned out the light and admired the New Year tree with its twinkling multicoloured lights. And then she realised what they were missing for the party. For the poetry of the winter night. She peeked into her son's room and asked him to run down to the corner shop for ice cream.

'Get the most expensive,' she said. 'The best there is, rich and creamy. Get some air too. All day in front of the screen. All that radiation.'

There was coloured confetti on the tiled floor outside the door. Mikhail winced at the mere thought of it sticking to the bottom of his shoes. He made his way to the lift, pushed the black button, and it lit up. One flight down, a man was standing in shadow by the window on the landing. He was looking at Mikhail, or so it seemed. Mikhail turned away. The lift arrived and the doors opened. Someone had stuck a wringing wet, grimy mitten behind the handrail. Mikhail did not get in; he turned back towards the man below. The lift doors closed.

Mikhail went down one flight. The man straightened up as he approached.

The actor.

He looked at Mikhail and gave an embarrassed smile. His head was closely shaved and his face showed a reddish stubble. He bore little resemblance to his former self; he was older, gaunt, his eyes sunken. But Mikhail recognised him instantly. He thought he had recognised the man even before he had looked at him properly. As soon as he had felt his gaze, he knew who it belonged to.

'Waiting for someone?' asked Mikhail, speaking quietly.

'Me? No.'

'So what are you doing, standing there?'

'Nothing. Getting warm.'

'Is it cold out?'

'Windy.'

'I got the impression you were waiting for someone.'

Mikhail did not go out. He could not walk away, just like that; he had to figure out why the actor was here, what he wanted. And the actor, in his turn, seemed to be waiting for something from him.

'You came out of flat sixty-seven,' the actor remarked. 'Do you live there?'

'No,' said Mikhail, lying for some reason.

'Dasha. Do you know her?'

The question made Mikhail jump.

'Whoa. Sorry?'

'Do you know her?'

Mikhail looked into the actor's half-crazed, darkened eyes, and decided to tell the truth. To get everything out in the open. To have the right to ask.

'Dasha is my sister.'

'Oh, is that so?' The actor was delighted. He licked his dry lips and moved closer to Mikhail.

Mikhail took a step back. 'So?' he asked coldly. 'How does my sister come into this? What does she have to do with you?'

The actor hastily unzipped his anorak, reached into his inside pocket, and pulled something out, something flat and trembling. Paper. He held it out.

A frayed, yellowed envelope. Mikhail took it and studied it. A letter. To the actor, in prison. From Dasha. Mikhail glanced at the actor. He was watching, anxious, expectant. Mikhail pulled a sheet of paper out of the envelope, and the actor bit his lower lip.

Greetings. I've wanted to write to you many times. You'll think I'm stupid. That's why I haven't written before, because you'd think that. But now I am writing, because everyone's badmouthing you, on the internet, the radio, everywhere.

I want to tell you that I also almost killed someone once. I flung a stone at a girl. It missed, luckily. Could have hit her on the head. These days I dream about you every night. We're walking together. I wake up with my face wet, crying. Answer my letter. A girlfriend of mine wangled your address from her Dad–he works at the Home Office. We'll write to each other, and you'll feel better. I love you very much. Dasha.

Mikhail lowered the piece of paper and met the actor's lost gaze. It was awkward to look at such a completely crushed, humiliated man.

The actor waited to see what Mikhail would say, but Mikhail remained silent. He folded the paper, tucked it neatly into the envelope, and held it out towards the actor. The actor could not bring himself to take the envelope. As if he no longer had any right to it–and never had done.

'I didn't answer her,' he said.

'Thank God.'

'Yes.'

'Did she write any other letters?'

'No, no.'

'Well, that is a relief. So what do you want from her now? What are you waiting for?'

'Me?'

'Well, not me, obviously.'

The actor was silent, at a loss.

'She's not at home now. She's with friends, seeing in the New Year. And she has a boyfriend. He's there too. Am I coming through clearly enough?'

'Yes, yes, of course.'

'Look. What were you waiting for? What were you hoping for?'

'I don't even know myself.'

'Suppose she'd been at home? What would you have said to her? Shoved this letter under her nose?' Mikhail shook the letter.

'No.'

'This letter puts her in your debt, mm?'

'No! I ... I don't know myself. I know I was being stupid.'

'You got no-one to see the New Year in with?'

'No.'

'No big deal. See it in on your own. Go to bed early.'

'Basically, I've nowhere to go. The flat's a goner. They're foreclosing.'

'I'm sorry for you, but Dasha has nothing to do with any of this.'

'Of course not.'

'Go to friends. Acquaintances.'

'I will. Of course. You're completely right.'

The actor's eyes had gone blank, and his gaze no longer contained any expression.

A door slammed upstairs, and there came a waft of cigarette smoke. The actor glanced at the envelope in Mikhail's hand. He left the window sill and headed quietly down the stairs, shuffling like an old man. Mikhail heard the front door open and close. He walked over to the window.

The actor was walking slowly across the courtyard. He slipped on the ice, swung his arms, recovered his balance. A hunched, black figure. Mikhail ripped up the envelope and the letter with it. The old paper tore easily. His hands were trembling.

March the 17th was a weekday, and they all got up early, before dawn. They sat down for breakfast together. The radio was burbling–their mother always turned it on to hear the weather. As soon as the presenter handed over to the weather forecast, she would say, 'Sshh. Sshh!' even if they were already quiet. And she would stop chomping and listen.

The forecast promised fog and ice, minus two in the morning, reaching zero in the afternoon. Straight after the forecast, the presenter of the morning show said that today would see the funeral of a famous actor, a man who two years before had been a success story. His co-presenter, a young woman, gasped, and started asking questions. 'Where did he die? In prison?'

'No,' said the presenter. 'He got out in December. There was an amnesty.'

'What did he die of? He was so young! How old was he?'

'I don't know how old he was. Maybe a listener will call in and tell us. He died in hospital, on Galushkina. They found him somewhere in Yauza district and took him in. Frostbite. Intoxicated, obviously.'

'Yes, he drank.'

'That's how he ended up in jail. Because he drank. Hardly remembered who he was.'

'Poor, poor man.'

'I don't know. I'm not the slightest bit sorry for him. It's his own fault.'

'Well I am sorry for him. He was very talented. Very.'

Dasha was poking around in her bowl, not looking up. Suddenly she let out a sob.

'Dasha,' exclaimed her mother, confused. Dasha buried her face in her hands and burst out crying.

Her mother stroked Dasha's back and hair, and looked helplessly at Mikhail.

Dasha ducked out from under her mother's hand and ran into the bathroom. The sound of running water was heard.

'What's got into her?' asked Mikhail's mother.

A doctor called in to the studio from the very hospital on Galushkina. The presenter was overjoyed to have such an important witness on air. The doctor said there was nothing he could have done, the actor was completely intoxicated and had frostbite; he'd got to them too late. There would be a send-off for the actor, he said, at the hospital morgue, and anyone who wanted to could come tomorrow at ten.

Dasha returned, tear-stained. Her mother poured her some fresh tea and stroked her hand.

'It's all right,' said Dasha. 'It's passed. OK now.' She assured them that yes, she had indeed calmed down, though she did ask her mother to switch to some other programme, without news, just music.

Mikhail took the day off from work and was at Galushkina by ten. He had been thinking that quite a few people would assemble there, but there were in fact just three people at the morgue, stamping their feet in the snow. An old chap with baby blue eyes, probably a relative. Two elderly ladies. They looked like old-fashioned theatre-goers, the kind who wear posh shoes to the theatre, powder themselves, smell of spring perfume, and never fail to present the actors with flowers. They stood there with chrysanthemums that drooped miserably. Virgin white, cold, and innocent.

Twenty minutes after the appointed ten o'clock, the doors opened, and they were invited in. The old chap tossed away his cigarette and it hissed in the snow. Mikhail was the last to enter the dank room.

The priest spoke. Mikhail paid attention, hoping to hear something important, something he didn't know himself. The priest spoke about forgiveness. The face of the man in the coffin was completely white. A stranger's face. Mikhail could not recognise the actor in him at all. He turned and headed for the door.

There was a young woman right by the door. The creature he had once felt so sorry for, whose fleetingness he had felt so keenly, to the point of pain. She stood there holding dark roses. Their eyes met. Mikhail knew she had recognised him. Instantly. She realised who it was she had mistaken for the actor that time, on the bus.

They did not exchange a single word.

Mikhail opened the door and stepped out under a grey, hazy sky. He set off along the path away from the morgue. At the gates, he looked back. For some reason he had thought the girl would be following him. But no-one was coming after him.

In the underground, the heat and the stuffiness, the monotonous movement, the endless coming and going of the crowds, the black windows, the rocking motion ... all combined to send him into a kind of stupor. He went past his stop, unable to summon the strength to stand up and make his way to the doors. He went further and further away from his own home, and wondered why she had come. Did she feel guilty too?

He had never, he thought, never lived his own life.

A TRIP

He told his wife that there were no olives of that kind, and she asked him to look in another shop, and if there were none there either, to come back home, as their guests were already arriving. He tucked his phone away, and headed for the car.

It was dark, already past seven o'clock, mid-December, slushy in Moscow.

He settled himself in the car, but did not drive off straight away. Wet snow was plastered over the windscreen, and he could no longer see what was happening outside. His world was confined to the cold interior of his car, shrunk to a pea, curled into a ball. He switched on the radio. A voice said, '...about zero'. There was a knock on the side window. The face behind the glass was blurred, as if it were melting.

He lowered the window. A woman said in a pinched voice, 'Excuse me, do you think you could give me a lift?'

Her breath was moist.

'To the metro. Two hundred rubles.'

He opened the door. She settled herself in and said, 'It's cold.'

It was about ten minutes to the metro. He drove slowly. He liked the woman, only he did not know in what way. He wanted to work it out before he dropped her off. At the traffic lights in front of the metro, he asked, 'You have far to go?'

'Into the region.'

The watch on her wrist. Old. He recalled his mother's. Something about her seemed to come from that long gone age. There were no faces like that now.

That was roughly what he thought.

You only saw them in photographs or newsreels.

The face seemed young; the half-dark had softened the wrinkles. Good; let it soften them. There were times when you wanted no sharpness, no clarity, no definition at all. Half-dark softens and resolves.

'This red is so long!' she exclaimed.

'Are you in a hurry?'

'My train's at quarter to nine. I'll have to wait two hours for the next one. I won't be able to stop myself nodding off somewhere in the waiting room. I haven't slept all night and I can hardly stand up. If I nod off I'll sleep till morning and then have to suffer all day again, because the person I'm going to see won't be home until evening and I need to catch him. It's a long story. Why's it still red? Perhaps the traffic light's broken?'

'Government cortège.'

'Damn!'

When she was speaking, the illusion that her face belonged to the past disappeared. In this way, as she alternated between silence and speaking, her face either went off into the mists of time or emerged from them and became prosaically intimate. It was exciting. He was also curious: was he alone in perceiving her that way or not?

The wipers stubbornly worked away at clearing the field of view, the field of the snow battle.

'The road's empty,' he said. 'We'll soon be going like the wind.'

'In that case,' said the woman, putting two one-hundred ruble notes on the dashboard, 'thanks, but I'll run. I'll make it to the metro quicker than you can.'

She began to unbuckle her seatbelt.

'Where exactly do you need to go?'

'Along Yaroslavka. It's not close. Past Pushkino.'

'Do your seat belt back up. I'll drive you.'

ELENA DOLGOPYAT

He could not quite make out her expression in the half-light, and it was obvious that she could not make out what his face was expressing; she was staring myopically, surprised.

'Is it on your way?'

'Yes.'

The cortège, meanwhile, had passed by at speed. A mongrel ran across the empty carriageway, or rather, walked across it. It was in no hurry; it somehow knew that it could take its time.

'I can pay another two hundred rubles, no more.'

The light went green.

Back home, the guests were gathering, and his wife was worrying, glancing at her watch. Nikolay Alexeyevich was taking a woman he did not know far away, out of town. He was committing an irrational act. And Nikolay Alexeyevich was a rational man.

He could not himself explain what had suddenly come over him. For some reason he did not want to let this woman go. She unsettled him, and he needed to work out for himself how. Yes, perhaps that was the key: he did not like vagueness.

She, meanwhile, had quietened down in her comfortable seat. She relaxed, and dozed off. He turned off the radio. He tried to drive smoothly, without jolting. His mobile phone rang. He pressed the button and said into the earpiece, 'Yes?'

He tried to speak softly, but his companion woke up. Night was covering any signs of time, hiding them away. Time had been stolen; they were driving outside it along the open night road.

He spoke again into his earpiece, clarifying. 'The law can be read in more than one way. The wording must be particularly careful. I suggest we go back to the first option.'

He switched off his phone.

They drove in equable silence, and he thought she was about to flake out and go back to sleep. Lights approached and were as quickly behind them.

'Are you a lawyer?' she asked.

'No,' he lied.

She stared ahead, at the road, abstracted, wholly given over to the movement, to their flight. Flying was exactly what it felt like in the darkness. There was no sense of solid ground, and the lights raced by them in space that was black, almost cosmic.

'I'm a restaurant critic,' he said for some reason.

He stopped the car and opened the door a crack to breathe in the quiet local air. He heard a rustling noise, and did not immediately realise that it was snow, rustling as it fell. His passenger put another two hundred rubles on the dashboard, said goodbye, and forgot about him.

He watched her get out of the car, walk towards the entrance, slip, and keep her balance.

Nikolay Alexeyevich saw from the car the window of the yellow-lit entrance. He saw her climbing the stairs. A picture in a magic lantern.

She reached the landing.

A light came on in a window on the first floor.

He went on waiting for something. He lingered, not leaving.

In the magic lantern, he suddenly saw her coming down a flight of stairs, holding on to the worn railing with her white hand.

The light was still burning on the first floor.

She came out of the entrance. Her earlier footsteps were already covered over.

The light in the window had gone out, but someone was standing there behind the darkened window, watching her go out.

The snow crunched.

'Get in,' he called to her.

She walked round the car and got in next to him.

'Why didn't you go?'

'I was waiting.'

'For what?'

'I don't know.'

She was silent, and peered out of the snow-plastered window. The wipers had jammed.

'Where are we going?' he asked.

'Don't you need to go home?'

'No. I'm on holiday.'

'Tell me straight, what are expecting from me?'

'Nothing.'

'I don't have any money.'

'I know.'

'And ... you aren't going to get anything from me.'

'I know.'

'You seem like a respectable man. Genteel, we might have said once.'

'I am genteel. When it comes down to it, your choice is limited. The man you wanted to see so badly didn't even let you in the door. And here you are, alone in a sleeping village, without money, without hope.'

She suddenly burst out laughing.

'What, then?' he asked. 'Back to Moscow?'

'The man I wanted to see so badly has gone away. And I still need to see him.'

'Where's he gone?'

The snow had stopped by morning. Far from Moscow.

His companion was asleep, and he pulled up at the side of the road and fell asleep too. He woke up at dusk. She was gone. He touched the empty, cold seat. Cars were racing by, splattering dirt. He got out and looked around. The place was sad. A grey sky, a snowy field. Lights were already on in the village across the way. On his side, at the kerb, an old man was standing, unable to bring himself to cross. Cars were racing by at top speed, and the old man was afraid. He would almost summon up the nerve, and then catch sight of the blazing, flying headlights, and step back again. Nikolay Alexeyevich trudged along the kerb. He did not go far, so as not to lose sight of the car.

He checked his pockets. Wallet, money, cards, everything was there.

Where could she have gone? What for? Perhaps she had stopped another car. Or got out to stretch her legs, and someone had slowed down, asked her what the problem was, and offered her a lift, saying it was on their way. But then she would at least have left a note. He rushed back to the car, in case there was a note and he'd missed it.

He looked everywhere, including on the floor, but couldn't see one. Somehow he remained convinced that there was a note, that while he was half asleep he had seen a white sheet of paper slipping off the dashboard onto the floor. He had trampled it down, carried it outside, and the note had disappeared in the porridge of grimy snow.

The old man was still standing motionless on the kerb. If he was ever going to cross, then everything would have to stop: the cars, time itself. Nikolay Alexeyevich took out a rag and wiped the windows and mirrors. In his zeal he pushed out his lips. The activity helped distract him.

He could not bring himself to start the engine and drive away. He felt old, older than the old man on the kerb. Grimy, lumbering, plain, abandoned, and stupid to the point of emptiness, to the point of a clanging in his head. The leading lawyer, respected man, father of a family: where was he? Lying dead in a Moscow alleyway.

Nikolay Alexeyevich felt like his own murderer. He was now alone in an airless space. The earth–his home, his cradle–was visible but not accessible; he was circling it in a distant orbit; there was still oxygen in his lungs, but it would soon run out.

Nikolay Alexeyevich tossed the rag into the boot. A truck went past, and he crossed to the other side, took the old man by his bony elbow, and brought him over.

The old man trudged along the kerb. Nikolay Alexeyevich watched him go, then followed along behind. Where the old man might lead him was unimportant. Not even interesting. He turned aside into a petrol station. The old man went on.

Nikolay Alexeyevich popped into the toilet, sluiced his face, and drank a horribly hot, charred coffee, so hot it was smoking. He was alone in the tiny eatery. He watched a grimy SUV being filled up. The driver was off to one side, smoking, on the edge of the asphalt circle. There is nothing interesting in such mindless staring, except that you're seeing but you're not there, you're not there but you are seeing.

He crumpled his paper cup.

Walked back to the car.

She was sitting there as if nothing had happened. A bag containing various packages was lying on the back seat. She was looking in the mirror, touching up her lips. He sat down, the car rocking under his weight.

'I've bought us something to eat,' she said. 'There's a nice little shop across the road.'

'Yes but you don't have any money.'

'I had a bit left. Where did you go?'

'The toilet.'

The light was fading, and they ate in semi-darkness. She picked up a rustling packet and asked him to switch on the light. She read everything on the packet: name, manufacturer, contents, expiry date. Out loud, in a steady voice. Read it and looked at him.

'It's fine,' he said. 'We won't poison ourselves.'

'Would you like some?'

'Not now.'

She tossed the packet into the bag.

'You must be a teacher,' he said.

They were already a long way from the kerb, and even further from his earth-cradle. They had entered a new and uncharted world.

'Wrong,' she said. 'Though I thought about it when I was a child. I saw myself in a severe black dress at the blackboard with a pointer in my hand. And silence in the classroom.'

She stopped talking.

'I wanted to be a spy. Seriously. Living in some foreign country, drinking whisky in a bar, waiting to meet a secret agent. A double life attracted me. An imaginary life and a real life. The imaginary one's obvious ...'

She wasn't listening to him. She was looking abstractedly out the window. She was not interested in him. She was in her own time, and he did not know the way there.

A large town was approaching. The open road gave way and streetlights appeared, but he turned the car onto a narrow, dark road along which they would travel all night.

'... in transit, from Belarus. We have relatives there, we're on our way home ...'

She said nothing, raising no objection and doing nothing to stop him rattling on about whatever he wanted, constructing the reality of his choice with her in the leading role. An elderly, good-natured policeman was sitting in the back seat, providing an audience. He'd flagged them down at an abandoned bus stop in the middle of nowhere. 'I've been waiting for an hour,' he'd said. 'Not a soul. No cars. The scheduled bus must have broken down. I'm so glad you ... I thought I'd spend the night there on the bench, but the bench was freezing and the wind was cutting right through my uniform jacket. Now I'll get home, steam my feet for a bit, down a shot of vodka, and go to bed.'

In the car he had gradually warmed up. He'd asked where they were from and where they were going; an old man's curiosity about people, he said. Nikolay Alexeyevich had launched into his tale about his relatives and Belarus. The woman looked perplexed and did not interrupt.

'We're tired. We miss our home. We have our own house, vegetable garden, a little flower garden. You can see the river from the windows.'

'That's good,' said the policeman.

'Most of all, obviously, we miss the children. Four of them. Their aunt's with them now, my sister. She's never been married.'

'Four kids is a lot. Rare, I mean. Who's got four now? I don't know. You managing?'

'We get by.'

'Still got to feed them. What do you do?'

'Restaurant critic,' said the woman, looking out of the window. He could not see her face.

'She's joking,' said Nikolay Alexeyevich, not breaking stride. 'What restaurants would they be? I have a small grocery shop. My wife does the bookkeeping, I do the deliveries, the staff; there's a lot of work. My sister helps us around the house, but I pay her, never fear, she wouldn't ....'

'That's good.' The policeman was more and more liking the picture Nikolay Alexeyevich was painting.

'My wife and I were in the same class. She got top marks, and I ... didn't. I didn't like anyone with top marks. I thought they were all idiots.'

The policeman burst out laughing.

'One time we were on duty together in class, cleaning the floors after school, and I cut my hand. There was glass on the floor and I didn't see it. She bandaged my hand with a handkerchief and I was amazed at how clean the handkerchief was and how nice it smelled, and she took me to hospital because the blood wouldn't stop. I even got stitches. Still got the scar. Since then I haven't been able to live without her.'

'That's good,' said the policeman. A stranger.

The policeman went on to tell them that his wife was currently ill and he had to do everything around the house himself. That he was tired of winter and wanted sunshine, and in summer his grandchildren would come and he would take them to the forest to pick strawberries.

'I like strawberry jam,' said Nikolay Alexeyevich.

They dropped the policeman off near the village. Nikolay Alexeyevich refused his hundred rubles.

They drove in silence for a few minutes.

'Yes,' said Nikolay Alexeyevich. 'A totally empty road, like in a dream.'

'You have a Moscow number plate,' said the woman.

'What?'

'The policeman might have seen that you have a Moscow number plate. He stood watching us go for ages. Did you not notice?'

'So what? Is it a crime to have a Moscow number plate? You think he'll put us on the wanted list? Because of an idle conversation? Like that's top of his list. He's already steaming his feet.'

A few minutes later:

'Do you really have a scar?'

'No.'

Chpok. Or that wasn't quite the sound. Drier. *Tstok.* Something like that. Ball against racket, with that sound. The game was boring. Boring.

Nikolay Alexeyevich knew that wasn't fair. That with the sun shining and the silence almost complete, the tension was drawn out, there were invisible power lines; he just had to plug in.

Tstok. Tstok. Discharge.

But not today, not now.

The sunny picture was flickering on the television in the corner of the dining room. Several people were watching it. Nikolay Alexeyevich and his companion were sitting far away from them. It was chilly in the room, and the food quickly became cold and unpalatable. Nevertheless, Nikolay Alexeyevich ate everything all up. The woman did not eat much. She put down a glass of unfinished tea.

'Are you all right?' asked Nikolay Alexeyevich.

'Tired.'

She glanced across to the far corner, at the flickering screen.

'When the tennis has finished there'll be a film. A comedy.'

She remained silent.

'What do you think of me?'

She turned and looked at him distantly, in almost the same way as she had looked across at the distant picture, from somewhere on the other side of the world.

'I don't know. Nothing. I don't really want to get into your affairs, to be honest. Are you offended?'

He did not answer at once.

Tstok. Tstok said the ball.

'Yes.'

'You don't need to be.'

She finished her tea, and politely wished him goodnight. She went to her room. To her own space, away from him.

The waitress collected up the dirty crockery, and he asked for a beer. He went on sitting on his own at the cleared table. The comedy had already started, and the people in front of the television were laughing. Young people. One young woman had turned her face away from the television and was looking at him. Looking without smiling, with eyes that appeared crazed. As if she had a high temperature, a fever. He, fat, unshaven, crumpled, was part of her delirium. Something like that. He averted his eyes.

On the stairs, he stumbled and cursed. He heard someone laugh. He looked around. No-one.

He went straight to the bathroom. Took a shower. Everything was basically clean, even new, but somehow rickety, unconvincing, untrustworthy. He could feel his own heaviness. From the bathroom he heard a knock at the door, but he did not hurry. He turned off the tap. The water ran away down the drain with a sob. There was something human in the sob.

There came another knock at the door. He took his time. Dressed. Walked over to the flimsy door. Cigarette smoke was creeping through the crack from the corridor. He turned the key and unlocked the door. On the threshold stood the young woman from the dining room. This time she was smiling.

She seemed to have forgotten the cigarette in her hand. A column of ash had grown and now toppled. Without a word, she stepped over the threshold. Nikolay Alexeyevich silently let her pass. She glanced into the bathroom, the light still on, and threw the cigarette butt into the toilet. It flopped into the water. She put out the light in the bathroom. And in the main room. In the main room she waited for him. He was still standing in the corridor.

She liked it that he was wet after his shower. He said nothing in reply. He had no time for words, so badly did he want this half-drunk, shameless girl. It was as if he himself was intoxicated. He could not get enough of her foul breath, and she did not give herself easily: she struggled with him– that was the way she liked it; she was very strong, and he was old and fat, but not now, all that was unimportant now, he was stronger than her, he could crush her, strangle her. The flimsy bed shook and groaned.

She wanted something more. He was lying there, motionless, wasted. She ran her hand over his chest, his stomach. He stopped her hand and pulled it away from him.

'Are you from Moscow?' She asked it in a sociable sort of way, and it sounded very funny coming from her.

ELENA DOLGOPYAT

'No.'

'There are lots of people in Moscow. Grandad says they haven't had a war there for ages.'

He roared with laughter. She burst out laughing with him. She did not really understand what their laughter meant, or what had caused it. Nikolay Alexeyevich finished laughing, and said, 'Forgive me. I can't sleep in this cot with you. It's too narrow.'

She stood up. He watched her looking for her tights. He could see where she had flung them down, but he kept quiet. She found them, and pulled them on. She stood in front of him.

'Can you lend me three hundred rubles?'

'Give me my trousers.'

The door banged shut behind her. He fell asleep almost at once. That night, he slept easily.

The last frontier separated them from their destination. The river.

At the downward slope, he stopped the car and switched off the engine. The pontoon bridge was removed for the winter, and people crossed over on the ice.

She was asleep. He was hesitating. He imagined suddenly that she had died. Not just now; a long time ago. There was no trace of her left. And no trace of him sitting beside her now. The car, the river, the night–all were gone without trace, without memory. The planet was also gone.

Nikolay Alexeyevich looked at his living hand. His fingernails had grown horribly long. He could hear the sleeping woman's breathing. The grey frosty air hung thick over the ground. The watch chirred on his wrist. In reality, none of this was real. It never had been. Nikolay Alexeyevich simply did not exist.

'Where are we?'

Nikolay Alexeyevich jumped. He all but burst into tears at the question, at the sleepy voice bringing him back to real life. It was already morning, and he could clearly make out the far bank, not so distant, and the small houses and the grey smoke above the chimneys.

Nikolay Alexeyevich did not answer the question. He started the engine.

'Just a second.' She stopped him.

She took her make-up bag out of her handbag. Looked at herself in a small round mirror. Powdered her face.

He drove carefully over the ice. Fearfully. A boy on skis coming towards him shot him a curious glance.

'Left.'

He turned into an alley, narrow, with black slatted fences, and snow heaped on both sides of the carriageway.

'Slow down a bit.'

She peered at the houses on the left side. Old houses, some dilapidated, some renovated, some with extensions, some still sleepy, some already awake.

'Stop.'

This particular house was still sleeping. A tit was pecking at a ball of lard and swaying with it. The branch of the apple tree to which it was tethered was also swaying. Snow was showering down. Inside the windows, the curtains showed white. The steps were dusted with snow. Cat tracks ran across them.

The woman opened the door a few inches, then looked round at Nikolay Alexeyevich.

'Thank you. And ...'

She did not go on to say what might have come after 'and'. She nodded, and got out of the car.

Nikolay Alexeyevich did not drive off. He lingered there.

She went up the steps and rang the bell. She stepped back from the door, so that the man inside the house who

ELENA DOLGOPYAT

had peeled back the very edge of the curtain could see her from the window.

The door opened and she disappeared through it.

Nikolay Alexeyevich waited. A woman walked by with an empty bucket. In the house across the way the stove was lit.

The curtains hung still and white inside the window.

A cat appeared. It stood on the steps, then jumped down.

Nikolay Alekseyevich waited.

Two girls came out of a house perched on rising ground and began to pound a doormat on the snow. Nikolay Alexeyevich imagined the fresh smell of the doormat as it lay on a cleanly scrubbed floor in a warmed room.

The door behind which his companion had hidden herself opened. A man came out onto the steps. He wore a crumpled shirt over his naked torso, tracksuit bottoms, and slippers on bare feet.

The tit had long since flown off, but the lard was still swaying.

The man fished out his cigarettes and lit up. Nikolay Alexeyevich tried to see his face, but it somehow did not let him; it kept slipping away into the shadows.

The man went on smoking. The door remained ajar. Nikolay Alexeyevich started the engine.

In the centre stood houses several storeys high, mostly old, merchants' houses, thick-walled, with arches into the courtyards. Nikolay Alexeyevich parked in front of the hairdresser's. A warm light shone in the wide windows, and a man in a white sheet was sitting in a chair.

Nikolay Alexeyevich asked the man to wash his hair, shave his face, and to neaten up his fingernails. The hairdresser was giving off a cold smell of cologne. He looked at Nikolay Alexeyevich suspiciously, and set to work reluctantly, as if he were doubtful. But when he had finished, he said in surprise, 'Look at you. A new man.'

Nikolay Alexeyevich warily met his own gaze.

On the third day he returned to Moscow.

He had been living with his wife for twenty years. They suited each other. They both liked tidiness, comfortable clothes, and their comfortable, well-organised, unhurried life. Their children brought them joy.

The wife told her girlfriend that she had no explanation. She said she preferred to forget the whole thing and not think about it. Nikolay Alexeyevich was insistent that he had called her that evening. He insisted that he had spoken with her that evening. About an urgent trip. That he'd said he'd be back in a week.

'I know he's lying,' the wife said to her friend. 'And he knows I know. But we pretend he did call and that for whatever reason I don't remember. It's more convenient that way.'

THE FACILITY

Hi Yulia! I got all your letters. I'm going to number mine, like you. Number 1 and so on. I know I didn't answer. I couldn't find the time. Now I've got time by the boatload and absolutely nothing to do with it. No, I'm not in hospital. It's a lot worse than that.

I expect you're surprised to get a letter from Borovsk rather than Yaroslavl. Right now I'm wondering why on earth I agreed–why didn't I stay in Yaroslavl? Why did I let myself be seduced by the subsistence allowance?

We arrived in Yaroslavl–'we' being me, Tanya Dyachkova and Galina Bakayeva. The hostel's new, not like ours. Not too big, and it's peaceful, a family place. A shower on every floor. True, the hot water's been turned off. We went to the baths. Pretty standard bathhouse, nothing unusual. Middle-aged women in the buff. A chap perched in a tree outside looking though the open transom.

The town impressed me. Clean, a big river, shops. Not like in Moscow, obviously, but still not bad. We picked up eggs and bread. Heated oil in the frying pan, crumbled the bread into it, poured on the eggs, and there you go, a proper evening meal. We had breakfast in the canteen at work. Porridge and tea.

After about ten days our boss proposed a move to Borovsk-23. He explained that we'd still be on the books at Yaroslavl (the parent enterprise), but live and work at the facility, which is cunningly located somewhere you can't find on the map; it's either in Moscow region or Kaluga, we don't know. Salary plus subsistence. Moscow only a little over two hours away. It's quite common, apparently, for a group of people to chip in and rent a flat, so as to get away at the weekends. Theatre, shops, all on your doorstep. The temptation was enormous. We signed the papers, received our expenses, and set off.

We rolled into Moscow on the train. Time was when we'd lived there, we'd been natives, we belonged, but now we were outsiders. Three nobodies. We walked for a while around the old places. You remember the *Shokoladnitsa* on Pushkin Street, with its grilled chicken and currant jelly? We spent a while in the *Shokoladnitsa*. There's a snack bar right next to it, the *Green Light*. Five years I lived in Moscow, walked past it a thousand times and never once looked in. That kind of made me sad.

Tanya said, 'It's probably an eatery for taxi drivers, you know, green light–taxi available.'

We finished our chicken (I miss it, I'm writing this and dribbling, hey ho) and our jelly (with whipped cream! Will I ever taste it again or is that it, gone beyond recall?). We went outside, looked at the sun, and dived into the *Green Light*. It was only two steps away.

A semi-basement. Dark after the sunshine. The clank of crockery. A man standing at a table (no seats provided) stuffing himself with dumplings.

Tanya said, 'So ... you happy now?'

We basically spooled around Moscow, like orphans. We got tired and were glad when it was time to go. Kievsky Station to Balabanovo. They make matches there. Have you ever taken a look at the boxes?

Our train was on time coming into Balabanovo, and we didn't have long to wait for the bus. We managed to be the first on as well, so we got seats. I was by the window.

Tanya said, 'Good omen.'

She says something at every opportunity. Galina's different. She keeps quiet and watches. She always seems disapproving. I'd feel awkward lighting up in front of her, so I go off somewhere.

The bus set off at 4 o'clock. It was still light. I enjoyed trundling along past unfamiliar places–fields, a copse, houses. The bus was packed to start with. Ladies clutching their purses, and a handful of men, one, a soldier, was the last to get on. A distinguished-looking chap. He should be in films playing White officers. Every now and then he'd turn his head, and I'd ogle him.

The stops came thick and fast at first, and people kept on getting off until the only passengers left on board were us, the officer, and a woman with a teenage boy. The officer found an empty seat and made himself comfortable. Looked out the window the whole time even though the only thing going past was forest followed by forest, more and more of it pine. The road was narrow and the pine trees were tall.

The driver had turned on his headlights, and inside the bus it was gloomy and chilly. The engine was giving out a low hum. Tanya moved to an empty seat and stretched her legs out. I was quite happy where I was and doing what I was doing, going along, looking at the road and at the light dancing in front of us. The soldier suddenly got up, went up to the driver, and caught hold of the hand grip.

'Commander,' he said, 'we seem to have been going a long time.'

The driver said nothing. The officer stayed by him, and the bus rolled on, jolting over potholes. I looked at my watch. We should have arrived about twenty minutes ago. The girls were dozing. The woman was looking alarmed. At least, I thought she looked alarmed. The boy was breathing on the window, making a little island of fog which he then wiped off with his palm.

The road became narrower, and the bus juddered frequently. I wanted to get there.

The bus slowed and then stopped. The road had come to an end at a crumbling wall topped by scraps of rusty barbed wire.

The soldier said, 'You've missed the turn, commander.'

'I'm new,' said the driver.

Tanya snorted.

The boy whispered something in his mother's ear.

'Hang on for five minutes,' his mother said.

The driver turned off the engine and opened the door. The boy jumped out and ran behind a tree. We all got out onto the old, pitted concrete. It was not as dark outside as it had seemed from in the bus; not all the light had yet gone from the sky.

Tanya and I slipped through a gap in the wall. Galina stayed near the bus.

We saw a parade ground covered with weeds, and a long grey building with an enormous ball on the roof. A birch tree was growing out of a hole in the ball, like out of the eye socket of an old skull. Green growth was forcing its way through every crack.

Everything was quiet under the clear sky. I lit up, and the lighter flame didn't flicker: there wasn't the slightest breath of wind. Like in an enchanted kingdom. The hum of the bus engine started up again.

The soldier told us we'd come to an old, abandoned facility, built by prisoners before the war.

The bus took us back, the soldier standing by the driver, watching the road lit up in the headlights. We went slowly, so as not to overshoot the turn a second time. It was pitch dark by the time we arrived. A lamp was burning at the checkpoint.

We were allocated a room in a local hotel. The hotel was in a five-storey house–all the houses here are five storeys.

ELENA DOLGOPYAT

An old building, past its best. In the foyer were a television on long legs, a settee, and a fig tree in a tub. We were given a kettle, and boiled it up in the shared kitchen. We filched tea from a cupboard, drank it, and collapsed into bed. Galina, stickler that she is, set her alarm; no lazing around for our Galina! She said her prayers as well.

Yulia, I'm sure you're wondering why I'm dragging this out, crawling along and not getting to the nub of it. I'm crawling along because I've got nothing to do except crawl along. Do you remember how we suffered Tolstoy at school? Those long sentences and disquisitions, like a goods train going by, wagon after wagon after wagon, endless, while you stand at the crossing and wait. My sentences are short and my disquisitions few (by reason of my feeble brain), but I have a whole heap of time. So I'm keeping myself busy, writing, recalling all the details. I'm writing about my life and at the same time kind of distracting myself from it. I've no-one to talk to about it. Who's going to listen to me? You'll read my letters, I know, and take pity on me and write back.

I slept deeply that night and didn't hear the alarm. Tanya shook me awake. Galina had already put the kettle on. The service bus left the checkpoint at eight o'clock sharp, so we ran. There we were running, while soldiers were marching on the parade ground and singing: *don't cry-y-y-y my little gi-i-i-irl*. The morning was quiet. I'd have liked to stay and take a walk in the forest, pick some mushrooms, sit on an old stump, have a smoke, look at the golden autumn. The gilded autumn. Cold rain will come and wash off the gilt.

The bus was full. It picked us up, shut its doors, and rolled away. There were civilians and soldiers on the bus, though more civilians. It took us about ten minutes to trundle from the town to the facility, from checkpoint to checkpoint.

We presented our passes, went through security, and headed along an asphalt path towards a long, grey building with white balls on the roof. The balls were whole and clean, not pockmarked. Aerials were picking up signals from space, from a satellite. Military secrets, perhaps.

I was struck by the wholly peaceful coexistence of new IBM computers and monitors and standard government-issue desks that looked out of the 1930s. There were plenty of new desks, but these, too, were from a previous era, heavy, with deep ink stains. To my delight, I was allocated one of the old ones.

Dear desk, did you come from that forgotten facility (practically from the next world)? Only yesterday, I was in your homeland; it's all overgrown with weeds there, but you've been rescued.

The desk, a few bits of telephonic apparatus, black like the coal my grandmother uses to light the stove. And uplifting posters on the walls: 'A chatterbox is a godsend for a spy!'

The room we work in is enormous, bigger than a sports hall. The programmers' desks are in two rows; there's plenty of space and no-one gets in anyone else's way. Engineers sit and solder along the long wall under a narrow window that stretches the length of the wall. There's a drift of blue smoke. We've each been given a stitched, sealed exercise book, pens and pencils. The exercise books are for writing our programs. At the end of the working day we have to give our exercise books in, and they're kept in a safe. To debug the programs we have to go into the display hall. No punch cards needed there! You just run the program and take your print-out.

The day passed uneventfully enough. Galina wrote her program quickly. Tatiana fiddled about doing hers, and I had no idea what to do. I doodled a Christmas tree. A bunny. We headed for the buffet for lunch. Impressive. Mozhaysk milk, and lots of it. Fish cooked in a recognisable way. An absolute mountain of mashed potato. Didn't stop me wolfing the lot, though. We hadn't had breakfast. Or dinner. My head was starting to spin. The pastry rings were ordinary but fresh.

ELENA DOLGOPYAT

The tea, obviously, was evil. But hot, and OK with sugar. I asked Galina about the program, and she pursed her lips, but after lunch she came and found me and explained. I tried to understand what she was telling me.

At 4.30 we handed our exercise books in to our boss. He had a look, leafing through the pages, then tucked them away in the safe. We gathered up our things and hurried for home. The long, dreary corridor with its doors and posters, and round the bend, the foyer and exit. To get out you have to present your pass. A soldier stands at the door checking them. I turned out my bag and rummaged through my pockets: no pass.

The soldier said, 'I can't let you through.'

What was I to do? The girls were already late for the bus. 'Run,' I said.

We all started running–the girls for the bus, and I to my workstation. I searched my desk, looked on the floor, poked in every waste paper bin. There was no-one to open the safe to let me look inside my exercise book: the boss had handed in the key and gone. So there I was, pretty much trapped. It was enough to make me cry. Except that I didn't want to cry yet.

I sat in the hall completely on my own.

White light from the fluorescent strips fixed to the ceiling. Have you noticed, Yulia, that they're incapable of glowing quietly. They give out this low whine. Not loud. When you sit for a long time on your own underneath them, you hear it.

The door opened to reveal a cleaner and a soldier. The cleaner took away the rubbish and washed the floors, and the soldier asked me to leave. He turned off the light and locked and sealed the door. I stood there for a moment, then another moment, and then wandered around the little smoking area. Squatted by the wall like a convict. Clicked my lighter. It was quiet. Godforsaken.

I finished my cigarette and got up and stretched my legs, which had gone to sleep. Trudged along the long corridor to the display hall. The door was ajar. Of course, people hang out here round the clock, analysing signals from space. We'd been warned that there were night shifts.

I went in.

The display hall was not large. Ten screens were glowing emerald green, connected to the IBM mainframe in the control room. People were sitting at the screens, like doctors, in white coats. I joined them; I took a coat from a hook and put it on, turning back the long sleeves, and settled down at a spare station. My screen was quiet, motionless; asleep. Twinkling green columns of figures were scurrying down the active screens, from top to bottom. It was easy to imagine that the screens were portholes looking into the depths of the sea, that the twinkling was green algae, and that our ship was going down, down, down, ever lower, ever deeper, but not reaching the bottom; there was no bottom.

Someone tapped my shoulder, and I came to.

A tall woman with a small, round face said quietly, 'Come with me.'

I asked no questions; I felt no surge of surprise or joy; I simply went. Her stride was long, like Peter the Great's in Serov's painting. What would I not have given to feel the wind and see the clouds banking in the sky. To be free. We stomped along the godforsaken corridor, lit only by emergency lighting. Swung into the foyer. The soldier looked at us indifferently from behind the barrier.

We turned towards the stairs, and when we'd gone down one flight, the staircase hid us from view.

We came to a door marked 'Technicians', which in this case meant cleaners. And sure enough, in a small room at an old kitchen table with a retractable drawer sat the same cleaner, drinking tea from a cup and saucer. Pails and mops were piled in one corner. Cloths were drying on the radiator which was, as it happens, cold–the heating hadn't yet been turned on.

The cleaner topped up her cup with boiling water from an electric kettle. She didn't look at us.

There was another door in the room. We went through it and found ourselves in a snug little place (it might have once been a pantry) with a settee, and a bookcase on which stood a sky-blue glass vase and a ticking alarm clock. A pair of friendly household slippers had made themselves a home on the floor by the settee.

The woman said, 'We'll unfold the settee and both sleep on it. Head to tail. For now.'

'For now?'

'Maybe you'll be lucky and find your pass. I've been looking for mine for six months. I've already given up looking, actually. Tea?'

Well of course, Yulia, obviously I said, this is impossible, we need to talk to the boss, we're not in prison. We're Soviet people.

'Yes, yes,' said the woman. 'You'll pop and see the boss and make your application, but meanwhile give me a hand. I want to sleep. There's a toilet on this floor but no shower. I just stand at the sink and douse myself with a dipper. Ask your friends to bring you soap, shampoo, and clothes. Books, too. There's a good library in town. I haven't read my way right through it yet. Call me Valentina, without patronymic.'

And can you imagine, we unfolded the settee, I stuffed Valentina's wrap under my head, and we somehow both got under one blanket. Valentina dropped off and started snoring, and I thought I'd never drop off, but I did. In the morning I couldn't immediately work out where I was, or why it was so utterly dark.

Over a morning cup of tea, Valentina told me that she had no hope of liberation, since there was no-one on the outside to petition on her behalf. She had plenty of acquaintances, and family too, but no-one out there missed her; whether she existed or not was not important to them. That set me thinking: who needs me that much? Enough for them to petition for me, and get a result. Mum, obviously, but Mum is not to be worried, no way. And it's awkward for you to petition for me, Yulia, you've got your little one, your work, and you're far away—your cries won't reach their ears. At the same time, I'm healthy, and I'm even writing letters. Before, when I was free, you'd get old waiting for a letter from me.

Whereupon, as they said in olden times, I pay you my respects and bid you farewell. Hoping for the best.

Sasha

6 October 1986. Borovsk-23. Letter № 2

I woke up and thought, either I've died or I've gone blind. Eyes open, eyes shut: just as dark either way. Stuffy.

An insect gnawing away at something. Wood or stone. Something.

Valentina sighed, and I realised I was lying up against her hot side on the settee in the windowless pantry, that the insect was my watch gnawing away at time, gnawing a way through it without ever managing to gnaw right through. Time, of course, is neither wood nor stone; it's a soft substance, transparent, but without end; once you're caught in it you're gone, bogged down, stuck there until you die. And what then, afterwards? Nothing. Emptiness.

The alarm started up its clatter. Valentina turned on the lamp and said, 'From bed to work just three minutes. A big plus.'

We washed in the cold, clean toilet. Valentina gave me some toothpaste and soap and turned up a spare toothbrush.

ELENA DOLGOPYAT

She was in a splendid mood, jolly, as if she hadn't in fact just served six months in jail without seeing the fresh air. She rejoiced in the morning and in the cool, clean water. She did exercises right there at the sink. Persuaded me to do a set of squats.

We drank tea at the cleaners' (technicians') table, and ate a slice of white bread. Valentina said, 'I don't have butter. We don't have a fridge.'

She ordered me to clear away our crockery, fetched out her make-up bag, and fell to what she called a mop-up operation. Dabbed cream on her face with her fingertips. Applied a helping of powder. Touched up her eyebrows and added eyeshadow and mascara, and rosy highlights below her cheekbones.

She gave me a warning. 'I'm not letting you use my make-up. Get your own. How are my lips? OK?'

'OK.'

'This lipstick doesn't make me look old?'

'No. It's fine. Artistic.'

'Claudia buys it for me. She's completely incapable of buying the right colour. I ask for the palest rose, you know, but it's all cherry with her. It won't do. It won't do at all.'

I asked her how old she was.

'Forty-five will come knocking in December. You probably think that's really old.'

'We got up early. There's still a whole hour before work.'

'I love getting up early. I don't want to let myself go. You know. Become flaccid. I want to go back out into the wide world in good shape. I want to live a bit, you know. I'll have my savings. When I go out I'll be a queen. I'll be married in a jiffy.'

'You don't spend any money?'

'You're a complete fool. Small and stupid. You know nothing of life. Don't pout, I mean no offence. Our money goes into our savings books, yes? Our salary and subsistence. Who's taking it out if you're not? No-one. So you won't get your hands on any of it. And you're not going to appoint an attorney. Meaning I have no cash, and soon you won't either. I've a friend who gives me some from time to time and records it in a book so that later, if I get out, she can present me with an account.'

'If.' You hear that 'if', Yulia? I shuddered to hear it.

We poured ourselves tea and talked a bit more. Just chit-chat. We even laughed. The tea, by the way, is not bad. 'Good Cheer'–you know the brand. I remember we had it in the bakery by the hall. What a splendid time that was. Such big windows–you could see for miles from them. The Ostankino Tower, the tallest in the world. Or not the tallest. Not important. I'm reminiscing like an old woman for whom everything's already in the past. Ridiculous! I'll gnaw an underground passage with my teeth. I'll get my brain in gear and come up with something.

Valentina told me which office to go to and when, to make a personal appointment with the boss.

'I made no impression on him,' she said. 'He forgot me as soon as he saw me. But you're a young thing, such a pale little face, like a child's. He'll take pity on you. You may be a small cog but he'll oil the wheels for you.'

'What did he say to you?' We were already chatting away like friends.

'He said he couldn't make out a pass for me here, only at HQ, in Yaroslavl, and only if I was there personally. Pretty much the same story as the money in the savings book. A vicious circle.'

Yulia, I read about something like that once. Admittedly, I only skimmed it. Sergey brought me a book. I told you about him when I arrived for the winter holidays after the end of the first semester. I'd fallen head over heels for him. I always get the hots for clever types.

A book: sheets of paper inside a jacket. 200 or so pages. Typed. Touch typed. No end, nor will there be. The hero can't get into the castle. He'd been promised work there. He kept waiting for them to let him in. For some reason he couldn't just say, 'Sod it' and go away. In his place I'd have said 'Sod it.' I can't say 'Sod it' where I am now. I've got nowhere to go. It's a lot worse for me than it was for him.

Can you see the difference? He didn't go away because he was thick, although he could have gone. I can't go. They'd shoot me. The soldiers have real automatic rifles. With live rounds. We've been given warning. So I have no sympathy for him. I completely and utterly sympathise with myself. And everyone else sympathises with me. I can see how they're all sorry for me, like for someone terminally ill. It gives me the shivers.

Galina toted in a whole mountain of magazines from the library. 'Read,' she said. 'Entertain yourself. There are interesting articles in them these days.' Tanya brought a pillow and a wrap. I squashed the pillow into my bag and wound the wrap around me under my coat. Smiled at security and they let me through. Sweets they brought too, and money, so that I could go to the buffet and get something. We all found ourselves weeping easily. We hugged, shed a few tears, calmed down, and stomped off to work, as if everything was as it should be, as if a living human being had not, after all, been walled up.

The day was routine. I don't know what I was expecting. Here I was, caught up in something unbelievable, and the day was passing normally. People got on with their work; the men talked about football, mushrooms, the local forests.

I sat in a torpor. The sun was shining through the narrow window (which doesn't open, forget that). I went over to the window. The men were soldering their circuits. Beyond the window was the road leading to the checkpoint, to the exit, to the bus, to the forest though which you can walk to our little town. The girls went home from work exactly that way yesterday, breathing in the air.

Galina wrote my program for me. Without crossly pursing her lips. She even tried to explain something in a friendly voice. And said she was praying for me.

Even so, everyone has already (already!) managed to get used to my crazy situation. Me too.

I'm sitting calmly at my screen, typing my program out from my exercise book. Galina writes the letter L exactly the way she writes a D. We march off to the buffet for lunch. I take enough food to make sure I overeat. I'll save a couple of donuts to have with my evening cup of tea. Eventually they'll make me fat. The girls say they're going to the cinema in the evening, and look at me guiltily. I ask what film.

'Something foreign. The poster's a guy with a gun.'

They'll tell me about it tomorrow.

Everything was normal until the working day finished.

We handed in our exercise books to be put in the safe. I asked the girls if they were going through the forest.

'If it isn't raining.'

I wanted to ask them to bring me a sprig of pine, but wasn't about to embarrass them.

I stood at the window and watched for a while, then spread out the magazines. I didn't want to read, and decided to do a bit of fortune telling. I stabbed my finger on 'he was the whole world; nothing outside himself had ever existed ...'. I felt sad, Yulia, as if I'd been torn away from Earth and was flying further and further away through space, into the blackness and emptiness of night.

I leafed through the magazines, waiting for the cleaner. She finally arrived, lugging her heavy bucket and chaperoned by the security guard. He stood in the doorway while she got down to picking up bits of paper off the floor. I hurried over to help her, and while I was at it I asked her if the facility had any other pantry or even just a nook where I could make myself comfortable until my case was resolved.

The cleaner said, 'I don't know.'

She washed the floor, I went out, and the security guard locked and sealed the door.

I still had a little time; it was only eight o'clock.

I wandered off to Valentina, hugging my pillow and wrap. I thought I'd drink some 'Good Cheer' tea, and cheer up.

The stairs. The sentry. He was sitting behind the barrier like a police officer on duty down at the station.

I don't remember if I was writing to you. Probably not. In my second year (I think) we were walking along a street one night. I've already forgotten its name. I'm twenty-two but I'm losing my memory like an old woman. Anyway, I don't remember. Or maybe I never knew. Not far from Butyrsky Val? Or Minayevsky Market? Happy days. One of the lads was carrying a splendid Japanese twin cassette machine, a Panasonic (I remember the make, at least). We had it on at full volume, of course. Pink Floyd 'The Wall.' Yes yes, I remember that too. Building the wall and tearing it down. On a street in Moscow, at night, in 1982, let's say it was. Autumn.

It was still warm. We were walking together, a little army, a reconnaissance squad, cool as Kalashnikovs, a musical bomb; look out!

We were detained and taken to the police station. The old guy on duty quietly asked us where we'd got the tape recorder from. Galina explained that her father had brought it back with him–he worked on a scientific research boat.

'Caught it in his net,' joked Misha.

'Not a bad catch,' the duty officer answered. He made a record of the incident and let us go. Ordered us not to make a noise at night, not to disturb people resting.

'They have to go to work tomorrow. Unlike you.'

I approached the sentry. He was studying the crossword in his paper. He finished writing the word 'asthma'.

'Hi,' I said.

No answer.

'Where are you from?' I asked.

No answer. He wrote the word 'galactic'.

'What words you know.'

No answer.

'All the best, soldier. I'm sorry.'

The corridor. The stairs. The cubbyhole.

Valentina and the cleaner were drinking tea. A half-litre tin of strawberry jam stood on the table by them. A bottle of Mozhaysk milk.

The table lamp was on, and they were sitting comfortably in its light. Steam was rising above their tea. Valentina dropped a cube of refined sugar into her glass and started to stir it, her spoon clinking and tinkling. I stood in the doorway in some confusion. Valentina was not looking at me, and the cleaner did not turn her head. Yet they must have heard me open the door and come in.

I wished them *bon appetit.*

The cleaner spread jam on her bread and spoke to Valentina. 'Not many strawberries this year.'

'There'll be a good crop of potatoes, though.'

'Yes. Thank God.'

'Class.' (This was me. I'd decided to join the conversation.)

Valentina slowly turned her head and looked at me with her bulging hazel eyes. 'Don't stand there. Go to your own room. And shut the door behind you. You're letting in a draught.'

'Meaning what? Where am I supposed to go?'

'Wherever you like. The world is huge. You don't like it here. Not that I know why. My bread is not to your taste, perhaps, or I'm in your bad books. It happens. Never mind. Go. Bird brain. She wants her own living space. Bighead.'

She finished, and turned away.

How was I to know, Yulia, that the cleaner would tell Valentina and Valentina would take offence? I had absolutely no idea where I was to go now, with my wrap and pillow and all my things.

I went out of the utility room in a complete daze.

The whole night was in front of me. Whole and indivisible.

Oh, Yulia, I've well and truly copped it. I've no strength for this.

Sasha

6 October 1986. Borovsk-23. Letter № 3

I'm writing the same day. More accurately, at night. I've already sealed up the first letter. Obviously I could steam it open, but I don't need to scrimp on envelopes.

After Valentina drove me out I went back to the sentry. Hugging my wrap and pillow, all exactly as before.

He sat behind his barrier and watched me. His look was vacant, like a fascist in a film.

'Hi', I said.

No answer. But at least he didn't drive me away.

'Finished your crossword?'

Silence.

'Where are you from?' I asked.

Still silence.

'I'm from Ust-Kamenogorsk', I said.

I told him about our river, our sugar loaf knolls, and about the two factories pumping out the sweet smell of lead and zinc and titanium and magnesium. The sun. The small, sweet melons, the live carp, the yellow autumn leaves, the stone bridge.

I don't know if he was listening or not. He was silent. His rifle was resting against the back of his chair. I tell him I've stripped a rifle with my eyes shut. The quickest in my class.

'How long did it take?' he asked.

Bingo! The dam breached, the fortress fallen.

I'm not saying he joined in the conversation. But he chuckled when I told him about our colonel measuring the boys' hair with a tape measure and sending the girls to the toilet to wash off their mascara.

'You be careful not to get like that,' I said. 'When you leave the service, take off your uniform, put on your civvies and dig your garden, go fishing, go to Crimea for the whole summer. Just don't go to school to teach basic military training.'

He chuckled again. 'I won't. I'm not going to be a soldier.'

'What are you going to be?'

'I don't know.'

'Does your stint here finish soon?'

'None of your business. Curiosity killed the cat. A chatterbox is a godsend for a spy. The less you know, the better you sleep.'

'Well. You are a one.'

'Go away. Don't distract me. I'm on duty.'

'Where? Where can I go?'

I burst into tears. I didn't mean to; it wasn't conscious. I stood there bawling my eyes out and couldn't stop. I didn't want to do it; it was about as welcome as snow at harvest time. I threw my wrap, pillow, bag, everything on the floor and howled. He was well flummoxed. Went pale, grabbed the phone. I didn't hear what he was saying. I was in absolute floods.

An officer arrived. The same one who'd travelled with us from Balabanovo. He wasn't as tall as I'd thought then. And this time I spotted a big star on his shoulder straps. Meaning he was a major: thank you, basic military training. He took one look at me and went away. He went away and my tears dried up. I was tired.

Leaving my stuff where it was, on the floor, I dragged myself to the toilet, washed in the icy water, and blew my nose. I didn't hurry back. I looked at myself in the mirror with a hatred with which I'd never looked at anyone before. Really and truly. I went out and headed back for my things, and there was the major.

'I'll help you,' he said.

He picked up my things from the floor and carried them. I set off after him. I didn't look at the soldier.

I followed the major up to the next floor. We walked along a corridor–such a huge corridor, a veritable street, and crooked to boot, like a street in Moscow. None of the doors had name plates, all of them were locked, and there was only emergency lighting and every other bulb was out into the bargain. Any minute now, I thought, a guy will step out of the shadows and ask for a light.

At the end of the corridor was a door flung wide. Light was coming from the opening, and soldiers were bustling about, carrying out a huge table and some other clutter.

'Nearly done?' asked the major sternly.

We waited another three minutes or so while they took out all the junk, wiped the floor (yes, really!), and brought in a trestle bed, a bedside table, a chair, and a table lamp. They fitted the whole thing out in a twinkling. The major carried out an inspection and said, 'Good work. Dismissed.'

He laid my things carefully on the bed, handed me the keys (!), and left. Thus I was given my own living space. It looked something like an old pantry.

It's fine. Cosy.

I spread out my wrap, tossed my pillow onto the bed, and lay down. I looked at the wall. Wall, wall. Painted with a green oil-based paint. Not the green of spring or the dark green of the end of summer, when the mornings already hold a whiff of autumn, but official, standard-issue green, the like of which there is nothing else in the world.

Cheerless murk. The gleam of the electric light did nothing to soften the impression.

Oh my God.

I wanted to cry again, but couldn't. I thought about the major. Dishy. Not a big man, only a little taller than me, but very nicely proportioned, with open shoulders, a straight back, and an easy gait. The back of his head was round, and his hair ... I've no idea whether his hair was soft or coarse. Next time, I'll ask him, 'May I touch your hair?'

Light hair, cut short.

I imagined him naked.

I went on thinking about him until I fell asleep. When I woke up, the lamp was still on and the wall was catching the light from somewhere. I looked at my watch–whoa, the working day was already underway. That's it, Yulia, my dearest friend.

Sasha

3 January 1987. Borovsk-23. Letter № 4

Hi, Yulia. I'm still alive.

I got all your letters (I can tell from your numbering). I couldn't answer. I didn't have the energy. I didn't have the energy for anything.

I found that room and then got stuck in it. I broke down. The only place I went was the toilet. I didn't turn on the light. I got so used to the dark I could see the photons; they found their way into me. Only joking. I wasn't totally blind, though. I could see the door being opened from the outside (they had spare keys, then; I really didn't care). The light hurt me, and I closed my eyes and turned my face to the wall.

The girls left sandwiches, sweets, and milk for me on the table. I ate, alone, in the dark. With photons for company.

I ate, I lay down; that was all. I didn't think about anything. I'd done all the thinking of which I was capable.

The girls stopped trying to reason with me. They told me that out there it was winter, cold, with white snow. And that soon it would be New Year. They were going away to Moscow. They'd taken a flat there. On Okskaya Street. A one-room flat in a prefabricated high rise, up under the roof. I imagined Okskaya Street as a river.

White snow. White snow. I could see it as I lay there; it glowed in the dark. The snowflakes rustled as they flew. Onto me. Snow drifted over me and covered me. I had no way to breathe; there was snow in my mouth and in my nostrils. I had to wake up; I had to get out of this or I'd die.

I started screaming, just to hear my own voice.

I groped for the switch.

I crawled out of my burrow to find the corridor festively lit, deserted and silent. I didn't know what time it was–my watch stopped ages ago. When my eyes had got used to the light, I went back to my room and picked up my soap, toothbrush, and toothpaste. And a towel. Someone had brought me a towel while I was in the darkness of nothingness. They'd brought me a lot of stuff, actually–all my things had been collected together and put beside me, and there was also a small transistor radio with a bright blue plastic shell and a black leather case with a thin carry-strap.

I'm grateful of course, but it's scary that they were all in here with me and I was with them, in my own room. It's scary that this is it now, for ever. I'm tired of worrying, though, Yulia. One gets used to everything. And in every situation one finds cause for joy. Well, not every.

In the toilet, I blocked the door with a mop and washed myself until I squeaked. Stared in the mirror. My hair's grown long and my eyes have sunk. No big deal. I'll live.

I suddenly realised that the toilet smelled like a New Year fir tree. The authentic smell of the forest. I thought it was some kind of hallucination, but I found fir branches and New Year tinsel in the rubbish bin. From which, as a true Sherlock Holmes, I concluded that the New Year had arrived. And not long ago.

The smell of pine seemed to throw a switch in me. I felt as if a miracle was about to happen. Or it had already happened and I just couldn't figure out what it was yet. I was suddenly happy, in spite of everything, and I was only afraid that this festive feeling would soon fade. I tried to preserve it, like a small fire in the hearth of a chilly house. Fuel, I needed fuel, so that the flame would catch. I threw myself into clearing up my cubbyhole.

The lamp was shining, and I gave the floors and walls a thorough clean. I suddenly caught sight of a picture. It hadn't been there before.

I say picture. Reproduction. It had been nailed to the wall with small parcel nails, in such a way as to be in my field of vision as I lay on my trestle bed, instead of the official, standard-issue electric glare.

The reproduction was of a field under a cloudy but light sky. You could make out a path in the field, and the dark of a forest on the horizon to the left, but the path turned to the right before it reached the forest.

No-one was walking along it. The landscape was deserted and could have belonged to any time in history. It was not clear whether it was morning, evening, or daytime. Peace or war. Who knows? I thought of this landscape as a pause. A halt in time and space. You take it easy, as they say.

I picked up the radio. Turned it on. Shhhhshhhhshhh. The voice of the ether. White noise. The ether was densely populated with it. As if every soul who'd ever lived was murmuring.

I turned off the radio.

Taking the radio, I left my hiding place, locked the door, and set off on a long journey, down the corridor, up the

ELENA DOLGOPYAT

stairs, up and down, to the place where Valentina lived. I was still happy. I wanted to ask for her forgiveness. It was New Year, after all. I didn't think about whether she might be asleep or working. I had to go. The staircases smelled of frosty air; it had found its way into our dungeon, and that brought a sense of alarm and hope at the same time.

The door to her cubbyhole was locked. I knocked.

Footsteps, and Valentina's sleepy voice: 'Who is it?'

'It's me. Let me in, please, dear Valentina. I did you a great wrong, and I want to make it up to you. Please let me!'

'Are you drunk?'

'No! How can you think that?'

She stood silent behind the door without going away, and I stood in front of the door without going away. Maybe something was happening out there in the world, or maybe nothing was. I switched on the radio. The souls murmured and trembled. I turned the dial and a man's voice sang out:

'Burnt by the sun ...'

Valentina opened the door.

I handed her the singing radio.

'... said farewell to the sea ...'

'This is for you. A present. Happy New Year.'

'... when you said you were losing ...'

'You can't come in.'

'... your love for me ...'

'Come in.'

We drank sweet liqueur. The radio was mumbling some news that had nothing to do with either of us, not me, not Valentina.

We drank liqueur and ate bread and sausage.

'You want to get out?' Valentina asked suddenly.

She was looking at me, and her eyes seemed huge.

'What a question.'

'I don't. I'm better off here. I'm not needed there. In Moscow, the flat's full of people. There's constant noise. No-one loves me. I can feel it. I cry, then I yell at them. I yell, but no-one hears me. In town, in my room, I can hear the neighbours laughing at me. Quietly, but I can hear them. No-one loves me. And really, why should anyone love me?'

I burst into tears and threw myself at Valentina, hugging her, stroking her hair.

I cried, and Valentina cried. I said that it was all nonsense, that people were good, that Valentina was good. She pushed me away. She blew her nose, and told me fetch her handbag.

'It's under my pillow, for safekeeping. Go and get it. I don't want to get up.'

I brought the handbag, and Valentina opened it.

'Everything I have is in here. The keys to my Moscow flat, and my room in town, and the key to this kennel. And your pass, in a secret pocket.'

She took out the pass and put it on the table.

'Take it. You're free. Forgive me, if you can.'

I didn't move.

'I stole it. I took such a liking to you. Such a simple soul.'

I was silent.

'Take it. Go.'

'And your pass. Yours is also in there, in the secret pocket?'

'Yes.'

I picked up my pass from the table.

Stood up.

Headed for the door.

And heard her say, 'I suppose you'll tell everyone?'

I turned round.

'No-one.'

That was a lie, because there's no way I can't tell you, Yulia.

That's all, my dear. Love and kisses.

Sasha

PS I walked into town, through the frosty night, through the forest. I walked with no fear, walked like I was singing a song. Electric lights lit my way.

I presented my pass at the checkpoint, and they let me through; a miracle.

I walked, the snow creaking. There was a huge fir tree in the square, topped with a glowing star. The major was smoking nearby.

I went up to him and stood looking at him. I started to sing, softly:

'Burnt by the sun ...'

He turned round. Threw his cigarette into the snow.

'... said farewell to the sea ...'

I put my hands on his shoulders.

'... when you said you were losing ...'

He hugged me.

We stood there, like that.

KATERINAA

You are reading Katerinaa's journal.

29 December 2012, 20:00

Katerinaa: Obviously I asked if the seat was free, just in case.

'No,' said the old lady.

She was sitting by the window. The seat next to her was being guarded by mittens.

People were still getting on. The old lady was looking confused, and I was hoping that no-one would approach her, that she'd have to clear away her guard mutts, and then I could sit down at last. I didn't have the strength to go on standing.

The old lady's mutts were of grey wool, a simple stitch, and one of them had a green eye patch on its thumb. A velvet patch, to boot. A dark shade, malachite, beautiful. God knows where that penniless old woman in her old man's jacket, her dark shiny skirt and felt boots with galoshes got such a beautiful scrap. Maybe she'd had a jacket like that when she was young. I tried to imagine her young and beautiful, in a dark green velvet jacket, face lightly powdered, scented with the faintest hint of Red Moscow. The old lady reminded me of mine in a way that made my heart squeeze.

The train started. The old lady, still hopeful, scanned the people making their way down the aisle. I didn't rush her.

She looked at me, and cleared away her mutts.

I settled myself in the seat. The crowd stood in the aisle, swaying in time with the train.

It was stuffy, sleepy.

The old lady's withered, yellowed fingernails suddenly touched my hand.

'My dear,' she asked, 'do you have a telephone?'

She unbuttoned her jacket and took out from a hidden inside pocket a sheet of paper folded in four. Yellowed graph paper, probably from an old school exercise book used by her grandchildren and kept in a closet somewhere, with marks and comments.

There was a number written on it in big letters gone over twice to make them clear. I dialled it.

A high male voice answered.

'Hello! Hello!'

'Hello. Your grandmother wants a word.'

I put the phone into the old lady's hand.

'Mitya!' the old lady squawked into the phone. 'I'm here! I'm on the train! I'm on the train! Where are you? Where *are* you?'

What her Mitya answered her, I don't know.

After the conversation, she calmed down, and pulled out from under her seat a much-battered dark blue school backpack. She unzipped it and fished out a bag which turned out to contain pies. From the Russian stove; that's what the old lady said. She offered me a taste. I didn't say no. I don't do any baking, but I've watched my grandmother many times. You get the wood in the stone firebox properly alight and burning, and then place a baking tray on the bricks over the coals. You cover the firebox with an iron screen, and there, behind the screen, in the bake oven, the pies and puffs rise and brown.

The old lady's pies were potatoes and fried onion. I ate and was happy. We parted friends. I even know her name now: Daria Sergeyevna.

I'd pigged out on the pies, so I was in no hurry to have dinner. I wandered around town, along the main street, glancing in and out of shops, but I didn't buy anything. Back home, I just drank tea. Tomorrow I think I'll go to Ikea to get a sofa. Mine's already fallen apart.

Snezanna: There's free coffee for breakfast in Ikea ☺. Or tea.

Dimon: Their coffee is disgusting.

Snezanna: You're being picky. As ever.

Dimon: I'm being objective. As ever.

Katerinaa: I like that everything there is flat pack. I've loved construction kits since I was a kid.

Dimon: You'll knacker yourself putting a sofa together on your own.

Katerinaa: I've managed a wardrobe. Been there, done that.

Dimon: Oh!

Snezanna: You know you can pay extra for delivery and assembly. Not that expensive.

29 December 2012, 23:40

Katerinaa: The phone woke me up. A thin male voice, like a sharp needle.

'Mitya. It's Mitya. My gran called me today from your phone.'

'And?'

'She's disappeared. She was supposed to make her way to the platform and wait for me there, and she's not on the platform.'

'Where are you calling from?' I ask.

'The platform.'

'What, you've only just got there?'

'Well, yes,' he said. 'Events ... I got seriously held up. Soon as I was free I dashed off to meet her at the station.'

ELENA DOLGOPYAT

'Have a little look at the time,' I said. 'How long was she supposed to wait for you on the platform? It is winter out there.'

'Yes, I know.'

'There's no need to shout. I don't know where she is now. Maybe she made it home. Does she have the address?'

'Basically, yes, she's got it all written down, but she's not at home, I've already been back there to look. Raced. No-one's seen her.'

'Well, perhaps there's a warm shop at the station.'

'I've already looked!'

'What are you shouting for? You think I'm to blame?'

'I don't know what to do. I'm going completely bonkers here.'

'Call the police. Ring round the hospitals. Keep asking around. I'm sorry, but I have to get up early tomorrow.'

'Of course, I understand. But while you were with her, was everything OK?'

'Everything was just fine.'

'OK. But it wasn't my fault! Honestly–'

I didn't listen to his explanations. And now I can't sleep. Where is that Daria Sergeyevna? Where's she wandered off to? I can still see her with her school backpack on her shoulders.

Dimon: It's not her you're seeing, it's your own grandmother. It's called displacement.

Katerinaa: Oh, you're not asleep either?

Dimon: Obviously. It's half past four in the morning here. I haven't gone to bed yet.

Katerinaa: What's the weather like?

Dimon: Thirty six.

Dimon: Minus.

Katerinaa: I got that.

Dimon: You don't have this where you are.

Katerinaa: Do you go out?

Dimon: In a spacesuit. Near enough. Warm underwear. Two sweaters. A down jacket. If it were up to me I wouldn't go out at all, I'd just sit by the stove.

Katerinaa: You have a stove??

Dimon: Radiators. A normal flat in a five-storey building with steam heating. Pretty much like yours.

Katerinaa: My grandma had a stove.

Dimon: You were saying. Pies. Was her house in a village?

Katerinaa: Almost.

Dimon: I wouldn't say no to that. Somewhere in your neck of the woods where the winters are milder and Paris is closer.

Katerinaa: Do you have any idea what it's like to live in a house like that? Water from the standpipe. Gas in cylinders. Coal and firewood ordered and ferried in, too. Ancient wiring, electricity barely up to raising a spark. Rooftop aerial picking up one and a half channels. Rotten beams. Leaking roof. Damp and fungus in the basement. It wasn't a house, it was a crypt. It needed dismantling and rebuilding, preferably somewhere else; might have been viable then. I went there every summer, helped her out and tried to get her to move in with me, but no, no way, she wanted to be on her own in her own house, the mistress. 'What would I do,' she said, 'in your city flat—look out the window and sit on the bench at the entrance clocking everyone going by?' She was right, there'd have been nothing for her to do here, she was used to freedom. But she was old! Shovelling the snow got to be hard work for her. She downsized the bucket she fetched water in, and she was afraid to go into the basement. But she didn't move. Dug her heels in. So she died there, all alone.

Dimon: What can you see from your window?

Katerinaa: Red Square. OK, there are houses blocking it. About fifty kilometres of houses and trees. Knock them all down and you'd be able to see Red Square. Through a telescope.

Dimon: You're angry.

Katerinaa: So would you be.

Dimon: I can't see anything out of my window even in the daytime. Med school's over the road, but fog's eaten the lot—buildings, people, trees. It's eaten me too.

Katerinaa: Why did you quit your job again?

Dimon: Tired.

Dimon: I'll get another job soon.

Katerinaa: Where?

Dimon: Same place. Ambulance service.

Katerinaa: You've had your rest, then?

Dimon: Running out of money.

3 January 2013, 21:35

Katerinaa: The grey cover rises a little. In the black lacquered depths, lights start to burn; the depths come to life. The cover slides off beneath a huge window the length of the wall. In the black depths beyond the window, lights are burning too.

A tall, thin man pulls back a chair and sits down at the piano. He lifts the lid and kneads his fingers. His eyes are lowered.

Few people in the large hall see the pianist. Many are asleep. A child is crying. An unshaven old chap, concentrating on each step, carries a steaming cup. The smell of coffee and the hum of the coffee machine could mislead you. If you closed your eyes and concentrated on just that smell and that sound, you could imagine you were in a café. Pick any city. Paris. Rome. Somewhere you've been or somewhere you haven't. Either way, it's an imaginary city.

The announcer tells everyone the train to Chita is now boarding. People can be heard getting ready.

Nadia opens her eyes. She is in the first-floor waiting room at Yaroslavsky Railway Station, with its huge panoramic window looking over the railway tracks and into the black distance. The piano seems out of place here.

Under its grey cover, the piano had attracted little attention. But then a tall man in a thick woollen coat had gone up to it, taken off his coat, folded it, and hung it on the back of the chair. He removed a stand with an advertisement that read:

CONCERT

DAILY

3:15 TO 4:00 P.M.

He lifted the cover.

It was time for Nadia to go. Fifteen minutes to her train; just time to get a seat.

The man starts to play. People waiting for their trains turn at the sound of the piano. Necks stretch. Some rise a little way from their seat. Others are on their way back to their seats with steaming cups. Some edge closer to the piano. The coffee equipment is still humming. The public address announces the arrival of a train.

The pianist plays popular melodies. From the seventies and eighties. Soviet and foreign pop songs. In a concert hall his playing would likely come over as dull, lame, even. But here his music sounds festive and bright. Strange. Here, he's Richter. God.

He plays out his forty-five minutes. Takes his hands off the keys. A few claps are heard. He rises, bows.

The grey cover slides back over the piano.

Snezanna: Great. I like it very much. And Nadia. Is that you?

Katerinaa: I sign articles for the newspaper 'Nadia K'.

Dimon: Is there even a word of truth in it?

Katerinaa: It's all true.

Dimon: I found myself envying your pianist.

Katerinaa: Me too.

Dimon: Mind you, I envy everybody now. I am of that stripe.

Dimon: Dare I ask what you were doing in the long-distance waiting room? Were you perchance heading for our part of the world. Lake Baikal and beyond?

Katerinaa: I was waiting for my local train. The one I normally catch was cancelled, and I thought I'd rather spend two hours in warmth and relative comfort.

Snezanna: Awesome. Is it really true: a piano and a musician, in a railway station?

Katerinaa: Yes.

Snezanna: Hard to believe. I wonder who he is.

Katerinaa: An amateur. Retired. Used to work for the railway. Probably. That's what I think.

Dimon: As far as I recall, you're not keen on Moscow. What took you there?

Katerinaa: Newspaper business.

Dimon: And how did Nadia K. find the capital at the beginning of the year? At the beginning of times, you might say.

Katerinaa: OK. Not many people.

Dimon: What took your paltry provincial newspaper to Moscow?

Katerinaa: An animator. He has a dacha in our district. He uses his Moscow flat to winter away the winter, and paints our provincial landscapes from memory. Not just the countryside. Paltry small-town backyards. An old five-storey building, for example, grown into the ground. A yard, washing on a line. Bedclothes, underwear, all out in the open. The multicoloured underside of life.

Dimon: You like him?

Katerinaa: Yes. But it's difficult talking to him. The whole time it seems like I'm asking something not quite right. That he's answering purely out of politeness. That he could tell me something much more interesting, but I can't find the right question. Maybe he's sitting there right now, drawing me from memory.

Dimon: Nadia K.? Katerinaa?

Katerinaa: Don't know. Who knows who he sees in me. I wouldn't hazard a guess.

Dimon: You've had a cultural day. An artist, a pianist. Although mostly that was Nadia K's day. Anything for Katerinaa?

Katerinaa: The pianist went off and I dashed away to get my train. There'd already been one after the cancellation, right before the one I got. Everyone went off on the first, and I got a seat on the second easily, by the window.

The heating was up high, and I was worn out and weary. I didn't sleep, but it felt like I was asleep. And that if I woke up, the carriage would disappear with all its passengers, including me, and the winter outside the window would disappear and so would the long stretches between stops and the lonely platforms. The only thing is, in my dream I didn't see what would appear in their place. And I saw it all kind of disjointed, with gaps. One moment there was a man standing in the aisle juggling balls. The next a woman walked in covered in snow and smelling of cold. But then I suddenly saw an icy platform, a bench, and a frozen grey mitten lying on it, looking out with a green eye. And I slowly worked out that the mitten must be the old lady's. And suddenly I was outside the carriage, on the platform, a flurry of snow whipping up in the wake of the departing train.

ELENA DOLGOPYAT

My dream ended on that little platform. I realised that I was standing there on my own, that the place was deserted, that in a somnambulant trance I'd overshot my stop by miles, and God only knew when the next train back would be.

The snowy dust settled, and I fished the mitten out through the railing. It was frozen through, and very like the old lady's. The wool was grey, and, more important, there was that green velvet eye.

I took out my phone and called Mitya, but he hung up. I tapped out the message *Has your grandmother been found?*

I waited a long time for an answer.

No.

Any news at all?

Pause.

No.

I think I've spotted her mitten on the platform. Tell the police.

No answer.

I thought: he'll call back.

I stood there holding the one-eyed mitten and had no idea what to do. I stepped down from the platform and wandered a little way along the tracks. In the wood a woodpecker was knocking.

A crossing. A small market. Dogs frisking about, jars of honey looking beautiful in the light. Five-storey houses nearby. A light burning in one of the kiosks. Cottage cheese in the window, sour cream.

I took a packet of nine percent; I thought I'd make some pancakes with it. I asked the saleswoman if she'd seen an old lady. The saleswoman was much higher than me in her kiosk–she must have had a raised floor in there.

'Yes,' she said. 'We got swarms of old ladies. Only thing is, I can't tell them apart. I caught sight of my own face in the mirror the other day and was, like, who's that strange old girl.'

'Is your cottage cheese good?'

'People buy it and don't complain.'

I asked around at the market, and drew a complete blank. I was freezing. I trudged off in the direction of the houses and popped into a chemist to warm up. I asked the guard there. No, he didn't know anything about an old lady. He gave the same story. Lots of them, he said. They don't want to die.

The old lady's mitten warmed up, too, and thawed out. Its green eye became darker and damper.

'Look,' I said to him. 'Look. You never know. You might see something.'

I headed back towards the platform, crossed to the other side, and looked at the timetable. A bit over an hour to hang about.

I bought my ticket and asked the cashier. Got the same answer.

'Loads of them. All look the same. Old things, off to who knows where. Why can't they stay at home? I get to be their age, I won't be gadding about.'

I went back over the crossing to the houses and looked in at the hairdresser's. I asked the receptionist if they would cut my hair. They didn't do a bad job, I must say. Told me that yes they do have old ladies who go there, and they only charge them a hundred rubles. Maybe mine's one of them, who knows. They were nice girls. They treated me to coffee.

Snezanna: What if it's not her mitten?

3 January 2013, 23:44

Katerinaa: When I was a child, I used to stay with my grandmother. The house had no facilities; I've already said that. So we went to the public baths once a week. On Thursdays, because on Saturdays there was a gigantic queue. We took our basins and our rubber flip-flops in newspaper, bast back scrubs, and chunks of bath soap. I used emerald-coloured shampoo which made my hair smell like apple. Grandma washed her hair with baby soap. We chose a place away from the steam room and closer to the shower. We washed and then towelled ourselves off and cooled down in the anteroom. We dressed without hurrying, went home, put on the kettle, and drank tea with jam, five cups each.

On one of our Thursdays at the baths there were old ladies in the anteroom. About twenty of them. Naked, bony, bent, ugly, some without breasts, with scars. They made their way barefoot to the entrance of the bathing room, stepping slowly and unsteadily on the slippery tiled floor, in a chain, holding on to one another. I watched as they disappeared one by one into the white steam.

The door closed behind them, and my grandmother told me that the old ladies had been brought in from the nursing home for their bath.

Dimon: You sorry for them?
Katerinaa: Of course.
Dimon: It's yourself you're feeling sorry for. You're afraid of getting old.
Katerinaa: And you? Aren't you afraid?
Dimon: I won't live that long.
Dimon: I hope.
Katerinaa: Why aren't you asleep again?
Dimon: I don't want to dream.

5 January 2013, 19:40

Katerinaa: I went to a village which shall remain nameless, on newspaper business. A town, to be precise. Almost eleven thousand inhabitants, lots of oriental faces.

Cats. Crows, tits, sparrows. Stray dogs, dogs with owners.

Cars half covered with snow in the courtyards. Lenin on a pedestal in the square. Milk delivered in drums. Pensioners milling about with cans and flasks. Some produced a piece of paper with an official stamp and were given theirs free. Local government supporting the hard up. The roads in the courtyards were iced with frozen lava lightly powdered with snow. Walking across it was no simple matter.

People sit in their homes, eating and sleeping. They go out infrequently, to the shops and back. The sky is grey and low. You open the fanlight and the grey sky flows into the flat. It's deadly dull. There's nothing worse than the urban settlements around Moscow. It's not a dacha under golden pine trees in virgin snow, like in a picture in a children's book.

The bus was old and clapped out, with plywood instead of glass in its doors and sneezing out blue smoke. I suspected that its engine on its wooden mounts and wire clips was actually not resting on them at all, but on fresh air and promises. That didn't stop them charging the full twenty-five rubles, not a kopeck less. They put the ticket prices up straight away, from the first day of the new year.

There weren't many people, because of the holidays. A boy of about ten and his mother, both of them with sleepy faces. Three fishermen with metal boxes. Me. A young woman with music blasting into her headphones.

We all took our seats, the bus set off, and the conductress got up, big and important, to collect our change.

The boy was sitting right in front of me.

It was cold in the bus, and the windows were frozen. The boy melted a little window in the ice with his hand and looked through it, like through a submarine porthole.

His mother's phone rang.

'We should make it,' she assured the unseen caller. 'If we don't break down.'

ELENA DOLGOPYAT

'We'll hold out,' grinned the conductress. 'We'll get to the aerodrome.'

The bus was taking us to the last local train before a long two-hour break. It seemed a miracle that it wasn't falling to pieces along the road. Maybe the conductress was keeping it going by the sheer force of her spirit. She was cheerful and warm, and bored just sitting there in silence. She asked the boy where his mother was taking him.

'The cinema,' the boy replied.

'You can tell me about it on the way back.'

'If it's another bus, I won't.'

'It won't be another one. Ours is the only one on this route. So pray it doesn't break down.'

The bus suddenly wheezed, slowed down, and lurched to an abrupt halt on Yaroslavka.

'We're all alive,' the conductress reassured us cheerfully. 'Still here.'

The bus opened its old doors with a creak. A bulky, middle-aged woman covered in snow lost her footing on the step, grabbed the handrail, and tried to climb in. Her foot kept slipping off. The boy's mother looked worriedly at her watch. One of the fishermen grabbed the woman and hauled her aboard.

'I have a pensioner's pass,' the woman announced.

'Pay anyway,' ordered the conductress. 'Oversize load.'

The woman settled herself on a vacant seat and fished out her purse.

'How much?'

'A hundred rubles. No, come on, come on, I'm joking. Don't take offence.'

'Offence taken,' said the woman. 'Here's your hundred.'

'You could get there in a taxi for a hundred. Don't take offence.'

The bus, meanwhile, was turning off Yaroslavka onto a country road.

From hill to hill and over the bridge across the river ran the country road. To the station.

There was no sign of the train.

'It's not been cancelled,' the cashier reassured us through her window. 'It's running late.'

The boy stood at the edge of the platform staring fixedly at the forest.

The forest was small, with well-trodden paths, but from the platform it looked like a jungle, an impassably dense thicket, a fairy tale darkness.

'Come away from the edge,' the mother ordered the boy.

He gave no sign of having heard her. He stared at the dense forest, eyebrows knitted severely. There was no wind, no snow; not even the sound of a car.

'Mama,' said the boy in the winter silence. 'I saw the old lady again.'

His mother took him by the shoulder and led him away from the edge.

'Where did you see her? There?' She pointed to the forest.

'No. I saw her from the bus.' He waved in the direction of the country road.

'Wonderful. That means she's alive.'

'Wait, what old lady, where? Where exactly?' I stepped towards the boy.

'What's the matter?' asked the mother, alarmed. She looked at me warily.

'I'm sorry, it's just that an old lady I know went missing somewhere in our neighbourhood, right before New Year, on the last working day, the 29th. She had one of those school backpacks with her.'

'That's right,' cried the boy happily. 'A backpack.'

'Her name is Daria Sergeyevna.'

'She didn't tell us her name.'

The boy's mother recounted how on the last working day of the old year, 29 December, late in the evening,

ELENA DOLGOPYAT

driving along the country road, they'd picked up an old lady. She'd been hovering about the bus stop, apparently waiting for a bus; she couldn't have known that the bus was at the terminus, broken down.

'Not the one that brought us here today, another one, newer. We were on our way back from over there, from the town, in our car, over the crossing, and on to Yaroslavka, home. We don't have the car today, Dad's got the car today. Anyway, we felt sorry for the old lady, slowed down, asked her where she was going. She looked at us and didn't say a word. Maybe she's hard of hearing. "Where are you going?" we asked. "To the village? Get in, we'll give you a lift." She got in. My Vitya was tired. I looked at him and his eyes were sticking together, and I was dozing off. It had been a hard day. I put on some music to wake us up. So there we were, driving up hill and down dale and the old lady was looking out of the window and I didn't spot exactly when she suddenly started trying to scramble out of the car. I quickly slowed down, opened the door, and the old woman went tumbling out of the car and hurried off into the woods. It was already pitch dark, by the way.'

'Did you notice if she was wearing one mitten or two?'

'None,' said the boy.

I asked for her mobile number and left my own, just in case. After all, they take that country high road pretty well every day.

She gave me her card. *Alla. Sales manager.*

I used to dream of being called Alla when I was a child.

Snezanna: Why didn't the little chap say he'd seen her straight away, on the bus?

Katerinaa: I don't know. He was wrapped up in himself, in his own world, in his magic circle of ice. He might not even have properly recognised her. I don't know.

Dimon: Why Alla?

Katerinaa: I was going to text Mitya but then I had second thoughts. I wondered if the little lad had imagined it. Or perhaps it was the wrong old lady altogether.

I let the train go without me. The train whisked everyone else away, and I wandered back, over the crossing, along the country road, along the verge. It took me half an hour to get to Yaroslavka. I didn't meet the old lady. Bitterly disappointed, I caught a bus coming from Sergiev Posad that got me to VDNKh.

Dimon: Why Alla?

Katerinaa: I bought Altai honey at VDNKh. I'm drinking tea with it at the moment.

Snezanna: Oh! I'm drinking tea with honey right now as well. Can you imagine?! ☺

6 January 2013, 01:20

Katerinaa: I sent Mitya a text message after all. I asked him: *Any news?*

The answer came back in a minute:

Do you have Skype?

I saw Mitya with my own eyes on my computer screen. It was excruciating, because there was a big delay on the line. I heard his voice, and then his face twisted as his mouth tried to get out things I'd already had time to answer. We were too far apart, at different ends of the earth.

Mitya's in Mexico. A very important business trip. On 29 December last year, I took his seat on the train next to an old lady, because he was late.

'That's the kind of job I have,' said Mitya.

He was trying to justify himself. To me, to himself, to the whole wide world.

'I simply got held up. She promised to wait for me on the platform. I got there as soon as I could, and she wasn't there.'

'And how long did she wait for you there?'

'I don't know.'

'Hypothetically. How long?'

'An hour and a half.'

'Rather a long time. In winter.'

'I see that, but what was I to do? I couldn't abandon everything, no way. I had to finish everything at the office. I was snowed under and had to fly out that night to Mexico. I already had my ticket and all that. And I went. You can think what you like but I couldn't not go. We had an agreement that I'd get her home, show her everything, and fly out. I left her a note on the door just in case, to call the neighbours. The neighbours had been warned, they had the key. The whole of my block was in the loop. She never showed up. The militia didn't know anything. The police, I mean. What would you have me do? I don't know.'

'I don't know either.'

'So get off my back, then.'

'Why was she going to yours in the first place?'

'Why do I have to report to you?'

'You don't.'

'She wasn't coping on her own, that's about the size of it.'

Dimon: Why Alla?

Katerinaa: Do you ever sleep?

Dimon: I'm afraid to sleep.

Katerinaa: Bad dreams? What do you dream about? Tell me. Soothe your soul.

Katerinaa: I've actually seen the street where you live. I think I even saw your window.

Dimon: In your dreams?

Katerinaa: *<link to Yandex.Maps, which offers not simply a map of the city, but the city as filmed by specially-installed webcams, enabling you literally to travel along*

the streets, all but glancing in at the windows of the houses and the faces of passers-by.>

Katerinaa: I may have seen you too. I don't really know your face. You don't post photos of yourself.

Dimon: I don't take photos of myself. And I don't look in the mirror.

Katerinaa: Do you shave?

Dimon: Sometimes. By feel.

Katerinaa: Is your house on the map?

Dimon: Yes.

Katerinaa: You don't seem to get much snow.

Dimon: The wind blows the snow away. I sometimes stand in the wind and think, I wish the wind would knock my thoughts out like that, and I could live empty and happy.

Katerinaa: I worked you out from the medical school. It's got two houses opposite, across the square. One of them's yours.

Dimon: Depressing.

Katerinaa: It's not that bad. Obviously the plaster's fallen off. But we're about the same here. The asphalt struck me. The asphalt on the pavements is all cracked.

Dimon: Harsh continental climate, hot summers, cold winters, permafrost.

Katerinaa: Sunny.

Katerinaa: Do you think my old lady is alive?

Dimon: I don't know.

Katerinaa: I want to believe.

Dimon: She disappeared on 29 December. Today is 6 January. More than a week. Winter.

Katerinaa: But suppose yesterday's boy really did see the old lady through his porthole. YESTERDAY. My actual old lady. Suppose it was actually her they picked up on the 29th. That means she's somehow survived all this time. I'm thinking she's found somewhere to shelter in that little patch between the railway, the high road ha ha, and Yaroslavka. It's pretty much a triangle. Pretty much a Bermuda triangle. It's a shame there aren't any webcams anywhere, not on any of the Christmas trees. At any rate, the internet doesn't know about it.

6 January 2013, 22:50

Katerinaa: I put on UGG boots with woollen socks and a Finnish down jacket; I don't think I'd have been cold even in Chita. I packed a rucksack with a thermos of hot tea, a bag of sandwiches, and chocolate sweets significantly called *Space Odyssey*. Knitted mittens I'd bought at the market last winter but had never once put on. I got to the station on the train, then wandered along the high road, not so much in the hope of meeting my old lady at the side of the road as simply to have a closer look.

It was getting lighter. And it was nice to stomp on the still-white snow.

There was no-one at the bus stop. I waited for a while. I don't know why. The occasional car went by. There was a path from the bus stop leading deep into the woods; people had already walked along it earlier, leaving tracks. According to my map, the path should lead to a dacha settlement. There was an access road going to it direct from Yaroslavka, but I decided to take the quiet back way, through the woods.

I walked. Stopped occasionally. Listened to the woodland sounds. Saw a squirrel.

The path broke off at a tiny narrow river. There was no bridge, so I tottered across the ice. A fisherman was sitting on his box in front of an ice-hole. Perhaps he was one of the fishermen on the bus that time, perhaps another one. The sky opened up. I so wanted to lie down on my back right there on the ice, arms outstretched, looking up at the sky until I fancied I was there, in the sky, lying with my arms stretched out.

I climbed up quite a steep slope on to the other bank. The path picked up again. A dacha appeared around a bend. Or rather, a house. Behind a huge stone wall.

I walked round it. I noticed several security cameras. I saw iron gates. I rang the bell. No-one answered.

A concrete path stretched away from the gates, scraped clean of snow.

I found a nearby pine tree, shrugged off my backpack, took out my thermos, and poured myself a steaming cup of tea. I stood there, leaning against the golden trunk, drinking my tea and looking at the iron gate. Pine trees rose up tall behind the fence as well. The sun came out of the fog. Above my head, it was as if the snow was falling of its own accord. I heard the hum of an engine. I splashed out what was left of the tea and put the lid on the thermos.

A car appeared on the concrete road. A Ford. Police. The car braked a few yards from the gates.

The front passenger door opened. An elderly chap in grey police trousers and a spotted jacket without epaulettes or any insignia got out of the car. He glanced at the snow sparkling in the sun, and headed towards me.

'Good day.' He ran a broad palm over his short-cropped grey head.

'Hello,' I answered.

'Lovely weather today.'

'Classy.'

'It's even warm in the sun. Out for a walk?'

'In essence.'

'Stopped for a breather?'

'Drank some tea.'

'Aha, tea, splendid.'

'Would you like some?' I held my thermos out to him.

'Thank you, I've just had a cuppa. Hardly finished it, call comes in: there's a woman snooping round the house, go and check. So I'm checking, pardon me. You'll want my ID. Uh-huh.'

He showed me his ID. I leaned forward and read his name and patronymic.

'Pleased to meet you, Sergey Petrovich. And I'm Katerina.'

'Well, Katerina, here you are, out for your walk, breathing the fresh air, taking a tea break, and here's me having to get in the car and come and see what's what.'

'I'm not going to tell you I'm standing here doing nothing at all.'

'Aye, aye, now then.'

'I'm waiting for the owners. I even rang the bell.'

'Ah well, word is they're not supposed to be in today.'

'So when will they be in?'

'What are we doing malingering out here in this frost? I came out without my hat, left it in the office. Sun warms you up, not saying it doesn't, but this wind goes through you. It's snug in the car, driver's probably nodded off already.'

Sergey Petrovich had a way of making me feel comfortable. He seemed to project a force field, a safe zone. Comfortable like home, ingenuous. A zone you didn't want to leave.

We settled ourselves in the back seat of their Ford. The driver wasn't sleeping; he was reading some battered little book. A muted muttering came from the police radio.

'They won't come today for sure,' said Sergey. 'You'd have waited all that time for nothing. Should have called them on your mobile, found out when they'd be about. Made an arrangement.'

'How could I? I don't know their phone number or anything. I'm just trying random things.'

I explained to him about my old lady.

'You never know, people might have seen her. Out the window, for instance.'

He heard me out carefully.

'There's no way anyone in this house could have seen her. They've been away for two weeks.'

'What about the security cameras? They've got them round the whole perimeter. What if the old lady happened to walk past.'

'We could take a look, why not? You give me a better idea of when she hopped out of that car. Plus when the young lad saw her from the bus.'

He fished a pencil stub from his inside jacket pocket along with a podgy notebook that was dirty, frayed, and miraculously still intact. He found an empty corner somewhere and started writing. As he wrote, he stuck out his lower lip the way a child might.

The driver suddenly chuckled. At something in his book.

'I've just had a thought,' I said, pondering. 'When the old lady went missing, that is, on 29 December, were there any other incidents in our neighbourhood?'

'Oh, sweetheart, we have incidents every day God sends.' Sergey Petrovich flicked his finger over his podgy notebook and smiled. 'Not a day without an entry in here. Beating, arson, a break in, joyriding.'

'I'm not talking about that. I mean something out of the ordinary. I don't know.'

Sergey Petrovich opened his notebook and started flipping through it. When he wrote he stuck out his lower lip, but when he read he raised his eyebrows and wore an expression that suggested his notes were bewildering.

The police radio burbled. The driver chuckled into his book.

'December twenty-ninth. Twenty-ninth of De–. Two days before. Before New. Before New, two thousand and thir–. Two thousand and thir–. Teen. Report came in at twenty-thirty. Uh-huh. Found. Body of a young man. Nikolay Ivanovich Kudryavtsev. Born 1994. Aye-aye-aye, so young. Found in the vestibule. What train were you on? Well, well. Which carriage? Even better. Your train and your carriage. Second vestibule in the direction of travel. Twenty-thirty, at the terminus, found by passengers. Body of a young man. In a red anorak, blue jeans, and Nike trainers. Blond hair. Cut short. You remember anyone like that?'

'No.'

'In the inside pocket of his anorak was found his student ID. And a personal stereo. Headphones attached to the latter. The player was paused during playback of the musical composition "Bullfinch" by Kill Shot. One earphone was in the young man's ear, the other had been taken out. Nikolay Kudryavtsev died from loss of blood. Working hypothesis: he was stabbed in the stomach. No murder weapon has been found. No witnesses.'

'It might not be connected,' I said.

'Quite,' agreed Sergey Petrovich.

'And if it is connected, how?'

'Beyond me.'

'Was she a witness?'

'It's possible.'

'It doesn't help much, anyway. It explains, but it doesn't help.'

'It doesn't explain much.'

'If she saw it, she might have simply taken fright and literally got lost from fear.'

'You and I, sweetheart, don't know whether she saw it or not. And if she did, then what?'

He tucked his notebook away in the inside pocket of his jacket. Glanced at his watch.

'Do you need a lift? Where would you have me take you?'

I need hardly say that I've found the composition 'Bullfinch', by Kill Shot, on the internet.

<link to music track on Yandex.Music>.

Doesn't do much for me. Still, I downloaded it; you never know.

I'd already gone to bed, turned out the light, closed my eyes, and was about to go to sleep when I realised I had to ask a question. It was after midnight but I couldn't wait till morning. I sent a message to Alla: *What music was playing in the car when the old woman went into a panic?* The answer arrived in the morning, at eight-thirty. A link, to be exact. To the very same composition 'Bullfinch' by the very same band Kill Shot.

No offence, people, but I'm disabling comments for now.

7 January 2013, 23:47

Katerinaa: I was in Moscow on newspaper business. A scientist hailing from our little town. Interview, childhood memories, this, that and the other. I found myself at the station just when the grey cover should have been slipping off the black piano. I decided to listen to the pianist and maybe actually meet him. But the piano was still under the cover. (For some reason I was reminded of trains with covered military equipment on open platforms. From my far distant childhood.)

Still showing up white on the stand was the notice about the daily concert from 3.15 p.m. to 4 p.m.

I asked the lady at the buffet, and she said the pianist was most likely ill. I asked her who he was and why he played here. She didn't know. The thought occurred to me that in England, say, these offerings in a large waiting room above the railway tracks would have become an unfailing tradition, uninterrupted by the performer's illness or even by his death. They would be picked up and continued, without fail. Someone cranky enough would be found.

Not here. Here, we can't manage more than a burst, a momentary flash. And then silence and twilight once more.

ELENA DOLGOPYAT

I didn't hurry for a train. I decided to wait for the one where I'd met the old woman. As if I hoped to see her again. As if I was actually getting on the very same train. As if a repeat were possible.

All the world's a stage, someone said. At any rate, it's a performance. I grabbed a coffee, sat down, and watched the passengers.

I made for the train in good time, unlike the last time. To make sure I got a seat. Standing in the crowd did not appeal to me.

Only I'd clean forgotten that the holidays were still going on. So I settled myself in unruffled calm in the same carriage, the same seat. And from that seat, I watched the passengers arriving.

The train eventually pulled off.

I was thinking the whole time that something had to happen, something of significance to me. I listened in to conversations. I peered at faces. The whole world was murmuring and swaying, murmuring and swaying. It was stuffy in the carriage, and I kept sliding off into sleep.

We'd passed Pushkino when I noticed a woman. Her face seemed familiar. She'd been travelling in the same carriage, on the same train, then, on the 29th. For absolutely certain. As she had been then, she was sitting with her knitting, and the sweater which had been barely begun on the 29th and was unrecognisable as a sweater was now, on the seventh day of the new year, nearing completion. The place next to the woman was free, so I moved to sit beside her.

'Hello,' I smiled at her.

She looked at me in surprise, but responded, 'Hello.'

'We caught this train on the 29th, just before New Year. Do you remember me? I was sitting there, next to an old lady.'

'No.'

'I expect you were coming home from work that day.'

'I'm coming home from work now. I work shifts.'

'She's disappeared. The old lady. The one I was sitting next to.'

'I don't remember, sorry. I don't particularly look at people. I get tired of people at work. I entertain myself knitting.'

'Yes, you were knitting then, too. You were just starting this sweater.'

'I actually thought I was starting a waistcoat. But I changed my mind.'

'It's lovely.'

'Thank you.'

The river. The road. Car headlights. The train was approaching my station.

The square in front of the station. The platform.

A torpor came over me. The driver announced the station and opened the doors. The carriage emptied out almost completely. A few people came in and brought the cold air with them.

'The next station is–' said the driver.

And announced our departure.

He paused, then shut the doors. The train started.

It was taking me away from home. And I wouldn't have minded being taken away as far as possible. Going on and on, for a whole day, two days, ten years. Yes I know the Earth is too small for such a journey. Still, I did what I'd many times thought of doing as I came into my station: I went on. Going I knew not where.

The train kept on going. One station. Another. The needles flashed in the woman's hands. Without taking her eyes off her knitting, she suddenly said, keeping her voice low, 'Do you see that man? Just got on. Across the aisle from us. Third lot of seats from the door. Yes. It's OK, he's not looking at us. I remember him. He caught

ELENA DOLGOPYAT

this train on the 29th, too. Got on at the same station. Sat next to your old lady.'

'You said you didn't remember the old lady.'

'I've just remembered. Saw him and remembered. They were talking about something. I mean I didn't watch them for long. I had to get out, I had a cake and a ton of presents from work, they completely overdid the present giving. I passed them with my boxes and something fell out of my bag, I don't know what, just some little thing, and the man picked it up and handed it to me. That's why I remembered. The 29th. Definitely. Just before New Year.'

The woman rolled up her knitting and tucked it away in her bag. Then she wished me all the best, and hurried towards the doors. The train was already slowing down at her platform.

The man had his group of seats to himself. I got up and went over to him. I sat down opposite.

His face was friendly, soft. Sparse grey hair. Neatly dressed. He noticed me looking at him.

I smiled, and he smiled back.

'I'm sorry,' I said, 'but I think I've seen you somewhere.'

'I always go home on this train.'

'No. Somewhere else, I think.'

'Do you live in this district? Have you ever had an X-ray?'

'You work at the hospital?'

'I'm a radiologist. So if you've ...'

'That's it. Probably. At the hospital.'

'We get referrals from all over the district.'

'Yes, yes.'

I didn't ask him about the old lady. Maybe it was a hunch, I don't know. But my tongue didn't twist itself into the shape needed to ask. I smiled, and took my personal stereo out of my pocket.

His look sharpened.

'OK, but don't put it on too loud.'

'What, not turn it on?'

'No, please, by all means listen, just not too loud. You know how sometimes it's, you know, playing through headphones but so loud that everyone around can hear it. It's oppressive. I want to be quiet.'

'Yes,' I said. 'But my headphones don't work. I'll just turn it on quietly.'

'No, I'm sorry, you get what I'm saying. I mean, you're a sensible person.'

But I'd already turned on my player. I wouldn't say very loud.

The composition 'Bullfinch' by the group Kill Shot.

That's when I realised that inspiration is a wave; it picks you up and carries you along. The main thing is to hold on.

'Would you be so kind,' he said extremely politely, 'as to turn it off.'

His eyes had gone icy cold.

I went on smiling and listening.

TaAAAmm-parRRAaam!

There were lots of empty seats in the carriage, and he could easily have got up and moved to another seat. But that taAAAmm-parRRAaam! seemed to get a hold of him and demand a response. He could no longer control himself.

'Turn it off!' he demanded, his voice jangling harshly. 'Immediately.'

I paid him no attention. I ignored him. He unzipped his plain black bag, placed the bag on his knees, turned it round so that I could see, and said, 'You see?'

Light was playing on a long, narrow, blade.

A knife.

I got up quietly and went into the vestibule. The doors closed behind me. I stood against the ice-cold metal wall. My stereo was booming fit to bust in my hand.

TaAAAmm-parRRAaam!

There was a teenager smoking in the vestibule. He paid no attention to me.

The doors swung open and the man entered the vestibule. His bag was hanging off his left shoulder. The zip on the bag was open. He shifted the bag to his stomach, reached into it with his right hand, and, I assumed, grabbed hold of his knife. He did not take his icy gaze from me.

I turned off my stereo. Suddenly I could hear the clatter of the wheels.

We stood facing each other. The man did not take his eyes off me. The train was slowing.

'Say sorry,' the man said quietly and calmly.

'Forgive me,' I said.

'"Forgive me, please."'

'Please. Forgive me, please.'

The train came to a halt. The doors opened onto the white, snow-covered platform. The man hesitated, and then jumped out of the door.

'Be careful–' began the driver.

The teenager stood there, leaning against the wall. Smoke drifted from the cigarette in his white fingers.

I'm disabling comments. I wouldn't be able to answer anyway.

Not at the moment.

8 January 2013, 03:15

Katerinaa: Let's suppose that it actually was her the little chap saw through his icy window. A week after she burst out of their car. Both events took place not far from the same station. She's hiding out somewhere near there. She's found herself a hiding place. Somewhere not far off. The self-same triangle.

She can't not eat or not drink in her hiding place, can she? Her backpack's unlikely to be magical, she's unlikely to open it up and pop! out comes a pie. She had a certain amount of money on her. She should at least be buying bread.

Five-storey houses beside the platform near the station building behind the small market. Little shops on the ground floors. Everything just as everywhere.

I texted Mitya. In the morning, he sent me a picture of the old lady. Taken in summer. Her face in close-up; good. Spots of light through the foliage. I photoshopped in an announcement.

<link to image: the face of an old lady in a patch of sunlight; above the picture, the caption: 'On 29 December, Daria Sergeyevna Kashchina (b. 1925) disappeared. She was wearing a man's black down jacket, a grey shawl, a long black skirt, and felt boots with galoshes. She had with her a dark blue school backpack. Relatives are ready to give a reward for any information. Phone number ...'>

I hadn't yet gone to bed. I was watching some stupid movie with fist fights. I made coffee.

Early next morning, while it was still dark, I trudged off to the bus stop. There were not many people there. The holidays were dragging on, and the windows in the houses were almost all black and blind. An empty bus arrived, and we climbed on, we few, and off we went to the station. Everything was so slow, so sleepy. And surprisingly, I didn't even want to hurry. I was in tune with time, the half-light was not weighing on me. The diffuse electric light, the conductress's slow movements: everything seemed right. Necessary, even. It was as if I was executing a script long since written and thought through, all the glitches smoothed out. And it was simply not right to rush. I was to execute every step meticulously. Clearly catch every sound. Miss nothing. Only then would the path lead me to my goal.

Such was the feeling I had.

Most importantly, I stayed calm.

We arrived at the station, and swung round. The dilapidated doors opened. I jumped down into the little square still covered by a night-time fall of snow. I went up onto the platform. I stood waiting for my train, looking to the west. I couldn't see the Kremlin, but I could see the red glow that lies above the city on even the darkest night.

The train pulled in. I was the sole occupant of my carriage.

It was chilly, and the light was on the blink. I could have moved to another carriage, but that didn't seem right.

Ten minutes later, I got off. The carriage rolled away completely empty.

I came down from the platform and trudged off towards the houses. Here and there, lights were already burning in the windows, and the shops were starting to open. The market was covered with snow and deserted. A dog skittered about between the rows. I stuck my announcements on front doors and in shop doorways. On the bus stop. By the ticket office on the platform. On the poles at the dump. On the trees in the children's playground.

It was dawn by the time I finished. I bought coffee in a plastic cup from a stall and scalded myself drinking the bitter liquid. I waited until the train arrived and went back to my own stop. There was a break in the bus schedule, so I hailed a taxi and rode home like a queen.

At home, I pulled off my anorak and shoes, shuffled into the main room, and crawled under the wrap on the sofa.

I had a dream. I seemed to be becalmed at sea, in fog. I was in a small boat. I couldn't see the shore. I leaned over the side, wanting to look into the depths of the sea, but I didn't have time: a bell rang, and I surfaced from my dream.

An unfamiliar number was showing on my mobile.

'Hello,' I said huskily into the phone.

Silence.

'I'm listening.'

Silence.

Click.

I waited a moment, then decided to call the number indicated.

Ringtone, connection, and again–silence.

'I'm sorry,' I said in my most polite voice, my most benevolent and even tone. 'We are very worried about Daria Sergeyevna. If only you could reassure us. Have you have you seen her?'

And after another silence, a little girl's little voice squeaked, 'Yes.'

'Is she alive?'

'I don't know.'

Little by little, in tiny stages, one word at a time, I coaxed the whole story from the little girl.

It seems that she and her friends were standing on the landing by the radiator.

'When?'

'Six o'clock.'

'Was it already dark outside?'

'Not yet.'

'Yes but it's dark at six these days. It's winter; the day's only just begun to arrive.'

'At three, maybe.'

'Before New Year? Or after?'

'I don't know. I don't remember anymore.'

A picture formed, its lines sharpening. This was it:

On the third floor an old lady lives all alone. She's small, hunchbacked, a hundred years old or a thousand, nobody knows. Everybody dies, but she goes on living. And a few days ago, not in the morning, not in the afternoon, and not quite in the evening either, this old lady came through the front door not on her own, but with another old lady who followed her quietly and obediently. As she passed past them, the submissive old lady looked pitifully at the girls. The girls fell silent and quietly followed her with their eyes. The poor old woman was bewitched; she had not a scrap of her own will left, and she walked under the spell of the sorceress.

The girls heard a door opening on the third floor, heard the rustle of footsteps and the click of the lock.

They never saw the abject old lady again. No-one had seen her.

'Did she have a backpack with her?'

'Yes.'

'Dark blue?'

'Dark blue. Or black.'

'Or pink?'

'No.'

'Tell me the address, please.'

'Will you give me a reward?'

'What do you want?'

Silence.

'I don't know.'

'Give me the address.'

I'm disabling comments again. We'll talk later. *Pardonnez-moi.*

9 January 2013, 23:50

Katerinaa: It seems like yesterday morning is being repeated right down to the tiniest detail.

The same hour, the same dead windows, the same quiet bus and the same carriage on the train, and everything seems to be repeating itself, everything; but I'm seeing, I'm noticing a little more than yesterday.

I notice a scar on the conductress's hand. I can't know if it was there yesterday; yesterday I didn't see it. I notice that one of the carriage windows is a strange greenish colour. Was it like that yesterday? I don't know, I didn't see. I notice something written on the wall in the vestibule:

Out of puff and out of luck? Grab this thing and pull like (the last word has been scratched out).

Was that there yesterday? I didn't see it. It's as if I'm re-reading the same book or watching a film again and being surprised at how blind I was first time around. If I had to live my life all over again, I'd live it exactly the same way, only with a difference: I'd see differently; I'd see everything I missed the first time.

The same platform and the same houses, only the morning is warmer, yes, it's definitely not yesterday's morning, there's no snow, although it looks as if it could start any moment. A snowflake swirls blindly into your face. Maybe the only snowflake to fall from the sky this morning.

I already know where the house I want is. I've seen it on the satellite map. How lifeless the map makes the world seem. It's the details that are absent from it: the scars, the writing on the wall, shadows, footsteps, voices, faces.

An ordinary five-storey building. An ordinary front entry. I know the code, *abracadabra*.

The landing where the girls were standing. I settle myself on the windowsill and get ready to wait. To hear the turn of the lock, footsteps. To see the hunchbacked old woman. She'll go for bread, for potatoes, for whatever's needed by every living thing, even a sorceress. I don't believe in sorcery; that's a child's world, and I live in a different one. But all our worlds overlap.

The house is waking up. Cigarette smoke drifts from upstairs. There's a smell of fried potatoes. A door slams somewhere and I catch a burst of laughter.

I glimpsed her through the window, out in the street, where it was already getting light.

ELENA DOLGOPYAT

Meaning she'd gone out in the early hours of the morning, checked all the shops, had a good look, had a good time. She hadn't bought much; she was clutching a single bag. It was transparent: I could see bread and sweets, two hundred grammes. A miserly existence for the girls' sorceress; she should have wished herself a richer life.

She laboured up the stairs.

Still, there she was.

'Hello.' I slid down from the window sill and smiled. 'My name is Katya. I've been waiting for you. I want to thank you for Daria Sergeyevna, for taking her in. How is she?'

She was silent. Looked at me with grey, wintry eyes.

'Mitya, her grandson, is absolutely desperate. You should tell her about Mitya. Tell her that Mitya is out of his mind with grief. Mitya's on a business trip at the moment, and I'm kind of standing in for him. How is she?'

Someone let out a yell overhead. 'Koolya!'

'At least tell me if she's alive.'

'She's alive.'

She said something. Finally.

'Can she remember who she is?'

'She hasn't forgotten everything.'

'Why haven't you at least called Mitya?'

'She hasn't said anything about Mitya. Who is he?'

'Her grandson. I told you, he's her grandson.'

'Young?'

'Yes.'

'She didn't say.'

'Where did you pick her up?'

'She was sitting in the post office. It was time for them to close, and she was sitting there.'

'You should have called the police.'

'Why? What for?'

'You don't know anything about her. Maybe she's forgotten her address. Her loved ones are going mad.'

She kept quiet, her lips pressed together.

Thinking, most likely, about the old lady's address, and her relatives.

But she'd done the wrong thing. She hadn't wanted to let the old lady go. She liked being with her. Talking with her, drinking tea, passing the time.

What loneliness does to a person.

Snezanna: But you saw her? Yes? How is she?

Katerinaa: I did. She's fine.

Snezanna: You're very smart. To guess all that. Unbelievable. You could write an article about it in your paper. A few articles. A series.

Katerinaa: Nadia K. writes for the paper, but that kind of topic's not her thing.

Dimon: You've entertained us.

Katerinaa: You're welcome.

Dimon: You get your sofa?

Katerinaa: Tomorrow.

ILLUSION

FOREWORD

2011. January. The first working day after the New Year. Dark and damp. I don't remember how it went. In the evening the train was hot and crowded, and the white fluorescent light was flickering and blinking. In the seats opposite me were a mother and her seven- or eight-year old daughter. They'd bought a stack of wooden toys that looked like the kind made way back when: a circle with chickens pecking at seeds, a doll with rope legs and heavy wooden clogs. The doll swayed on a spring and smiled a painted-on smile, serene, happy.

The driver announced that the train would not be stopping at Stroitel, Chelyuskinskaya, Tarasovskaya, Klyazma or Mamontovskaya.

'Calling at all stations,' sighed the little girl.

'No,' her mother objected.

'All stations,' said the girl, refusing to yield.

What a stupid girl. That was my thought. But the girl was smart, smarter than us. They got out at Mytishchi. Meaning that for them, Stroitel, Chelyuskinskaya, Tarasovskaya, Klyazma and Mamontovskaya did not exist. They were stops that came after they'd left the train, after Mytishchi. It's a fact that most of the world does not exist for us; it is of no significance. No apparent significance, at any rate.

A young lad was sitting a little in front of us and across the aisle. He had his back to me, but he turned round from time to time, so I had a chance to look at him. It was immediately clear that he was a bit lacking upstairs. I don't know how it was clear so quickly. His face seemed completely expressionless. No tiredness, no joy, no thought. Even the doll's wooden face was wearing some kind of expression; the artist had had a go at daubing one on.

The train went on its way, and I mostly watched the girl playing, the hens nodding their beaks into the millet glued onto the wood, the doll smiling and swaying on her spring. Then I tired of them, and shifted my attention away. Turning, I saw, a little in front of us and across the aisle, a hand. It belonged to the simple-minded young lad. He'd stuck it over the back of the seat in front, and, without looking, was running it over the shoulder of the passenger sitting in the seat. The man had his back to the lad. He was asleep, and the hand was touching his shoulder, stroking it; it seemed separate from its simple-minded owner, living its own life. The passenger woke up, jerked, turned round, saw the strange hand, and shouted, 'Get your hand off!'

The hand instantly disappeared.

Several more times the lad forgot what he was doing and stuck out his hand, the hand stroked the passenger on the shoulder, was shouted at, and disappeared. The shout was one of fright, disgust, hatred. As if what had touched the passenger was not a human hand but a spider's leg. I was afraid I would have cried out exactly the same:

'Get your hand off!'

CHAPTER 1. THE BROWN FACE

I see my face in the photograph and don't know if I've always been so preoccupied and sad. The face in the photograph is much too expressive–a closed, melancholy face. I hope it hasn't always been like that, that there were times when it was cheerful. But there's no photograph with a laughing face; just this one. This is the only one I have at all from that time. And I don't even know exactly how old I am in it. Seventeen or eighteen. I'm not wearing glasses, and I can see, just badly, by the look of it–my eyes are black because my pupils are huge, not to mention that the quality of the photograph is too poor to convey subtle tones. It's black and white, and small; the whole thing fits easily in the palm of my hand.

I'm trying to figure out if any boy would like me looking like that. Hardly. He'd most likely be frightened by my preoccupied face, my crazy, unseeing eyes. None of the relationships I've made in my life started with that expression. I wish, I so wish there was another picture. I'd like to look at it.

1981. My first autumn in Moscow, a long way from my parents' house. At that time I wrote home often. The letters have not survived, but I remember that my handwriting then was like a child's, and that in literally every letter I described the weather. I don't know if you could have trusted those letters, even when it came to the weather. I'm not sure. As for my inner life, that was not reflected in them. They were a false mirror, those letters, always upbeat and dashed off in a hurry.

I used to come back from the institute on the number three trolleybus, from Novoslobodka. A man on the trolleybus asked me where I was studying. I answered honestly that I was at the Institute of Railway Engineering. To this day, if I meet someone and that someone–it doesn't matter who it is–asks me my name, where I work, where I live, whether I'm married or as good as and do I have children, I answer every question honestly and directly. It's like I've been injected with truth serum. And the stranger finds out that I'm not married and that God has not granted me children. Back then, on the number three trolleybus, the question of children did not arise; I was a child myself.

I answer questions truthfully, but people don't always ask; sometimes they guess for themselves. In which case I always confirm their guesses. 'There's someone at home waiting for you.' 'Aha.' 'Your husband.' 'Right.' 'Military, I'm guessing.' 'Well, yes.'

So on the one hand I'm incapable of lying, but on the other, I provide complete freedom to be fooled.

The man on the trolleybus was very sunburned, not a gentle holiday resort bronze, but overly dark, a working man's tan. His eyes were light against his brown face. He made no assumptions. He got truthful answers to his questions: I live in hall, I'm a first-year student, my father's in the army in Kazakhstan. Why he spoke to me in the first place I can't really say now. In all likelihood our eyes met by chance. We just saw each other; it happens.

He told me to meet him in Sokolniki at eight o'clock that evening.

In the time it took me to hunt down an iron in hall and iron my blouse and brush my teeth and put on mascara in front of the tiny mirror and ride the number three trolleybus to Novoslobodka and make my way underground from Novoslobodka to Sokolniki, I had already married this brown guy in my mind and given him a son and our son was with me on the metro and I was stroking his fair head and everyone was looking at us and smiling.

At eight o'clock it was already getting dark and the streetlights were coming on. I exited from the metro and was afraid I wouldn't recognize him. Maybe I'm different in this respect from other people, but I can't remember a person's face from the first meeting. The second time I see someone, I always note with surprise that they're not as I'd been seeing them in my head. A picture more or less corresponding to the real person forms around the third or fourth meeting, and even then I'm not sure what colour their eyes are. Knowing the colour of someone's eyes requires a special intimacy.

It turned out that I'm not particularly different from other people. The man standing at the metro was also looking at me uncertainly. Uncertainly and expectantly. At length he made up his mind and approached me.

'Hi.'

'Hi.'

Who knows if he was really waiting for me, if it was him I saw on the number three trolleybus? Anyway, we set off together along the asphalted avenue into the park. The sky was still light, but dusk was gathering on the ground. The man had no flowers with him. I'd been supposing that there must be flowers, but there weren't, and I decided immediately that there didn't have to be. That's another one of my traits: I go along with what's happening and don't argue with reality or demand anything from it. Others know better how things should be, and I bow the knee to them.

The broad avenue turned, narrowed, and became more remote, and we involuntarily slowed. Cautiously, he took my hand. I felt my hand lying in his as if it were dead–a sign of how scared I suddenly was that I was alone with a complete stranger in a remote corner of an enormous deserted park. And no-one knew where I was.

'Shall we sit down?' he suggested. We sat down on a bench lit by a sad electric light. That kind of light makes things look different, and it seemed to me that my stranger's trousers were shiny with age, and his face was grey rather than brown. Grey and unhealthy and smooth and looking fundamentally incapable of growing a beard. We were no longer holding hands; I'd extracted my hand to straighten my raincoat when I sat down.

He inched closer. I didn't move a muscle. He covered my hand with his, snaring it.

'What are you thinking?' he asked.

'That you're a maniac.'

He looked at me, at a loss. He realised I was not joking. He quietly unclenched his fingers and released my hand. We sat there not saying a word, and I could sense that he was afraid of me. Afraid that I would take fright at something–a rustle, a cough–and start screaming. Most likely, he was thinking I was crazy, paranoid. I got up warily from the bench and set off along the narrow avenue enclosed by dense thickets. He remained on the bench. He's still sitting there to this day–in my memory. The man with the brown face.

CHAPTER 2. OH–MAMA

We were on the number nineteen bus from Maryina Roshcha, me and Rita, my roommate. It was already winter, and we were on our way to our hall, standing on the rear platform. The windows were weeping and my roommate was reading me a poem.

Tongues, like snakes, exchanged caresses
in the depths of two mouths joined as one.

'Isn't that great?' asked Rita.

'Yes,' I answered uncertainly.

The bus was jolting, and beyond its fogged windows lights were burning. My companion's eyes were shining; she was seeing something in those lines of which I, innocent thing that I was, had not even a tenuous grasp. She was a participant in poems like this; I had still not got there.

'Yes,' was what I always said. 'It's great.'

I wished I could feel the verses as she did.

A black cloud of birds was rising over the brewery: the bus was already trundling along Ogorodny, where our halls were. On one side were our halls of residence, residential blocks with shops on the ground floor, a nursery school, and an ice cream shop and café, and on the other side were the brewery, a meat-packing plant, a milk-processing plant, and an experimental confectionery factory. From the window of our room we could see the Ostankino Tower; it would sway in the wind and hide inside dark clouds descending on the city. We could hear the railway. There was a narrow alleyway between the towering stone walls of the brewery and the meat-packing plant, and you could use it to cut through to Ostankino railway station on the Oktyabrskaya line. In the daytime, it wasn't scary.

I used to skip through this gap, this trap that stank of decay; I was afraid of the yard dogs. I skipped along it to get a train to Leningradsky railway station, from where I'd cross the square to catch another train from Kazansky to the town of Murom, where my grandmother lived at the time. All my trips there were trips into the past, into my non-existence, because in that far-off past I did not yet exist. Moscow was also the past for me, but more about that a little later.

The house in Murom was a wooden house for four families. Each family had a garden and a vegetable patch, and you felt you were living quite separately from everyone else. There was a stove, a standpipe, a toilet in the yard, and near the barn a log pile covered with roofing felt against the rain. An ancient life, frozen in another time, gone to the bottom. At the very bottom, the passage of time slows. On the surface it runs, but the deeper you go, the calmer it is, and in Murom I found myself in the very depths, wondering if I'd ever surface again. I'd lie down on a cot with metal knobs and listen to the radio with its glass frequency marker, take a cup from the sideboard, a black one with a fish on the side, and look at black and white pictures in an album. One night I was woken up by the voice of Yury Levitan reading a Sovinformburo report. I looked out of the black window with dilated pupils and believed I had woken up during wartime, that I'd gone that far down. Dogs were barking far off somewhere. I guessed that Levitan was in some film or other; the neighbours' television was on. Did it really matter? I was in that time; I had stepped into its waters.

I found out about Moscow's distant past, too, in Murom. My little brother was with us one summer. He asked me to read me him a fairy tale before bed, and I read, *'Petrovsky Castle, gloomily ...'*, a passage from a fifth form reader. I liked saying those words over and over, and he liked to listen; he would fall asleep to my quiet, measured voice, in the dark, at the very bottom of time.

I went out there on Saturday nights to be back on Monday morning, in time for my first class. Not too often, but I went. To Murom with presents from Moscow, sausage and sweets, and back with presents from Grandma, buns I called kisses, cherry jam, pickles.

And so, November. Again the train to Murom. A light, third class carriage.

I couldn't read. I got travel sick if I read. We'd been going a long time. The conductress was serving freshly-brewed tea. I tore open the paper wrapper, tipped sugar into my glass, and began to stir and tap the hard, unyielding sugar cube. Steam billowed from the glass.

'So?' A young man said to me sternly. 'Shall we get acquainted?'

He was sitting opposite me with his tea, but was in no hurry to tip sugar into it. He spoke sternly, but looked at me cheerfully. I felt somewhat uncomfortable, but I answered his questions.

'What is your name?'

'Lena.'

'And how old are you, Lena?'

'Seventeen.'

'A fine old age. Where are you going?'

'To my grandmother's.'

'What are you doing in Moscow?'

'Studying.'

ELENA DOLGOPYAT

'I'm studying in Moscow, too. I've done my stint in the army. I'm finishing up, it's my last year. Writing my diploma. I already know where I'm being sent. The Urals. Will you come with me to the Urals, Lena?'

'I'm still in my first year.'

'Yes, I realise that. Do you live in hall?'

'Yes. Your tea will get cold.'

'Relax, Lena, don't be so stiff. I don't like my tea hot. Tell me what you like.'

'My stop's coming up soon.'

I got off in Murom, and he went on to Kazan. It's amusing that I was walking from the station to Kazanka, our district, and the train was taking my companion to Kazan. We'd left Moscow from Kazansky railway station. The Kazan Bermuda Triangle. And a paper icon of Our Lady of Kazan stood on my grandmother's sideboard.

In December, the cold arrived. It transpired that I'd grown out of the new winter coat I'd bought in the summer. I went on growing until I was twenty.

It wasn't yet New Year, but there wasn't long to go. The scent on the air was not of mandarins, as it had always been at New Year when I was a child, but oranges. Tons of them were delivered to the shop on Ogorodny, and we got them and ate them every day. It was an orange winter, that one, with peel on the floor, the windowsill, and even in the bed. It's surprising, but I've never gone off the taste or smell of oranges. We lived like it was wartime, the blackout. The wind blew in through our window, and it got terribly cold. We stuffed the cracks, but the wind percolated through and permeated our bones, so we came up with the idea of covering the window with a standard-issue blue blanket, fastened to the frame with the tiny nails that were used back then to attach the mail boxes. It was warmer, though without the view out of the window.

I was reading on my cot with the lamp on. A head poked through the door.

'Lena, someone's asking for you.'

The head disappeared, and a stranger came in and said sternly, 'Hello. Is it night where you are?'

I closed the book.

'Good evening.'

'Oh please. So formal.'

I looked at him uncertainly. I'd heard his voice somewhere. His face did not seem familiar.

'Don't you recognise me? "Ker-dunk, ker-dunk, went the wheels."'

The guy from the train?

'I recognise you,' I said cautiously.

'Well, that's good. Do you have any wine glasses? Or are we going to be drinking out of tumblers?'

He put a bottle of champagne on the table. 'Sovetskoye'. Sweet. I didn't like it.

Champagne gave me a headache, but I couldn't bring myself to refuse. There were no glasses or tumblers, so I fished out cups. In the meantime, he walked around our little room. Three cots, one wardrobe for all of us, a table against the wall nearer the door, three bedside tables, three bookshelves. The wardrobe was facing into the room with its back towards the door, demarcating a sort of vestibule.

We sat down at the table and he pulled out the cork, carefully, cautiously. I didn't know you could do that, without thunder and gunfire, with just a little pop and a puff of vapour wafting from the neck. He poured out the champagne just as carefully and gently, without foam.

'There,' he said. 'Cheers.'

He watched me drink, appraising. 'Well now,' he said sternly. 'You've gone a little pink. Livened up.'

'Did you finish your diploma?' I asked.

'Shall we drink to *Brüderschaft*, mmm? You and I?'

'No, thank you, I don't want any more.'

We said nothing for a while. There was a radio pushed up against the wall, and he pressed a button. The radio gave a shout, but he turned it off before it had a chance to say anything comprehensible.

'Whose is that painting on the wall?' he asked.

'Kramskoy. *Portrait of an Unknown Woman*. It's a reproduction.'

'I don't mean who did it. Who put it up?'

'She did.' I pointed to one of my roommate's cots.

'Romantic,' he said. Another silence, and then: 'Where is she?'

'At home. She rarely sleeps here. She lives in the Moscow region.'

'Far away?'

'Zagorsky district.'

'That's crazy. How much does she spend on travel? What for?'

'She misses her family.'

'A romantic young lady. Tell me something interesting about the other one.'

'She recites poems by heart.'

'Impossible.'

'So, for example, she'll recite standing in a queue, to take her mind off it. Not out loud, obviously.'

'Romantic young ladies.'

He was quiet again. He touched the knob on the radio, but didn't turn it on.

'Well, what about you?'

'I go to the Illusion.'

'What's the Illusion?'

'It's a cinema. Old films.'

'Romantic young ladies,' he repeated for the umpteenth time. And poured more champagne into our cups.

'I don't want any.'

'Nor do I.' He picked up his cup. 'But we should finish it. It'll go flat.'

We clinked cups, and drank.

'Got anything to eat?'

'Sausage.'

'Fetch it.'

'No bread. I could pop out and blag some.'

'Don't worry.'

He took a mouthful of sausage and washed it down with champagne.

'Back there, on the train, I thought you were older.'

'I'll be eighteen in February.'

'Yes. But you look thirteen, no more.'

'That's because I've had my hair cut.'

'Yes, true, a haircut makes you look young. I feel disgusting. Like I'm getting a child drunk.'

A head poked through the door.

'Lena, did you take notes on the maths lectures yesterday?'

'No.'

The head disappeared.

'Why didn't you take notes on your lectures?' he asked sternly.

'My glasses are broken and I can't see anything on the board.'

'You need to order new glasses.' He looked at his watch. 'Time to go.'

He got up, went behind the wardrobe, and put on his rustling anorak there. He shut the door behind him quietly, carefully. I sat and waited while he walked all the way down the long corridor to the lift, then trudged out of the dark room into the shared kitchen, which was as wide as the building. The white light from the kitchen window dazzled me, a reminder that it was daytime.

I turned on the hot water. I watched it flowing, steaming, and thought something like this. *I wonder why he dragged himself over here, a good-looking guy. Doesn't he have a girlfriend, or have they had a fight, or broken up altogether, or maybe he really liked me on the train. Why on earth did I have to get my hair cut, stupid, worse there was a queue and I sat there for almost an hour, and the hairdresser dropped her scissors, twice.*

I left the water and rushed out of the kitchen to the lift. The lift was busy, so I skittered down the stairs and flew out into the street, onto the icy pavement.

The guy was standing at the bus stop, waiting for a bus. In his dark blue anorak, slim, good-looking. He didn't see me. I didn't dare approach him. The bus arrived and took him away. That's when I noticed I was wearing slippers and a thin sweater and that a frosty wind was blowing, cutting right through me.

There was a crowd at the lift, and I dragged myself up the stairs, one flight then the next, to my room on the seventh floor. A girl I knew was standing on the landing, a cigarette smouldering in her fingers.

'Hey,' I said, 'let me have a smoke.'

'Do you know how?'

'No.'

She taught me to smoke. 'Look. When you breathe in, it's like you're saying "Oh." When you breathe out, it's "Mama." Breathe in–Oh. Breathe out–Mama. Oh–Mama, Oh–Mama.

Breathe in. Breathe out. Breathe in. Breathe out.

My head spun.

CHAPTER 3: THE BEST BOOKS

The best books were in Murom.

Tom Sawyer. I read it in the summer, on a bench under the under the apple tree.

Tom!

No answer.

Nikolenka's Childhood. A slim book with a hard cover and stiff, slightly yellowed pages. It lived on the veranda, squeezed into a bookcase beside a bunch of *Quant* magazines, all in one single, cramped row. It froze, warmed up, smelled of grey, slushy snow. I would take it inside and read it by the light of a strange lamp on a very high pedestal under a tiny bright red iron lampshade. The shade fitted directly onto the lamp and got so hot you could burn your fingers.

The third best book is *The Pickwick Papers*. I bought it one winter in Moscow, at a second-hand bookshop, a *bukinist*, brought it with me to Murom, and read it by the stove. The door was ajar and I read and watched the flames. So every page of *The Pickwick Papers* carries a trace of our stove with its peeling, bluish whitewash and the glow of the flames and the ticking of the round clock on the sideboard. And a picture of my mother as a baby.

Childhood is imbued very specifically with the tea I used to drink while I was reading–Georgian, number thirty-six–and the maths problem I simply could not solve. My neighbour came round, knocked the snow off her felt boots, sat down on the edge of the sofa right by the door, thought about the problem with me, and drew a complete blank.

Tom Sawyer rustles with the shadows of the leaves of the apple trees on the pages where they're on the island and everyone thinks they're dead but they're alive in their boyhood paradise.

In Moscow, when I was seventeen, I read Dostoevsky. *Crime and Punishment.* It had been a set book at school. I read it as if for the first time. The action seemed to be happening in Moscow. The streets of St. Petersburg were in Moscow. Raskolnikov lived somewhere in Maryina Roshcha. Lectures would finish, and I would be walking away from the Institute knowing that he was following me, immersed in his feverish thoughts. His fever infected me, and my forehead burned. I would turn round and so nearly catch sight of him, but I never met his eyes. I could hear his thoughts.

It is surprising that I was being stalked by a man who had no idea that he was stalking me, who had no idea that I existed, and who didn't actually exist himself. Although I for one am convinced that fictional characters exist. They exist for me in much sharper definition than the billions of people of whom I have not the slightest notion. All I know is that they exist. But who are they? I can't imagine their faces, their occupations, their ways of thinking, their worries, their pain. Well, I can, but only in the most general, universal sense. Not concretely, not in such a way that all these billions become alive to me. And in the same way, I don't exist for them. And I never will exist. As if I weren't in this world at all.

The made-up hero Raskolnikov occupied my thoughts to such an extent that I felt his living presence. He walked along the same street I walked down from the institute. I'd be able to see him if I looked round. I had no doubt of it. There's no shaking off that kind of stalker. No shaking him off, no getting away from him, no tricking him. You can double back, jump on a bus, hide in the crowd, and your stalker won't fall behind by as much as a step or a second.

I was out of sorts on that bitterly cold night when my companion was plotting his murder. His fever infected me, and I felt sick.

My saviour turned out to be a lad from our intake. There were three groups of twenty-five in our intake; each group had its own seminars, but we attended lectures together, the whole intake. The boy was walking slowly, and I caught up with him. I didn't remember his name.

'Hi.'

'Yes,' he answered, as if agreeing with my greeting.

'Where are you going?'

I needed to shake off my ghost, and I forgot all about my shyness and threw myself at this living man. Luckily for me, he answered my questions, eagerly and good-naturedly.

Perhaps he even remembered my name.

'I'm going to the *Maryinsky Mostorg*,' he said. 'I want to buy a teapot. To replace the one I broke last night in strange circumstances.'

'Really? We don't have a teapot.'

'So how do you make tea?'

'In a mug. A half-litre enamelled mug. We put a saucer over it. It makes really good tea, but obviously it spills when you pour it into the cups.'

'If I were you, I'd acquire a teapot.'

'We had one but it broke and I don't know who broke it. There I was in the morning, looking for it, no teapot, shards in the rubbish, and no-one's ever owned up. I have my suspicions, but I keep quiet. I'd buy one, but I want the person who broke it to buy it. That would be fair.'

I walked easily beside him, as if with someone I'd known a very long time and we'd often walked along together just like this, now chatting, now saying nothing. He smiled a lot, and I got to know his smile. I got to know his look. It's strange to find yourself suddenly in the company of someone who feels like one of your nearest and dearest, though you can't even remember his name.

There were no small teapots, so he bought a big one. He said he would fill it a third full of boiling water. I remarked that it was a teapot for a large gathering, and that it would attract guests to itself; guests would flock to it like moths to a flame, and now he wouldn't have to drink tea alone.

'God forbid,' he replied seriously.

We went as far as hall together. On the ground floor we checked the mail, which was distributed among alphabetically-ordered open boxes. Then we went up in the lift. I got out at the seventh, and he went on up to the top floor, the eighth. In the lift, I managed to ask him about the strange circumstances in which he'd smashed his teapot.

'The circumstances were these: I was alone, and suddenly someone called out to me and I jumped, and the teapot was unlucky. I was alone. No-one had called me. I imagined it.'

In his voice there was, or so it seemed at the time, a special trustworthiness, directed only towards me.

Rita had lugged a parcel home from the post office that day, a huge plywood box. She couldn't wait to open it, but the nails had been whacked in as far as they would go and we couldn't even slide a knife under the lid.

'Wait,' said Rita. She was flushed and panting. 'I'll be right back. Don't touch it without me, understand? Don't touch it!'

She rushed off, leaving me alone in the room.

That evening I felt the whole time as if I was listening out for something, both when Rita and I were trying to rip off the lid and when I was alone. The night was looking in at the window; the moon was its pupil, yellow and pale, its rim liquescent. I sat with the knife on the floor beside the plywood box. The box, for certain, was hiding surprises. Rita's father worked on a research ship, and they called in at foreign ports. It was hard for me to imagine the streets and shops there; all I saw and held in my hands were presents from those places: blouses, beads, mascara. It was all special, utterly not ours, amazing, alien.

The door swung open, and Rita ushered in Yasha.

He ripped out the nails out with pliers while Rita held on to the box. They were laughing. I laughed and held on to it too, but I kept listening out for something.

There were chocolate sweets in the parcel, tightly packed. Every parcel without fail contained either chocolate or chocolate sweets, and in the letter which always lay right at the bottom, so that we had to battle our way to it as well, there was always a note: '... and for Lena, a chocolate souvenir.' When we very first started sharing, Rita wrote to her father that I had the silver foil wrapper from a chocolate crackling in every pocket, that I chomped chocolate sweets right there in the street and it had made my cheeks round and ruddy, and that I spent half my grant on chocolate, and the only ice cream I ate was chocolate and the only cakes I ate were chocolate, and I put chocolate spread on my bun when I had my morning cup of tea. I must, she said, be ill. And Rita's father, whom I've seen only in pictures and whose face I can't now remember, started sending me chocolate souvenirs, and it amazed me that he never forgot, and I even came to feel a little as if we were family.

I dreamed about him not long ago, although I don't remember his face, and I don't even know if he's still with us. Such a strange visitation from the past. I'm not going to try and retell the dream. I've tried many times to retell my dreams, but every time I end up composing them anew rather than retelling them. Dreams unravel in the light of day.

We unpacked the parcel and sat down for a cup of tea. With the chocolate we'd been sent, of course. Yasha liked it too, though he said our Soviet chocolate was far better. I don't know; back then I liked any kind at all. I asked them over tea if they knew the lad from our intake who lived on the eighth floor.

'Someone lives there,' said Yasha.

'His last name starts with an "a".'

'My last name starts with an "a" too.'

'Your last name starts with an "s",' laughed Rita.

'When I forget it and I'm trying to remember it, it starts with an "a".'

'Because there's an "a" in the middle.'

'More like in the first quarter.'

I was listening to them and at the same time I was listening out for something. I suddenly remembered that my mother had been listening out in exactly the same way one night a while ago. We hadn't gone to bed. We were sitting in the kitchen drinking tea and playing silly games. I was rabbiting on about something or other, and Mum was listening to me and listening out for something else that wasn't me. My brother was supposed to come over that night.

I went out of the room and up to the eighth floor. It was quieter and cleaner than the seventh. Mostly families lived there; there was a pushchair on the landing, and a tricycle. The smell wafting from the kitchen was of borsch rather than neglect. I walked around the quiet, warm floor, looking at the doors. I got as far as the lift and then headed back. I went down several flights of stairs, and asked for a cigarette.

CHAPTER 4: HE

Moscow seemed to me a city alien and cold, a city forever turned towards the past rather than the future, a city that didn't see me or know me, for whom I had never been born. Moscow was collapsing, its walls peeling. The cake shops sold coffee and milk in faceted glasses, and when I drank it I felt as if time had turned down a dead end. I didn't feel like a girl; I felt like an old woman who had already lived her life. I wouldn't have been surprised to see my still child's hand withered and wrinkled, with protruding veins and yellowed fingernails.

And yet I loved walking around Moscow as a non-existent person. I never thought that one day I would come into existence. That it would happen, even if not for long.

I slept badly that night. I lay there looking at my luminescent alarm clock. Outside the window, over which we'd hung recently purchased net curtains, the warning lights of the Ostankino television tower were glowing. I tried to persuade myself that I would definitely see him tomorrow, that he would not fall ill or die that night. And I wouldn't fall ill or die either. We would see each other. I'd walk up to him and say hi. Everything would be fine. I'd never wanted anything so much in my life as to see him and go up to him and say hi. Without him, without the certainty that I would see him, it was as if I was losing my balance, flying towards the Earth like a chip of stone.

The alarm rang, the morning began, and I went to brush my teeth. Over the washbasin in the shared bathroom hung a spattered, grimy mirror. I took a piece of toilet paper out of my pocket and cleared a little island in the mirror so I could see myself. Could he really like me looking like this? The mirror must have seen a lot of faces peering in and asking that question. It's fine; a dab of mascara will make all the difference. Without it I'd be a chip of stone.

He hailed me at the bus stop. He was standing in the crowd, and I didn't notice him with my myopic eyes. Meaning I was not the one to say it to him: he said 'Hi' to me. And again it came out as if we'd known each other for a hundred years, so long we'd had time to forget all about each other.

'I didn't see you,' I said when we were on the bus, the crowd pressing us against the glass on the rear platform, against the handrail. 'Don't be surprised if I walk by without greeting you. I can't see very well but I don't wear glasses. They don't suit me. Anyway they fog up when it's cold.'

'You could wear lenses.'

'Lenses make my eyes hurt.'

'I can see all right, but I get lost in my own thoughts. I could walk past without seeing you. So we're equal.'

The bus braked, jolting me so I touched his hand. His hand felt hot. The bus was approaching Novoslobodka.

We walked along the alley to the institute in silence. A garish tram was rumbling along the tracks. We were walking very slowly.

ELENA DOLGOPYAT

'Do you smoke?' he asked suddenly.

'Yes.'

'I have asthma. Smoke makes me lose my breath.'

'I don't smoke much. It's an indulgence.'

The alley turned, and there was the institute behind its ancient fence.

'I don't feel like studying,' he said.

'Yes.'

'I get where I don't want to study and I don't go.'

'So what do you do?'

'Wander about somewhere.'

We came to the black bars of the gate. The lesson had started, the lights were on in the windows, the morning was dusky. We walked past the gate. Another tram overtook us with a clang of alarm. Or maybe I was the one who was alarmed.

We ended up in a courtyard, quiet, enclosed. I don't remember how. The swing creaked; the wind was setting it swinging, and whipping the snow across the bare asphalt. We stopped at the same time, and looked at the house.

'Would you like to live here?' he asked.

'Why not? It's quiet. Brick house, old, cast-iron radiators, probably high ceilings. Yes, it would do me.'

'Where? What floor?'

'Third.'

'Where?'

'That window there.'

'Where the cat's sitting?'

I took my glasses out of my bag and put them on.

'What cat?'

'It's already jumped down. Probably gone to eat.'

He was looking at me with smiling eyes.

'What? Glasses don't suit me?'

'I don't know. I don't know whether things go or not.'

'What about you? Would you like to live here?'

'Very much. Only higher up. You'd get a good view, the whole of Moscow.'

'Risky on the top floor. The roof will leak in spring.'

'No, not here it won't. It's been renovated recently, and it's well heated. I like warmth. I'd be like a cat sitting on the window sill over the radiator. They've got wide window sills. I'd sit and look.'

'How do you know it's well heated?'

'Look at the fanlights, you idiot. A lot of the flats have got them open.'

I looked from one window to the next. With my glasses I could see with unaccustomed sharpness. My head was even spinning slightly, because far-off life had suddenly emerged from the fog and come right up to me in all its detail.

'The curtains are still drawn in that one,' I said. 'They're still asleep?'

'I'd still be asleep too.'

'I wouldn't. I'd be up by now. I'd be making breakfast.'

'What exactly?'

'Don't know. Porridge. Oatmeal.'

'With milk?'

'Well yes, milk tastes better. A soft-boiled egg.'

'I wouldn't make anything. I'd go to the bakery on the ground floor, get fresh rolls, white coffee.'

'And what's stopping us from going to that bakery?'

In the bakery I noticed he wasn't wearing gloves. He said his hands never get cold. I touched him. His hand was hot. Like on the bus when I accidentally bumped it.

I was usually self-conscious. I was somehow altogether not quite at ease. But with him, I felt peaceful. He was pretty much admiring me. Whether I was wearing glasses or not. Even when I spilled my coffee and coughed. We walked for a long time that day, popped into several cake shops and drank coffee, and I didn't feel like an old woman. I was a girl; we were both children, and he took my hand with his hot hand and it was like I could feel his blood flowing, as if we were two beings with a single bloodstream. I don't know if the country we were in then was enchanted. I just know that on that day and that evening, when it was already dark and we came to Zamoskvorechye, where we'd also found a house in which we'd made our homes, and where my window was lit by a lamp with a red iron lampshade but his window was dark, he did not turn on the light. He just put on a record and lay on the floor listening. Something classical, thunderous, sounding from the heavens.

I never asked his name. I'm not sure he remembered mine. He didn't use it once.

In hall, we were going up in the lift. Not just the two of us; there was a crowd. Our eyes met. His look was the look of a stranger. Maybe he'd fallen into thought, and that was why he couldn't see me anymore.

'My floor,' I reminded myself.

'Yes. Good night.'

I got out, and the lift closed its doors and took him to the eighth floor, under the roof. He must have talked the supervisor into giving him a room at the top. Or perhaps they let him up there because of his asthma. There's less smoking on the eighth floor; there are children up there.

'Well, OK,' said Rita. 'Have you at least kissed?'

We were sitting at our table against the wall. Green deer were running across the buckram, and Rita had made tea and it was steaming in the cups. I looked out of the window at the tower, swaying in the breeze.

'Well, it's as plain as a pikestaff that he likes you. Meaning it's all going to plan. Personally, I don't like him very much, but that's by the by. Oh, and just so you know, he's a candidate for expulsion after the exams. He likes partying too much, and our class head's the kind to make sure all his absences are noted. So listen. Don't get kicked out with him.'

'Did you and Yasha kiss right away?'

'No.'

She was silent for a moment, then read these lines:
Close to you for a heartbeat
I found myself in that country ...

I don't know what came before or after those two lines, but Rita was right: they were about me.

She told me his name, I might add. It was as if she had christened him. Because before Rita, he didn't have a name.

The next day, Rita gave me a jumper, brand new, from her latest parcel. Italian, ribbed, the colour of ripe cherries. She gave me a pendant made from a black translucent stone, square, heavy, on a silver chain. Said if I lost it I wouldn't live to tell the tale. Said my mascara was disgusting and my lipstick didn't suit me, so I put on some of her French mascara and her French lipstick. It was pale pink, and Rita said my lips were seriously eye-catching. I tried on a pair of her jeans, but they were too big for me. Rita was upset; she hadn't thought that she was so much fatter than me, and she really didn't want me to wear my own, bought in the Maryinsky for thirty rubles. Nothing for it, though. She wouldn't let me wear my hat. Said it was time I threw out that abomination or took it to my grandmother: she could unravel it and knit it into socks. It's not that cold out, you'll survive without a hat–that's what she said. She also told me not to screw my eyes up and to smile more often.

'Because when you're not smiling, it looks like you're crying inside.'

Only it was all for nothing, because he wasn't there. Not at the bus stop, not on the bus. On the bus I still had hope: he might have gone earlier or be coming in later. He might even have taken the trolleybus; there were options. In class I was still hoping that he was late and was just about to knock on the door and walk in with a guilty mien or make it to the second class in time. But he didn't come, and I sat there miserably drawing faces in my exercise book and thought about how he was rambling around Moscow on his own and had forgotten about me, finding a house where he would live, without me, of course. Or perhaps he was ill and not rambling. He was lying there rambling, or perhaps he was rambling while he was rambling, and if so, then he was rambling with me. And what I wanted more was that he'd fallen ill and even died, but with me in his thoughts, and I was sorry that he hadn't seen me in my cherry jumper with my black pendant or feasted his eyes on my pale pink lips; they even smelled like roses, morning fresh.

From the institute I went straight to hall. Standing on the rear platform by the weeping window, watching the road run away, it seemed to me that my life was ending. I went up to the eighth floor and crossed to his room. Rita had told me the number. Behind the door there was silence, utterly undisturbed. I knocked cautiously, timidly; nothing stirred behind the door. I thought: what if he's actually lying there unconscious or already dead, and out of fear, I started to bang on the door with my fists. A neighbouring door opened and a woman's haggard face peeked out.

'I've just got my baby off to sleep.'

'I'm sorry.'

'There's no-one there.'

'Yes?'

'He went away this morning and hasn't come back yet. The walls are cardboard here.'

'Does he ... does live alone?'

'Almost. The other one has a girlfriend in Moscow. As far as I know.'

Several times that evening I climbed up to the eighth floor, up the cold stone stairs. On the eighth, I was enveloped by the warmth of home, the sounds of home, the smells of home. I'd go up to his door and knock cautiously.

Rita had gone to a film with Yasha. I took a book and went up to the eighth. I listened to the silence at his door, knocked, and went over to the window near the kitchen and climbed on to the sill, wide, stone and warm, the cast-iron radiators beating underneath it. I sat on the sill, just like him in that fantasy of his where he was a cat on a window sill. My book lay in my lap and the lights of the night-time city were shining below, but I wasn't looking out the window or at my book for fear of missing him. The floor was living its domestic life. Food was being prepared in the kitchen. The child was let out into the corridor on his tricycle and zoomed about pedalling as hard as he could and ringing his bell. They took him off the trike and carried him back in for dinner. He didn't want to go and was screaming till he choked, looking back at his trike.

He came out of the lift just after ten. I quickly dropped my eyes to my book. I was hoping he'd notice me and be glad, and come over and ask me what I was doing there. And I'd tell him I lived here, on the window sill. It's really not bad, I'd say. True the wind comes in through the window, but the view's fantastic.

He didn't notice me. I supposed he was sunk in his own thoughts. I watched him walk along the corridor, skirt the trike, and take the key out of his pocket. He didn't know anyone could see him, and it was like he was himself, he was more himself, at least that's what I thought–but what was I seeing? Just his receding figure. I don't think his gait would have changed if he'd known I was watching him. A weary gait. He opened the door and stepped into the room. I heard the click of a switch. The door closed. He didn't see me.

The corridor went on living its life. I felt as if I didn't exist. I could see, hear, and understand in part, but I didn't live here; I didn't live anywhere.

'Who stopped you from knocking on his door?' asked Rita. 'You knocked on it when there was no-one there.'

'I thought he was tired. His gait was tired.'

ELENA DOLGOPYAT

'*When a tired submarine comes home from the depths,*' muttered Rita.

We lay on our cots in the darkness. The luminescent hands showed just past one o'clock in the morning. I asked Rita if I could wear her sweater again tomorrow. But Rita was already asleep.

CHAPTER 5. MATHEMATICS

I could hear my alarm but I lacked the strength to wake up. Rita swore she hadn't even heard it, and that if I hadn't shaken her, she would have gone on sleeping until the year 2000, the threshold of the new millennium. Back then we were very preoccupied with that distant year. We kept working out how old we would be, and we tried to predict what would have become of us and who we might have turned into. I thought I would live to see the year 2000, but 3000 ... no, never; none of us would see that year–that was eternity: 3000 years from the birth of Christ. It had a solemn ring to it: from the birth of Christ. We would not be there to see it.

We were fifteen minutes late. The lecturer turned as we slipped into the auditorium, and the class head reluctantly scrubbed our non-existence from the register. We sat at the edge, where there were empty seats. I looked around. He was here, in the back row by the wall. He was looking straight at me. With a serious, attentive look. I smiled. He held up a warning finger. At the break I moved to join him. He sternly instructed me to put on my glasses so that I could see what the lecturer was writing on the board. I said I wouldn't understand anyway. He said there was nothing complicated about it and he'd be happy to explain and could do it right away if I had no other plans. I wanted to say, like Piglet, that I was completely free until Friday, but I kept quiet. What if he'd never seen that cartoon? I thought it was very special, very different from anything else.

I found myself in his room that same evening, behind the same standard-issue door, on the same quiet floor. His window also gave a view of the Ostankino television tower. Of course you'd expect it to be visible, but somehow it seemed strange to me that he could look out at the same tower as me. Granted, from slightly higher up. But that didn't matter to the tower. Given its own height, this was an imaginary number of which no account was taken.

On the way back from the institute, he said he was unable to explain anything on an empty stomach. At the bakery on Ogorodny Passage we picked up some of his favourite buns with raisins and nuts, and chocolate for me. His room turned out to be smaller than ours, designed for only two. He said he lived with a post-grad who wanted to get married, but the girl was afraid he was only after the residence permit, and was hesitating. As a matter of fact, that's how it was, although it wasn't the only reason. But you couldn't leave the role of the permit out of the equation, otherwise you couldn't solve it.

'Would you get married for a permit?' I asked.

'I might do.'

'In that house, up under the roof.'

'In that house–definitely, without hesitation.'

'Even to an old woman?'

'That's a really good option. She wouldn't have long to suffer, and nor would I.'

'A shrivelled old woman who'd seen Napoleon.'

'I'd hear about Napoleon.'

'She'd have sclerosis.'

He made tea in his big teapot, and I said I was right, the teapot had attracted guests, namely me. We drank out of glasses. Exactly the same kind of faceted glasses from which we drank sweet milky coffee in the bakeries. He said he'd

ELENA DOLGOPYAT

filched them from the bakeries, four glasses, one of which he'd already broken. First of all, it had saved him money, and secondly, he liked drinking out of faceted glasses. The spoons were also stolen, aluminium. The silver leaf rustled and crunched. He said I was covered in chocolate and asked me to run a chocolatey finger across my upper lip. He wanted to see if a moustache would suit me. No-one had ever seemed closer to me. We were sitting right next to each other, and I suddenly smeared his upper lip as well with my chocolatey finger. He was at a loss. Without a word, he wiped the chocolate with his hand, but of course he didn't wipe it off as such, more smeared it around. With a grunt of 'Be right back' he strode out of the room. I went to the mirror and saw my moustache. I felt an urge to have him lick it off. The thought embarrassed me, and I fished out my handkerchief. In the mirror behind me was a map of Moscow, broken up into squares with coloured felt-tip pens; three of the squares were numbered. When he returned, his face washed clean and serious, I asked him if he was a spy. He said the squares were markings from the walks he took. The numbered streets were the ones he'd already walked and studied. The unnumbered ones he was planning to walk. Pushing the glasses and the rustling leaf against the wall, he said it was time to get down to work; linear algebra was waiting for us.

He wasn't looking at me. He tore a page out of his exercise book, and said coldly, 'Let's consider a non-homogeneous system of linear equations.'

He was explaining too fast and I couldn't keep up. He threw his pen on the table and watched as I read everything he'd written so far. He remarked aloud that my lips were moving as I read. And added that presumably my brain was also moving. I asked him to explain the Elimination Method again.

'Nope.'

'Why not?'

'Because it's elementary. Elementary and obvious. Explaining obvious things twice is for nursery school. Why did you come to study here in the first place? You have no aptitude for maths.'

I was at a loss. There was such animosity in his voice.

'Why did you?'

'To avoid the army.'

'But you don't study. You wander about Moscow.'

'I don't study, but I know my stuff.'

'You'll be expelled after the exams.'

'Why on earth? I'll pass them all.'

'And they'll expel you. For skiving.'

'So we'll both be expelled. Me for skiving and you for stupidity.'

I left.

I went down to the second floor. There was a man there, smoking on the landing. He gave me a cigarette and said I'd better quit smoking, it was bad for your health. I promised. He'd come to visit his daughter for a few days. He wanted to see how she was doing. Said she was all grown up now. She used to need him before, when she was little, but now she didn't, now she was ashamed of him, and he'd never felt so lonely. He'd get through his last two days here and go back home.

'I'd marry Valentina,' he said, 'but I'm kind of afraid.'

I didn't know why he lived alone or who Valentina was. I didn't want to know and didn't ask.

Rita came back after one a.m., or so the luminous hands of the clock said. I lay looking out of the black window at the red lights of our tower. She was behind the wardrobe pulling off her boots, drinking water from the kettle.

'Do you argue?' I asked.

'Sometimes.'

'What about?'

ELENA DOLGOPYAT

'I didn't like the film yesterday. Yasha said it wasn't his fault, he didn't make it. I said a film of his would be even worse, and he flew up at me. Must be full moon.'

'No. The moon's on the wane.'

'Strange.'

'So have you already had a second kiss?'

'Well, almost.' Rita finally came out from behind the wardrobe.

'Almost?'

'I pulled away.'

'Why?'

'I don't know. I got scared. I thought he might be catching.'

'What are you on about?'

'Seriously. I spent the whole day looking at my lips in the mirror to see if anything had come up.'

She lay down on her cot without undressing or making the bed. She turned her face towards me.

'Why aren't you asleep?'

'I'm thinking.'

'*What is it? The fires of love? The fires of hate?*'

I closed my eyes. Right in one. How could the poet know about me?

CHAPTER 6. 'WHERE ARE THE SORROWS, WHERE IS THE SWING, WHERE DID WE PLAY, JUST YOU AND I?'

I slept badly, disturbed by the lights of the tower and the whirring of the clock. And his contempt, which I could not forget. For as long as that night lasted, his contempt seemed to be the only sincere thing about him. The night passed slowly, painfully; time barely moved. I thought it might be worth dismantling the clock and greasing the mechanism; perhaps it would go a little more cheerfully, and we'd skip through the night to the glow of the hands.

At four o'clock I decided to get up. I doubt if I'd ever been up so early in hall. The only time I'd been up this early was as a child, in Murom, when we went mushroom picking on the suburban work train, Mum and me and Grandma and Granny Katya and Misha.

In the kitchen, a forgotten gas ring was still burning. There was a puddle on the floor. Potato peelings were strewn around. A cockroach was running across the tin-topped table. I brushed my teeth. Quietly, so as not to wake Rita, I got ready. I eased the alarm clock closer to her. And I left. I really didn't want to meet him, so I thought it best to get out early, not at my usual time, not at anyone's usual time.

I rode a half-empty bus through the early streets, the streets that belonged to no-one. They're always no-one's, belonging to no-one, but it's only at this hour that you realise it. The institute was likely to be still closed, so I dawdled, walking quietly, peering in at windows and finding I didn't want to live in any of the houses. I noticed an alleyway I'd never been down before, and turned into it. The alleyway was a dead end, blocked off by an empty house with strips of paper criss-crossing the windows. Like in the war. So that bomb blasts wouldn't blow out the glass. The paper crosses held it in place. Though if the blast was nearby, they wouldn't have done. With my mind I understood, of course, that the house was not from the war. It was probably being used for filming and they'd taped up the windows. I understood, but my understanding was an imaginary number. Like with Levitan that time in Murom. The significant and important quantity was the feeling that I'd walked straight into an early morning in 1942. And I wasn't scared. And if I'd come back from the dead-end street in some time other than my own, if I never made it out of the war, I wouldn't be scared. I'd stay and make my life there as best I could. But I walked out of the dead end

ELENA DOLGOPYAT

into 1982, towards a garish tram. I stopped, and followed it with my eyes. OK. I'll live here and see what happens.

The auditorium had just been swabbed down by the cleaning lady. I went in. Snowflakes were swirling in through a fanlight. I climbed up on to the sill and closed the window. The snow fell quietly, heavily. March had begun, the first month of spring. I felt as if I were floating above the ground with the snow.

I jumped down from the sill and settled myself by the window in the front row. I took out my exercise book and pen, put on my glasses, and the electric light was immediately reflected in the glass. I opened my exercise book and began to reread the lecture carefully, concentrating, switching off from the footsteps and voices. I didn't want to see when he came in. I didn't want to know if he came in at all. Didn't want to see, didn't want to know. So when the lecturer began his lecture, I had no idea if he was there.

I tried to concentrate on the lecture, and eventually I really was concentrating. I became absorbed in it, I understood what it was about, and when the lecturer asked a question in the course of establishing the proof, I answered. I was surprised to hear my own voice.

'Well done,' said the lecturer.

I looked round at the audience, suddenly wanting him to be there, to witness me being praised, my success.

He was there, in the back row, right by wall. He met my look, smiled, and held up his thumb in approval. I poked out my tongue. I was happy. Completely happy.

We went to lunch together. There was a massive queue in the canteen, as ever. I usually worried that the bell was about to ring any second and I'd have to run to class hungry while the ill-mannered pushed in and the serving lady stood gassing with the lady from stores and basically did absolutely nothing. The bell did ring, but not for us. The people dispersed and the serving lady asked us what we wanted, though she was unable to grant our every wish. He had some of his favorite buns, and I had sausage and black bread. I was going to buy chocolate, but he said he'd get it for me, as a treat. Coming from him, that was quite a gesture. He didn't like to splash out, and anyway he had nothing to go on the spree with. His scholarship was forty and his mother sent him thirty and that was enough, he said, for his lifestyle, and in the summer he hoped to earn a bit extra.

From that day on we went to the institute together, sat in lectures together, skipped classes together, came back together, went to the cinema, and in the evenings drank tea from faceted glasses in his room. People thought we were living together. I didn't try to dissuade them; I've already said that I don't like to spoil other people's ideas about me. I'm usually just too lazy to spoil them, to explain how things really are. Who cares what the truth is? Let people think what they want to think. In this case, admittedly, I would have liked it to be the way people were thinking. But it didn't happen. He wouldn't allow it. I couldn't even kiss him. The furthest I got was holding his hand. It was as if my kiss would make him melt away or turn into a frog. There was something strange about it all, incomprehensible to my childish mind, unreal. I cried into my pillow at night. I thought the problem was in me, and I asked Rita what was wrong with me. She explained that he was the one with the problem, not me, and urged me to chuck him, the sooner the better. I agreed and I couldn't. I couldn't do without him. Or ... I was a chip of stone.

Summer came. His asthma and my short-sightedness got us out of the construction brigade. The two of us were left on our own as the halls and institute and laboratory emptied out. The lab was in an ancient building, in the basement, and was reached by way of the basement. The grey wooden planks of the flooring bounced under our feet. Thick pipes wrapped in shaggy cloth ran along the wall. The

ELENA DOLGOPYAT

days were hot, but we were freezing behind the thick walls; we had neither day nor night, the electricity was on, the tall metal computer cabinets were humming, we were running programs, debugging, turning in printouts, chatting. He asked me about my childhood, about the places I'd lived with my parents–Central Asia, Transbaikal. He'd never been there. He had been to Murom. He'd passed through and seen our fortress-like railway station. We established when he'd passed through, what year, what day, and I tried to remember (or invent) where I was and what I was doing at that very moment. It was summer, so I was definitely in Murom, at my grandmother's, during the holidays. We even decided that I'd been at the station watching his train and had seen his silhouette through the window. We liked our invented meeting.

Everything was fine. Everything was unbearable. So close, and the last step impossible.

Planned renovations were underway on the seventh, and the supervisor gave me the key to a vacant room on the first floor. The lower down, the worse. More dirt, noise, smoke, cockroaches, cracks in the windows. We heaved Rita's and my things down there, along with stuff belonging to a girl who was registered to our room but didn't live with us. We didn't forget the *Portrait of an Unknown Woman*, either. He said he was tired, he'd gulped in a lot of smoke. The lift had broken and we'd dragged the stuff down the stone stairs, past the smokers, though there weren't many of them still there that summer. He left right at the beginning of the evening.

I was a long way away from him in my new place, and I couldn't even see the tower. The window looked out onto the other side, onto the courtyard. I used to look at the tower and think that he was looking at it too. It always seemed to me that we were looking at the same time. Now I was looking at the lilac bushes, long since over and gone dark. The bushes suddenly started rustling: it was raining. I listened to it falling for a long time.

I picked up the standard-issue kettle with the room number on its aluminium side in order to go to the kitchen, put some water in it, put it on to boil, distract myself. I had only just grasped the handle when I heard a key turn in the keyhole. Quietly, noiselessly, I put the kettle down where it was, on the filthy, unwashed table. The door swung wide open, and into the room came a young lad, soaked through. He saw me and stopped dead, a puddle instantly pooling around his shoes. In his right hand was a key, and in his left an ancient plywood suitcase with iron corners, the kind my Dad used to take on business trips years ago.

'Two hundred and nine?' he asked, bewildered.

I turned the side of the kettle with the number on it towards him. He squinted.

'Hell. The supervisor told me this room was empty.'

'The supervisor's an idiot.'

'You got that right.'

He hesitated for a few seconds and then went off to sort it out. I stepped over the puddle and shuffled into the kitchen. Here the houses blocked out the tower. No height, no flight; the first floor was grounded. I felt cut off, alone, lost.

I came back with the boiling, steaming kettle. It was heavy–I'd slopped too much water into it. And, following my logic, the big kettle attracted a guest. He knocked on the door, waited for my 'Come in,' and came in. He had already changed into dry clothes; granted, all his new, dry clothes were too big for him. Huge white trainers were barely peeping out from beneath sagging trousers. I sniggered: Charlie Chaplin.

'What?'

'Nothing.'

'Look, can I have a cup of tea with you? I've brought cake.' He brought his hand out from behind his back and showed me a white box tied up with string. His hand sticking out of the big sleeve of his T-shirt looked utterly childish, boyish.

'Where'd you dig that up from? The shops are shut.'

'OK, I swiped it from the guys, out the fridge. They've put me in with these blokes, they don't just have a fridge, they have a TV and a cassette player, all that stuff, basically, they're fine with me taking something to eat. They're asleep and it's boring snacking on your own.'

'What's the cake?'

'Not a clue. A bite of sausage would have been just the thing, but they didn't have any. Sausage.'

'Well, have a look in the fridge, you might find some.'

I spread a buckram cloth on the table and fetched cups. He found a tin of mackerel in the fridge. I tossed him the tin opener.

'Your trousers are falling down.'

'Trousers, shoes, the lot. Because they're not mine, mine are soaked. Picture the scene. I open my suitcase and there's water slopping about in it.'

'That's a hippy suitcase you've got there.'

'Uh-huh. A hippy would know. I used to have a normal bag. It got lifted. Borrowed the suitcase from my grandad. It's even been abroad, this suitcase.'

'What country?'

'Socialist.'

He sneezed.

'I'm getting ill. I need some vodka to warm me up.'

'No vodka.'

'The supervisor always has some.'

He was crystal clear. Straightforward. As if he were not from our time, but from somewhere like the sixties, the early sixties I'd seen in films, when strangers would smile and let you stay overnight and lend you money. And you could walk down the back streets without fear, and every man was a friend and everyone could look forward to a life full of meaning. A beautiful morning world.

He and I drank the supervisor's vodka. A third of a cup, another third, the same again, warm and light as never before, and tongues came loose: you're lovely, yes, you're like a brother, no, why brother, I'm not a brother, I want to kiss you, can I, I don't know how, seriously, yes, I'll teach you, wait, you can stand up, simple enough, my head's spinning, hug me, hold me, be quiet, at least let me breathe, breathe through your nose, don't laugh, you silly girl.

He was shorter than me but strong, with firm muscles. When he dropped his trousers, his feet were purple up to his ankles. He explained that his socks had got soaked and run. I laughed like a drain.

I told him I'd never done it before, that this was my first time. Me too, he said. Don't be afraid. Let's chuck the mattress on the floor because this cot, you know, my head's going and the cot's going, better the floor, the floor is firm, close to the ground, first floor.

Look, you're short-sighted too. How do you know? You're squinting.

You okay?

I'm fine.

It's my first time, too.

Yeah, right.

The phosphorous hands showed just after eight. They glowed in the half-dark. Here in this room, behind the dense lilac, it was always half-dark; morning began higher up. I felt sick; my head was aching. By morning, the lad was frozen, wrapped in a grey, standard-issue blanket, golden stubble appearing on his face.

I got up, found my toothbrush, dropped the soap, picked it up, and it slipped away again. He didn't wake up. In the bathroom, I shoved two fingers down my throat and threw up, but it didn't help.

ELENA DOLGOPYAT

I took the brush and the soap dish into the half-dark room. He had rolled onto his back and his mouth was a crack open as he slept. A purple leg had crawled out from under the blanket. Wincing from my headache, I dressed quietly.

The lift was still not working. I had to drag myself up the stairs to the eighth, breathing in the stinking smoke. After the fifth flight I sat down on a stone step to catch my breath. There was a tree growing outside the narrow, dust-streaked window, and a branch was resting against the glass. A small grey sparrow was sitting on the branch. Our eyes met. It was as if the bird and I were alone in the world, no-one but us. Only for an instant, but there it was.

On the quiet eighth there was a smell of burnt milk. I walked down the long corridor and knocked on his door. I heard him get up from his creaky cot, move a chair, walk. He threw open the door and stared at me with bright, surprised eyes.

'What's up?'

'What?'

'You not well?'

'I'm fine. Just feeling sick.'

'What's fine about that? Come in.'

'I had vodka last night. Everything's still ... not where it should be.'

'Come in. I'll make some tea. How much did you drink?'

'All in all a bottle between two of us.'

I settled myself at the table and he went to put on the kettle. He came back, made tea, set out the glasses and the sugar bowl. Then he picked up what I'd said.

'Between two?'

'Yes. The thing is, there was this guy, long story, he got caught in the rain, we started kissing, well, and other stuff. You know what I mean?'

He was silent. Poured me one glass of black brew and tossed in four lumps of sugar.

'That's going to be horribly sweet,' I said.

'Drink.'

He sat down and watched me take tiny, tiny sips.

'So?' he asked.

'It's hot.'

'I'm not talking about the tea.'

'Fine. Why?'

'Nothing. You have any plans?'

'Don't know. Let's go somewhere.'

'Where?'

'Don't know. The Tretyakov Gallery.'

So we did. We went to the Tretyakov Gallery and wandered from room to room and looked at the paintings and even discussed something or other. We walked all the way back to hall. Zamoskvorechye, Red Square, Dzerzhinsky Square, Kirov Street, the Garden Ring, Prospekt Mira. Streets and alleyways. Houses in which the lights were burning. Houses in which we could never live. A courtyard, with a swing. He sat down on the seat, swinging. I went up to him. He took my hand and sat me on his lap. He pushed his face against my back and fell silent. The courtyard was quiet, secluded. There were men at the garages, fiddling with a car, digging about in the engine. He lifted his face, gave me a nudge, and I stood up. I turned round and saw that he was crying. We went back to hall in silence. He went to the lift and I went to my room on the first floor.

The door was open. The guy was sitting at his desk, writing. He saw me and smiled happily.

'Look, I'm writing a letter to my mother. Help me out.'

'Write about the weather.'

'Done that.'

I picked up the kettle.

'Fill it up, make plenty. I drink a lot. Eat a lot, too.'

His name was Kolya. He had legible handwriting and a kindly disposition.

THE FLAT

He had no classes, and slept through until eleven o'clock. He hauled himself out of bed and got himself across to the window by way of the sun-warmed floorboards. He sluiced his face, took a gulp of water from the kettle, pulled on his clothes, and scooted out for a pack of ciggies. He noticed a white glimmer in the round opening of the little iron door.

The letter had journeyed for seven days. It had been despatched to Moscow on 12 September 1970, postmarked in Moscow on the 17th, and received on the 18th. Seven days. Two hundred and eighty-one kilometres. It would be possible to work out its average speed. A primary school maths problem.

Garik opened the envelope right there on the landing. His mother always spent money on airmail even though planes did not fly from their town to Moscow, and letters made their way quietly in mail and baggage trains or postal wagons. This was not something his mother wished to comprehend.

... So we get by, son. Our neighbour Vasya still plays his harmonica and they're promising to bring the trolleybus to us. Getting to the city will be easy if they do that. Not like now. The other day I waited forty minutes to get back from the market ...

Their house was in a workers' suburb, by the factories. There were many such houses there, built of wood, with metal roofs on top and stoves inside, and small plots of land where apple trees and cherry trees and potatoes and cucumbers grew. The houses had been put up before the revolution by a former owner of the factory, a German, whose surname Garik did not know.

... There've been lots and lots of apples this year. I've been going to the train to sell them. I've made jam and been giving it away. There's jam in the cellar. Currant liqueur as well. What else? My health is OK. This evening I'm going to the cinema with Rita Andreyeva. Do you remember how you did that maths question with her, you'd been given it for homework? She kept saying, 'Don't be miserable, Igor.' Oh, how we laughed ...

Igor had been given the nickname 'Garik' in Moscow.

There's news of Svetlana Yerofeyeva. She arrived yesterday from Leningrad, maybe for a week, maybe longer, she doesn't know yet. She came on her own; says she's got divorced. With a child, a boy, lovely-looking little chap, curly hair, hazel eyes. I told her they'd kept you on in the department; she might as well know ...

Garik tucked the letter away inside the envelope and went back into his flat.

He walked slowly back, but once inside, he suddenly started hurrying. He swept up money from the bottom of a carved jewellery box, in which he also kept documents and letters, grabbed a backpack from the wardrobe and shoved a sweater into it, had a quick look round, straightened the blanket on the couch, threw his backpack over his shoulder, and headed into the hall. He took his cap and anorak off the hook.

He waited a long time for a bus, stomping along the edge of the pavement. He tried to stop the few taxis that went by, then lost patience and set off walking. The bus, of course, overtook him. One way or another, he reached the metro forty minutes later, and forty minutes after that he got off at Komsomolskaya and made for Kazansky railway station.

There was a crowd languishing at the ticket office. An announcement declared that the passenger train was boarding, and Garik hurried onto the platform. The third class carriage was at the rear. People were pushing through the door with packages and suitcases; someone was shouting, 'Varya! Varya!' A child was crying.

Garik was pulled into the carriage, past the conductor.

He climbed at once onto the luggage rack, up against the ceiling. Tucked his backpack under his head, and fell silent. People kept on coming and coming, four or five to a seat, even on the side benches, with their backs to the window. All the top shelves and luggage racks were taken, and in some places two people squeezed in.

The train was hardly in motion before Garik closed his eyes. Nobody asked for tickets. The conductor didn't show up; he'd vanished.

The doors to both vestibules had been opened wide because it was so stuffy, and the smell of smoke came wafting in. Garik remembered the cigarettes he hadn't bought; remembered and forgot again. He slept and didn't sleep, heard all the conversations and exclamations, the clinking, laughing, coughing. The train was barely moving, frequently stopping. Garik occasionally hung his head down to look out the window, and saw what seemed to be the same thing: the embankment and the darkened grass, run to seed. The sun came out, then hid. People made their way towards the exit down the clogged aisle.

The train had left Moscow at one-thirty, and it reached Garik's station seven long hours later, in the autumn twilight, after eight o'clock in the evening.

People hopped down onto the low platform and walked across the tracks to the station. Garik was afraid that someone would recognise him, call out, start talking to him and hold him up, so he slanted away from the station in the direction of the depot, a short cut Garik knew as perhaps he knew no other road in the world, a path travelled and travelled again, in summer, in winter, in all seasons of the year. He thought that if he were blind, he could still have made his way along it without going wrong; he knew every pothole and twist and could orient himself by scents and sounds: here was the factory canteen, and here was the narrow gauge track with a train moving along it; he'd have to wait it out.

Garik did not hurry; he did not run, as if drawing close to his goal was spooking him. He passed the kerosene shop and turned onto Krasnaya Presnya (so named for its three-storey red brick houses). He crossed the road and came to the common. To his right, behind the humming substation, stood Svetlana Yerofeyeva's house, the same kind of house as his and his mother's: wooden, with a metal roof.

There was a glimmer of light in the curtained window.

The narrow pathway paved with red brick. The dark bush of prickly wild rose. The steps. Three of them. All familiar. It was all as if he were dreaming the same dream for the umpteenth time.

Washing was drying on a line between the apple trees: women's knickers, a camisole, children's T-shirts, underpants, a sheet.

Garik stood looking. Suddenly the curtain was pulled back and a face appeared in the lighted window. It moved closer to the glass. Familiar and long-awaited, it seemed to Garik to belong to a stranger. Perhaps the yellow electric light was to blame, or perhaps time, which had kept them apart for so long.

Garik beat a retreat back to the path, and stepped out towards the station. His mother did not find out that he had been.

He went back to Moscow on the night train. He travelled in comfort, in the open sleeper coach. He made his bed, lay down, and could not drop off. He tossed and turned on the narrow shelf, listening to the breathing of those sleeping around him. Eventually he slid down and went out to smoke in the cold vestibule. A man brought up a burning match to his cigarette, and asked, 'You sick?'

* * *

Nikolay said the neighbourhood was great, a place you could feel at home. He was talking and smiling. 'You haven't changed at all,' he said. 'Not the slightest.'

He asked if she was hot.

'You know, I'm awfully glad you'll be able to use it. Old friends, you know.'

Vera remained silent.

His phone rang, distracting him. Thank God.

'Yes. Yes it's me. Yes. Got it.'

He gave vent to a loud yell.

'Bollocks! They need me. Now now now. I'll drop you off at the metro. Have a look at the flat, and if there's anything you want changed, we'll discuss it. Take the keys.'

'Are you sure?'

'Absolutely. I'll park up here. It'll be fine for you. You'll see. Make yourself comfortable. Call me if you need anything. Any time, day or night.'

He gave Vera a sudden peck on the cheek.

At one time they'd been in the same class, and Kolya had forlornly chased after her, wearing her out in the process. Alla had persuaded her to call him, giving her his number. She knew everything about everyone.

Vera was left on her own, her surroundings as yet unfamiliar. She looked around curiously. The streetlights burned, shop windows glittered, cakes and coffee scented the air. And something else, hot and satisfying. Vera couldn't resist buying a coffee in a paper cup and a pastry with something like meat.

The coffee was blazing hot, and she waited a long time for it to cool, gawping at passers-by. One man tipped her a sudden wink.

She finished her pastry and drank her coffee. Pigeons pecked up the crumbs.

Vera walked along an asphalt path, rounded a tower, and made her way past a grey prefabricated hulk. She turned and saw the only five-storey building in the area.

My new old house.

Cars jostled for space in the yard.

The fourth entrance. The code.

The entry phone beeped, and Vera pulled the door towards her.

The main entrance was not bad. Clean. Double-glazed windows. Naturally, the belated brightening of the motion-sensitive energy-saving bulbs annoyed her. There was a smell of stale cigarette smoke, and advertising fliers lay in piles on the window sill and on the floor beside the mailboxes.

Vera hunted out a small key from a bunch and opened her (from this evening) mailbox. She fished out the fliers, had a look at them (pizza deliveries, flat repairs, more repairs), and added them to the general heap on the window sill. As if to legitimise her stay in the building. Then she walked up the worn stone steps to the top floor.

The door was a wholly unremarkable standard metal door, upholstered in black faux leather. Two locks. A spyhole.

Vera fetched out the keys and unlocked the locks. And at last stepped over the threshold of her new dwelling. The door quickly banged closed. She heard a click, and yanked the handle. The door did not budge.

She would have to go carefully with that kind of latch. God forbid that she should leave without her keys.

She fumbled for the light switch, gave it a push, and a lamp lit up the hallway.

A bare lamp on a twisted cord.

Vera stared at the lamp, which was somehow dim and blinding at the same time. At the wallpapered walls, the brown oil-painted wooden floors, at the lonely man's slippers with their tramped-down soles.

A man's black coat hung on a hook, dust across its broad shoulders.

This was a surprise.

Nikolay had spun her a bunch of stories about a European-style renovation, stretch ceilings, Italian light fittings.

Vera looked around. On the inside, the door was wooden, plain, painted with the same paint as the floors, only somewhat lighter. And there was only one lock, an old so-called English lock that clicked shut. And no spyhole in the door.

Vera went through into the small kitchen. She switched on a lamp under an old-fashioned glass shade.

A draught was coming from a crack in the ill-fitting wooden frame. The lights of the distant tower glowed. Dirty dishes were piled in the sink. On the buckram covering the table, a drop of water glistened amongst the crumbs and sausage skins. Vera touched it, as if she wanted to convince herself that it (or she) was real. She wiped her wet finger on her skirt. Turned off the lamp. She went on through into the main room.

A comical three-arm chandelier lit up the room. It was exactly like one in Vera's grandmother's old house. Her great-grandmother's, to be precise, though Vera called her grandmother. And the couch was exactly the same. So too the polished three-leaf wardrobe.

Opening the door, Vera was ready to encounter her grandmother's blue crêpe-de-chine dress, but was greeted instead by a man's jacket on a hanger. In the second compartment, on the shelves, were bedding and a man's underwear. And a carved jewellery box, also exactly like her grandmother's. Vera lifted the lid and saw a dark green passport on top of letters in envelopes. The passport was exactly the same as her grandmother's, identical (in those far-off days, we had passports exactly like that in our everyday life).

Vera opened the document.

A young man in a black and white photograph. Dark eyes, a dark fringe, a small, straight nose. A white shirt, a tie. Igor Vasilyevich Nikodimov, born 1944, Russian.

Vera put the passport away, locked the box, and closed the cupboard. She decided to call Nikolay without further delay.

Her smartphone had no signal. Not in the main room, not in the kitchen, not in the corridor. Vera thought: fine.

She was too tired. When it came down to it, the flat was old-fashioned, but not dilapidated. On the contrary, all this old stuff, including the gas cooker, the television, the taps and, most surprisingly, the passport, seemed new. So Vera tucked away her useless smartphone. It was not as if she had anywhere to go.

She lifted the seat of the couch and set it in its upright position. In the drawer under the seat, just as Vera had been thinking, was a blanket in an old-fashioned slipcover, a sheet, and a pillow. The linen did not look exactly fresh to Vera, so she took it out and tossed it onto the floor against the wall, and pulled a clean set, with sewn-on laundry tags, out of the wardrobe.

She made her bed, showered, climbed under the covers, looked for a moment at the lights of the distant tower, and fell asleep.

* * *

The train arrived after one o'clock in the morning. The station façade was lit up with festive illuminations. This

ELENA DOLGOPYAT

year the centenary of Lenin's birth was being celebrated. Garik approached a car with a green light. The driver was sitting in the cabin with his eyes closed.

Garik knocked on the glass, and the two agreed three rubles.

They drove in silence along the deserted night roads, all of which seemed alien. It was warm inside the car. Garik sat in the front beside the driver. It took them about thirty minutes to get there. To fly there, more accurately: the driver hammered the car. Garik was sorry that the journey was over so quickly. He would not have minded sitting for much longer in the warm car, and driving, driving, somewhere, anywhere, far away.

Outside his house, Garik looked at the dark kitchen window.

He went up two flights, opened his mailbox, took out a newspaper (he subscribed to *Izvestia*) and, without hurrying, reluctantly, set off upstairs to his top-floor flat. He fetched out his key as he climbed.

He stepped into the darkness of the hallway and the door slammed. The lock clicked.

Garik tromped into the main room without taking his shoes off, tossed aside his backpack, and caught sight of something white on the floor. A heap of something. He bent forward. A sheet. A slipcover. Garik looked around and saw a woman asleep on the couch.

A hand on the white slipcover.

Carefully, Garik crept closer. The woman was breathing. Sleeping. She smelled of apple. Antonovka. The curtains were open, and beyond them the sky was dark. Except that even back then, the sky over Moscow was not impenetrably dark.

Garik stood looking at the sleeping woman. The alarm clock with its round face was ticking.

He eased away from the sofa, unlaced his boots and pulled them off, and silently returned to the hall. He bumped into something and stopped. Listened carefully, quietly. He bent down, and his hands fumbled over the shoes Vera had left there. He took his heavy winter coat off the hook. In the main room he shifted a mountain of laundry, spread out his coat, lay down on it, and tucked up his legs. He was so worn out and weary that he had no energy left to think about, much less puzzle out, why this woman was in his flat, in his bed, who she was, and how she had got in.

Probably Lyokha, decided Garik. *Definitely. Tomorrow. I'll sort it out.*

He closed his eyes. His own body felt heavy, cast-iron.

He was falling–through the floor, through every surface, through the ground, and on, on, on.

Vera woke up before it was light.

She opened her eyes, closed them. She lay there listening to the cars going by in the street below, to the old fridge rumbling in the kitchen.

A snore.

Vera opened her eyes and propped herself up on her elbow. She saw a man sleeping on the floor by the wall. She didn't cry out, or gasp. Very quietly, she slid off the couch onto the icy floor. Without taking her eyes off the sleeping man, she got dressed.

He did not move. His breathing was laboured. Like he had a cold. Vera grabbed her bag and made her way into the hall. She put on her shoes in the dark. Fumbled for the lock.

She hopped out onto the landing, slammed the door, and raced down the stairs.

The banging of the door woke Garik up. He could not understand why he was lying on the floor in a jumble of bedding. His arm had gone to sleep. He sat up and started chafing it, wriggling his fingers. And froze, remembering the woman. She was not on the couch. Garik stood up, listening hard.

The alarm clock was chirring. Voices could be heard on the landing.

That cool smell of apples.

Garik made a tour of the flat. He glanced into the toilet and bathroom.

On the kitchen table he caught sight of a thin rectangle. More precisely, something like a rectangular plate, maybe five millimetres thick. It was metal, smooth, and one of its sides was glass. The glass was black, opaque, cold. There was a small round indentation in the glass at the metal edge, a dent just where his finger was. Garik stroked the indentation, gave it a press, and the glass lit up. Small coloured pictures appeared. Under each one, an explanation:

Messages. Calendar. Photos.

In the upper left corner, in tiny letters, it read: *No network*.

Garik gingerly touched the picture labelled *Photos*. On the screen (Garik had already realised that it was a screen, of course) a large number of small images appeared. Garik touched one of them. The image expanded.

In the colour snapshot he saw a woman.

She was sitting on a bench. In a park, probably. A patch of sunlight rested on her round cheek. The picture had been taken in summer; it was sharp, and Garik just wanted to look at it and not stop looking. He touched the cheek in its pool of light, and the photo shrank.

A miracle.

Garik left the mechanism (no, that was certainly not the right word) on the table and headed for the bathroom. He looked at his face in the mirror, and fetched out his razor. When he returned from the bathroom to the kitchen, the screen was inscrutable. Garik decided not to disturb it. He finished the rest of the water from the kettle, put on his shoes and anorak, and left the flat.

Around the corner by the bakery was a phone box. It was occupied. The door was not properly shut, and Garik could hear the conversation.

'No, you don't understand. And never will. And he doesn't eat bread.'

Garik could not get through to Lyokha; he succeeded only in wasting two rubles. Back in the flat, the amazing gadget was not on the kitchen table (nor was it anywhere else in the flat; Garik ransacked the whole place, even the mezzanine).

Vera was at the door of the metro in the already weary early morning crowd when she remembered her smartphone. She extricated herself from the throng and ran back to the house, scooting along the curb against the flow of people coming the other way.

She rang the doorbell several times. No-one answered.

Vera unlocked the locks. Without crossing the threshold, she peered into the semi-darkness of the hall. Nothing. Not a shadow, not a rustle. Vera stepped into the hallway, leaving the door open behind her to secure herself a retreat. Then she flew into the kitchen, looking neither right nor left, grabbed her smartphone from the table, and tore back out of the flat. She slammed the door and raced down the stairs.

'What the hell?' exclaimed a man, barely getting out of her way in time. He was labouring heavily up the stairs.

Vera leaped out of the front door and switched on her smartphone. The connection was restored. Vera dialled Nikolay's number. He answered instantly.

'Vera? Good morning.'

'Yes, Kolya, it's me. Why did you lie to me? European-style renovation, the whole shebang. What for? Some guy in there. Grateful he didn't kill me in my sleep.'

'Vera, sweetheart, what are you talking about?! You've lost me completely. I'll come over right away. Where are you?'

'Just coming up to the metro.'

'Wait, I'll be right there.'

'Get a move on. I'm giving you back your keys.'

The kiosks were all open, smelling of cheap coffee. Vera bought herself one. She sat down at a high table, and sipped a little of the sugary drink. Her lips felt as if they were sticking together.

It soothed her, that cheap instant coffee with milk; three-in-one, pure chemistry. It soothed her and reminded her of her childhood. It lulled her; that was exactly what it did. Vera used to drink it in the mornings from a huge mug. Her mother would still be asleep, and Vera would get ready for school on her own. She would switch on the television in the kitchen, turning the sound right down; she did not want her mother to be woken suddenly by a loud yell and come running in and start saying, 'Why don't you make yourself some porridge? Look, it's right here, you're a big girl, we agreed, you should keep your word.'

Pictures would be flashing across the screen, flickering and going out. Something like a primitive fire, a hearth.

Vera would wash her face, drink her coffee, dress, turn off the television, and leave the flat, locking the door. Her mother boasted about how independent she was, how responsible, how calm and tough she was. Level-headed. When she was a child, Vera struck herself as being already very old, long established, someone who understood this life completely.

A car pulled up. Nikolay got out, turning his head this way and that.

Vera watched him angrily, and waited. Tall, with a small head on a thin neck. At length he saw her, broke into a smile, and ran towards her.

'Vera!'

'Let's go.'

She tossed her empty cup into a bin and strode off along the asphalt path away from the metro. Nikolay caught up with her and took her elbow. Vera felt his fingers trembling, and yanked her arm away.

The front door, the ragged steps, the lamps flickering like in a film about the end of the world. The door upholstered in black faux leather. The two locks. The black, blind spyhole.

Vera unlocked the door and threw it open. The semi-darkness of the hall opened out before them.

Vera turned round towards Nikolay, fixed him with a look, and stepped over the threshold. Nikolay followed, flicked the light switch, and the hall filled with light.

Gone was the old (though new) wallpaper, the old-fashioned hanger with hooks and the shelf for headgear, the coat, the tromped-down slippers. Nikolay had not lied. There were the suspended ceilings, the plasma TV, the coffee machine. Everything, as promised, without deception.

On the table in a round glass vase, irises glowed a soft blue.

He watched her. Vera was at a loss, embarrassed.

'So what's wrong?' Nikolay inquired gently.

'I don't know. I was somewhere that wasn't here,' mumbled Vera. 'I. Really am. Going mad.'

Nikolay hastened to reassure her. 'You could have mixed up the entrances, and the keys might just have matched, you know, like in *The Irony of Fate*.'

'Rubbish. No. Same entrance.'

'The floor?'

'Right one. Top floor.'

'And the roof, pray observe, is not leaking. We've had a major refurbishment, really successful. I told you.'

'Yes. I'm sorry. I don't understand.'

'Me neither. But if everything's OK, let me make some coffee. There's a packet in the fridge. I left it there. You know you have to keep coffee in the fridge?'

'No. It's not important. I don't want any.'

'Vera?'

'What?'

'You can live here free. As long as you want.'

'No, Kolya, I don't need it to be free.'

'OK.'

'I want to be alone.'

'OK. I'm on my way. Only. Have a look in the fridge anyway.'

He left her, thank God. His presence was excruciating.

Vera walked around the gorgeous flat, touching the wonderfully even walls in the main room as if they were marshmallow.

She pulled out her smartphone. She had signal, and lots of it. Vera called Alla and said she would be in somewhat late owing to unforeseen circumstances.

'Maybe you should take some time off. You have time off owing.'

'I have an appointment at twelve.'

'Well, be a good girl, don't be late. You'll tell the director, though.'

The coffee machine was of a light-coloured metal, and solid. Not so much a coffee machine as a coffee factory. Vera decided to see what kind of coffee she would get from it. She glanced into the fridge, also made of a superior, light metal. It fitted into the tiny kitchen without cluttering it; everything in the flat had been thought-out, calculated, and the furniture was obviously custom-made. A cake sat solemnly in the fridge, in a transparent box. Vera looked at it in bewilderment, and shut the door.

Vera made coffee, a tiny cup of thick espresso, and drank it as she stood by the window, looking out at the distant towers, trying to imagine people sleeping in them, or perhaps having breakfast, or going out, leaving their dwellings and it being dark and quiet inside them.

OK, enough coffee for today.

Vera picked up her smartphone and took a picture of the distant towers.

She washed up her cup. She put on lipstick at the oval mirror in the hall, turned out the light, and went out onto the landing. She banged the door, but for some reason the lock did not click. Vera put the key in the keyhole and turned it. She had gone down one flight when she remembered that she had left her smartphone on the windowsill again.

Ah, come on, what am I ...

She had to go back, fish out her keys, and unlock the locks. A voice was burbling on the landing.

There was a man in the hall. He looked round and stared in amazement at the open door.

Whether he was the one who had been sleeping on the floor against the wall the previous night, or someone else, Vera could not tell for sure.

'I'm sorry. I ...' Before Vera could finish, the man flung the door shut with a bang.

He did not seem even to have noticed her.

'Well, what do you know,' said Vera. She pressed the bell.

She could hear the doorbell ringing in the flat. There was no sign the man was even thinking of opening the door.

What was she to do? She could not call the police; her smartphone was imprisoned behind the iron door, and while she was running for help the man would vanish without trace. Already had vanished, likely enough. Madness. Madness.

I'm going to open the door, walk in, and get killed, thought Vera and started to open the locks (both were locked).

Vera stepped into the entrance hall with its painted wooden floor and wallpapered walls. The coat hung on the hook. Boots. Vera tripped over them.

Garik, knife in hand (he was slicing bread), headed into the hall, towards the noise.

Vera shrieked.

'Ah,' said Garik. 'It's you.'

Vera did not take her eyes off the blade, the dagger blade, charged with menace.

Time was, when he was a child, Igor (and Goryun–those were his names back then) had had it whetted in the railway workshops by some lads he knew. The handle was beautiful, decorated, and comfortable. A hoodlum's dream. His mother, of course, took it away, but when he went to Moscow to study, she gave it back to him. Like a weapon for a knight preparing for a journey.

'I'll kill Lyokha. He might as well start writing his will. Was it him gave you the key?'

'Nikolay. I forgot my phone.'

'I don't know about a phone, but you did leave some sort of thingummy here.'

'A smartphone. Please be so kind as to give it back to me.'

'I can't. I ran off to call that idiot Lyokha, couldn't get through, came back, and it was gone. Vaporised. What is it? Some kind of new-fangled gadget?'

'I took it. I forgot it twice. It looks like I came back while you were out making your call, and then I came here with Nikolay and forgot it again. It should be in the kitchen. On the window sill. I was standing there, taking pictures of the view from the window.'

'It's not on the window sill. Honestly. See for yourself. Please. Come in. You can keep your shoes on.'

Vera went through. She realised that Garik (the same man who had slammed the door in her face), was, despite his blade, harmless.

In the kitchen (Vera had already realised what kind of kitchen it would be and that, of course, there would be no smartphone in it) Vera wanted to ask if the man had noticed anything strange in his flat, and burst into tears. That had never happened to Vera before, except when she was a very little child.

Flustered, Garik hurried to sit Vera down on a stool and gave her some water.

Vera took a sip, sniffed, and asked permission to go to the bathroom.

'Of course, of course!' cried Garik, and ran off to fetch a clean towel.

Vera washed herself in cold water. Garik handed her the towel, and said, 'I've made tea.'

He poured tea for her, poured tea for himself, and offered her the sugar bowl and some bread and sausage.

'Don't say no. Drink, eat. We will find your smart. It's all Lyokha, all this, who else could it be. He's got nothing to do, the jerk, he lives like he's in the movies, all adventures. Lands himself flat on his own arse.'

Garik came up with an explanation for what was happening.

Vera (he had already asked her name and told her his) worked in a secret research institute. Lyokha had clearly got to know her–he was acquainted with academics and cosmonauts. The amazing device which Vera had left on his table and then somewhere else was her invention. No-one knew about it; it was a military secret. The twit Lyokha (why did I give him the keys to my flat, now who's the moron), that swamp thing Lyokha had told the girl that she could spend the night here (for some reason she had nowhere else to sleep; how was he to know why that was?). She'd had the smartphone with her. Yes. And Lyokha had swiped it. For a joke. A hugely funny joke. There were inconsistencies in this version, but it offered some kind of explanation, however thin and meagre, and would do as a patch.

Vera was silent, and Garik did not bother her with questions; he too sat in silence.

She sipped her tea, gave what sounded like another little sob, and looked out of the window.

A grey haze, windows twinkling in the distant towers. A haze outside, but in the kitchen, on the buckram, was a patch of light. A warm ray of sunlight. Vera reached out her hand and wriggled her illuminated fingers.

'Where's the sun come from?'

'The window.'

'And what's there, out the window?'

'Well, the sun.'

'What else?'

'The sky.'

'Blue?'

'Blue.'

'What else?'

'A vapour trail. In the sky.'

'What year is it?'

'What year's it supposed to be?'

'I'm serious.'

Garik took a newspaper from the window sill and handed it to Vera.

'Today's.'

'*News of the People's Deputies,*' read Vera. '*1970. 19 September. Saturday.* It's Tuesday where I am. *2017.*'

Woho, thought Garik. *So that thing was a time machine.*

It was not that he instantly believed Vera to be from the future, but he did not dismiss it out of hand and write her off as crazy. He lived in an era when the future seemed to be a kind of paradise, a promised land; there was a longing to look at it. And sci-fi writers were looking, and the question of a time machine remained an open one.

'And what have you got out the window?' asked Garik.

'Slush.'

Vera looked like she might be a foreigner. A Frenchwoman. Though French girls were all skinny, like schoolgirls, but Vera was like a ripe apple. And she smelled like an apple, like an orchard. And of coolness. Her shoes were spattered with mud, and so too was the hem of her raincoat. Dirty and not yet dried out. It certainly made one think.

Raincoat, shoes, long skirt in an oblique check. The raincoat was blue, and bright–a blue fireball. There's no such thing as a blue fireball, but there will be. No ring on her ring finger.

'You don't believe me.'

'Why not? That smartphone was absolutely fantastic.'

'It's a phone. Without wires. Basically, a little computer. But you probably don't know what a computer is, do you? Fine. I'm on my way. I'll try, I don't know, something. Anything.'

She got up and headed into the hall. Garik hurried after her. He opened the door.

'Your Lyokha's got nothing to do with this,' said Vera. She stepped over the threshold onto the landing.

And immediately melted into thin air.

A dazed Garik followed her quickly out onto the landing, missed the door, and it slammed shut.

A cool smell of apple. Melting with her.

Vera stood on the landing and stared at the slammed door.

Black faux leather. The spyhole giving off a dull gleam. The two locks, the keys to which were in Vera's bag. She took them out, then dithered; she could not bring herself to undo the locks. She heard footsteps, laboured and halting. They were coming closer.

A heavy-set man was coming up to the landing on the top floor. The man she had narrowly missed knocking over the other day. He was on his way up the last flight. One-two. Pause. One and two. Pause. That kind of rhythm, more or less.

He arrived on the landing, frowned at Vera, and headed for the neighbouring door.

'Excuse me,' said Vera. 'May I ask you a favour?'

She asked him to open the door for her, saying that her key was jamming but that perhaps it would work for him.

He hesitated, but opened the door. He stepped back, and Vera heard the ring of her smartphone. A tune from the TV series *Sherlock*.

'Vera-Vera.' It was Alla, secretary (and overseer), onetime classmate (and head girl). That was all she said.

Vera got to work just after midday. Her clients had already been waiting for her for twenty minutes, thankfully without grumbling.

Vera made up for her lateness (two and a half hours) by working until 10.30 in the evening. She headed out of the office, her eyes unseeing, her tongue unable to wrap itself round a single word, her legs barely moving. She did not even feel like eating. Least of all did she want to call Nikolay. What would she say to him if she did? That if she opened the door herself (by herself, and probably without witnesses, though she needed to check that), she would find herself in the flat in 1970. The same flat, that was obvious. The same flat, the same house, the same city, the same country—but in a different time.

Vera-Vera, as Alla said.

Asking someone to unlock the door so that she might get to her modern, marshmallow, practically edible flat: no, she was not brave enough for that. So Vera went up to her top floor, the white flashes making her squint. She unlocked the black cyclops herself, and went in to Garik in his 1970. She walked in and said, 'It's me,' as if she were entering her own home, as if she were expected.

Perhaps she was expected and perhaps she was not; no-one heard her. A guitar was being strummed, voices were chattering, the air smelled of smoke.

Oh no, anything but that.

Vera decided to go straight back to 2017. Except that she did not have time. A cheerful fellow, hair stuck to his sweaty forehead, glanced into the hall. Vera thought she knew the cheerful fellow's face.

'I'm sorry,' said Vera.

'Not a word. I know everything. Your name is Vera, you appear and disappear, you have the keys to Garik's flat, and he thinks I gave them to you, and I didn't, but he doesn't believe it.'

The voices rose and fell, the guitar rattled.

'You are obliged to rehabilitate me. Come on.'

'I'm dog tired. I've been stupid. Please excuse me, I'm leaving.'

'I'm not letting you go. Not for anything!'

Quick as a flash, the young man slipped past her to the door and blocked it.

'Have a heart.'

'It may surprise you, but I do. Come on, Vera, come in and be with us, eh? They're all good people in there.'

'I don't like groups of drunks, Lyokha (there you are, I know your name too). I need to rest.'

'We're not drunks. We're cultured people. And you'll get your rest. We've got potatoes. Just boiled. Crumbly, you know. Garik brought them from his mother's. She lives over there, beyond the woods.'

'Blah blah blah,' said Vera amiably.

Lyokha fell silent and looked at her tenderly, affectionately, like a good-natured yard dog. Quite suddenly, Vera wanted to join them in their little kitchen, in that world, the world she had only seen in films (films from Khrushchev's thaw, or maybe a little later). Comradeship, love.

And taking turns, the rain and snow, ta-ta-ta-tari, pronounced the guitar.

'Potatoes,' said Vera. 'Do you have butter to go with the potatoes?'

'Not sure.'

They boiled the potatoes in their jackets and ate them with coarse, shiny salt. There was vodka on the table and Vera did not say no; she downed a shot. Garik peeled her a potato (took off its jacket) and watched with shining eyes. He introduced her as a scientist from a secret research institute; Vera voiced no objection.

Lyokha, Garik, a guy with glasses and the guitar, and a young woman, Olga. They were talking. Vera was not paying attention, but she suddenly realised they were talking about *The White Sun of the Desert* (someone exclaimed 'Gyulchatay'). It seemed the film had not long been out.

'Bergman! Now there's the real thing.'

The sound of their voices was pleasing to her. Her eyelids were drooping.

'People,' said Garik. 'I declare this meeting closed.'

And all of them, even the tireless, sparkling, sunny (probably even while he was asleep) Lyokha, said their goodbyes and hurried off their separate ways home. Vera was left alone with Garik in a kitchen that stank of cigarette smoke, in silence. Although the silence was only for Garik, his night-time silence of 1970. Vera could hear the howl of a car alarm and a heavy bass, apparently coming from the neighbours downstairs. Her 2017.

'I'll make your bed on the sofa, and I'll sleep here in the kitchen.'

'Where here? On the floor?'

'I'll put down a rug. I've got a rug up there on the mezzanine, you know, multi-coloured, from the country. I sort of inherited it.'

'Wonderful. Make up a bed for me on it.'

'No chance. I'll be more comfortable in the kitchen. That's point one.'

'Point two: what do you use to wash the dishes?'

They cleared the table. Vera washed, Garik wiped ('Bring a clean wiping up towel'–and he did). He dried the plates and put them in piles in the cupboard.

Quietly, without a word, like people who were already used to each other, like relatives.

'I'll show you my view from the window,' said Vera when they had finished wiping the table completely dry.

Vera switched on her smartphone, opened photos, and expanded the last picture to full screen.

A window, and beyond it, the lights of the distant towers.

'Now what can you see? Wait, don't tell me. Try to snap it. I'll show you how, it's easy peasy. Turn the light off.'

Garik lined himself up and touched the white circle at the bottom of the screen carefully, as if the smartphone were something like a trough of water and he was afraid of spilling or even slightly shaking it (then the image would disappear).

Outside Garik's window, the moon was lighting up the distant fields.

Vera put the smartphone down on the table. The screen went black. Garik leaned and touched his lips on the round lobe of her elfin ear.

'I'd like a shower,' said Vera.

'What for?'

They fell asleep on the sofa together. Garik set his alarm clock for seven. Its luminous hands and luminous digits showed pitiful and pale from a dark corner.

Garik woke up at five and stared at the dial that was so like a little face, and did not move. Vera was breathing on his shoulder. Garik thought about time. In the fantasy books of Garik's day, a meeting with the future was scary: it changed the past, it changed history.

Ah, never mind, thought Garik, and closed his eyes.

Vera was in the crowd at the metro when it struck that her that Lyokha reminded her of an actor. Naturally, Vera could not remember his last name. She had to ask Alla.

'There's this film. A beautiful woman, a spy, turns his head. He's daft as a brush but a good guy, his uncle's at the factory, an engineer, builds planes, and she's got to get to his uncle through him, to the blueprints. Old film.'

ELENA DOLGOPYAT

'I know,' said Alla, stopping her. '1935. Stepan Kowalski played the young man. Drop-dead good-looking. They shot him in 1940.'

Wikipedia, however, was certain that there were witnesses who had seen Stepan Kowalski in a camp in Magadan in 1942. And one K.S. Udodov had met Stepan at the front, in a penal battalion, in 1943.

... It is known for certain that Kowalski was arrested on 5 May 1940, and on 21 January 1941 his wife Claudia gave birth to a son, Leonid. From 1966, the son's resemblance to his father was observed to be striking, and the young man began to be recognised in the street (several films in which Kowalski starred have not lost their popularity to this day; the actor had charisma, as we say now).

Leonid inherited his father's face, gait, voice and, most importantly, his charm. He was not trained as an actor (he barely scraped through building institute), but he was invited to play parts in films. Leonid Stepanovich's filmography includes one feature film and two documentaries. In one of these he played his father, and many are still convinced that the film was actually newsreels. Leonid also appeared on stage, in an experimental youth theatre, in minor roles.

After 1970, he began to change. People stopped seeing his father in him. He put on vast amounts of weight. He drank. He worked variously as a stevedore and a stoker. After 1973, all trace of him is lost. At any rate, we have found no more material evidencing his life. Nor do we know anything about his death.

Vera closed the Wikipedia article, poured herself some tea, and set to work.

* * *

Black olives, green olives.
Black and green tea.

There must be a joke in there somewhere.

Vera ambled round the supermarket, pushing her trolley, and could not come up with a joke.

The evening was calm, quiet, unlike the previous day. The streetlights were warming up but the sky was not cooling, not going out. Vera walked home imagining laying out all her gifts on the little kitchen table, including the green avocado and black plums.

Black and green. What could she come up with?

Garik had promised to get brown bread and boil the potatoes. The fundament, so to speak, of the repast. She needed to embroider the theme. Black and green.

Something a little pink: trout. And French rosé. And brownies, dark brown, almost black. And green salad leaves. Aha!

There were to be no guests, just Vera and Garik. They would draw the curtains. That was how it would be. That was how it was.

Garik took a look at the laid table and broke into song:

'*Red, green, yellow, violet …*'

'I know that!' exclaimed Vera. 'I know that song!'

A miracle. Miracle of miracles.

* * *

The heavy-set neighbour phoned Nikolay. The new lodger smoked, he said. Cigarettes. 'Mount Vesuvius. I'm scared to go into the kitchen in the morning. Suffocating.'

'Vera, sweetheart,' complained Nikolay on the phone. 'He's not going to calm down. He'll nag us both to death. He's the other side of your wall and sniffs out anything and everything. A rat.'

Vera explained that she did not smoke and did not receive guests who smoked. Nor, indeed, guests who did not.

ELENA DOLGOPYAT

'Maybe the smoke's coming from downstairs.'

It was afternoon when Nikolay called, and Vera was at work. She spoke quietly, with restraint. Nikolay apologised for taking up her time, and assured her that he would sort everything out.

Just over an hour later, he was entering his own flat.

The neighbour was undoubtedly mad. There was not a trace of ash. The only thing the place smelled of was dust. The dust surprised Nikolay. No-one had been here for a long time. Vera was paying for a flat she did not live in. What for?

Nikolay checked the meters. No water or electricity was being consumed. He recorded all the readings in a special notebook.

He called the neighbour and showed him the flat. The neighbour frowned but did not back down.

'Doesn't smell now but smelled then. She'll burn you down. Me too.'

'She doesn't come here at all. There's an absolute carpet of dust.'

'She comes here every night. 8.30, give or take. Lugging bags from our supermarket. I see her.'

'You're getting flaky in your old age.'

'I'll write to the police.'

'You do that. Have them come with forensics. If you can talk them into it.'

The neighbour slammed the door.

Nikolay walked around the house. The irises had wilted, and the water in the round glass vase was cloudy and stinking like a swamp. The cake lay untouched in its transparent box in the fridge. Like a princess in a crystal coffin.

Nikolay got back in his car and went off on his own business. He was back by eight. He stood by the window and sure enough, his wait was rewarded: Vera arrived. Exactly as the neighbour had predicted, with bags from the supermarket. In one of them Nikolay made out a bottle.

He waited, listening out, then tiptoed into the hall and looked through the peephole, but there was no sign of Vera. Nikolay went out onto the landing. No. At some point after nine he left. He did not know what to think.

Perhaps she had met someone on one of the lower floors and that was where she went, and was living there. But why pay for a flat she didn't need?

Nikolay did not like riddles.

Vera had offended him. It seemed to him that she was being uncivilised. She was using him. His feelings for her.

* * *

Nikolay called to ask her to meet him.

'I can't right now,' said Vera. 'I have clients.'

'It's urgent, Vera.' Nikolay's voice was unexpectedly sad and serious. 'I'm selling the flat. Circumstances.'

'Well not today, at least,' said Vera. 'I don't even have a place to stay overnight. You know that.'

'Stay at my place.'

'No, Kolya.'

He sat in silence. The silence drew out and out.

Mercifully, Vera's clients waited quietly, without becoming irritated. Nevertheless, they did not fail to report on Facebook how patiently and indulgently they had waited.

'OK,' he finally decided. 'Let's try to thrash it out. This evening. Eight thirty. I'll book a table.'

The restaurant was in one of the steep, quirky lanes between Maroseyka and Solyanka. In a semi-basement, with candles burning on heavy tables, and vaulted ceilings. In Vera's imagination the whole thing looked like a catacomb church, where people exchanged low whispers, where they did not eat but took communion, their faces hidden in the shadows. The only things that could clearly be seen were the white

ELENA DOLGOPYAT

plates, large and flat and traced with secret signs written in sauce: scarlet, yellow, green. Hieroglyphics.

'It's my fault,' said Nikolay. 'My fault, my treat.'

'If you need money,' pleaded Vera in a thready voice, 'I can take out a loan.'

'There's no need, sweetheart. Why get into debt? I've found you a flat, in this neighbourhood. You can move in straightaway, today.'

He topped up her glass with cool wine.

'Vera-Vera.'

'I'd like to stay in your flat. I'll find the money. I will. I'll buy it.'

'I've already found a buyer. You don't seem to be backing down.'

'I'll talk to him.'

'Ah, Vera. Mysterious Vera. Why do you want my flat when you don't even live there? I was there yesterday. Dust and desolation.'

Nikolay seemed to be enjoying her confusion.

'Most remarkable of all: I saw you. I waited by the window and along you came. You went in the front door at half past eight. I checked my watch. But you didn't get as far as the flat. And I can't work out what you need with my flat if you're living with someone else. Even if it is in the same block.'

Of a sudden, Vera was calm. She looked directly at Nikolay.

'OK. I'll have to show you. I'll wait for you outside.'

She got up from the table and headed towards the exit from the catacombs.

Nikolay hurriedly paid the bill.

He stepped out of the half-dark onto the narrow pavement.

Vera was examining a glowing shop window, looking at the ridiculous, idiotic souvenirs: books with blank pages

(*Dead Souls*, *War and Peace*, *War of the Worlds*), a bendy knife, an alarm clock on bird's legs. An aluminium flask radio.

Nikolay came up to her. He thought he had made no sound, but Vera looked round. Looked at him without excitement, even with something approaching boredom.

They came to the modest five-storey building, went in through the front door, and climbed to the very top.

'I'll go in,' said Vera in the tone of one giving orders. 'You wait a moment and then follow. And please don't watch me open the door. Turn round, look the other way.'

'So you can do a runner?'

'Where to? There's nowhere to run.'

'Why then?'

'So you don't jinx it. Turn around and don't peek. Be patient and all will be revealed. Are you not curious?'

'Kids' games,' muttered Nikolay. He turned away.

He distinctly heard the key enter the keyhole and turn. And the second key enter and turn. The door opened and immediately closed again.

Nikolay turned round and grasped the door handle. Locked. It would not budge. Nikolay rang the bell once. A second time.

That bloody Vera.

He fetched out his own keys.

He searched every nook and cranny. Vera was not in the flat. Nor was there the scent of her, apple, fresh.

Nikolay came out of the uninhabited flat onto the landing, and pulled the door to. He had no idea what to do next. He stood there in the pitiful, pale light. Suddenly the door he had just closed opened, and Vera stepped out of the darkness of the flat.

'What's this, a trick?'

'Almost. Open the door. We'll go in together now.'

They went in.

She instructed him to follow her. Nikolay was confused and submissive.

They sat at the bare table in the kitchen.

'It wasn't a trick. Your flat is special: people can go in and not come back out. It's under surveillance. And believe me, it's in your interest to keep quiet about what you've seen today. I personally don't care what happens to you if you blab. It's not my concern at all. I'm just warning you.'

Nikolay said nothing.

'Yes?'

'Yes.'

'Let's hope so. Have you been letting this flat a long time?'

'Five years. A family with a kid. Russians.'

'Why'd they move out?'

'More comfortable in a different neighbourhood. I suppose. I didn't poke my nose in. Did the renovation after them.' He glanced around the small kitchen.

Walls like buttercream. The homely ceiling light of green glass.

'My grandmother lived here. Moved in in '94 and stayed till the end. Her end. 2011.'

Vera was silent. Then she issued another order. 'Leave me.'

He went. At last.

Vera wandered round the flat, turning the lights on and off, running the water and shutting off the taps again. She listened carefully: muffled, heavy sounds.

Music. Where from?

She ran her palm over the smooth, sugary walls. Looked out of the window.

A man was standing in the yellow light of the streetlight. He was wearing a black overcoat and black hat to match and looked like a noir hero; he could have been a detective or a killer. Light snow was swirling, right on cue. A cigarette showed white in his fingers.

Vera put out the light in the bathroom (she had forgotten she had turned it on), checked the taps, left the flat, and returned–this time to 1970. Except that beyond the window she could still see 2017. A yellow circle of light, and in it, the man in black.

Garik was telling her about a French film. It had been a closed screening, and Garik had provided simultaneous translation.

'The French just never stop talking,' complained Garik. 'A miracle I coped. Easier to unload wagons, and I should know. I used to do it.'

Vera had grown fond of watching him. The way he lit a cigarette (always shielding the flame in his palm, even indoors with not a breath of air). The way he hacked the bread with his bandit's knife (yes, bread, a brown loaf with a firm, crispy crust). The way he laid a sheet, smoothing out the folds. The way he shaved, looking seriously in the mirror. She had grown fond of his smell, his dark blond curls (she cut them herself; she could not bear the thought of anyone else touching his hair). She had even grown fond of his cough. She lugged sweets and wine and expensive clothes for him from her 2017.

'I'm just afraid,' Garik said more than once, 'that one day you won't come. I'll be waiting. I'll wait and wait. I'll always wait for you.'

One day, close to New Year, to the smell of oranges and pine needles, Lyokha (he used to visit them on Sundays, towards the evening; more precisely, he used to come round to warm up), would not leave Vera alone. He hung round her, repeatedly asking her to come to his première. He did all he could to persuade her. He even got angry.

'Vera, you mysterious woman,' he said. 'What would it cost you to go out with Garik? Into the outside world. There'll be respectable people there, and champagne by way of refreshment. And me on stage. Exactly five minutes. Do I need to kneel? Come on, Garik, let's get on our knees.'

'How about come on, Lyokha, calm yourself down. Or I'll calm you down, and your première won't happen, or it will happen without you. They'll find someone else, for five minutes, and you'll be in A & E with a broken nose. And you'll never come round here again. I won't let you in.'

Garik spoke with such vehemence that Lyokha did indeed calm down, as if he had sobered up, as if he had not been a tad under the influence. He sobered up and became sad. He finished his tea and took his leave.

Looking out of the window, Garik said that Lyokha was wandering along the icy pavement, quite lost. Sometimes they would both stand at the window and tell each other what they were seeing. And if someone from the seventies had checked out their kitchen from the other side of the glass, they would have been surprised to see a man talking to himself. Kissing the empty air.

On the second day of the New Year, all the kiosks by the metro were closed, their eyelids shut, sleeping, and there was no more than the occasional light showing in the windows of the towers. Holiday rubbish cluttered the street–bottles, papers, peel. Garik went out to work, to the institute–they did not have long holidays there–and Vera became bored on her own. She decided to go into the centre and have a walk, and if she should chance upon a café suddenly opening, she could sit down with a cup of coffee. She was pining for an espresso; such a thing had not yet reached Moscow of the seventies. Garik brewed sweet, thick coffee in a Turkish pot.

At the metro, Vera switched on her smartphone. Nikolay had called several times and, of course, had not got through. Vera did not call back. She made her way to the centre and, as she had been dreaming, even found the open doors of a café on Kamergersky.

Vera asked for an espresso, saying, 'Not a double. Triple.'

Her phone rang.

'Yes, Kolya, Happy New Year.'

'Yes, right, Happy New Year. Do you have connections there? Can you help?'

'What with?'

'You don't know? That is a surprise. You should be the first to know. Our house is being knocked down. You have to help. People don't want to leave. Lots of them don't. It's in your interest.'

'Yes. Got it,' said Vera, and turned off her smartphone.

Bitter morning coffee.

Lying side by side, the glimmer of a winter morning, a Sunday, each one hearing their own sounds through the walls, the rolling surf of their own time, the rattle and hum. They each had their own time and their time in common. How it had come to be, they did not know. Why was it that Vera, and no-one else, opened the door and walked in to Garik, to 1970, no, it was already 1971?

'I don't know. I don't know,' said Vera. 'It's the only miracle I've ever experienced in my life. There's never been anything else. I haven't seen ghosts, I haven't read other people's thoughts. I came to work in Moscow because there are no jobs back home. I've lived in rented flats, first one then another. I've never fallen in love with anyone before you. I mean, I had relationships, but they were here today gone tomorrow, like flimsy thread. They all fell apart.'

'I'm nobody without you,' whispered Garik. 'That's why.'

Of the fact that their house would be demolished in 2018, Vera said not a word.

Come March, the tenants were moved out.

The house was still standing, but the electricity and water were turned off and the gas pipes capped.

But the house was still standing, and Vera took to going in the front door with a torch, stun gun at the ready.

The worn steps. She could walk up them blindfold.

On the very last day of March, the 31st, Vera climbed to the top floor (with each passing day it seemed higher). The door to the flat had been torn off. A dark opening yawned. Vera stepped into it. She lit the floors and walls with her torch. Someone had already fouled the place, and all Nikolay's beautiful renovation had gone to ruin.

The window in the kitchen was broken. It had been a house, a living body. Now it was a skull.

Alas, poor Yorick.

In 1980, Garik (Igor Vasilyevich Nikodimov, b. 1944) would marry a French woman and go to Paris to live with her. He would teach at the Sorbonne. In 1981, he would have a son. In 1984, a second. He would publish commentaries on medieval philosophers. He would translate a dozen crime novels into Russian. In 2005 he would become a grandfather.

All this Vera had read online shortly after she had met Garik.

She said nothing to him.

THE SECOND HALF

Anya woke up. She didn't open her eyes and didn't move, but he knew she wasn't asleep. He was looking at her; she could feel him. The feeling weakened as she drifted back into a deep sleep. He wanted to put his hand on her belly, but couldn't bring himself to do it. What if the child in there was sleeping the same sleep as its mother? And if they were having the same dream? His hand would be like a shadow falling across it. What dream? He'd have to ask.

The day began. He made breakfast, rustling up oatmeal porridge and brewing a pot of tea. Anya joined him in the kitchen. He placed a cup in front of her.

'Do we have any cream?' she asked.

He went to fetch it.

Over breakfast, he told Anya that his day was timetabled in minutes. He was curious about hers. 'What are you going to do today?'

At any given time he wanted to know what she was doing. He needed to know, to preserve his equilibrium.

She said she couldn't count out the minutes as accurately as he did. 'I'll start by washing the dishes, or maybe go back to bed for a bit. Listen to music. Galya will ring, for sure. The only question is when.' She smiled. 'Unlike you, Galya is not predictable. Me, though. No mystery there. Read a book, play patience.'

'Don't sit at the computer. Go for a walk with Galya. If she smokes when she's with you, I'll kill her. Make sure you tell her that.'

ELENA DOLGOPYAT

'I won't tell you whether she smoked or not.'

There was mockery in her look. It was not a look he liked. It made him feel an idiot. Or rather it devalued his intelligence, diminished its significance.

'You won't need to say anything. Your hair will smell of smoke.'

'I'll wash it.'

'OK, suit yourself.'

'Don't sulk.' She leaned over and pinched his cheek. 'She won't smoke. I promise. I love it when you've just shaved. Your cheeks are like silk. And your lips.'

Meeting.

Out to the depot.

On the way, it started to rain. He pictured them in the park without umbrellas, and called. Anya said they were watching TV.

Talk with manager.

Answer emails.

Meet important client.

The client didn't want to meet at the office, and they chose a café on the outskirts. Sasha arrived five minutes early and ordered coffee. The client phoned in a flap, apologised, and cancelled the meeting. He did explain, but afterwards Sasha couldn't remember what he'd said. Burglars? His car had been stolen? Heart attack? Anyway, it meant that Sasha suddenly had an empty time slot at the end of his day. A window ... out of which he took a crashing fall.

An hour, unoccupied, uncluttered, empty; to Sasha it seemed like eternity. He was at the edge of an ocean, waves rolling in and retreating, whispering through the pebbles.

Sasha looked around. The café was small, its lights low and music discreet. Sasha made himself comfortable in a soft armchair, and took out his mobile phone.

A waiter brought coffee. Sasha called his wife. She was at the hairdresser's. No, not her hair, of course not; having your hair done when you're pregnant means bad luck. Galya's hair.

'We went for a walk. It's stopped raining. The wind's dropped.'

For some reason he didn't tell her he had a window. As if it telling her might have slammed it shut.

He drank his coffee unhurriedly. It was an unaccustomed and pleasant feeling. He didn't look at anyone, but he knew there weren't many people there; their voices were barely reaching him. He looked at the lighted window and imagined that the pastries displayed in it were magic. One presaged death, another long life and health, another love and longing. But which one meant love and which death, no-one knew, not even the confectioner. The visitors pondered their choice and took their chances. They ate at their leisure, watching out for inner changes. Spoons tapped against plates.

He didn't take a pastry or the risk that went with it; he was an outside observer.

Sasha grinned at his fantasy and imagined telling Anya about it. Anya would be delighted but a little frightened, realising that she didn't know him at all yet. He hadn't known himself that he could think of such a thing.

He looked at his watch and was disappointed to see that his eternity was coming to an end. He called the waiter over, paid, and went to the bathroom.

Rinsing his hands, he saw a familiar face in the mirror, one of his old teachers, who had taught second-year linear algebra. 'Hello,' he said cheerfully.

A surprised look greeted him.

He opened his mouth to remind the man of the institute, of the labyrinth of corridors in Building No. 4, the staff cafeteria where there were never any queues. Then he closed it again, realising that he'd been mistaken. The reflection in the mirror was a stranger's.

'Have we met?' asked the man, studying Sasha closely.

'No. I was mistaken. Sorry.'

'Who did you think I was. Just curious.'

'It's not important.'

'Even so.'

'A teacher. Must be ten years. I took you for him. Sorry.'

Sasha turned away from the mirror. When he was embarrassed, he invariably became gloomy and appeared angry. He dried his hands and crumpled the wet napkin.

His way was blocked by a short, smiling man. The man moved aside, but not enough, and Sasha brushed him.

'Sorry.'

'It's OK.'

Sasha thought: the guy's tipsy.

He stepped outside and was surprised to see the streetlights already on. It was overcast, dusky. A fine rain was settling on the car. Sasha ran his palm across the bonnet, leaving a damp mirrored trail. He shook the water off his hand, opened the door, and climbed in. Turned on the wipers.

There was a knock on the window. It was steamed up and pockmarked with raindrops. Sasha rolled it down.

The short man and the man he'd taken for his teacher.

'Would you be able to give us a lift?' asked the man, still smiling.

'If it's on the way. I'm in a hurry, sorry. I've got a way to go, out of town.'

It turned out to be on their way.

The 'teacher' got in the back, while the short man settled down next to Sasha. He made himself comfortable, and looked quite at home.

'Fasten your seat belts, please,' said Sasha.

They had the wide main road practically to themselves. Sasha drove easily, smoothly; even Anya did not get carsick when he was driving. She said that driving best revealed his character.

The short man observed, 'You drive so ... delicately.'

Sasha kept glancing in the mirror at the man in the back. He thought he'd offended him by mistaking him for someone else. He decided to extoll the teacher's virtues.

'He did linear algebra seminars at our school. Only seminars–he hadn't got his masters. Even the lazy students didn't get low marks from him, and it wasn't because he was lenient. He always helped clear up tricky questions, right in the exam, so that eventually a person would begin to understand and no longer deserved a bad mark. In any case, Boris Samuilovich didn't give them one.' Sasha had a sudden thought. 'You don't have anything against Jews, do you?'

The man in the back made no reply, but Sasha's companion said reassuringly, 'No we don't.'

'Boris Samuilovich ran a music club. On a strictly voluntary basis. There was a House of Culture at the institute and they let us have a room. We met twice a week, in the evenings. Boris Samuilovich would tell us about conductors, performers, composers. Brought in records for us to listen to and discuss. Once he brought along Schnittke, who was working on an opera about Faust at the time. We listened to excerpts.'

'I'm curious as to the fate of this remarkable man,' said Shorty. He only seemed to be smiling the whole time; that was the natural repose of his features.

'He went to America, I believe.'

'And knowing this, you took it into your head that you'd just bumped into him on the outskirts of Moscow?'

'He might have come back to Moscow to see his family.'

'He has family here?'

'I don't know. OK, out of curiosity, then. Or on business. The fact is I took you for him as he was then, ten years ago.' Sasha looked in the mirror and addressed the silent man. 'As if he wasn't a day older. He's actually probably changed so

ELENA DOLGOPYAT

much that I could sit in front of him for forty minutes and not recognise him.'

'Why forty?'

'I don't know. OK, forty-five. Or a week. A year.'

'Yes,' agreed Sasha's companion. 'People change.'

No-one said anything for a while, and Sasha relaxed a little. The awkwardness passed and he almost forgot his passengers altogether. He was worried about Anya, what she'd had for lunch, and about his upcoming negotiations with the director of a factory near Moscow.

They passed through a village, and Sasha marvelled at how many apples there were this year.

'Stop here, please,' his companion said suddenly. Sasha pulled in to the side of the road.

They thanked him and got out, closing the doors gently. Sasha waited a moment, watching them cross the road, walk along the kerb, and then turn towards a church.

Beyond the village, the road widened, and a view of autumn fields opened up, and dark clouds scudding across the sky. Three kilometres further on, Sasha started to feel ill. He managed to brake and pull into the kerb. Then he lost consciousness.

Only a minute later, a battered Lada stopped next to him. A man of about fifty climbed out.

Sasha's engine was still running. The man from the Lada came up and peered through the open window. He looked around, opened the door, and got in next to Sasha. Sasha seemed to be sleeping. The man took out his mobile phone.

At ten o'clock in the evening, Anya became worried and called Sasha on the office telephone. An unsteady voice told her that Sasha had had an accident.

The funeral was two days later. It was well-attended: colleagues, neighbours, university friends, even a few from school. Anya seemed dazed: what was happening, why were all these people here, most of whom she didn't know from Adam? Why had she come, to this hospital yard? Why were they all standing in this raw wind outside the low morgue building? Why were they talking so quietly? Why were they all looking at her while trying not to? Why had each and every one of them brought flowers?

The doors opened, but for some reason no-one went in. Anya stood looking into the black square of the entrance. Galya took her arm and led her inside, before the others. A stranger was lying in a coffin wearing Sasha's new suit. Anya looked at him intently, quizzically. New shoes that he'd never worn, the laces tied in a way Sasha would never tie them. Anya wanted to re-do them, and even leaned towards the coffin, but the air drifting from it was cold. Galya took her elbow and ushered her to one side.

The wake was in full swing when Galya led her away from the table, put her in a small room, and closed the door tightly. Even through the door voices could be heard. Someone said quite clearly, 'I reckon his heart played up before and he kept quiet so as not to worry the wife and all that.'

An older voice replied, 'Worked himself to death.'

Anya lay on her back, eyes wide open. Galya switched the table lamp on and the overhead light off.

'Sleep,' she said. 'Let yourself go. Think of the child.'

Finally, the tears came.

Sasha woke up in a small room, like a closet. Through a tiny window he could see branches laden with frost. The window was open a crack, letting in chilly air, but the wooden panels at his back were giving out warmth. A corner of the dark ceiling was a mass of grey cobwebs. A light bulb dangled from a twisted cord. Sasha lifted his head, but it started to spin and he dropped it back onto the pillow.

A vial containing medicine of some kind stood on the table under the window. Sasha could smell its bitter scent. Someone was making their way behind the wall, coughing. The door, knocked together out of boards, opened, and the Lada man appeared–as yet, of course, a stranger to Sasha.

The stranger pulled a stool from under the table.

He sat at the head of Sasha's bed and rolled up the frayed sleeves of his jumper, which smelled of the stove. Stubble showed silver on his weathered face.

'Where am I?' asked Sasha. He could hardly hear his own voice.

'I'll get you some soup,' said the stranger. 'Give you the strength to talk.' He coughed into his fist.

'I need to phone home.'

'Of course.'

After his soup, Sasha fell asleep. When he woke up, it was night.

Outside the window, a tree was rustling in the cold wind. A streetlight behind the glass made the snow stuck to the window seem black. Shadows flitted across the wall. It took Sasha a while to realise that it was the branches making the shadows. He crawled further under the warm blanket and went back to sleep.

In the morning the stranger gave him baby cereal and a drink of tea.

'Do you remember what happened to you?' he asked.

'I started feeling bad in the car.'

'Were you alone?'

'Yes.'

'You sure?'

'I had passengers with me, but they'd got out.'

'People you know?'

'No. That's just it. No.'

Sasha told the stranger about his mistake, and about the good man Boris Samuilovich. If he'd been taken for a man like that, he said, he'd have been proud, not offended.

'He was offended?'

'At first I thought so. Then I figured he didn't believe me. Like I knew him really but used Boris Samuilovich as cover instead of admitting it. He looked at me like he was trying to remember. I've only just seen that.'

'Is there a Boris Samuilovich?'

Sasha's turn to take offence. 'Ten years ago there was.'

'Wonderful,' said the stranger, and stood up.

He went out. Sasha was annoyed that the man had not even introduced himself and Sasha had not thought to ask. More important, he'd not got as far as asking about Anya. And why was he here, in this closet, and not in hospital or at home?

The door opened again. An elderly woman in a headscarf entered. She approached Sasha, touched his forehead with a soft hand, and said that she'd heated some water and was going to give him a wash.

'What should I call you?' asked Sasha.

'Miss Pasha.'

'What happened to me?'

'Poison.'

'How? Why am I here and not in hospital?'

'You should ask Vasil Andreich.'

'Where is he?'

'He's gone to town.'

'What town?'

Miss Pasha pulled the blanket away. Sasha was not even embarrassed, probably because her eyes were like those of an old, world-weary mongrel and there was not a glimmer of womanly interest in them.

'There's nothing of you. Like a skeleton.'

She helped him up and led him into a dark bathroom, where the tap yielded not a drop of water. Miss Pasha sluiced him with a dipper, scrubbed him with a rough flannel, and hummed. The lingering melody sounded familiar, but Sasha could not remember where he'd heard it.

After she'd washed him, Miss Pasha dressed him in old hand-me-downs. They were at least clean.

She gave him potatoes and a drink of tea with currant jam. The room they were sitting in was large and bright, and the stove was alight and hot; it was also warming the closet wall.

'There you go,' said Miss Pasha, blowing on the tea in the blue saucer. She was looking out of the window, and Sasha followed her gaze.

Sasha's stranger, Vasil Andreich, was walking briskly along the path towards the house. Miss Pasha left the tea and hurried to the door. Something in the cupboard jingled.

Miss Pasha warmed up the same potato for Vasil Andreich, and he ate straight from the frying-pan, picking the potato out with his fingers, sniffing with pleasure as he warmed up. He told them that although there was no frost out there, it was very cold and the wind had made his eyes water. He was clean-shaven, and this alone changed his face: with its stubble it had seemed rather simple and inexpressive, but without it, intelligent and important, impossible to ignore.

Sasha asked no questions. He watched Vasil Andreich eat his fill and then wipe his hands with a paper napkin and roll it into a ball. Observed the oily ball lying in the empty frying-pan while Miss Pasha poured Vasil Andreich tea. Sasha had no energy to put any questions or make any demands, or perhaps he had stopped wanting answers to his questions. On the one hand, he felt comfortable in the room with the white stove at his back and did not want, physically did not want to disturb the equilibrium and lose the cosiness. On the other hand, the cosiness seemed a snare, a sticky tar in which he was stuck, gummed up for ever.

Vasil Andreich took a sip of tea and added more sugar. Stirring it with his spoon, he began to speak in a casual tone.

'Did you know Boris Samuilovich's wife?'

'I saw her. Once. I met them both by chance, on the Arbat.'

'She's a mathematician too.'

'I didn't know.'

'They have three children. The eldest boy is into computers. The have a house in Boston, not in Boston itself, in the suburbs. The frogs croak loudly at night.'

'How do you know? Is that where you've just been, by any chance?'

'Near enough.'

'Quick turnaround.'

'The man you mistook for Boris Samuilovich actually does look like him when he was young.'

'Who is he?'

'A man who hides his past. I think he believed you really had confused him with someone else, that you were not from his past. But he took you out just in case.'

'What do you mean, he took me out?'

'Killed you. It's been three months since you were buried. You've got a tombstone.'

Sasha didn't believe it, or pretended not to. He laughed, and looked at Miss Pasha. She crumbled sugar into the jam pot with tongs, fished out a lump of jam-soaked sugar with her teaspoon, and finished her tea with it.

'Are you trying to say I'm in the other world? Purgatory, unless they lied. It's not bad here. Warm. Food.'

Miss Pasha collected the dirty dishes and left the room. Vasil Andreich looked at Sasha with studied detachment. Then spun a yarn that sounded straight out of a Hollywood action movie, except that somehow the hero of the story was Sasha.

'You were driving the car. The man beside you was asking questions, finding out what you knew about the man in the back. He pretty much believed you knew nothing but decided to get rid of you just in case. Or rather, it wasn't his decision. You set the mechanism in motion as soon as you looked at the man in the mirror and said hello.'

'But I didn't know ...'

'You were injected with a needle dipped in a special solution.'

'Do they always carry needles dipped in a special solution with them?'

'I think it looks like a simple biro. Only instead of ink, it has a special solution in it. And the pen doesn't write, it pricks. You were supposed to have died in about half an hour. Cardiac arrest, as the doctors would say. I got into your car 20 minutes after they injected you. I had time to give you the antidote.'

'You also carry special pens around with you?'

'You were lucky. I've been watching them. You suddenly entered their orbit. I didn't understand your role, so I resurrected you to find out.'

'So I'm not actually in the other world?'

'Not unless I'm an inhabitant of the heavens.'

'If I'm not dead, who did they bury?'

'A suitable corpse from the morgue.'

'Why?'

'So your killers wouldn't suspect anything. If they think you're alive, they'll find you and kill you properly. Slice off your head, for instance.'

'What on earth for?'

'You never know. Maybe you do know something after all.'

'What?'

'Who knows. That's what frightens them. The not knowing. The uncertainty. Your resurrection would demonstrate that you were a player. A significant player, I should say. However much of a bit part you really have.'

Sasha sat in shocked silence.

Miss Pasha appeared outside the window and began to clear the snow from the path with a wooden shovel.

'How's Anya?'

'She's had a son.'

'Already?'

'Slightly early. From the shock, I guess.'

'And she's named him ...?'

'After you.'

'How is she in herself?'

'Fine.'

'And the baby?'

'Fine.'

'What do I do now?'

'Start a new life. New name. New face. New past.'

'Where am I going to get a new face?'

'We'll do plastic surgery. Sort you some new ID. Invent you a new past.'

Outside the window, Miss Pasha stopped for a break. She stuck her shovel in a snowdrift and tightened her headscarf.

'Why would you bother? To make me a new face and past. So much trouble and expense. It would be much easier, as you put it, to get rid of me. You've got all the detail you need from me. You don't need me anymore.'

'I haven't been sleeping well lately. I'm afraid of dying in my sleep. So many sins. Maybe your life will earn me forgiveness.'

'Are we far from Moscow?'

'Not at all.'

'Where will ... my face be ... done?

'We'll do it here.'

ELENA DOLGOPYAT

'What, in this shack?'

'It's quiet here. And we have no choice, neither you nor I. My superiors also think I've eliminated you. I'm taking a big risk.'

'Appalling.'

'My doctor's reliable. He needs me. He'll do his best and keep his mouth shut. Mind you, it's your choice. You can get dressed right now and go wherever you like. But I wouldn't put a kopeck on you living long.'

'And if I get a new face, how much then?'

'If you stick to the rules, you'll most likely die a natural death.'

'And the rules are ...?'

'Stay away from your old place. Don't come into contact with people who knew you before. Try to forget your past completely and replace it with the new one. We'll make you the simplest backstory we can. Modest, no contradictions.'

What was to happen to Sasha in the more distant future was already out of Vasil Andreich's hands.

* * *

He glanced at the house where he was now living, and returned to his car.

The lights were already on in the long block of flats. He sat behind the wheel and tried to decide where to go. His name was Kostya now. He seemed taller; he had lost a lot of weight and no longer stooped. He walked differently too—lightly, with barely a sound. His nose sported a new hook, the set of his eyes was different, and his eyebrows met over the bridge of his nose. He'd cut his hair short, making his forehead seem higher. Some of the colour had gone out of his voice, as if he'd aged. Vasil Andreich had assured him that no-one would recognise the old Sasha in him. Provided, of course, he took no risks and followed the rules.

It was late summer. Sasha–Kostya–was driving an almost new Volga which he'd bought as soon as he entered the world with his new name and face. The world was enormous. He could travel, far away, and his new life would become a road movie, with a kaleidoscope of meetings and brief rendez-vous; life would become a long road, or to put it another way, the road would swallow up his life and he wouldn't even notice how it swallowed everyone on it and was never satisfied.

The sun set and darkness coloured the air. A window was flung open in the house and a voice yelled, 'Vitaliiik!!!!'

Kostya drove slowly away.

In his old life he'd been used to having no time; every second had been accounted for. Now he was driving without purpose, falling into a void.

In fact he did have a goal, although he was trying not to see it. It was not of his devising; it was simply there, the one thing he wanted–and was not to have. It troubled him ... and called to him. He did not strive for it; it attracted him. He was a chip of matter that had entered its orbit.

Kostya joined the main road and turned west. He flapped a hand and yielded to the call, and having yielded, drove quickly, confidently. It was completely dark. Lights swept by in the opposite lane. He felt that he was rushing through black space, his speed increasing as he neared his goal. He drove through the night, not stopping anywhere, not engaging in conversation, as if on a tangent to the flow of life.

Early the next morning he found a parking space on a road in one of the capital's northern districts. It was about seven o'clock, but people were already hurrying to the metro. Not all the kiosks were yet open. A small, swarthy man was pulling a flat trolley laden with all sorts of stuff: boxes, coloured cloths, something shiny and lacquered. A road sweeper was clearing rubbish. Lights glowed cosily in

McDonald's. Early as it was, a middle-aged lady was already selling papers near the metro, a pyramid of magazines and newspapers teetering on her cart, samples fastened to the handle. Kostya took one carrying classified ads and headed towards McDonald's, popping briefly into a shop where he could pick up a mobile phone.

The morning was cold with a nip of autumn, and Kostya felt sorry for the news lady, out there in the wind. He had a good view of her through the wide window. McDonald's was warm and not yet full. Kostya bought a white coffee and cheese on toast. He browsed through the advertisements, smelling the news type and seeing it black on his fingers. He fetched out his mobile. Vasil Andreich had given him some starter money, still hoping his sins might be forgiven.

'Good morning,' said Kostya in his colourless, transparent voice. 'Is it too early? Yes, your ad. Yes. I wish.'

He jotted some figures beside the ad and called the next one.

When he left the restaurant it was already rush hour. The kiosks and stalls were all open, and crowds were pouring into the metro.

A musty smell struck him, as if the flat had never been aired. Indeed, the window frames were covered with yellowed sticking plaster, though it had started to peel off in places. Burned porridge added its odours to the mix. The stout landlady showed Kostya his room. There was no lock on the door. Kostya expressed his unhappiness.

'Lawd, put a lock on it then. Do repairs, whatever, just don't make any noise at night and don't bring women here.' She gave Kostya a sour look. 'Don't bring anyone here. Understand?'

Kostya sighed. But he was hardly likely to find a cheaper room.

Kostya flicked the switch, and light filled the squalid room.

'Don't use electricity during the day.'

'You want me to live in the dark?' The room was like a cave, with trees outside the window blocking the light.

'I'll charge you more.'

'Goodbye.'

'Wait.' She was silent, considering. Breathing heavily from the exertion of thinking. 'Stay a month,' she said, deciding. 'And then we'll see. Pay in advance though.'

Kostya took his wallet out of his pocket and counted out the money. She couldn't take her eyes off the notes. She moved closer.

'Receipt,' said Kostya, not letting go of the money.

She stared at it. Sniffed. Finally mumbled, 'I got no paper or pen.'

Kostya fetched out a pen, and a notebook from which he tore a page.

She perched at the rickety table and thought for a long time. Spent a long time writing. Kostya stood watching. She put the pen down.

'Sign it,' said Kostya.

'Put the money on the table.'

He laid it down but kept his hand on it.

She signed, then inched the paper towards him, keeping her hand on it in her turn. Kostya let go of the money and she instantly grabbed it; he managed to snatch up the receipt.

'When will you move in?' she asked, recounting the money.

'I already have. Give me the key.'

The landlady was unhappy that he had no things. He said he'd left his wife and left all his things there.

'What does she need your stuff for?'

'I'll get it eventually. What are you worried about?'

'What if you escaped from jail?'

'Anything's possible,' said Kostya seriously.

ELENA DOLGOPYAT

She stood in front of him, staring, struggling to process some kind of thought. Without a word, she went to her room and shut the door. Kostya went through to the kitchen and saw a pile of dirty dishes in the sink and a cockroach ambling along the greasy window sill. The radio burbled.

The toilet cistern was leaking and there was no paper. Laundry, already mouldy and ripe, was soaking in the bathroom.

The telephone stood on a unit in the hall. Kostya picked it up. A faded reproduction of Kramskoy's *Portrait of an Unknown Woman* hung in his sightline. Kostya dialled the number. A familiar voice at the other end answered softly, 'Hello?'

Kostya could not bring himself to answer straightaway.

'Hello?' came again.

'Good morning,' he said.

'Good morning,' replied Anya.

'May I talk to Sasha?'

She was silent. He could hear her breathing.

'I'm an old acquaintance of his, from Novosibirsk. We haven't seen each other for fifteen years or more. I just ...'

'Sasha's not here.'

'When will he be back?'

'Never.' She hung up.

The landlady was bound to be pressed up against the door hearing everything. The toilet gurgled. Kostya dialled the number again.

'I'm sorry, I really am. I just wanted to see–'

'You can't. He's dead.'

She said it so simply. 'He's dead.' Only then, hearing those words, did he realise that it was truly and irrevocably so.

'Oh my God. How long?'

'A whole year.'

'I'm sorry. I'm sorry, but could I drop by? Just for a minute. I owed Sasha some money.'

When Anya was carrying her child, she felt as if she already knew his character and appearance and almost everything that would happen to him, but had forgotten, and her child's entire future would be a restoration of lost memories. At weekends they took walks with Sasha along the boulevard, Anya leaning on Sasha's arm. Anya would tell Sasha how she could feel their son's future, though she couldn't express it.

'But will he at least be happy?' Sasha had asked once.

'I don't know. I'll be praying.'

One day after work, Sasha had stopped by *Children's World*. The shop had seemed even bigger than he remembered from his childhood. Majestic, like an ancient Egyptian temple of the sun. Sasha wandered around the huge sales hall, stood rooted in front of the little cars, soldiers and fantastic creatures, took them in his hands, imagined them in the hands of his son. As if he had picked them up with his son's hands. He wanted to buy an aeroplane, but didn't dare. Anya said you mustn't buy for an unborn baby, it was a bad omen. Regretfully, Sasha replaced the winged machine. He'd looked round as he was leaving; one last look.

Kostya spotted the aeroplane behind the glass window of a kiosk, next to some rubber balls and a toy mobile phone with idiotic pink buttons. Saw it and was pleased, as if it were an acquaintance with whom he shared fond memories.

The flat cardboard box would not fit in his pocket, so he bought a bag.

Walked out onto the street from the metro. Slowed.

Impossible. He was seeing what he should not: the street on which his own house stood.

He glanced into the little shop into which he used to walk so easily with no feelings, neither happy nor sad, not even feeling it as an event. Now there was something grandiose and improbable about walking into this shop in its small glass pavilion, seeing what he had seen many

ELENA DOLGOPYAT

times before and what he was now seeing against all the laws of nature.

His indistinct reflection in the glass of the shop window.

He saw it and did not recognise himself in it; he'd forgotten. Remembering distracted him, and when the woman asked him what he wanted, he couldn't immediately find the words. He stared dumbly.

She was new to him; he did not remember her.

'Have you just started here?' he asked, taking the sweets she'd put on the counter.

'Six months.'

'So fast.'

'Sorry?'

'Everything changes so fast.'

He stepped inside the entrance, and froze. Touched the smooth wall, apparently recently painted. It was as if it had withdrawn from him, become different, and the old chipped wall was out of reach; it no longer existed. He was afraid that Anya would have become a stranger too.

The door opened at once.

She stared at him intently, and stepped back.

'Come in, please.'

She was still the same. Her clothes were all the same as he remembered, even to the touch. It had been a long time, though, and he had to reaccustom himself to seeing her, and to the fact that he was standing right in front of her unrecognised, like a masked man at a carnival.

She led him into the room and sat him on the couch.

He looked through the window onto the balcony. Clothes were drying on the line. Baby clothes. Tiny. Touching.

'You have a child?'

'Yes. A boy.'

'How old is he?'

'Nearly one.'

Kostya picked up his bag and took out the sweets and the aeroplane in its box. The bag rustled with every movement, annoying Kostya intensely. He handed Anya the sweets and the box, crumpled the crackling bag, and slipped it into his pocket. The bag continued rustling dryly there, all on its own, but Kostya couldn't fish it back out; he had no idea where he would put it then.

'I didn't know if you had a child, so I bought a toy just in case and guessed.'

'Thank you.' She made out the aeroplane behind the plastic window in the box. 'You guessed it was a boy, too.'

'I thought a girl would like the plane too. She can fly to far-off countries. Paris, or Egypt.'

'Wonderful. Thank you.'

'Where's your boy now?'

'Asleep.'

They both glanced towards the closed door of the other room.

'Sasha probably didn't tell you about me,' whispered Kostya.

'Don't worry, he won't hear us. He sleeps very soundly. Unfortunately I don't remember Sasha talking about you. Would you like tea? Coffee?'

'If it's no trouble. Thank you.'

In the kitchen he pulled out the stupid bag and shoved it in the bin.

'I expect you'd like to wash your hands.'

He'd put up the bathroom mirror himself, with his own hands. It remembered his hands. His old face too–but couldn't reflect it any more. Everything in the bathroom was almost as it had been when he was there. The same soap they'd always used. Only the terry dressing gown was gone, vanished from the hook.

Has she thrown it away or just hidden it?

He couldn't exactly ask her.

His deodorant was gone, and his razor and aftershave. Thrown away, most like.

Kostya turned on the water and washed his hands long and thoroughly. It struck him that he had not just Sasha's memories, he had his fingerprints, too, and it was as if he was trying to wash them off.

'Do you have your coffee with cream?'

'No, black. I like it black with lemon.'

'I've got lemon.'

He dipped a lemon wedge into the cup, and added a dash of sugar, half a spoonful. Anya watched intently.

'Sasha liked coffee with lemon, too. And exactly half a spoonful of sugar.'

'We liked a lot of the same things.'

'It's strange he didn't talk about you.'

'We fought. He probably didn't want to remember me.'

Anya poured cream into her coffee and spread butter on her bread.

Strange business. He was dead, and she was drinking coffee and eating bread and butter, and taking care of the baby, washing his clothes, feeding him, telling him stories. Sasha was dead and life went on. Not everyone got to see quite so plainly how life goes on.

'What happened to him?'

'Heart attack.'

'He never complained about his heart.'

'Not to me either.'

She opened his box of sweets. Took one from the edge. Tasted it. Chocolate with liqueur.

'Nice?'

'Very. You guessed right again.'

She cocked her head, listening. 'Excuse me. Sorry.'

She went out. Kostya figured she'd gone to look at her son. He got up and followed her with his silent tread.

The door to the other room was ajar.

He padded up to it and peered in. The curtains were drawn and there was little light. Anya was leaning over the cot. He couldn't see inside the cot. Anya straightened, and he retreated quietly.

Anya returned to the kitchen. He was putting sausage on his bread, and raised his head when she came in.

'What happened to you in Novosibirsk?'

'I was living there, and Sasha came to do an internship.'

'Yes, I know, after his second year.'

'1990. There was practically nothing in the shops. Coupons for everything–cereal, sugar, pasta. We bought stuff at the market. I was an intern at the same research institute as Sasha. Only he'd come from Moscow and was living in a dormitory, and I was from Novosibirsk and living at home, so I took Sasha to my place for lunch and dinner. We had pickles, jams, and potatoes from our own allotment. We became friends. Not just because of the lunches. We had the same interests. We talked about James Bond, Buddhism, politics. Things we differed about, they were interesting as well. Girls, of course. We had a fight about a girl. That's probably why Sasha didn't tell you about me. He was kind of a non-combatant in it all, put it like that. She had the hots for him, and I'd been chasing her for two years and getting nowhere. Made me jealous. We had a fight. He went away, we didn't say goodbye. A week later I got a money order, 'for the lunches'. I was offended, naturally, and sent it back. He tried again. Made it out to my mother. She's kind of tight-fisted. Kept the money.'

Anya grinned. 'And you've decided to return it?'

'Money's not the same now, and anyway it's not about the money. So many years have passed. It's just I was in Moscow for the first time in years and wanted to see him.'

'Did things work out with the girl?'

'I kind of cooled off after the fight.'

The phone rang, and Anya hurried to pick it up.

ELENA DOLGOPYAT

'Hi. No, he's sleeping. I've got company. An old friend of Sasha's. No, you don't know him. OK. Done.'

She hung up. 'My friend.'

Kostya just stopped himself from saying, 'Galya?'

'Galya. She's worried about me.'

'Thank you for the coffee. It was delicious. I love coffee made in a Turkish pot.'

'Like Sasha.'

'What was Sasha like?'

'Oh, that's hard.'

'Was he easy to be with?'

'It varied. He had no self-confidence.'

Kostya was amazed. 'You think so? Really?'

'I don't know, maybe you didn't notice back then, or didn't understand, or maybe he was different. He liked order in everything. Even the chairs had to be in set places. If one of them was moved, he'd put it straight back. The things in the house were like a single system to him, like a planetary system. Any planet slipping out of its orbit meant catastrophe. The system would collapse. Chaos would ensue.'

'It'll ensue anyway, we all know that. The law of entropy.'

'Sasha tried to get round that law the whole time. I was part of his planetary system as well. I had my own orbit and had to stay in it. It wasn't easy, it wasn't always easy, but I tried, otherwise he'd flounder, be helpless, even.'

'Did you love him?'

'I suppose so.'

'Did he love you? What do you think?'

'I think I occupied an important place in his coordinate system. Fundamental, maybe. Family meant a lot to him. He could hardly remember his parents. He was brought up by aunts.'

As they said goodbye, already on the way out in the hallway, she said, 'Thank you for asking me about Sasha. I haven't talked to anyone about him for ages. The other day I was afraid I couldn't remember what colour his eyes were. I rushed off to look at photos.'

His eyes are looking at you right now!

'Well, all the best.'

'Would I be able to come and see you again before I leave? I would really like to see your son.'

'Yes, of course. We'll talk on the phone.'

'Do you work?'

'I'm going back next year. I teach physics.'

He knew she was watching him from the window, but he didn't turn round.

At 12.45, fifteen minutes before their lunch break, he was already at Mu-Mu. He ordered tea and a salad and waited for them to arrive. They were late, and he was nervous.

Just after one, Lara and Nadia finally arrived and joined the queue. He strained to hear their chatter. All chit-chat, but it seemed to him important and meaningful.

Lara was talking about the boy her daughter was dating. 'He looks twenty, he's actually fifteen, and inside he's just a child. Masha dances round him. I say, look, Masha ...'

Kostya remembered the very Masha. She'd come to his flat at New Year about five years previously, pigged out on sweets and fallen asleep right at the table. Sasha had carried her to the little room and laid her on the bed. His hands remembered the child's weight.

The others arrived. Misha, Kirill, Oleg, Inna. And some young chap Sasha didn't know.

They took a table by the basement window, from which only the legs of the passers-by were visible. Kostya picked about in his salad. He couldn't hear what his former colleagues were saying; he just watched their faces, smiles, gestures. The new lad was shy, and spent most of the time eating and saying nothing. Kirill and Misha were

ELENA DOLGOPYAT

discussing something, their heads close together. Football for sure. Nadia lit a cigarette and stared out the window.

Kostya didn't wait for them to finish. He wiped his lips with his serviette and stood up, pushing back his heavy chair. The chairs at *Mu-Mu* are very heavy.

He walked along the narrow pavement past the window behind which they were sitting, eating, talking about the most ordinary things, and it was all as distant from him as the other end of the universe. He was still interested, but it had gone out of his reach. That new lad must be his replacement. He'd be sitting at Sasha's computer, drinking tea from his mug. Why not? The mug with the pagoda painted on it. A present for his last birthday.

Kostya spent until evening walking through the old places, along streets he'd loved, tied up with such fond memories. The streets were all still in their places, but his past life no longer existed. So strange. No; they weren't quite in place, not quite where they had been. They'd shifted slightly, leaving Kostya wandering in a world that was somehow skewed.

It was dark. Kostya entered a yard and saw in front of him the house in which he'd rented a room.

A light was burning in the kitchen window. Kostya imagined the landlady picking scrambled eggs and sausages from the frying pan, her lips stained with yolk and her face shiny. The old fridge shuddering from its exertions. Cockroaches lurking in the cracks.

'Why would I go in there?' he thought. He headed out of the yard towards the metro. He'd left the car at Medvedkovo, in a paying car park.

Proper night was setting in as he passed beyond the Moscow Ring Road.

The most banal of truths settled on him: you can't bring back the past and you can't catch up with it. The memory of you will disappear, and if her son's eyes are not there to remind her, even your own wife will forget the colour of your eyes.

He made a home in Novosibirsk, where he had once done an internship at the research institute. The institute itself no longer existed. Kostya bought a diploma and got a job as a programmer. Rented a decent flat, acquired friends. Eventually he thought of getting married. He began to forget about the first half of his life. The past Vasil Andreich had invented for him seemed more real.

JOHN

It was morning. John was getting ready for work. He grabbed a biscuit off a plate on his way by. His wife Ann was tying his tie. His daughter Annie was lugging his big shoes over to him. While he was pushing his feet into them, the little girl climbed onto the sofa and drew something with her finger on her father's shirt-covered back, and he tried to guess what it was. Sunshine, a car, the word DAD.

Coffee was brewed, and a large mug poured for him. They sat with him at the table while he drank it. With biscuits.

A family idyll.

In the hall, they hugged, kissed, and arranged to meet at the shopping centre after work. To watch a film there and relax in a café. He promised to buy presents for his girls. The family dog scampered around, and John gave it a rub behind the ear.

He went out, and the door closed behind him. The moment he was out he remembered something, and started hunting in his pockets. Not finding it, he rang the doorbell to his own flat. No-one came hurrying to open it. He pressed the bell again.

He looked in confusion at the round spyhole. All was quiet. John knocked. Harder, louder. The neighbour's door swung open. A tall, skinny, sleepy man stuck his head out and barked angrily, 'What's going on? Who are you?'

'It's OK,' replied John. 'My folks aren't opening the door and I've forgotten my wallet. Something's happened. Call the police. You do have a phone?'

The neighbour disappeared into his flat, banging the door behind him. John felt tears threatening. Almost at once, the neighbour's door swung open again, and the neighbour came out. He went up to John's door and started pushing a key into the keyhole. John became agitated, gabbling something about when the door was locked on the inside you couldn't open it from the outside. But the door had already opened with the neighbour's key.

'Please,' said the neighbour. 'You can go in. What is it you've forgotten in there?'

John looked through the doorway in complete confusion. It was dark, like a cave. The neighbour waited.

John stepped over the threshold. It was dark. Dark. Quiet.

'Ann!' called John. 'Annie!'

He hurried into the dark main room and fumbled for the switch on the wall. There was a burst of light, and John saw a dusty, abandoned room. The curtains were drawn right across the windows. There was no furniture. It was quiet.

John turned round.

The neighbour was leaning against the lintel.

'Is that everything?' he asked John sarcastically.

'Uhh, it's ...' mumbled John. 'Excuse me. The key. May I? Have a look.'

'You may.'

The neighbour handed John the key.

'This is not my key,' mumbled John.

'Well, no.'

'I don't understand anything.'

'Me neither.'

'Have you been living here long? I don't remember you.'

'I've lived here a long time. First time I've seen you. Give me back my key. If you'd be so kind.'

The neighbour took the key from John's flaccid hand.

'I don't understand anything,' whispered John.

ELENA DOLGOPYAT

'Go home.'

'This is my home.'

'If you say so. You can stay. Shut the door on your way out.'

The lanky neighbour went out.

John wandered around the flat. It was long unlived-in. He looked out of the window and saw a girl in a bright anorak far below. The child was standing on the edge of the pavement, preparing to run across the road. John yelled, 'Annie!'

He rushed into the hall, to the door. But the door was locked and John couldn't open it, couldn't get out, the lock wouldn't budge. John ran, shouting, back into the room and over to the window. He looked down. The little girl was no longer to be seen.

There were cars on the road. It was a grey morning.

John returned to the hallway and leaned his forehead against the cold door. He heard voices. Heard the lock turn. The door opened. John nearly fell over.

A policeman was standing on the threshold. Behind him loomed the lanky neighbour.

'I'm sorry,' mumbled John. 'I'm not doing this to annoy you. I'm a bit tired. I had a hard day yesterday.'

'Do you have your papers with you?' inquired the policeman politely.

John reached hastily into his anorak pocket. He fished out his card and offered it to the policeman.

'My driving licence.'

The policeman looked at the picture on the card, then looked at John.

'It's me,' said John.

'Possibly,' replied the policeman.

He returned the card.

'Is your car far away?'

'Downstairs. In the car park. Can I go now?'

'I'll come with you.'

John walked past his neighbour and looked at him.

'What?' asked the neighbour.

'I'm sorry.' John stopped suddenly. 'Is this your flat?'

'It's mine for now. It's for sale. You decide you want it, you're welcome. Seven hundred thousand and the keys are yours.'

John dropped his head and made for the lift. The policeman had already pressed the call button.

The policeman was calm, polite. At times it seemed that he was looking at John sympathetically. In the lift, neither spoke. The policeman was looking at John's shoes, his polished, thin-soled boots. Suddenly he asked, 'Expensive?'

'What?' John looked at his boots. 'Yes.'

They came out in the underground car park. John headed confidently ahead and to the right of the lift.

Cars were standing around, silent. Electric lights were burning. Alarming. John stopped, then approached a blue convertible, confused. He looked round at the policeman.

'Your car?' asked the policeman politely.

'No.'

'So where's yours?'

'I don't know.'

'Did you leave it here?'

'No. I don't know.'

'Perhaps it's been stolen?'

'No. I don't think so. I don't know.'

'So how did you get here? It's raining out. Your shoes are dry.'

'In a taxi?'

'You've forgotten?'

'No. Probably.'

'Do you remember where you live?'

John answered after a pause, in a lowered voice. 'Yes.'

'Wonderful. I'll give you a lift.'

They got into the police car. The policeman looked at John. The car sat there.

'What?' asked John, frightened.

'The address,' the policeman reminded him peaceably.

'Ah, yes.' John named the street.

The car drove through the big city. John looked attentively out of the window. At the people, at the houses, at the advertising hoardings. Abstractedly, he said, 'It's exactly the same city.'

The policeman looked curiously at John. John said, 'To tell you the truth, we're on our way to my work. The address I gave you was my office. I should have been at my workplace an hour ago.'

The policeman drove on calmly.

'I'm an engineer,' John added for some reason.

The policeman did not answer.

He stopped in front of an enormous glass building and asked John politely, 'Here?'

'Yes. Thank you very much.'

There was a note of relief in John's thanks: he recognised the building. He hurriedly opened the door.

'Wait a minute,' said the policeman, stopping him. 'I'll come with you.'

'No. Why? You don't need to do that. What will they think of me?'

'OK,' said the policeman, agreeing unexpectedly easily.

'Thank you. You're very ... you're very obliging.'

'Think nothing of it.'

John got out of the police car, banged the door shut, and ran towards the building. He entered the enormous foyer and joined the queue for one of the lifts. Everything was just as usual–the faces, the greetings, the jokes. John suddenly noticed a man in the queue for the next-door lift. The man was reading a small, frayed book as he waited. John hailed him.

'Michael.'

The man pulled himself away from his reading and looked absently at John.

'Hey, Mikey! How's it going?'

'Wonderful,' replied the man indifferently.

'How's Charlie?'

The man was silent, puzzled. His queue was moving forward quickly. The lift doors closed behind him.

John came out on his own floor and walked along the long, curving corridor. He stopped at a door with a brass plaque. Etched on the sign was the head of a bird with a predatory curved beak. John swung open the door and entered the room. There were men sitting at a long rectangular table. All of them turned round and looked at John.

'What brings you here?' asked the man sitting at the head of the table. 'What do you want?'

The policeman was in his car chomping peanuts. His service radio burbled. The policeman chomped his peanuts and observed the enormous office building. Passers-by walked by, cars drove by. It was spitting with rain. Nothing out of the ordinary. Suddenly the policeman stopped chomping. John was coming out of the glass doors. He came out and stopped. The policeman looked at John's lost figure, and shoved his bag of nuts into his pocket.

John looked around, spotted the police car, and headed towards it.

The policeman leaned back in his seat, watching John approach. John came up, and the policeman rolled down his side window. They looked at each other. Finally, John said, 'Drive me to the hospital.'

John was put into a deep hypnosis. A calm, soft voice asked him to talk about his wife and child.

'What are their names?'

'Ann and Annie.'

John's voice was recorded on tape. John's voice talked.

... Ann is painting the wall very studiously. John takes the brush from her and draws a funny face on the wall. Annie spreads the paint with her finger and the face grows a moustache. Ann takes the brush away from John and paints over the face ...

John's voice:

It's gone nowhere, that face with the moustache. It's there, under that layer of paint. It's guarding our home.

... Evening. John, Annie, and their dog called Hector are walking in the park. Ann has stayed at home with a throat infection. Little Annie takes John by the hand. She looks up and laughs. John pulls her cap over her forehead. He buys her candyfloss ...

The low voice:

'Where do you live? Say the address.'

John's voice:

Here it's not far. Can you see the house?

... ducks are diving into the black water ...

John blinked. He was in a quiet office in the hospital. In a restful chair. Electric light was reflected in the glass doors of a cabinet.

'It's all right, John,' said a calm, even voice. The doctor explained. 'You obviously have false memories. Or partly false. I'm going to put you under observation. All will be well.'

John was on the hospital ward. He was sitting up in bed. He adjusted the pillow behind his back to make it more comfortable.

The television was on. John morosely watched a baseball game. The people in the stands were screaming furiously. John turned off the sound. The spectators, struck dumb, went on opening their mouths wide. In the silence, John heard a pattering. He turned his head. Beyond the window was rain; the patter of rain. John looked at the streams running across the glass, and made up his mind. He threw back his blanket and stood up barefoot on the floor. He took off his hospital pyjamas, opened his locker, fetched out his jeans, and pulled them on.

Head down, John walked quickly along the hospital corridor.

John's doctor was at the lift, talking with someone.

John quickly turned away from the lift, and hid behind a service door.

John ran down the service stairs.

He found himself in the basement.

He scurried around the catacombs, yanking at the doors. Locked.

John slumped to the floor against the wall. Above his head, a lamp alternated between flooding with light and going out. John appeared and disappeared along with the light.

Tears left a wet trail across his motionless face.

John pricked up his ears. Some kind of quiet sound. Zummm. John got to his feet and walked cautiously towards the sound. He realised quickly enough that the sound was the voice of the street. Probably a car droning by and honking its horn.

John rounded a pillar and saw a young lad clicking away with small scissors. A nail clipping fell. The lad frowned and swore. The voice of the street was coming from a television screen. The lad was sitting in its hazy glow. John looked at the television's rainy street. The glare of light on the wet asphalt; the honking. He stared as if spellbound.

The lad turned in his swivel chair and looked at John from under his brows.

'How did you get here?'

'I came down.'

'What for?'

'I was thinking.'

'What? Go away.'

'I'd be happy to. I'm lost.'

The lad looked at John and suddenly stretched his hand out towards him, fingers splayed.

'Help me out here. I can't use my left hand. I'm one snip away from hacking off a chunk of flesh.'

John went up to the lad, took the scissors, and cut his fingernail.

The two of them walked through the basement, their footsteps audible on the clean stone floor.

'You done a runner?' the lad suddenly asked.

John did not answer.

'I'll never do a runner,' said the lad. 'I get lost in the open air. This place is just the job. Accommodation and work, I got it all here. I'm a specialist in electrical veins. I can slice them and stitch them.'

There were wires running along the walls in bright binding. John and the lad were walking inside an enormous stone body.

The lad unlocked a door in the wall, stepping back to avoid seeing the opening. John went out.

Black wet asphalt. Quiet, steady rain. John looked around. The metal door had already closed behind him. Above the door was the eye of a video camera. The lad could doubtless see John on the television screen. John raised his hand in acknowledgement.

John ran to hop on a bus.

The glass office building. It was still raining. The electronic clock above the entrance showed the time. People were coming out of the building. Heading for their cars. To the bus stop. To the steps down to the underground.

The flow of people swelled. John stood on the other side, watching. He went up onto his tiptoes and squinted, his eyes flitting from one face to the next. He did not have time to make them all out; there were too many people, a great rolling wave of them at the end of the working day. John squeezed his eyes shut in despair, and opened them again.

The crowd was no longer so great. It was thinning. Drying up. The wind was chasing the litter along the pavement. John looked at the glass doors, lowered his head, and turned round. He saw Michael standing there, hands shoved into his pockets.

'I wanted to ask,' said Michael. 'Who are you looking for?'

'Me? Nobody.'

'What are you hanging around here for?'

'Nothing.'

'Are you following me?'

'Yes. No.'

'Yes or no?'

'No. I ...' John went quiet.

'What did you want from me this morning?'

'Nothing. From you. I mistook you. I thought you were someone else. But I was hoping. Actually I was looking out for you. Well him, really. This crowd, though. It's impossible. An acquaintance of mine looks awfully like you. His name's Michael, too. He has a wife, Sally, who teaches children in junior school. They have two sons, Tim and Bob. We're family friends. Saturday nights Michael and I play poker. His neighbours come over.'

Michael interrupted. 'I don't have a wife,' he said with a frown. 'Or children.'

'I'm sorry.'

'Go home. To your wife.'

'I don't have a home. Or a wife. I have nothing and no-one. I used to. Now I don't. It's all gone to pieces. I won't bother you again.'

John walked away from Michael along the black, deserted pavement. Michael stared at his hunched back. Suddenly he called out, 'Hey!'

John turned round and gave a tired look.

'Do you really play poker?'

The metro. A half-empty train.

They travelled together in silence, not looking at each other. John scrutinised the few passengers. Michael read his tattered book.

They played poker in Michael's tiny bachelor flat. John, Michael and a few other men. John was drawn into the game; he forgot himself, and smiled fleetingly when he won.

'Oho,' one of the men exclaimed, glancing at his watch.

He finished his beer and stood up.

The others stood up after him. They said goodbye, shaking hands with the host. John stood up, too. He dragged himself towards the door. His face was lost.

'John,' Michael called out to him. 'Come on, get this rubbish.'

Michael was sweeping beer cans and nut shells into the bin.

'You don't walk in your sleep, do you?' he asked John.

'No. I don't think so.'

Night. John was lying on the floor, on a mattress spread with a sheet. Under a cosy plaid blanket. His shoes were drying by the radiator. John rolled over and adjusted his pillow. He opened his eyes a crack and saw Michael sitting up in bed. Michael was reading his book by the light of a small wall lamp. He turned the page carefully. John closed his eyes. He heard a car go by, and a distant siren (an ambulance, perhaps, or a police car). He opened his eyes again.

Michael was asleep, his head hanging down.

John got up and quietly went over to Michael. He peeked at the open book. The font was small, the paper thin, translucent. The book slipped out of Michael's weakening grip, and John just managed to catch it. He closed it, and put it on the bedside table. It was the Bible. Worn, creased. A cheap paperback edition. John put out the lamp.

John woke up. It was light in the room. Michael's bed was made. John lay there, listening to the silence. Slowly, he got up. On the table were several banknotes and a note: ENJOY YOURSELF.

John went into the bathroom. He looked in the mirror at his stubbly face.

On the shelf was a brand new, cellophane-wrapped razor. John unpacked the razor. He cut his finger with the blade. He washed the blood off under running water.

A smooth-shaven John made his way into a coffee shop and sat down at a table. There were no customers. The television was burbling. A woman emerged from behind the counter. She went up to John and asked, 'What'll you have?'

'I don't know. Anything.'

'Pancakes?'

'Yes, why not.'

'They're very tasty. Fluffy. My recipe.'

'Yes, yes. Pancakes it is.'

'You're bleeding.'

John looked at his finger. Blood was oozing from the cut.

'Razor,' he explained.

'I'll get a plaster.'

He lifted his head and looked at the woman. A sweet, kind face.

'Are you married?'

She answered peaceably. 'No.'

'What time do you finish work,'–John read the badge on the woman's blouse–'Liza?'

A snow-covered park. John ran after Liza and caught her up. Liza tried to wriggle out of his grasp and they both fell over in the snow, shouting with laughter.

'I've lost my hat,' said Liza, her voice a whisper.

John snatched off his own hat and tossed it aside. He kissed Liza.

Hand in hand, they walked along a narrow avenue.

Coming towards them were John, Ann, and Annie. As if nothing had happened.

They walked. Drawing closer together.

Liza and John.

John, Ann, and Annie.

Liza and John walked past John, Ann, and Annie.

John, Ann, and Annie walked past Liza and John.

They noticed nothing. They did not see one another.

The avenue was deserted. Snow fell quietly.

THE STEPPE

She'd already slept five nights up on the shelf. On a scrawny mattress, to the clack of the wheels. How many more such nights lay ahead of her in her life, she had no idea.

The lieutenant went to lift her suitcase from the luggage space and exclaimed, 'You've got gold in here!'

'Of course,' she answered.

'Coins or ingots?'

'Coins.'

'What mint?'

'I don't know. They're old.'

'Oho! A whole suitcase of old coins.'

'Enough to keep me fed.'

'Far from it! My dear young lady, you're quite wrong. These coins will be no use where you're going. You'd have done better to pick up a winter jacket. August is seeing out its last days. Blessed August, as my dear mother used to say. All this sunshine and warmth is illusory, mere appearance, a deception. The reality is a colossal forty degrees of frost, brought in over the steppe by the wind, faster than our train. And the night sky above the steppe is black, like a hole. You may laugh, young lady.'

She was not laughing; she was smiling. Outside the window, over the steppe, the sun was shining, clouds were lolling in the blue sky, and fresh air was pouring in through the lowered window. Blessed August: later, she would remember and repeat that more than once.

'Don't laugh,' repeated the lieutenant.

ELENA DOLGOPYAT

'Why not?'

'Because I'm being serious.'

'Will you take my suitcase down to the platform for me?'

He maintained a stern silence. Looked at her. Thought. Tried to make up his mind.

'If you don't want to, you don't have to. I'll ask someone else.'

'All right. I'll give you a hand.'

An old lady on the side shelf sneered loudly: 'Well, God be thanked.'

The lieutenant darkened. Repeated with dark seriousness, 'I'll give you a hand.'

'He's doing you a big favour,' said the old lady, winking at Liza.

The lieutenant easily picked up the huge, heavy suitcase tied up with twine, and set off with it towards the exit. The train was slowing down.

Liza wished everyone in the carriage a pleasant journey, and they all wished her happiness, success, health, and love. Thus she parted from her fellow-passengers, having received their blessing for her future life. The lieutenant, with his two little stars on each shoulder strap, was already in the vestibule. The train was coming to a stop.

The conductress opened the iron door and wiped the yellow hand grip with a rag. The lieutenant picked up the suitcase and jumped down from the bottom step onto the cracked asphalt. Liza lingered on the step. The sun was blinding. She jumped, and the lieutenant caught her. He set her down on the asphalt, but instead of letting her go he held on to her in a strong embrace. She dared not move a muscle. Her thoughts, too, froze. The lieutenant's heart was beating against her forehead, and she was breathing him in. She felt as if she were inside him, protected from the whole world by his big, strong body; he seemed enormous, enveloping, swallowing all of her.

She sensed the train moving off, but the lieutenant hugged her tighter still, squeezing her closer to him. He started to rock back and forth quietly with her. The train was picking up speed; she could hear it going, she could hear voices shouting to the lieutenant. He suddenly let her go and took a step back.

The train was departing. They stood together, still close.

The lieutenant was looking at her intently, his eyes shining. Suddenly he spun round and broke into a run. Liza watched him go. She saw him dash alongside the rear carriage, grab hold of the hand grip, and make a leap for it. She thought he would look round when he was safely up, but he did not.

The roar of the train was dying away; already she could hardly see it in the distance. The rails shone in the sun. Liza suddenly burst into tears. Through her tears, she saw a small brick station, and a cart. A man was standing by the cart and appeared to be watching her. He tossed aside his cigarette butt and came across the rails.

There were lots of rails, a huge, glinting network. Liza's platform was like an islet, an asphalt rectangle.

The man crossed the rails, reached her islet, scrambled up onto it, and stood in front of Liza. She sniffled.

'It's not that bad,' he said. 'He's not going off to war.'

'It's not that bad,' agreed Liza.

'Yelizaveta Sergeyevna?'

'Yes,' she answered quickly, startled.

'Pyotr Andreyevich. Director.' He stretched a large hand out to her.

Liza shook it distractedly. The director himself had come to meet her! He was carrying her suitcase. Helping her into the cart. Taking the reins.

The horse trotted along quietly. Liza gazed into the distance. Her eyes were wide; she was thinking about the lieutenant.

He was a strange one. The whole way, day after day, he'd paid her no attention. He'd gone to the restaurant, returned in the company of some gnarled little chap, and proceeded to drink vodka with him all night. Through her sleep she'd heard them saying 'Shush!' and the lieutenant giving an occasional laugh, to which the other man responded with something like 'Ahhh!'; she never heard him laugh. The lieutenant had slept long into the morning on his top bunk, woken up towards midday, stretched, lowered his bare feet, jumped down and pulled on a pair of shoes with trodden-down backs–civilian shoes, old and worn. Off he'd gone to the toilet, slap, slap, slap. In the whole long journey he had not once struck up a conversation with her. Once he'd treated everyone in their nook to omul which he'd bought at a station en route. She'd eaten with them. The fish was tasty but expensive. When the train had come to a sudden stop at Baikal, he'd dashed off for a swim, not worried about being left behind. Later, he'd reported that the water was ice, pure and simple. Liza could not think why he'd hugged her goodbye in that way. Perhaps he'd really liked her but been too shy to say, and then when he'd been faced with their parting he'd plucked up the nerve. Liza was sorry that they had not chatted even once, that they were unlikely ever to see each other again, and that the future held nothing at all for them.

The lieutenant was what might have been. Liza did not grieve about it. The whole of her life was in front of her.

The cart rolled over the hard ground. Clouds grew in the depths of the sky. A single shadow made up of the cart, the horse, the director and Liza lengthened in the setting sun. When the sun had dispatched to earth its last, farewell ray and sunk below the horizon, this shadow would cover the whole steppe.

The houses had not yet come into view, but there was already a smell of smoke, of habitation. The horse became more cheerful and picked up his pace. The whole thing was like something out of a nineteenth century novel. Liza felt herself to be a heroine from the previous century. As if someone had already written her life. As if she were living out something already written and read.

'Do you know how to light the stove?' asked the director.

'I do,' answered Liza. 'We have a stove at home. A Russian one.'

It was perfectly true. A Russian stove provided the heating for their house. Except that when it came to stoking, the stoker was not Liza. She'd thrown wood onto the fire and raked out the ashes with an iron shovel. She'd brought firewood in from the shed, and eaten pies and potatoes cooked in the oven. She'd crawled inside it when she was little and hidden behind the curtain in the dry warmth. But her mother had been the one to light the stove. Why had Liza not admitted that? What was she ashamed of?

'We'll bring you coal,' said the director. 'There's a shed in the yard. Make yourself a vegetable garden in the spring–put down manure, fix some cloches. So ... the permafrost. In summer it can get up to 40 degrees, but deep underground the earth stays frozen.'

He looked at Liza and saw the dismay in her eyes. 'But our potatoes are tastier than yours,' he said. And after a little silence, he added, 'And we have a lot of sun.'

He put her suitcase down just inside the door and walked across the broad floorboards to the window. He leaned towards the windowpane, looked out, and pronounced, with satisfaction, 'Good.'

Taking his leave, he shook Liza's hand and told her that she needed to be at school the next day.

Liza went out onto the step and watched the cart head off.

The house she had been allocated was out of the way, but on a rise, so Liza could see the whole village. The steppe here was not smooth and even, as Liza had imagined it would be. She looked at the village, already in the shade. Lights were starting to come on in the houses.

A big village. Almost a town. There were big houses, too, several storeys high. The director had said that there were two cinemas. And a club. She'd have gone straight into town, but that would have meant making the scary walk home in the dark when everywhere was deserted.

It was chilly standing on the step, and Liza went back into the house and bolted the door.

She sat on a chair by the window and fell to watching the sun go down. The red ball touched the rim of the earth and started to sink behind it. The clouds began to lose their red highlights, just as burning coals fade as they cool.

Darkness arrived swiftly, and Liza turned on the light and fell to unpacking her suitcase. She undid the twine, opened the plywood lid, and took out her dress. Dark blue, shaped at the waist, specially sewn for her graduation by a local seamstress, a present from her parents. A grey, sheepskin, stand-up collar.

Liza tried on the dress. There was no mirror in the room, and she went to the window to look at her reflection in the black glass. She turned sideways, spread her arms, then fancied that someone was looking in at her from the other side, from the night, and hurried away from the window. She resolved to buy curtains the very next day. She hung the dress on a hook by the door, and stood her black felt ankle boots with their rubber soles underneath her dress. From the bottom of her plywood suitcase she fetched out a white sheet and sat hugging it on the edge of the narrow iron cot, breathing in its smell.

The sheet had absorbed the wormwood air of her little town. It even held something of the mushrooms Liza had cleaned in the garden, bringing them in from the forest one quiet morning not long ago. Liza had sliced the mushroom stalks with a sharp knife, and dried the sheet on a sagging line nearby. Water had been trickling off the sheet and dropping onto the leaves of a currant plant, creating the impression of a light rain. A placid sun had been shining, not at all like the one here, whose whole aim seemed to be to blind rather than illuminate.

Liza spread the sheet on the flat mattress. She shoved her trunk under the bed and undressed a little further away from the window, by the wall, wriggling into her long, ankle-length nightdress, which also smelled of home, the clean air of her homeland. She settled herself in bed, covering herself with a Chinese wool blanket she'd bought in Moscow. She had her own feather pillow, given to her by her grandmother as a moving-in present. The blanket prickled.

I'll buy myself a blanket cover out of my pay, thought Liza. *And a table lamp. A radio would be good too, to hear a human voice. Curtains straightaway tomorrow, though. That's the first thing.*

She left the light on, so as not to be all alone in the dark on the outermost edge of the inhabited world.

She dreamed that the lieutenant was walking outside her window and looking stern–he was guarding Liza's dream. Outside the window it was winter. He was wearing a mid length sheepskin coat, and the snow was scrunching beneath his lieutenant's boots. *The bride is dreaming of her groom in her new home,* Liza thought. And she came awake out of her dream.

Beyond the window there was barely a glimmer of light. It felt very early; the view to the west was still in shadow. Liza had not taken her watch off when she went to bed, and now she lifted her arm to look at the time. Her watch had stopped. Liza breathed deeply; the air had cooled overnight. With a decisive movement, she flung off her blanket, and lowered her bare feet to the floor. Yelping at

ELENA DOLGOPYAT

its icy touch, she quickly searched with her feet for her slippers, new ones, bought in Moscow.

She felt like a cup of hot tea. The kettle was already full of water and standing in the hearth, and there were logs in the wicker basket. Liza decided to light the stove. First, she placed logs inside the stove. Then she found an old newspaper in her suitcase, tore it into strips and shoved the strips in between stove lengths of wood. Everything exactly as her mother had done. She even hacked chips of kindling off the stove lengths with a large kitchen knife, and pushed pieces of kindling in among the logs and laid more on top of them. She lit the kindling and the newspaper, remembering to open the flap so that the fire could draw.

The flame caught. Liza watched it, sitting on her haunches by the open stove door until her legs went to sleep. She closed the door and eased the kettle into the middle of the hearth, where the fire was hottest.

She made her bed. She wiped a track with her palm in the steamed-up window; through the track she could see blue sky. The kettle started to rattle and came to the boil, sending water hissing onto the red-hot cast iron.

In the cupboard beside the stove, Liza found a packet of compressed tea and a box of refined sugar. 'Thank you,' she said, acknowledging whoever been considerate enough to make sure she had supplies.

The director, most likely.

Liza made tea in a large porcelain cup she'd brought with her from home. She spent a long time draining her big cup to the bottom, the way her family drank tea at home after a bath. Strong, sweet tea. When she'd finished it, she cleaned her teeth at the washbasin in the chilly corridor. The water swilled out of the sink into a bucket.

Liza put on her cornflower-blue summer dress. It had become thoroughly crumpled in her suitcase, but she could not find an iron in the house. Nor was there a single mirror.

This house is like a hut in the taiga, thought Liza. *Supplies for people passing through. An island of salvation.*

Liza went out onto the steps to greet the sun. She stopped and looked at the village below. She made out the white, four-storey school building. Smoke from the factory chimney was dissipating in the blue sky, vanishing completely. Liza took another deep breath of the new air, and went down the two steps onto the path. The path led her downwards, then made a right turn, and the village disappeared from her field of vision. Liza became unsure as to whether the path was taking her to the village or not. She was walking in a gully beneath the bright sun and was quite ready for anything at all, including that the path would wind round and bring her back home, that the village was a mirage, and that Liza herself was currently on another planet a thousand light years from her native land, like in a fantasy novel.

Liza quickened her step. She was starting to feel that she had already been walking for a long time, and her stopped watch was no help in telling her the time. The path abruptly came up against a grey fence. Liza looked at the fence uncertainly. It was high, preventing her from seeing what was behind it, and its boards were close-fitting. Grey and dry, and shot with silver in the sunlight. The path divided into two, offering a choice of walking beside the fence to the left or to the right. Liza turned left, downhill.

She walked along the fence, and as she walked she spotted a skew-whiff board. She caught hold of its edge. It was held on by a single nail at the top, and Liza was able to move it aside and look through the gap. She saw an asphalt road, cracked, and glinting in the sun, so empty it looked positively abandoned. Liza moved the board further aside and slid herself into the gap. Stepping through the fence, she saw that the village started just across the road.

Liza heard the hum of an engine; grinding its way up the road was a lorry. It slowed as it drew near, and the driver yelled from his cab, 'Want a lift?'

Liza shook her head. The driver gave a laugh, and with a roar the lorry sped off up the glinting road. Liza watched it go, straightened the hem of her dress, and crossed over to the other side.

It's a big village, she thought. *The footpaths are wide, there are poplar trees, and the wooden houses have iron roofs. I suppose there's a forest somewhere nearby and they use the trees for firewood and building. The street is really long but there's no-one on it.*

In a yard beyond a low picket fence, a man and a woman were sawing a log with a two-handled saw. The saw caught and buckled, and they lifted it up a fraction and carried on carefully: *wheek-wheek.* The steel glittered in the sunlight.

There's the school. Brick, plastered, white, big windows. The classrooms are light, I should think.

Liza stopped at the front steps of the school, raised her head, and saw a grey-haired, wrinkled woman looking at her from an open window on the fourth floor.

The foyer was cool and dark after the street. Liza headed for the stairs. Wide stone banisters had been painted brown. Liza went up to the third floor and made her way along the parqueted corridor to a high door marked 'Staff'. She knocked.

The director was not there, but Liza was expected, and was greeted warmly. A young teacher was celebrating her birthday and had brought a cake. A kettle was boiling on an electric ring. The cake was dark brown with white frosting. The teachers asked Liza to guess what kind of cake it was. It was delicious, and like chocolate, which prompted Liza to say, 'Chocolate.'

Wrong. The cake was chokecherry. In these parts, people dried chokecherries and then ground them up very fine.

After the cake, they washed the classroom windows. Liza studied the teachers, thinking she would recognise the woman who had been looking at her from the fourth floor, but she did not. After the windows came a staff meeting. Liza was told that she would be teaching physics in the sixth class. It was a difficult class, but she would be given help. After the meeting, they went their separate ways. Liza dawdled, and was the last to leave. She asked a passing man the way to the bakery, and he showed her. Liza bought a half loaf of brown bread, and then picked up a tin of Chinese stew in a grocery store. She carried her purchases through the street in her hands. The bread smelled delicious.

Someone hailed her. The teacher who had treated them to cake was digging her vegetable garden.

'Do you have another spade?' asked Liza.

The teacher's name was Valentina. She gave Liza an old tracksuit she wore to school for PE, and they turned the soil together. They cleaned themselves up in the garden, pouring water on each other's hands with a dipper, then cooked up some potato and opened Liza's stew.

'I don't celebrate my birthday at home,' said Valentina.

'Why ever not?'

'I don't know. I just don't. Well, if we do, we have a drink with our evening meal. Homemade. Do you want some?'

Liza said decisively, 'Yes.'

The sun was sinking towards the west. Valentina said that her husband would be home from work soon. Thinking about the walk home started Liza feeling scared, and her fear prompted her to drink plenty of alcohol.

'Eat something, eat something, or you'll get drunk,' said Valentina. 'I've done lots of potato, plenty for all of us.'

ELENA DOLGOPYAT

Liza ate more than enough, and then said it was time for her to go. Valentina saw her as far as the wicket, and stayed there to wait for her husband.

The alcohol made Liza forget her fear completely. She walked along under an ash-grey sky, stepping out firmly. She walked west, where the sun had already set. The air was cooling, but Liza was altogether warm, and felt very beautiful in her cornflower dress. She was sorry that the director had not seen her in it.

He would see it, but the lieutenant never would.

Liza crossed the road, found the hole in the fence, and slipped through it onto the path. She set off along the path confidently and calmly. A pale afterglow still lit the sky. Liza reached home before it became completely dark, and looked back from her step at the lights of the village, twinkling below. She opened the door.

She went into the dark room and saw the window, dark with the night. Without turning on the light, she went over to the window and felt for the back of her chair. She sat. Sat for a while in the silence. She felt that she'd been wrenched away from everyone alive; she was on the edge of the world. She cried a little. Touched the silent watch on her wrist. Wound it up by feel. Brought it to her ear. The watch was ticking.

THERAPY

1. 1986

The sheet of paper lay on my desk. I looked at it and said nothing.

An application for leave. Three lines. I suspect he couldn't fathom why I was spending such a long time reading it. Not that I have any idea what he was thinking, standing in front of my desk, waiting. I've never had any idea what another person might be thinking, even about me; I don't have enough imagination. Not to mention that I've never experienced any desire to find out.

'Have I done something wrong?' he asked, finally taking the plunge.

'Something special happened to you in 1986, then?'

He was flummoxed, naturally enough, by this ridiculous question. He thought hard. I must say, I'd have thought hard as well. It's not that simple to recall events from 1986, a quarter of a century ago. Unless there's something particular associated with the year.

Me and 1986? Not a thing.

'Perhaps you were allocated a flat in 1986?' I asked. 'Got divorced? No? Well, I don't know. You went somewhere on holiday? Bulgaria. I remember you telling us something about Bulgaria.'

'Bulgaria was '74.'

'Excellent. So in '86 what, then? Something really nice? You had a lover, perhaps?'

'I've never had a lover.'

There are four in my department. Leonid–the one waiting for my signature–will soon be sixty. His patronymic's never caught on; he's always called by just his first name. Masha's on maternity leave. And then we have Larisa and Gennady. Whispering to each other, whisper, whisper, like mice. They rarely talk to each other in normal voices; everything's a secret with them. I've no interest in what they're talking about, but their 'whisper, whisper' irritates me. They live together as well. They haven't got tired of each other: remarkable. When I put my lover question to Leonid, they stopped whispering and went quiet. Looked at us, wide-eyed. No clue what was going on, naturally.

'It was probably something really bad, then,' I said to Leonid. '1986. Think.'

'Perestroika started.' A faint cheep from Gena's desk.

'Who cares about perestroika?' I said. 'Or maybe we do care?' I looked intently at Leonid.

'I don't know,' he said, still flummoxed.

'Your son died? What year did your son die?'

This was an awful question; I was perfectly aware of that. The mice kept quiet. They were waiting for the answer, too. Afraid of the answer.

'Sasha died in '88,' said Leonid in a flat, even voice. 'Hit by a car.'

'Yes, I know that. It was his fault, I believe. He ran across on red.'

'He was in a hurry.'

'That's OK then. In '86 he was still alive. You don't need to pull such a tragic face. I'm asking you about '86. Your son's still alive. Maybe he finished school that year?'

'What do want from me, Sergey Nikolayevich?'

'Nothing. I'm just curious what made you date your application 1986.'

I pushed the paper towards the edge of the table. He picked it up. Flummoxed, of course. Squinted.

'1986. It says 1986, trust me. Your glasses are on your desk. Go and have a look. And write your application out again. I'm leaving in five minutes. The director's called a meeting.'

The mice kept their heads down. The radiator gurgled briefly. Leonid's pen started scratching across the paper.

I was looking out of the window during the meeting when an ambulance pulled up at the front entrance and doctors came dashing out of it. They'd been called to Leonid, it transpired. When I got back to my department he'd already been whisked away. Heart attack. The mice didn't look at me, just tapped away at their keyboards. I wish they always applied themselves like that. They sat there in silence until the end of the day, not saying a word to each other.

Off they went. Patter, patter. Bye, bye. I finished the program I was writing and shut down my computer. Leonid's computer was still on. I sat down at it, nudged the mouse, and the screen lit up.

I looked at his photographs and went into his inbox. He was absolutely alien to me. Uninteresting. I looked indifferently at his face. He looked older in the pictures, especially in the ones where the sun was out and he was on holiday, on a street in some Mediterranean place, or by the sea.

If I'd been my normal self, I wouldn't have wasted a word. I'd have asked him to rewrite his application, bang, conversation over. I've always kept my distance. Involving yourself in someone else's life is boring. And a nuisance.

2. EVENING MEAL

Our evening meal at home has its own routine. I listen to the radio, eat, and say nothing. My wife's a housewife, and my son's in his third year of secondary school. He's getting on OK with his studies and is into some kind of Japanese fighting, all the rage these days. He was telling Valya a funny story and couldn't help laughing himself, but it hurt him to laugh. He's just had a tooth out, and was eating with unusual care–he usually just wolfs everything straight down. It upsets Valya that he doesn't give himself time to taste his food, and she calls him her little animal–fondly, of course. She's a splendid cook, actually. One of life's pleasures for me is our evening meal at home. Eating tasty food in comfort. Banal as it may sound, this is one of the pillars of my existence.

That evening, though, I had no sense of taste. The radio, too, was irritating me, so I got up and turned it off–an occurrence so unusual that my family went quiet. My son stared at me wide-eyed, and Valya gave me a bewildered smile. It wasn't really about me being irritated, though. I wouldn't even call it irritation. I wrote that I had no sense of taste, but I actually had no sensation of anything. I was in a state akin to being asleep. I wanted to bite myself on the arm. I had the feeling that the people crowding round the little table with me did not exist, even though I could see and hear them. Or that they existed somewhere far from me and were moving further and further away. The universe is expanding; we know that. I didn't know what to do. My 'condition' did not begin that evening, but it was exacerbated that evening. Or maybe we should see its exacerbation as starting with Leonid? It was as if everyone had distanced themselves from me, and too far at that, scarily far.

I speared a slice of meat with my fork and casually asked my son, 'Can you help me with something?'

He went on chewing carefully, looking at me expectantly.

'There's a chap needs killing.'

My son stopped chewing. Valya looked at me, startled.

I carried on unperturbed. 'He's got a top floor flat. Only the attic above him. He has to go down two flights to get the lift. All you've got to do is throw him down the stairs when he's heading out for a walk with his dog. Somewhere around midnight's a good time, people are basically asleep then. He's an old guy, coming up for 80. Already tired of living, is my guess. His dog's tired of living as well. You'll be doing a kindness, and picking up a bit of extra cash at the same time.'

My son listened with interest. I'm ready to take an oath to that effect. It may not have been his ambition to find this interest in himself, and perhaps he didn't want it, but he was interested; it showed.

'Sweetheart, would you mind passing me some bread?' I asked my wife.

'Sergey, what are you doing?' said Valya reproachfully, perplexed. She passed the bread.

'Thank you, dear.'

My son and wife watched me as I bit off a chunk of bread, chewed it, and washed it down with lukewarm tea.

'What's your price for giving the old man a shove?' I asked.

'Seriously?'

'Absolutely.'

'10,000 Euros.'

'You're nobody's mug. What will you spend it on?'

'A motorbike.'

'Who'll sell you one? You're still a child.'

'You'll buy it.'

We looked each other in the eye, as if we were playing who blinks first. My son was the one to look away. I set down my tea and rose from the table. On my way out, I heard Valya whisper something to our son, but I don't think he answered. I returned and put five one hundred-Euro notes on the table in front of him. He looked at the money, then at me.

ELENA DOLGOPYAT

'An advance,' I explained.

I sat back down at the table. 'Do you mind pouring me some more tea?' I asked Valya.

She said not a word and moved not a muscle. Our son slowly gathered up the money, picking up one note then the next. My wife watched him, fascinated. Watched him fold the notes over double and secrete them in the back pocket of his jeans. And then tuck into his bread.

'Misha.' Valya tried to catch his attention.

He did not look at his mother. He wiped his bread around his plate, mopping up sauce. Dispatched the bread into his mouth.

'Your hands are dirty,' said Valya. 'From the money.'

Our son did not answer. He finished chewing, and asked, 'Is he fat?'

'The old man? Yes. Meaning he's clumsy. A good push and he'll be a goner. Put on something a bit less noticeable. That anorak of yours is too bright. You need a black one. You should be all in black–hat, trousers. Like a uniform. There are thousands dress like that. No-one'll be able to identify you.'

'I don't have a black anorak.'

'Go down the market and buy one. You've got the money. Make a small investment in the undertaking.'

Valya silently followed our conversation. Flummoxed.

'And keep your face away from the surveillance camera over the front door. And when you go back out, don't run. Walk calmly. Limp, even.'

'What for?'

'Limp in, and limp back out. That'll throw them off. They'll be looking for a cripple.'

'The dog bothers me.'

'She's old. No teeth. She can't bite you.'

'Even so.'

'Look, kill the dog as well, if you like.'

'Sergey, what is this drivel?' Valya tried to make me look at her. 'Misha, don't listen to him, for God's sake.'

'Does he live a long way away?' asked my son, business-like.

'I'll give you the address tomorrow.' With that, I got up from the table.

Valya stopped me. 'What are you playing at?'

'Playing?' I asked, surprised.

I don't know what they said to each other. I went off to my room, the room I call my office. My books and computer live there. I shut the door and no-one comes in. It has a balcony which I go out onto at night to smoke and look at the city. The city's practically invisible, with only its various lights to tell you anything. A window: people live there, though who they are and what kind of life they have is not my business. Car headlights: where they're going and who's in the car is not important. Streetlights.

Sometimes I don't go out. For whatever reason, I don't feel like looking at the lights twinkling in the darkness, and I sit in my chair near the open balcony door. Even in winter. I fancy I can hear the snow rustling as it falls. And the cigarette smoke drifting towards me. Or maybe I should pick another verb here. No; I can also hear smoke. I practically never smoke–I haven't caught the habit–but sitting reading in my office in the late evening I'm drawn not to the cigarette, but to its red glow, to the drift of the smoke. I basically don't have any harmful habits. I'm in excellent health. I'll live to be a hundred if I'm not knocked down by a car. Underneath the car, I'll contemplate the God whose love of theatre permits him to resolve all insoluble problems, unpick all plot twists, and enrage his critics by being a hatchet man. That's a point. I could also get a hatchet in the head.

I didn't want to see the city, and drew the curtains across the window. Settled in my armchair. The curtains are heavy, and it was so dark I was as good as blind. My wife was talking on the other side of the wall. Maybe with our son, or maybe on the phone–I couldn't hear another voice. Next door seemed to be rearranging their furniture. Then they turned on the television. Sounded like a love film. Long, lyrical, musical interludes. None of it got through to me. None of these sounds had the slightest relevance to my life. Eventually they quietened down. Not all sound died away, though. Water gurgled in the pipes. Cars went by outside the window, along the main road. There was a sudden scraping noise in my office, and the sudden scrape, so close, startled me. As if someone besides me was in the room. I turned on the lamp. Gilded letters glittered on the spines of my books. What a lot of gilded letters there are on the spines of my books.

3. THE BILLIONAIRE

My wife was reading in bed. She glanced at me, then returned to her magazine. Travel. Some exotic country somewhere. I studied her face as she read. She turned the page.

I settled down on my half of the bed, wriggling under the blanket. My wife was radiating warmth. She hardly ever gets really cold. She walks about in sub-zero temperatures wearing light boots. My feet are permanent blocks of ice.

'Can I ask you something?' My wife turned towards me.

I closed my eyes at once.

'What was that circus about?'

I kept quiet and did not open my eyes.

'Misha respects you. I overheard him once talking you up to his friend, Fyodor. Obviously you won't remember Fyodor. You know nothing about your son's life. Have you ever taken any interest in him? How he's getting on? Not that I remember. As for heart-to-heart conversation, you have no idea what that is. "Hello." "Goodnight." "Pass the bread, please." That's the sum of what you say to him. But he still loves you, remarkably enough. And he wants you to like him. Are you aware that he wants you to like him? Tell me what made you suddenly start all that crap about the murder. What do you want from him?'

I said nothing, kept my eyes shut, breathed evenly.

'Who is this old man?'

I heard her throw her magazine onto the table. She clicked the switch and off went the lamp.

I opened my eyes. The night sky twinkled beyond the window.

'You remember Malamud chasing after you at the institute?' I asked. 'You nearly drove him to poison. Or was he going to throw himself under a train. I can't remember. Perhaps he got into a fight and ended up down the police station. He's in Switzerland now. A billionaire. Not married. Does charity work. Everyone does charity work these days.'

She said nothing.

I turned to my wife. Propped myself up on my elbow.

She lay there, eyes open.

'Do you really not think about it?' I asked.

'About what?'

'"What a pity I let him go back then. I could be living like a queen now. In Switzerland. How much better and brighter my son's future would be." That kind of thing. Or your daughter's. Or you might have given him six children.'

'Yes,' she said. 'I have thought about it. I could in fact be in Switzerland right now.'

I was lying back on the pillow, arms behind my head. 'No you couldn't.' I smiled into the darkness. 'I have no idea where Malamud is now. Somewhere in Samara, possibly. Ashdod. Scraping a living in New York. I made up the Switzerland thing.'

No answer.

ELENA DOLGOPYAT

'Although of course he might be in Switzerland and he might be a billionaire. There's got to be a sporting chance.'

I turned away, tucked my frozen feet under me, and closed my eyes.

4. MORNING

Outside the window, the sky was growing light. My feet had warmed up, and I was enjoying the feeling. I could hear the water making its noises, voices in the kitchen, the clinking of crockery.

They spent ages getting ready, walking up and down the corridor, turning lights on and off, talking to each other. They left me in peace, though.

The door closed and the key turned in the lock. They were gone. I'd already run out of time for breakfast. I grabbed a shower and got dressed, then went into the kitchen to check that the gas was off. In the sink was a cup with a few slops of tea. There was something very lonely about it, cast off, abandoned. Like on a cooled planet. No warmth—no life.

I found my key in my anorak pocket.

I got to work in no time. Lights went green as I approached and jams dissipated instantly. Meaning I wasn't late. I rolled the car almost up to the front entrance; there was a spot there still empty. I didn't get out of the car. I sat and watched people going into work. It was cold out— the air had almost a touch of winter in it. The wind was biting, and people were turning their faces away, lowering their heads, and hurrying.

Despite the cold, there was a mosquito. On the windscreen, the street side. I expected him to fly off, but he didn't budge. It was as if he was hoping the glass would vaporise and he would suddenly find himself in the warm, close to a living human body. I felt uncomfortable, as if the glass might actually dissolve. I turned on the wipers, and they swept the mosquito away.

The working day had already begun. The entrance was emptying out.

A trolleybus trundled up, and out got my mice. They'd dressed up snug and warm, and were not hurrying. They weren't afraid to arrive late–I'm pretty relaxed about late arrival. I wasn't a demanding boss at all, although my mice were afraid of me. Everyone was afraid of me at work.

Their faces were red in the cold wind. They were quite close to my car, and I lay back in the seat so that they wouldn't see me. The car radio was burbling. I always have the radio on. Even when I was a child, I couldn't do my schoolwork without the radio. It has a calming effect on me. Tomorrow will be colder still, it said, with a possibility of snow. The mice had gone past, so I pulled myself back up. The security guard had come out onto the front steps and lit a cigarette. I started the engine and set off. Away from work. Just away from work. My movement had no other goal of any kind.

I got caught in a traffic jam, like in a trap.

Sitting there for ages irritated me, and at the first opportunity I turned off through the arch of a big house and drove into a depressing yard. I got out of the car.

There were five of them. Black anoraks, jeans, trainers, black knitted hats. Exactly how I'd advised my son to dress for the murder. They were standing around in a children's play area. While I was making my way towards them, one of them settled himself on a swing and started to rock gently, making no great effort. I caught their conversation. A lad with a cigarette was talking. Something like this:

'America perceived the work of Scott and Byron not simply as unique literary achievements, but as part of the current of the English romantic movement.'

He gave the lad on the swing a puff of his cigarette.

ELENA DOLGOPYAT

The youngest of them, a little runt of about twelve, not a day more, declared:

'America has never found its own Byron. The nearest anyone has come to fitting the bill is Edgar Allan Poe.'

The one standing and smoking took a drag and blew out smoke. 'The most Byronesque of the American states was, obviously, Virginia.'

I went right up to them and joined their circle. They fell quiet.

Everything was as I described–the swing, the cigarette, the runt of a boy among older lads. Just the conversation was different. I lied about Byron. I copied that from the foreword to a book of Poe's poems. I need hardly say, they could not have had a conversation anything like that. Or could they?

They were talking about the little one breaking into a night club that his older mates had been turned away from. They hadn't passed face control. Through a toilet window. He'd reached the window by the fire escape. Knocked on the window, and someone–O miracle–had opened it for him. It was the ladies' toilet. His mates were sceptical. The toilets in clubs don't have windows, they were saying.

They went quiet when I joined their group. I understood–I could feel it–that the leader here was the one rocking on the wooden swing. The cables to which the swing was fastened squeaked.

'You found a wallet?' I asked the leader. 'Black, lacquered, silver monogram. Well, not silver, obviously, just white metal. I put it down here. Exactly in this spot.'

They seemed to find the ground interesting, suddenly.

'You not seen it?'

'Unfortunately, no,' said the leader.

I'm not lying about 'unfortunately'. That's precisely what he said.

'A lot of money in it?' asked the little one.

'Nearly 40,000.'

'You leave it a while back?'

'About 20 minutes ago. No more.'

'You sure about it being here?' asked the leader.

'Yes.'

'Why didn't you pick it up?'

'I forgot it.'

The little one started laughing.

'OK I forgot. What's so funny? Forgot and came back.'

'We've been sitting here for over an hour. You can't have put anything here twenty minutes ago. You weren't here twenty minutes ago. You get my drift?'

'I see,' I said. 'I see very clearly. You've got my wallet. Yes? Give it back, boys. It's not good to take someone else's stuff. It's a sin.'

'Nobody's taken your wallet,' said the little one.

'Unfortunately,' added the leader.

'Unfortunately,' echoed the little one.

'Show me your pockets,' I said to the leader.

'What?' He smiled.

'Stand up,' I said roughly, 'and show me your pockets.'

He stood up, keeping hold of the rope swing.

There was a tense silence in the group. They were watching his every movement.

'Pockets,' I ordered.

'Right,' he said, and whacked me in the face. I would have fallen over, but one of them standing behind me caught me. A boot landed in my stomach. The guy behind me let me go, and I collapsed, trying to shield my head from the blows.

A piercing female shriek sent them running.

The owner of the shriek came up. I was sitting doubled up on the ground. She took a look at my face.

'Shall I call an ambulance?'

'No.'

'There's no point calling the police. Grisha's own Dad works for the police.'

'Who's Grisha?'

'The little chap. My neighbour. Trails round after those jerks. Take this,' and she held out a paper handkerchief.

'It's OK,' I said.

'Your nose is bleeding.'

'It's OK, I'm fine. Go. Really, go. I'm fine.'

She went. I lay on the ground. Lay there looking at the sky. It was snowing, so lightly you could hardly see it, and the wind was making the swing creak. The blood stopped flowing. I was frozen.

5. THE CHIROPRACTOR

I have seen my own skeleton while still alive, like the hero of The Magic Mountain. My bones were unbroken. The surgeon told me I was lucky, and tidied the pictures away. The sign on his office door said 'Surgeon', but he introduced himself to me as a chiropractor.

'Who painted you these nice colours?' he asked, interested.

'Boys. Teenagers.'

'You know them?'

'No.'

It was just the two of us in his office. The nurse had asked for the day off–relatives had arrived from abroad, apparently. There was a queue in the corridor, but he didn't hurry. He spent a long time looking for a form on his table, rustling papers, dropping his pen and watching it roll and then going to fetch it. I was sitting on a couch covered with a white sheet. In the twilight it looked clean, but when he turned the light on, I could make out faded spots. Blood?

He picked up his pen and muttered, 'I hate teenagers.'

'It wasn't their fault. I provoked them.'

He looked at me, perplexed and curious.

'What for?'

The lamp's reflection shone in the dark window.

'Have you never had the feeling that you're not really here? You're alive, healthy, everything's great, but actually you're not here, and haven't been for ages.'

The chiropractor made no reply. He returned to the table and settled himself back down on his revolving chair. Drew a sharp line across the form with his pen. Asked, without looking up, 'And? That helped?'

'Yes.'

'Meaning that now you're ... alive.' He laid his pen aside and stared at me. There was a curious change in his tone. More intimate, somehow.

I looked at my fingers and wriggled them, as if trying to assure myself that yes, I was alive.

'You need to see a psychiatrist. A psychotherapist, shall we say.'

'I've already seen one.'

'Seriously?'

'Handed over a ton of money.'

He crumpled the form, screwed it up and lobbed it at the bin. Missed. Looked at the ball of paper long and hard. The ball suddenly rustled, uncrumpling itself, giving the impression that it, too, was alive. The chiropractor took a new form. Leaned over the paper and started to write.

'I'm giving you a phone number,' he said. 'Anatoly Ivanovich. You won't be able to get an appointment with him, but he owes me one.'

'What's this with the sudden favour?' I asked.

He put his pen down and rolled his chair away from his desk in the direction of my couch. He held out the form. There was nothing written on it except a phone number.

'My father died at forty-six in unexplained circumstances,' said the chiropractor, looking closely at me. 'He was found on the railway track beneath a pedestrian bridge. No-one saw whether he jumped or was thrown off. Not long before he died, literally a couple of days, I came upon him standing in front of a mirror. I saw the way he was looking at himself. I've remembered that look my whole life. You had exactly the same expression when you looked at your battered face in the mirror.'

He pushed himself off with his foot and rolled his chair back towards the desk.

'What kind of expression?' I asked.

'None. You weren't seeing yourself. You weren't ... looking at yourself.' Then he added, 'I'm not a writer. I can't describe it.'

6. EVENING

Nobody opened the door, and I had to look for my key. Make my way into the flat, dark, and cold as if it had been deliberately chilled, although the radiators were hot and the tight-shut windows were keeping out the raw air. They let in the night-time blackness, though, barely diluted by the streetlights.

I settled myself on the settee in the main room–it doubles up as a bedroom, after all–and stared at the television. More accurately, at its empty grey screen.

A note lay on the kitchen table. 'Soup and pilaf in the fridge. I've changed and ironed the bedding and bought bread and milk. Paid the bills. We're at Mum's.'

It was such a relief to sit on my own in the house in front of the blank TV.

I was peckish, and warmed up the pilaf. I didn't turn the radio on over dinner–there was no-one to hide from behind its noise. It occurred to me that noise is a cocoon, and inside it I'm defended, like in a pre-birth state. My wife and son were in a neighbouring street, not that far away. Probably already asleep.

In the morning I woke up before the alarm, but I didn't get up, just peacefully waited for it to go off. Headed for the bathroom. My face looked scary in the mirror after yesterday. Cleaning my teeth and shaving were painful, but I endured it bravely and shaved meticulously until my face was baby-smooth. I swilled down a painkiller, had a bite to eat, and dressed as if for a reception: white shirt, expensive black suit, dark cherry tie. Pity I didn't have a tail coat handy; I would have dressed up in that, too.

My mice greeted me at work with bright, wary eyes. I said hello, and they instantly looked away without answering. Buried themselves in their work.

Emanating from them: hatred and bewilderment. These things each have their own smell, it seems. Hatred and bewilderment. So do love, fear, pain. Not literally, I don't suppose: not literally a smell. Something akin to it, though. Something you pick up straightaway.

I got the feeling they'd decided to ostracise me after yesterday. To test my theory out, I asked how Leonid was, in hospital. No answer. Nonetheless, my question seemed to unsettle their mighty conspiracy. They were flummoxed, you could say. My battered face had disconcerted them. The combination of battered, thug-like face and ceremonial dress. I couldn't help noticing that we reached lunchtime without them exchanging a single word with each other, never mind with me.

Lunch starts at 1 p.m. I go to the cafeteria. They bring their own. Their desks are close together, end to end, so the effect is something like one long table for two. They spread a napkin in the middle, and set out dishes, slice bread, turn on the kettle. I reckon that Gennady has a smoke after lunch. I suspect that he opens the window, locks the door, and has a nice little puff. I've never once caught him in the act, but airing the room still doesn't get rid of all the smell. There are flecks of ash on the window sill as well. Leonid also goes to the cafeteria as a rule, and even keeps me a place in the queue, allowing me to join it in front of him. I hate cafeteria food, but I can't be done with lugging my own in from home. And eating at your desk is revolting. The cafeteria's at least something of a distraction. A source of entertainment, at times.

My computer was showing exactly 1 p.m. The mice looked up from their monitors.

A minute passed. Another. I did not get up and did not go out. I sat at my computer, tapping away at my keyboard. Time ticked on. The first to get up was Larisa. She put on the kettle. Gennady shifted papers aside and spread out the napkin. They set out dishes and packets. The kettle came to the boil. Larisa took the dishes out of the microwave, while Gennady sliced bread.

I got up when they started eating. Took a mug from the cupboard, tossed a teabag into it, and poured in hot water.

I headed towards them with my steaming mug. Gennady looked up at me with something like fear.

Larisa kept a cool head. 'Pass me the bread,' she said. Gennady hastily latched onto the bread as a convenient distraction.

I put my mug on the edge of the table, near their wondrous picnic. Brought up a chair and settled myself down opposite. They tried to ignore me, and went on eating. Larisa spoke to Gennady in a quiet voice, one she might use at home. 'The cabbage rolls have fallen apart anyway,' she said.

I was sitting opposite them with my mug. Smiling. Although it hurt to smile.

'Are they good?' I asked suddenly. 'May I try?'

Gennady froze. I took the fork from his stiffened hand, stabbed a slice of cabbage roll in his dish and dispatched it into my mouth. Both silently watched me chew. The roll was soft, and chewing it was bearable.

'Splendid,' I said. 'Delicious. Wonderful. Your wife is a wonderful cook. I'm hopeless.'

'I'm the cook,' he mumbled.

'Terrific!' I stabbed another morsel. 'Magnificent. I wish I were married to you.'

He looked at me with fear, she with hatred.

I took the last morsel and swallowed it down. Then I aimed my fork at her dish.

'May I?'

'No!' she said roughly, and pulled the dish away.

'You burned a hole right through my eyes,' I said. 'You burned through the mirror of my soul and ended up inside me. That's more vital than sex, you know. Such closeness.'

I turned to him. 'She's just been unfaithful to you. With me.'

Gennady sat there, pathetic, lost.

I suddenly asked Larisa, 'Did you have a nickname when you were a child? I did. Wet Vanka. Just so that you don't think the wrong thing, it's a flower. I wrote in an essay that on the window sill at home we had a Wet Vanka. Well, you're finding out some of my deep secrets today. You're an honest person. Your honesty compels you to be mine.'

I swallowed some tea. Put my mug on the table. Stood up and left the office. I was like a drunk.

8. EVENING THEATRE

Darkness was falling, and lights were starting to come on in the house opposite. My coffee arrived but I didn't drink it. I was very tired. It was as if my soul had been pried out of my body following the lunch break. I'd become indifferent to my fate. Whatever will be will be. Something like that.

ELENA DOLGOPYAT

Not that there are such things as souls and fates. They exist only in literature; they're a great big myth. Literature is a fairy tale about the way things are, the attribution to reality of significance and meaning, of something wonderful or frightful, elevated or ugly. Of something, at least. Not meaning, no; more like a longing for meaning. Any word written on paper, said aloud or left unspoken, is a justification of the way things are.

I find this a dark thought, and I don't want to think it to its conclusion. I'm sitting in a café, by the window. A lot of lights are already on in the house opposite. Electric lights. Gas too, maybe, if the house has gas stoves. I don't care what kind of stoves it has. Or what kind of people live there. I can picture these people all too easily as it is. They crowd before me and jostle around me. I drive them away but they take no notice and go on standing stubbornly in front of my eyes. Yesterday I called the number the chiropractor had given me. A dry voice introduced itself: 'Anatoly Ivanovich.' He did not want to meet me, and limited himself to a telephone conversation. Asked me questions, listened, and made recommendations. Now I was preparing to put them into practice.

I was sitting there, feeling empty, in front of a black coffee. It was twinkling and juddering. A metro line ran underneath, and the whole building was juddering. The whole street, including my black coffee, which had long since lost its aroma and gone cold. Touching your lips to a cold coffee is the same as touching a dead body. No life.

Around eight o'clock I called the waiter over and asked for the bill.

I crossed the street and approached the building I'd been observing from the café window. Inside its first entrance was the black door of a semi-basement. I rang the bell, and with a click of its lock, the door opened. To the left of the door sat a security guard at a narrow school desk. A lamp illuminated his large hands. He was doing nothing, and gave no sign of having noticed me walk in. I thought I'd better stop and say what I'd been told to say. By way of clarification I added, for some reason, 'Art therapy.'

'Along the corridor on the right,' he said, and recorded in his log: 'Art therapy.' The pen looked like a matchstick in his great paw, but he formed his letters with surprising elegance. They came out light and shapely, though a little immodest, like a tipsy ballerina, if you can imagine such a thing.

'Do you have a cloakroom?' I asked.

'Nope.'

I set off along the narrow, bare corridor.

In the small, ten-row auditorium, only the stage was lit. I could make out a wooden floor and a long, narrow table. Two people were sitting at the table, a man and a woman. I don't know whether or not they saw me from their circle of light; I was standing below them, in the darkness.

They sat in silence at the table, not talking to each other, not moving. I even wondered if they were mannequins. Then the woman suddenly turned her head and looked, squinting, into the dark abyss of the auditorium.

I walked towards the stage along a narrow aisle. To my right, in the auditorium, I discerned a dark figure, and stopped. From the stage, the woman intoned, 'Can you not be a little quicker? We've been waiting for you for ten minutes.'

'My watch is slow,' I answered amicably.

'Put it right then. We charge by the hour, you might like to know.'

For some reason, I expected the stage boards to creak under my feet, but they were quiet; not a peep. I approached the table. A lamp hung over it, low, intent.

'Sit down,' the woman directed me.

'Where?'

'There are plenty of seats.'

'Is Anatoly Ivanovich coming?'

She glanced into the darkened auditorium. 'I take the art therapy sessions. Anna Ignatyevna, at your service.'

She was sitting at the end of the table, and I took a seat at the long, unoccupied side, facing into the auditorium. There was a bald, middle-aged man across the table and to my left, facing me, his back to the black abyss. The way he was holding himself spoke of an especial calmness, a certain poise. I would have found it uncomfortable to have the black abyss at my back, from which Anatoly Ivanovich, whom I had never seen, was looking at me.

'Were you prescribed a sedative?' Anna Ignatyevna asked me.

'No. I've taken them before. Various types. All useless. They make me slow. I can't work. I don't even want to watch detectives. I get lost in the plot, like I'm stuck in a labyrinth. Crossing the street becomes an unachievable task.'

'Very good,' she said, and turned to the bald man. 'Victor.'

He was sitting, sunk in himself, self-absorbed, but he reacted immediately to the woman's voice. He pulled a strip of tablets from his pocket, pressed one out onto his palm, examined it with fastidious curiosity the way I might examine a beetle, then hastily tossed the tablet into his mouth. A bottle of water stood in front of each of us. He took a gulp from his, and wiped his wet mouth with his hand.

Anna Ignatyevna also took a tablet, her face stern and concentrated as she did so. Then she took a pair of glasses with thick black frames from her bag and sat them on her narrow nose. She went into her bag again, this time for some sheets of paper, which she smoothed out and separated into three sorry-looking piles. She pushed one pile across the table towards me, and another to the man.

'I'll be reading the part of Safonova,' she said to me. 'You–Aleksey. Victor, you read the stage directions and the chap with the imposing voice.'

Scene 1, read Victor in a dull, expressionless voice. *A front door. The door opens. Aleksey enters. He shakes off the snow and clops across the floor in his boots, heading for the lift. The cleaner, Safonova, is mopping energetically. Distorted reflections of the electric lights can be seen in the wet tiled floor. Safonova catches sight of Aleksey, stops work, and stands watching him, leaning on her mop. He goes up to the lift and presses the call button.*

Safonova: Don't seem to have seen your wife and boy around.

Aleksey: They're away.

Safonova: Holiday?

Aleksey: Of a sort. My wife's taking time off work, and my son's school has broken up.

Safonova: They're good people, your folks. Your son's nice and polite. Always says hello. A Grade A boy.

Aleksey: Grade B.

Safonova: Your wife's polite too. Strict, though. Kristina, I call her. That's just my name for her. I've made up names for everyone here. You too.

Aleksey (*slightly annoyed*): Marvellous.

Aleksey looks wearily at the lift. The button refuses to light up. The impression created is that the lift has broken down and become stuck. Talking, coughing and laughing can be heard booming down from the upper floors. Aleksey seems to be a restrained character, but this is only because he is usually detached from what is going on around him. If he is deprived of the opportunity to be detached, to withdraw into himself, to be unnoticed and out of sight, he becomes irritated almost instantly. He continues to be polite, but goes bright red, as if he's heating up.

'I what–go red at this point?' I asked.

'Up to you,' answered Anna Ignatyevna, and moved straight on to her next line.

Safonova: My name for you is James.

Aleksey: Why? By analogy with whom? With what?

Safonova: You're like a foreigner. An Englishman. You're not our type. Maybe I could call you James to your face?

Aleksey: James Bond, if you like.

The lift finally begins to hum: it is on its way. Aleksey cheers up.

Safonova: James Bond doesn't suit you. *(Thinks.)* So I think I'll call you Nikolay.

Aleksey: What exactly is your issue with Aleksey?

Safonova *(thoughtfully)*: Nikolay suits you better.

The lift doors open. A noisy crowd pours out: several adults and children, and a dog. Aleksey makes to enter the newly-emptied lift.

Safonova: Just a minute, I'll give the lift a wipe. Quick as you like. I'll be that quick you'll do well to see me. That lot and their muddy boots.

She bustles about the lift with her mop, keeping the doors open by pressing the 'hold' button.

Safonova: My son's vanished.

Aleksey watches her wiping the tiny lift at great length. The sight wearies him. Safonova is clearly spinning things out; she has something to say, and wants to detain Aleksey until she has said it.

Aleksey *(with growing, barely-controlled irritation)*: There's a sense in which I'm glad. I mean I'm sorry, of course, and I'm sure he'll soon be found, your son, but if I may speak plainly, it's a lot quieter now on your side of the wall. I couldn't for the life of me work out why. I see now. I've nothing against your son, but the music he listens to is lethal. My heart hurts from the racket. And the glasses in the cabinet rattle and shake. It's not music. It's an earthquake.

Safonova (*offended*): We don't yet know who's going to be in there, the other side of your wall. They might start up music enough to make my boy's seem like the singing of heavenly choirs.

Aleksey: Who's going to start what up? What on earth are you talking about?

Safonova: I've sold the flat. To bail my son out. He hasn't disappeared, like disappeared, like. He's lost a load of money. They were winding up to murder him. He still hasn't paid it all back, he's still in debt, but they're not killing him, as of now. He's working it off. At least they've spared his life. Meaning I'm flatless at the moment, Nikolay. I'm at my neighbour's, while she'll have me. I clean her floors, cook her meals, do her washing. She's an invalid. On her own. Boring for her. When I start getting on her nerves, she'll throw me out, that's what she said. Said she'd throw me out when I start getting on her nerves.

Safonova has managed to say what was burdening her. She finishes wiping the lift floor and comes out. Aleksey enters the lift. Before the doors close, he has time to ask a question and receive an answer.

Aleksey: What do you call your son?

Safonova: Vanya.

Next scene, said Victor. He fell quiet, sinking into thought over his sheet of paper.

'Are you tired?' Anna Ignatyevna sounded concerned.

'No. I'm fine.'

'I can see you're tired. Let's take a break.'

'No, no! No! Please. I'm just searching for the right intonation.'

'Intonation?' This irritated me. 'You're reading the author's comments.'

'You think the author had no intonation?' Victor was offended.

ELENA DOLGOPYAT

'As far as I'm concerned, all the comments are just instructions. Go left and then straight on. They're no different from how to assemble a settee. Take nail number seven and knock it in straight with hammer number eight.'

'You're talking complete rubbish,' observed Anna Ignatyevna coldly. 'As you know perfectly well. You simply want to annoy Victor.'

'What mood you're in when you hammer in a nail makes no difference,' Victor put in, sounding fraught. 'But when you're on stage, your mood is very important. The directions give clues not just to things like where and how people move about, but also their state of mind. They show you the meaning of the scene.'

'It's better to be in a good mood when you're hammering nails, so they don't go in crooked,' I said, smiling.

'To stop them going in crooked takes experience! Nothing more!' Victor was distressed.

'It goes without saying that it's better to be in a good mood when you're hammering nails,' said Anna Ignatyevna, amicably agreeing with me.

'Especially into a coffin!' shouted Victor.

'Into whatever,' said Anna Ignatyevna mildly. Then she turned to me. 'But on stage a nail might occasionally have to go in crooked, so that someone bursts into tears, for example.'

'Of course,' I agreed. 'Then he'll write *Exit left in a bad mood. Trips on the way and bursts into tears.* I agree, it's important and necessary. But why does a recommendation about mood have to be read with a particular intonation? Kindly explain.'

'So it's easier for you to get the point,' said Victor dully.

'Please calm down,' said Anna Ignatyevna. 'You're not going to change his mind. He's provoking you. Take another tablet and keep reading.'

Victor was silent. He looked fixedly at his sheet of paper. Then he picked up his bottle and took a gulp of water, without a tablet. Anna Ignatyevna waited patiently. Victor placed his elbows on the table and his palms to his temples, as if using his palms to protect himself from us. He started to read in a dull, expressionless voice. *Aleksey goes in the front door. He shakes off the snow, heads towards the lift, and then stops. A small house has appeared beside the lift. It has a big glass window, in which a light is burning cosily. Its walls are plywood, decorated on the outside with an imitation-brick pattern, which makes the house appear at first to be real and solid. Aleksey glances in through the window. He sees an armchair, a low table with a television, a rose in a clay pot, and a rug on the floor. There is no-one in the house, although the light is on, as is the electric kettle.*

Safonova *(behind Aleksey)*: Hello, Nikolay!

Aleksey jumps, startled, and steps back from the window.

Safonova: You like it? Me too. I sit inside for a while, then come out and have a look from the outside. I like it so much I could happily live right here.

Aleksey: It's for you, then, this house? Meaning you're now our concierge? Congratulations on your promotion. Who's going to clean the floors now?

Safonova: I'll still clean the floors. In my position, you can't chuck away good money.

Aleksey: I'm pleased for you.

Aleksey heads for the lift, but Safonova stops him.

Safonova: You and me need a chat, Nikolay.

Aleksey presses the lift button.

Aleksey: I'm in a hurry. Sorry.

Safonova: I won't keep you long.

She stands looking at Aleksey. The lift arrives and the doors open.

Safonova: Life and death. That's what we need to chat about.

Aleksey: In an abstract sense, or concrete?

The lift doors close, but Aleksey presses the button again, and the doors slide apart.

Safonova: Extremely concrete.

Aleksey looks at her questioningly.

Safonova: In private.

The lift doors close.

Victor took his palms away from his temples and turned the page. Sipped water from his bottle.

'Is everything all right,' asked Anna Ignatyevna.

Victor made no reply, merely looked stubbornly at the next page. He was obviously reading it to himself, groping for the right intonation. When he started again, his voice was changed, somehow muted.

Going inside the house, Aleksey nearly knocks over the kettle. He manages to catch it and steady it.

Safonova: Careful. It's hot.

Safonova is clearly very concerned to preserve her fragile world.

Safonova: Sit in the armchair, Nikolay.

Aleksey: It won't break under me?

Safonova: It's a strong armchair. Almost new. Dasha from number 54 gave it me. Our children were in the same class, only her daughter's in England now. Flourishing. And my boy's disappeared. Your folks called you lately?

Aleksey: So we'll be having more of a secular conversation, then? I thought you wanted to talk about life and death?

Safonova: That is what I'm talking about. Life and death.

Aleksey looks at Safonova in alarm. They hear the front door opening and someone coming in. Safonova twitches the curtain shut and turns on the television, so that passing neighbours hear the television rather than the conversation.

Safonova: When did they call you?

Aleksey: Lunchtime. Everything's fine. Everything's really good, they said. They've been skiing on a really high slope.

Safonova: Thank goodness! I'm pleased for them. Let's hope their health goes on getting better and better, while you and me sit here and sort out our business.

Aleksey: You'll forgive me I hope, but what kind of business can you and I have?

Safonova: You're right, you're right. You're there and I'm here. You think I don't know that? I don't know my place? It's Vanya. He's put everything into a muddle. Won't let me sleep. Gives me no peace. But I can't abandon my own flesh and blood. You understand that, Nikolay.

Aleksey is quiet, looking guardedly at Safonova. The television burbles.

Safonova: Vanya asked me to tell you that your folks'll be fine. You don't need to worry.

Aleksey *(worried)*: I'm not worried.

Safonova: He only wants 10,000. You've got it, and more, don't tell me you haven't.

Aleksey raises his eyebrows in surprise.

Safonova: Couldn't stop himself, he couldn't, Vanya. He's started playing again. It's like a drug, he says, can't give it up, even though he knows he can't win, they'd never let that happen, he knows that, but he can't help himself. Now he owes them 10,000 Euros. If he doesn't hand it over, they'll chop his arm off at the elbow. Given him a day. Help us out, Nikolay. Vanya'll be waiting until midnight for your answer.

Someone knocks on the window from outside. The knock is restrained but insistent. Safonova gives Aleksey a reassuring nod, goes to the window, peels back a corner of the curtain, and lifts the sash a fraction.

Impressive Voice: Does Alevtina live here, my lovey?

Safonova: What's her surname?

ImpressiveVoice: I don't know her surname. I gave her a lift yesterday. Brought her right to this door.

Safonova: I don't know any Alevtina.

ImpressiveVoice: You're saying she lied? Took advantage of an old man?

Safonova: I don't know.

ImpressiveVoice: She said she lived here. Maybe she really lives in Bibirevo.

Safonova: I don't know.

ImpressiveVoice: Have I got the right name? It could have been Ksenia. Is there a Ksenia living here?

Safonova: I don't know.

ImpressiveVoice: You seem to be the world's least well-informed concierge. What is it you actually do, lovey?

Safonova: I don't know.

Safonova lowers the sash and puts the curtain back. She turns the television up and faces Aleksey.

Safonova: He says that if you haven't agreed by midnight, he won't let your folks go alive.

Aleksey: I talked with them at lunchtime. They skied down the slope.

Safonova is quiet.

Aleksey: Where is this Vanya of yours?

Safonova: I don't know, sweetheart.

Aleksey: He talked with you on the phone?

Safonova: No, my darling. He sent me a letter. I found it this morning in my letter box.

Aleksey: Show me.

Safonova: I can't. I burned it. Those were his instructions.

Aleksey: The letter was written on paper?

Safonova: What else?

Aleksey takes out his mobile and calls a number. There is no answer. Aleksey turns his phone off. He looks intently at Safonova, then turns his phone back on.

Aleksey (*dialling*): I'm calling the police.

Safonova: You'll never see them again, then. Vanya asked me to tell you that you'll never see them again, alive or dead. He's got nothing to lose. Asked me to pass that on as well.

Aleksey turns off his phone and looks tiredly at Safonova.

Aleksey: Did he ask you to pass on anything else?

Safonova: No.

Aleksey: And how will he know if I've agreed or not?

Safonova: If I've put a geranium on the window sill come midnight, it means you've agreed.

Aleksey: The window sill?

Safonova: In the kitchen.

Aleksey: And if I don't agree?

Safonova: I won't put a geranium.

Aleksey: What makes your Vanya think I've got that much cash on me?

Safonova: Guilty as charged, Nikolay. Don't shoot me. I blurted out that you had 10,000 handy for your ma-in-law's operation, might be needed at any moment.

Aleksey: How do you know so much? I don't think I told you.

Safonova: You didn't tell me. You told someone else. I know a lot about people, Nikolay. Too much. Life's a lot more peaceful when you don't know.

There is a tap on the glass, persistent but restrained. Safonova goes to the window, turns back the corner of the curtain, and lifts the sash a fraction.

ImpressiveVoice: I had a thought, my lovey. I'll describe her for you. Tall, practically my height. In heels, obviously. Red-haired. Cheerful. Blue eyes. Which flat does she live in?

Safonova: I don't know.

ImpressiveVoice: What kind of concierge are you?

Safonova *(thinking)*: Wait, wait! Red hair? Blue eyes?

ImpressiveVoice *(hopeful)*: Cheerful.

Safonova: Does she have a habit of touching her nose when she's thinking?

ELENA DOLGOPYAT

ImpressiveVoice: You *do* know her! Oh, you beauty!

Safonova: She lives on Frunzenskaya Embankment.

ImpressiveVoice: Really?

Safonova: I've got a friend there. House number 100. She went up in the lift with your red-haired girl. Or down, maybe.

ImpressiveVoice: You're sure?

Safonova: She's got a red mobile.

ImpressiveVoice: Oh, you beauty!

Safonova lowers the sash and straightens the curtain. She turns to Aleksey.

Aleksey: There's a red-haired young woman here. Number 73.

Safonova: She asked me not to tell. What's your decision, Nikolay?

Aleksey is quiet, watching the television.

Aleksey: How will you get the money to him?

Safonova: There were instructions in his letter.

Aleksey: Complicated instructions?

Safonova: Not simple.

Aleksey: You're not going to mess this up?

Safonova: There's nothing wrong with my memory.

Aleksey is quiet. He twirls his mobile in his hand.

Safonova: I'll be off to set the geranium?

Aleksey gives Safonova a long, hard look.

Aleksey: I'll think about it.

Safonova: Course you will.

Aleksey gets up, setting the armchair rocking. Safonova steadies it.

Safonova: Careful now.

Aleksey's flat.

'Wait a second,' I said, stopping Victor. 'One second. Let's take a break.'

'I was just groping for the intonation,' grumbled Victor without looking up from his papers.

'My legs have gone to sleep,' I complained. I got up from the table and went to the front of the stage. I made out a dark figure in row seven.

'I'd like to know who wrote this idiotic play,' I said.

Silence behind me. Silence from the chap in row seven.

'Sergey, come back to the table, please,' asked Anna Ignatyevna.

'I'll be better off going home.'

'There's only a tiny bit left. Let's finish reading, and then you can go home.'

'What are you going to do at home?' asked Victor with interest.

'Sleep.'

I looked round. He was sitting at the table, half-turned towards me. He said, 'I'm going to eat. I've got dumplings in the fridge.'

'Homemade?' asked Anna Ignatyevna.

'Bought.'

'I want my money back for this moronic art therapy session,' I said to the chap in the auditorium.

No reaction.

'I'll give you your money back,' said Anna Ignatyevna. 'If you're still saying it hasn't helped when we've finished the reading, I'll give it you back.'

'Promise?'

'You have my word. I speak before witnesses.'

'I have no faith in your witnesses,' I observed. Nonetheless, I left the front of stage and returned to the table. When I'd settled back into my seat, I looked into the darkened auditorium and said, 'I know what this session reminds me of. The Last Supper. I guess it's the long table.'

'You can't have a Last Supper without Jesus,' objected Anna Ignatyevna.

'He's here,' said Victor, his voice trembling. 'He's always here.'

ELENA DOLGOPYAT

'Please, read,' I begged him.

'Yes, Victor, please.'

'What's the right intonation at this point?'

'Measured. Cold. As detached as possible from what's going on.'

Aleksey's flat. The dining room. Aleksey is sitting on the settee watching television. His eyes are directed towards the television, but he is not seeing what is happening on the screen. Aleksey is sunk in his own thoughts. On the coffee table in front of him are two telephones. One is a mobile, the other a land line. The mobile suddenly rings, and Aleksey snatches it up. He sees the caller's name in the window, and the excitement dies from his face. Disappointedly, he presses the button and brings the handset to his ear.

Aleksey (*with pauses, in which the caller's voice can be heard*): What? The report for which month? Of course, yes. Yes. Look carefully. Very good. I'm glad. You're welcome.

Aleksey switches off his phone, then turns it back on. He dials a number, and listens to the buzzing on the line for a long time. He turns off his phone and looks at his watch. It is 11.30. The television is showing the news. There are items on the economy and crime, and the weather forecast. Aleksey snatches up the remote from the settee and turns off the television. He looks at his watch, then picks up the handset of the landline and dials a number. At the same time, his mobile rings. Aleksey sees the caller's name in the lighted window, and snatches up the phone.

Aleksey (*excited, with pauses*): Hello! Masha! Lord! Where are you? How ...? How ...? How's Leon? Lord! Good news. No, no, I was simply dreadfully worried, calling and getting no answer. How was the excursion? I'm so glad. So glad. Let Leon have a word. Hello, my boy. How's the skiing–you an expert now? I never doubted it. Do what your Mum says, OK? Give her the phone now. Of course I've missed you, sweetheart. No, I've been eating. Had some potato. I have lunch at work. All is well in the stomach department. I'm managing to remember. Night night! Night night. Give Leon a kiss for me.

Aleksey disconnects and leans back on the settee in relief. Then he remembers the handset of the land line. Or rather, the handset itself reminds him of its presence. A dull voice reaches him from it.

Safonova *(voice from the handset)*: I'm listening. Speak. Speak. I'm listening.

Aleksey brings the handset to his ear and is about to say something into it but changes his mind and replaces the handset. He lies back on the settee, hands behind his head. He closes his eyes. The big hand catches up with the little one; the clock shows midnight. The big hand moves on. It is now past midnight.

Victor finished reading and laid aside his sheet of paper. Unscrewed the top from his bottle and sipped his water. Looked sullenly at me. He seemed to be waiting for some kind of reaction from me. A question, perhaps. He looked at me, and waited.

'You'll get the intonation right, I hope?' I asked.

He placed his elbows on the table, squeezed his temples with his fingers, and continued.

Aleksey puts out the light in the hall and opens the door of the flat. A strip of light falls from the landing. Aleksey goes to step over the threshold and notices a fat white envelope on the floor beneath the door. The envelope is not sealed, and Aleksey shakes a photograph out of it. Pictured on it are the bodies of his wife and son.

Victor turned the page. After this page–the last–was a photograph, which he pushed towards me. It sailed easily across the slippery table top.

The picture showed the bodies of a boy and a woman. My son and my wife. Misha and Valya. They were looking at me with glazed, dead eyes. Valya had her mouth wide open, as if she'd been laughing at something just before she died. Misha's face was peaceful, calm.

I picked up the photograph and examined it carefully.

'Photoshop,' I said.

They were silent. I got up from the table. I could feel their eyes on me as I went down the ramp into the auditorium and made my way towards the exit. Eyes from the stage and eyes from the auditorium.

The security guard did not pay the slightest attention to me.

In the car I fished out my mobile. My hands were shaking.

Valya's mother picked up.

'Olga Nikolayevna, how are they? Can I have a word with Valya? Hi, Valya, love, how are you? And Misha, bless him? No, no, I've been eating. There's still some of the soup left. Nothing. It's just ...'

VERA

And it seemed to her that it was breathing with her, moaning, with something like a pre-death sob. The whole room. Shallow breaths, rising and falling. Stopping. And Vera was lying like the wreckage of a ship, thrown onto a level shore, Vova's head on her belly. The nape of his neck was wet, and there was water in the hollow between his shoulder blades.

She had a belly, oh, and legs, and arms, and that part of her body ... Vova had come up with a name for it, a nickname, almost like for a puppy. Enough of that; it's an 'in' thing, stupid to outsiders.

They were sleeping. Vera and Vova. The clock was going shurr-shurr, like a mouse. There came a sudden sound, thin, pitiful.

Vera half-rose, then sat up.

The clock was round, not blinking, not lying. Shurring: fourr-shurr-fourr. It should have been light, it was June, but beyond the uncurtained window it was still half-dark. Storm clouds, probably. Great news, in its own way.

Vera got up without disturbing Vova and stepped off the mattress onto the floor. Their mattress was on the bare floor. So was the clock. Their clothes were in a heap. The sound was coming from the street, thin, pitiful, drawn-out. The door to the balcony was wide open.

Vera pulled on Vova's shirt, one button dangling on a thin thread. She went out for some air, but there was no air; it had been eaten.

Their floor–the second–was not large. Down below, an old woman was walking with a trolley. The trolley was moaning. Keening. It was hazy.

That summer the peatlands were burning. It was hell in Moscow. Where Vera and Vova were staying, outside the city, as recently as yesterday there had been air. That was yesterday; today, the air had turned to ash. Smoke filled the lungs. There was no light to be seen.

Vera held on to the railing with her narrow hand. Three steps and the old woman was gone. A bluish haze and a moan.

Vera went back and knelt in front of the sleeping Vova. She brought her face close to his shoulder and touched it with the tip of her tongue. Salt and bitterness.

They packed in a hurry. The flat belonged to someone else, and they didn't know where anything was. They looked for coffee, couldn't find any, and drank plain water instead. They brushed their teeth with the same brush. There was a shelf in the wardrobe, a sewing box on the shelf, a needle in the box. Hidden like Koschey's death. Vera sewed the button on firmly. She pricked her finger, and Vova licked the scarlet bead. No time for anything except to fly. Pity. Lock the door, wrap the key in a piece of paper, shove it in the letterbox. The landlord would find it when he came. He had snuck away from the fires into the country beyond the curtain–beyond the screen of smoke.

The truck was parked by the pond. Vera's house with its metal roof would have fitted into it, like into a whale's belly, along with the chimney, the terrace, the two apple trees, the black bird on a black branch, and the bench, and her mother, and her little sister Sonia, and the cat, Milka.

'I don't need any help,' said Vera.

She scrambled into the cab, into the driver's seat, and placed her narrow hands on the steering wheel.

'Action! Start her up!' cried Vova.

'Engine, sir!'

She turned the key once, twice, and started the great beast rolling.

'Only as far as the turn,' Vova warned her sternly.

'I'll go round it. I can do it.'

'No. Stop before it.'

'To the main road.'

'To the turn.'

'I'll throw you out of the cab.'

'Quiet! Yo!'

She took the turn anyway. As he had taught her. With her own slender hands. Vova bit his lip but did not interfere. He was running with sweat.

'Smoke. Put the headlights on. That's enough. Get out, Vera. That's it. I'm serious.'

They swapped places. He eased the truck out onto Yaroslavka and stopped at the kerb. They kissed.

'Drive carefully.'

'Relax.'

'Call.'

'Affirmative, Comrade Commander.'

Vera was Vova's Comrade Commander. Of course.

She had sewn his button on and smoothed his curls. He looked good.

'Time.'

She jumped off the running board and stood below, small, not waving, watching him go off into the haze. Still, he was going away from the fires, and would soon emerge into the light, into the air.

She stood at the roadside. The smoky haze swallowed up the cars, the headlights. Summer. June.

A big bus to Sergiev Posad rolled by. Behind the illuminated windows (each one a magic lantern), people were sitting. One of them turned. It all happened so fast, like lightning.

ELENA DOLGOPYAT

Vera suddenly shouted, 'Hey!'

And rushed after the bus.

She could have run to Sergiev Posad, thirty kilometres, oh, comfortably, easy as you like. She was cheerful, and the smoky air did not hamper her breathing at all. She was young, strong, alive. She turned down into the still-sleeping village. What time was it there? Not yet five, Sunday morning, the morning of resurrection.

Her steps were weightless, and the grey air was hiding the corners, the bushes. Vova was on his way, and she was running.

At the sports ground by the school, she stopped. The parallel bars. She stroked the smooth, dry wood. Secured her grip, and broke away from the ground. Underswing. Dismount.

Vera landed and saw a small figure, short, frail. Curly-haired Kolya was standing by the bars. His hands were full: in one hand he had a box and in the other he had a box. The two white hulks were tied with ribbons. Vera jumped down and bowed. Kolya, at a loss, bowed back. Small, skinny, freckled. Vera burst out laughing. Her teeth were white and even, and her eyes crinkled when she laughed. Kolya smiled back, his mouth wide.

'Been watching long?'

'No, I was just walking.'

'Far?'

'Home.'

'Oh, Kolya, you spent the night away from home? Congratulations.'

'No. Thank you. No. I was at home. But you can still congratulate me. It's my birthday. I've been to my aunt's to get cakes.'

He lifted the white boxes an inch or two.

'She bakes. You have to get in early 'cos she takes them to Moscow, to order. She takes a big order to Moscow. They cost an arm and a leg. You've never eaten anything like them. You must come. We're starting at seven this evening. I've invited everyone, we'll all be there, about twenty of us, totally, everyone's coming.'

'That won't be enough for twenty.'

'They're ginormous. Plus they're from Palych.'

'"They're from Palych" is not a recommendation. "They're from Palych" is a minus.'

'Come. Pretty please, Vera.'

'There's something strange about your invitation, Kolya. Random. Polite people give out invitations in advance, but here you are, out of nowhere, on the fly. I'm offended.'

Vera was saying she was offended, but her eyes were crinkling and she was laughing, green cat fire in her eyes.

'No, look I've been thinking about you all the time. I even went to your house. Stood there. Went away again. Scared.'

'What, you're afraid of me?'

'You make fun of me.'

'Well, Kolya, all the more reason not to invite me. You don't want me there scaring you. You have fun. Dance.'

Kolya was silent, unable to answer. Vera headed off. Soon she would be hidden in the grey mist.

'Vera,' Kolya called. 'Dimon'll be there.'

Vera looked round.

'He got in from St Petersburg yesterday.'

Vera kept going. Her voice came from the gloom, shouting: 'Happy birthday, Kolya!'

It was going to be a nice day. Hot, dry. Smoky.

It smells like hell, was what Vera's mother said. She had lost the ability to laugh; she was tired of life. She was a little over forty, but looked like she had already swapped her fifth decade for her sixth. It was not that her hair was grey; it was the colour of chestnuts, and her face was unlined. But it was obvious at once that this was someone who had been on this earth a long time. Living, losing her lustre, declining.

There was a light on in their house. Vera was surprised to see it so early. She stood by the picket fence, observing the window. She pulled a leaf off a currant, and chewed.

All right, no point standing here. Go in.

They had already had breakfast, but not yet cleared the table. Vera was suddenly pleased that there were crumbs on the table, the knife and a slice of bread on the board, and the smell of porridge and milky coffee.

Her mother did no more than bark out, 'Look who's here.' She didn't say much. She was tired of saying useless words; she only ever kept to the point. She was tying a bow in Sonia's plait.

Vera settled herself at the table and smeared a slice with softened butter. Her mother gave her an angry look. Sonia stood quietly, patiently, in her blue chiffon dress, squinting at her reflection in the half-open mirrored wardrobe door. It was twilight in the looking-glass, and a smell of lavender wafted out from it, the smell of a world where autumn had not yet arrived. In the room, though, there was the smell of burning.

'Water the tomatoes, water the cucumbers and apples. The potatoes. There's porridge in the pot. Tidy away the crockery. Don't turn your phone off.'

'OK, OK, yes, obviously. How far are you going?'

'You only think about yourself.'

'We're going to the theatre,' said Sonia.

'Yes, that's right.'

'And afterwards to Galina's,' said Mother. 'We're spending the night there.'

'Yes, I remember. Yes.'

'Don't smoke, OK? You'll burn the house down and we'll be begging on the streets.'

Mother left Sonia and fished a long, pearl grey coat out of the world behind the looking-glass.

She dressed, dusted herself with pale powder, and put in earrings as clear as her eyes. She was transformed. Not younger, but different, unfamiliar. Alien. She squirted scent from a faceted bottle.

'Me too!' (Sonia.)

'Shut your eyes. Tight.'

Sonia did.

'That's enough,' said Vera. 'Open up. Come here, I'll fix your sash. There you go. You smell tasty. The wolf will have his eyes on you instead of Little Red Riding Hood.'

'Why are you frightening her?'

'I'm not scared!'

'Sonia's the new generation, she's not afraid of anything.'

'Except for crumpling her dress.'

'Oh, Sonia, really? What about when you're on the bus?'

'I'll stand.'

'And the train? A whole hour!'

'I'll stand.'

'And the metro?'

'Stand.'

'Yes but the theatre. They won't let you stand there. The play won't start until you sit down. The audience will be yelling at you.'

Sonia said nothing. She went red, and was ready to cry.

'She'll be very careful how she sits. I'll help. Nothing's going to get crumpled. And nobody's going to start yelling at you, don't listen to her, child. Come on, let's go, or we'll miss the bus. We need to pick up water at the station.'

At the door, Sonia turned round and stuck her tongue out at Vera, and Vera answered by shaking her fist, small and strong.

How good, how wonderful that they had gone away, that today was Sunday, and she was off duty and the whole day lay ahead, big and round like a ripe apple.

ELENA DOLGOPYAT

Vera collapsed onto the couch and lay looking into the corner with its tapestry of grey cobwebs. This room was their kitchen-dining-room (gas cooker, sink, sideboard), mother's bedroom (couch, wardrobe), and a sort of living room (two pairs of creaky old chairs). Vera and Sonia had their own little room (two bunks, a mini-wardrobe, a table, a couple of bookshelves, a toybox). On good evenings they would whisper and play silly games or draughts and Sonia would fret when she lost and Vera would be happy to let her win. Not always, though.

Vera lay there, idle, not interested in moving or talking, not even with Vova, if he should suddenly call. She nodded off, woke up, stretched, and went on lying there. She heard someone knocking on the door and coming in (that's right, the door's unlocked, come right in, you cocky fellow). And still she lay there, not moving.

Footsteps in the solarium. Along the corridor. A knock at her door.

Vera was silent.

The door opened a crack and a head poked through.

'Hi.'

Vera did not answer.

'What's up? Are you on your own? Are you ill?'

'I don't know. What do you want?'

Not answering at once, Irina, Vera's onetime classmate, came into the room, sat down sideways to the table, and pushed at a crumb. She looked darkly at Vera, and asked, 'Are you going?'

'I'm lying down.'

'This evening. To Kolya's.'

'Don't know. No.'

'Good, thank you.'

'I thought you were here to try and persuade me.'

'No. I'm here to talk you out of it. I came to ask you not to go.'

'Why?'

'You know why.'

'I don't.'

'Yes you do.'

'Well, let's suppose I don't know. Tell me.'

'Vera, you're a snake.'

'You won't talk me out of it like that.'

Irina suddenly dropped from the chair onto her knees and crawled towards the couch.

'Vera, please, I'm begging you, don't go. Dima's arrived, he'll be there, you know how I ... what do you want with him, you already have a boyfriend and you know how I ... and if you go he won't even see me, *caput*, *finito*, sure as God made little fishes.'

'OK I won't go.'

'You mean it?'

'Word of honour. Get off your knees. I'm not an icon.'

'Thank you.'

Irina stood up. She barely restrained herself from bowing to the floor.

'Hey.' Irina had reached the door when Vera stopped her and addressed her skinny back. 'Wait.'

She opened the wardrobe, both leaves. In there were kept her mother's things, Vera's, and Sonia's. Mother said: a communal wardrobe.

When she was very tiny, Vera used to play in the compartment, and inside the compartment it was always the dead of night. Only a narrow strip of light oozed in where she had not quite pulled the door to. Her father had explained that she must leave a crack for air, and once upon a time Vera had pulled the door tight shut without leaving a crack because she really wanted to die, but nothing had come of it; the air had got in anyway, and thank God, she had cried a little and come out.

'Look,' said Vera. 'A dress. Never been worn. A dress like this ... sizzling.'

'It's blue.'

'A blue sizzle. And with your eyes ... look out, boys. It's German. My father sent it to me. I don't want to wear it and I won't. It's just taking up space.'

'No, no way. What are you doing, Vera? What's your point?'

'Try it on.'

'I'm sweaty.'

'Everyone's sweaty these days. So.'

'Turn away.'

Vera went over to the window. She looked at the apple tree with its silver leaves, some already fallen. She felt sorry for the apple tree and all living things.

'OK.'

Vera turned round.

'Ooh, that is *so*.'

Ira said nothing. She went on studying herself in the mirror. 'You won't be sorry?'

'That's not me. I can't be sorry about stuff.'

'I'll tell them you've come down with something.'

'Don't say anything. And don't say anything about the dress, about you got it from me, OK? Why even do that.'

'You've really never worn it?'

'Not even tried it on. I promised mother I wouldn't throw it away, to stop her crying.'

'Can't you forgive your father?'

'Stick to your own knitting.'

Ira left with the dress in a rustly bag, and Vera drifted around the room. The window was closed tight, but the air was still bitter and turbid. Vera went out into the garden, and at first it seemed a little easier out in the open air. She set to watering the bedraggled plants with the hosepipe. She felt they were thanking her. The plants, the little creatures, the earth itself.

Vera hauled an old camp bed out of the closet and lay down in the shade, under the apple tree.

The canvas was sagging, and lying was uncomfortable, but Vera had no interest in getting up or even moving. She looked at the motionless leaves, then dropped her hand and touched the grass, damp after her watering. She closed her eyes. Tuned in to the sounds.

The distant hum of Yaroslavka.

'Kostya! Kostya!'

Come on, Kostya. Answer.

Shhhh.

What's shhhh? Shish? Shish who?

Ah. The neighbours were watering their garden. *They should crank it up, turn it into rain, then we could breathe.*

Vera jumped awake in twilight. Her tee-shirt was stuck to her sweaty body.

I need a drink.

Vera turned her head. The cat was sitting on the porch, watching.

I need a drink.

That was who had been asking for a drink. The cat.

Vera turned onto her side, and she and the wheezing, clattering camp bed toppled over onto the grass, long since dried.

They drank, Milka from a little bowl, Vera from a mug. Vera splashed the rest on her forehead.

'What time is it?' she asked Milka. She stroked the cat's little head.

Six-thirty came the reply from behind the neighbour's fence.

The radio. Or the television. Not important. Early for twilight. Smoke everywhere, eating up space and time.

'Milka, chop-chop, let's go in.'

In the house it seemed freer. There was a reason why Mother had battened down the windows. Vera fished some sausage out of the fridge. A slice for herself, a slice for the cat. Turned on her laptop. Watched a couple of episodes of *The Living Dead*. At the beginning of the third, when he suddenly turns round and there are holes instead of eyes and his mouth has rotted, Vera heard a muffled, measured knock. She crept stealthily across to the window. Not that she was frightened. Standing on the steps wearing a garish shirt was Dimon. In person. Dimych. Dmitry Olegovich.

He would not come in. Said he would wait on the steps. Said he'd promised everyone there that he'd bring her.

'The birthday boy got down on his knees and begged. Pleaded.'

Vera, of course, refused, but if truth be told, without energy. For the sake of order (her father used to say: to provide a veneer).

'You've talked me into it. Rogue.'

'I'm waiting.'

'Wait.'

He stood on the steps. Nothing stirred in the little garden.

'Why are you smoking?' someone was saying. 'Breathe the air. The difference is precisely zilch.'

Vera decided to dress simply, nothing too flashy. She changed her T-shirt and gave herself a squirt of her mother's perfume. She thought for a moment, then opened the sideboard and chose a mug with Gagarin on the side.

She and Dimon ambled along, in no hurry. Past the five-storey houses, beyond the pond, across the sports ground. Dimon told her how he was settling into St Petersburg. Vera listened, smiling. Dimon had once nicknamed her Mona Lisa for her smile or, rather, her half-smile. But he rarely called her that. And never in public.

'So, Lisa, what's with you?'

'Nothing. Didn't get a free place. I'll try again.'

'You'll get in. You're smart.'

'I'm a scatterbrain.'

'Get a grip.'

'Uh-huh.'

They walked round an old Lada, eaten away by rust, and looked in its dusty mirror.

'I hear you're at the hospital now? Good decision. You'll pass. You're a shoe-in for an external place at least. You seen dead bodies?'

'Yes.'

They'd got as far as the fire station. There was a bus parked at the terminus, empty, doors wide open. The driver was in the cab reading a book with the window down.

'Probably a detective story.'

'*War and Peace.*'

'Shall we ask him?'

'No.'

'Don't you want to know?'

'No.'

'Vera, come to Petersburg as well.'

'I have a boyfriend here.'

'So I've heard.'

They reached Kolya's house without saying another word. Like Vera's, Kolya's was a one-storey house, but somewhat bigger and newer, with a bigger plot. Music rumbled through the wide open windows.

'I'm going home.'

'No, Vera, no. I promised Kolya.'

'Well next time don't promise. Here. Give him this mug from me. Tell him to reach the heights. Like Gagarin.'

She walked along the street of one-storey houses, and the rumble of the music quickly faded into the distance. She picked up an ice-cold beer at a corner shop. She settled herself down not far away, at the bus stop, perching on the bench under the canopy. Like in a cave. She sat there, sipping at her beer. The time ... was whatever it was. Vera had left her phone at home, and there was no-one to ask. Nor did she even want to.

It was dark. Night. A car found room for itself alongside the pavement across the road. Music boomed and growled. Mother would say: Poor neighbours.

Vera finished her beer and was sorry she had picked up only one bottle. She could pop to the shop ... no. No. Too hot. And the smell of burning from everything, from her own hair. Two cars rolled by, one after the other, taxis. No light on inside, windows down, laughter, talking. And a third taxi. Laughter, talking.

Vera went on sitting.

The music had pretty much died down. Nothing. Not even half a sound. Silence like death. Footsteps.

Ha. Kolya. Slicing straight down the road, along the kerb, waving his arms.

Vera did not hail him; she did not budge. He passed by, and thank goodness for that. The air was heavy, even though she was in an open space. There were garages across the road, and beyond them a field.

Vera lay down supine on the bench, hands behind her head, legs bent at the knees. A dog came over and sniffed at her.

'Go away,' commanded Vera.

The dog went. Animals always obeyed Vera. They recognised her.

Footsteps. Kolya. Coming back. Not empty-handed. He was carrying a bag. Beer, possibly.

Vera whistled. Quietly, but Kolya heard it and stopped, on his guard. He came closer and peeked under the awning.

'Beer?'

He opened the bag. Bread. 'Vera, what are you doing? he said. 'Let's go to my place.'

'I don't want to be in a crowd.'

'There isn't a crowd. They've all cleared off. Dimon's got a plane or a train, I don't remember, long story short, they went to see him off.'

'Train is my guess. Sapsan.'

'Probably.'

'Who you carting bread about for?'

'My father. He'll come back after his shift and have a bite to eat. He doesn't eat anything without bread. Not even porridge.'

'He have ice cream with bread?'

'He doesn't like ice cream. Come on, Vera. There's no-one else there.'

'Any food left?'

'Loads. Mother, you know, a ton of everything: salads, pies, meat.'

'Her magic cake?'

'Scrumped.'

'Well, I don't know. I was thinking cake might tempt me.'

'Vera, pretty please. Let the pie tempt you. You know what kind of pie it is. Lemon!'

'How come it didn't get finished?'

'I saved some. For morning. For when I'm soaking up the quiet ambience.'

Vera sat on the bench, swinging her leg. Kolya stood like a supplicant, waiting.

'What about coffee?'

'Coffee! The real thing! I have a coffee machine. I'll make you coffee you won't get in any café!'

Vera grinned, got up, and walked off down the small street. Kolya kept up, trotting along the kerb like a slave, like a submissive dog.

'You afraid of your father?'

'Eh? No.'

'You went scampering off to buy bread for him.'

'Like that's a big job? I understand him. He has it hard. Mother too. I'm sorry for them.'

'You're a good person, Kolya.'

'Me? No. But I do try.'

'I don't try.'

'You can do it without trying.'

'I don't know. I don't bother.'

Kolya's house was right at the back of the plot, behind the cherry trees.

The windows were wide open and pitch dark. A light suddenly flared. Vera and Kolya froze at the wicket.

'Who's there?' whispered Kolya.

'Your parents?' Vera whispered back.

'No! How? Why?'

'Why didn't you close the windows? It's not like you. Such a thorough, thoughtful chap, goes to get bread for his dad, and what do you know, windows.'

'I thought I'd air the place. It's reeking of smoke.'

'The air we've got at the moment, you can't ventilate a thing.'

'The air's all right now.'

The sound of delicate glass clinking came from the open window.

'Interesting,' said Vera.

She opened the wicket and headed soundlessly across the grass towards the window. At that very moment, in the frame of the lighted window appeared the figure of a young lad. His mouth was shining with grease and he was chewing, his eyes squinting above prominent cheekbones. He was standing quietly, his powerful shoulders squared.

'The Boar,' said Kolya.

'Ah,' said the lad. 'There you are.'

He filleted Vera with narrow, sharp eyes.

There was indeed a mountain of food. Kolya's mother had excelled herself. The party had packed plenty away, but there was as much again left, if not more.

Kolya set out the bread. The Boar noiselessly flipped out the blade of a folding knife, rapidly planed the bread into slices, and began to wolf it down with melting aspic, Olivier salad, dressed herring, pickles, and potatoes boiled whole. Kolya fetched ice-cold vodka from the fridge, and The Boar tipped back one shot and chased it straight down with another. He poured one for Vera, and she did not refuse. Kolya drank flat apple juice from his Gagarin mug.

Introductions did not take long. Kolya said, 'Vera, my classmate. The Boar. I mean Sergey. We work together.'

'So what should I call you—The Boar or Sergey?'

His behaviour was not marked by inhibition.

'The reason I'm late,' said The Boar, crunching his way through a spicy Korean carrot, 'is I was looking for a present. No point buying a bottle—you're teetotal. And I don't know what you like. So I thought perhaps I could buy you a shirt—would always come in handy. Then I thought, what am I, a girlie, giving shirts? I'll give you a thousand rubles to buy yourself whatever you want. So that's what I'm doing. Here you are. It's yours.'

'Thank you.'

Kolya picked up the thousand-ruble note The Boar had laid out, rolled it up, and tucked it into the pocket of his light summer trousers.

'You thought about that for ages,' remarked Vera.

'Wrong. I thought fast. A lot, though. Because at that point question number two came up: what to wear. There are going to be girls, I was thinking. I want them to like me. So I shave and brush my teeth and take a shower. But what to wear? That stumped me. Impossible to breathe outdoors, impossible to breathe at home, same shit in the car. Even so, shorts and a tee-shirt? Please. Short-sleeve shirt. That's a thought. Except I don't have a short-sleeve shirt. Flog myself down the shop? Hmmm. Trousers. Something summery. Nope, cupboard's bare. Shorts and jeans. Pinstripe suit, except that's for a funeral–mine, basically. Time marching, me fuming, shop closing. I make up my mind: OK, that's the way it's got to be. I'm not going anywhere. A ton of people, all strangers, no-one I know except, of course, the birthday boy. Good health, my friend. Turn on the TV, lie down on the sofa, watch some kind of crap, fall asleep, wake up when it's practically evening. I think, that was a weird day. And why am I lying here? I want to go and be with people and what difference whether I'm in shorts or wearing a tie. Which, by the way, I don't have. So I get on the road. As you can see. I walk up to the house and hello great clanging silence. Strange. The windows are all open and beyond the windows it's as dark as night. Have I hauled my butt to the right place? I knock on the door. Quiet. But the smell wafting out the open windows is lipsmackingly good. And I'm hungry. Come on, I think, at least have a gander at what's in there.'

'What a motormouth,' said Vera.

'Exclusively under the influence of alcohol.'

The Boar poured himself another shot, and a shot for Vera. Kolya looked at The Boar with delight and at Vera with fear and adoration.

'Good health, my friend.' The toast remained unchanged.

The Boar had eaten his fill, and now fished out his cigarettes. He offered them to the lady first.

They smoked. Kolya, of course, refused.

'You know what your problem is,' said the Boar. 'You don't know how to relax. You're always on the alert, always in control. That's not helpful. It makes people throw themselves in front of trains.'

'I'm not planning to do that.'

'The thing with control is, the more there is of it, the worse it gets. It's like tightening a nut. One turn is good, two turns is good, but three and you break the thread. You need to know how to switch off.'

'Teach me,' Vera volunteered suddenly.

The Boar looked at her through narrowed eyes.

'You really don't know?'

'Not the way I'd like.'

'People, you are a mess. What about you, Kolya? Don't you want to learn? It might come in handy.'

'Yes, he does. Come on, teach us.'

Vera reached for her shot glass, where a drop of vodka remained undrunk. The Boar intercepted the glass and pushed it away.

'If you're going to relax, you need a clear head.'

'Alcohol relaxes you completely.'

'That's not quite right, my dear. As you see on boxes of medicine, there's a whole heap of side effects. For example, you want to stand up, but can't. The floor comes out from under your feet and other such miracles. No, my little friends, that is not our way. First, we'll have an invigorating coffee and sober up.'

'I am sober,' objected Kolya.

'You've overdosed on fumes,' grinned Vera.

The Boar cut them off. 'Everyone will drink coffee,' he announced.

'I'm fine with that. I'll make it.'

'No, my friend, I'll make it myself. You two sit here and have a rest.'

'I've got a coffee machine.'

'Calm down. I'll manage.'

He went out. Something clinked in the kitchen, a bit of rustling. Then the rumble of the coffee machine and the sweet smell of coffee.

'Arabica,' boasted Kolya. 'From Kenya. Premium grade.'

Vera smiled her Mona Lisa half-smile and did not answer. Kolya became awkward and fell silent. But he never took his eyes off Vera, as if he really had gulped down an excess of alcohol fumes and become brave.

The Boar brought in three cups on a chopping board instead of a tray.

'That's not a machine you've got there, it's a locomotive.'

He placed a cup in front of Vera. He placed a cup in front of Kolya.

He settled himself down. Grasped the thin, rounded handle.

'Well, cheers.' He drank his down in two gulps.

Vera sipped her coffee slowly. Her head really was clearing. Kolya seemed to be waiting for something, and kept looking at them.

'You should drink espresso hot,' said The Boar. 'Cold espresso is dead espresso.'

Kolya obediently picked up his cup and drained it.

'Not bitter?'

'No.'

'Thank goodness. I was afraid the tablet would make it bitter. I dissolved a pill in your coffee, each of you. It'll start working soon.'

'Meaning?' Vera became flustered.

'Your control will weaken, and you'll become authentic.'

'You nuts?'

'Well you agreed.'

'Not to a tablet I didn't.'

'So what did you want? Hypnosis? I can't do that. No, this tablet's the right answer. Tried and trusted. And it's not a drug, don't be afraid. No side effects. Word of honour.'

They sat there looking at one another.

'So?' asked Vera. 'What now?'

'I don't know. We'll see.'

'You didn't fail to dissolve a tablet in your own, I trust?'

'Failed. Didn't feel like it.'

'Pig.'

'I'm a boar, Vera. Remember that.'

Vera made no reply. She plastered some bread with butter and started chewing.

'Where do you ply your trade?' The Boar asked her.

'Where I'm needed. Today in Mum's garden.'

'She works in town, at the hospital,' Kolya suddenly butted in.

'Nurse?'

'Orderly.'

The Boar put his questions to Vera, and Kolya answered.

'Your tablet is having a peculiar effect on him,' remarked Vera.

'Should I lie down so you can examine me?' asked The Boar.

'You'd like me to take your bedpan out when you're done? You're welcome.'

'A bedpan is too much.'

'So what do you want?'

The Boar did not answer. He fixed her with a stare that was very watchful, and, most likely because of that, very serious.

'She hasn't gone to med school,' said Kolya, picking up his cue.

'I'm going to take you on as a secretary, Kolya. In a voluntary capacity.'

'What department have you applied to?'

Vera looked at Kolya, and he responded instantly. 'Paediatrics.'

'Good choice. You'll get in.'

'I don't know. I'm not sure.'

'I'll get in next year, I'm sure of that,' said Kolya loudly and clearly. 'You think I'm going to be your errand boy forever, Boar: bring me this, wash that, close this, open that, hose, oil, polish? Suck it up. I'll get in. I'm preparing. I'll be someone and you'll stay in this backwater and croak. Ten years from now I'll come and take a look at you and you'll be so happy to see me you'll kiss my hands. You too, Vera. What are you so proud of? You look after stinking sick people? They slip you a hundred roubles and you're happy.'

'Oh,' said Vera. 'Well, well, well.' She burst out laughing.

'And what are you going to be?' The Boar asked good-naturedly.

'I'll be in politics.'

'Shooting for president?'

'Emperor,' said Vera.

'Why wait? I'm doing this right now.'

The Boar got up, walked round the table, bowed at Kolya's feet, and caught up his hand and kissed it.

Kolya looked contemptuous.

'How long does your pill last?'

'About an hour. Or a bit longer. About that.'

'Oh. Ages yet.'

'You bored?'

'Well how about you? You having fun?'

'I'm not bored, I'll say that much.'

'Why isn't it having any effect on me?'

Kolya suddenly turned to her. 'What about you? Aren't you going to kiss my hands?'

'Wash them with soap.'

'Kiss them like this. As they are. Then I'll feel sorry for you later.'

'OK, I'm off. Knock yourselves out.' Vera started to get up.

'Wait a minute.'

'Wait for what?'

'Finish your sandwich.'

'Where's he gone? Hey, Kolya!'

'Gone to get his crown.'

'The things he wants, though.'

'Nothing special.'

Kolya had meanwhile returned, silently, with dignity. Water was dripping from his wet hands. He approached Vera.

'I've washed them. Kiss them.'

'What stopped you drying them?'

'The towel's filthy.'

He stood there, waiting, looking at her coldly.

Vera smirked, and stepped towards him. Bowed. Kissed one hand, kissed the other. The Boar let out a bray of laughter. He was enjoying himself. Vera undid the buttons on Kolya's shirt. She pulled off the shirt. Kolya stood, arms outstretched, like a little boy. Lost. Pathetic. Vera unbuttoned his trousers and his trousers fell down. Vera pulled Kolya's pants down, down his legs and onto the floor. She spoke softly, like a pigeon cooing. 'You're as skinny as a minnow.'

She stroked his scrawny blue body with her hand. He knelt. The Boar grunted. 'Ouch, this is not easy to watch.'

He watched anyway.

Kolya saw nothing; tears had blurred his vision.

All of a sudden, Kolya went limp and collapsed on to the floor, clocking his chair and sending it toppling. Vera got down on her knees and looked at him lying there. She stood back up and, unruffled, said to The Boar: 'Help me.'

They heaved the naked Kolya onto the couch and covered him with his own shirt. They looked at each other.

The Boar raised a large hand and gently stroked Vera's head. He looked into her face. Cupped his palms around her head. Kissed her on the lips. Vera found a perch on the edge of the table. They hurried; the table shivered, the crockery toppled over, a stain spread beneath the vodka glass, adding to the stains already decorating the tablecloth that Kolya's mother had spread out white and pristine.

His mother had set out the crockery and roasted the meat in the oven. She'd sliced up salads, working through the night until morning, and had left some money in case there was anything else they needed to buy. Then she'd kissed Kolya and left for her sister in Korolyov. Kolya's father was working that day. He was due back by ten o'clock the next morning. Mother had warned Kolya that she would be back early, by eight o'clock, to give herself time to clean up, so as to greet Kolya's father with peace and quiet and an atmosphere of contentment.

She arrived as promised, and found the house in perfect order. The dishes had been washed clean and put away, and the floor was shining wet. The heavy linen tablecloth was in the laundry basket; understandable. A fresh liner had been tucked into the rubbish bin.

Kolya was not in the house, and his mother decided that he had gone out to take the rubbish to the container.

Kolya's mother was not exactly overjoyed by the cleanliness. There was something unsettling, unnatural about it. She went through the house and found a cigarette butt on the window sill. Her anxiety eased a little.

The floor was drying out. Mother went out onto the steps. Beyond the fence, a heavy, overcrowded bus lumbered by. Mother made her way down the path, and heard a dull thud. She rushed towards the barn without realising what she was doing or why. She pushed open the door and saw Kolya sitting on the earthen floor. Around his neck was a noose. A piece of frayed rope hung from the beam overhead. Mother rushed to son, wailing, repeating over and over, 'What have you ..., oh, oh, I'm here now, it's alright, it's alright, oh, oh, oh.'

She brought him into the house, washed him, changed his clothes, gave him a sedative, put him onto the tightly-made cot in his quiet bedroom, drew the curtains, and sat down beside him. She stroked his hand as he fell asleep.

Until a few hours previously, the bed in his parents' bedroom had been a wreck. Vera and The Boar had slept with their arms round each other. They woke up simultaneously, and simultaneously moved away from each other. Vera got up as she was, naked, without a word. The Boar, too, was silent. He didn't move a muscle; merely watched. Vera went into the main room. Kolya was still lying on the couch, only his back was turned and his face was pressed into the backrest, his legs tucked up. He might have been breathing and he might not. Vera dressed and went out. Kolya stared into the couch back, at the herringbone fabric, of which he had known every line since he was tiny. He heard The Boar blunder in and also get dressed. Only not silently; swearing softly, indistinctly. He went out, too. Kolya heard a train chuntering by, a long, long way off. They were about five kilometres from the railway: a long way. Kolya stood up, to all appearances calm. He dressed, and set to the business of clearing up. He became more and more wound up, burning with rage. As far as he was concerned, he was very definitely thinking of nothing at all the whole time.

When his father returned, Kolya was still asleep. His mother made no mention to his father of the noose around their son's neck. Kolya told his mother privately that he had only a hazy recollection of what he'd been doing.

'I mustn't drink, I've got that much. Not a drop.'

And never again in his whole life did Kolya let alcohol pass his lips.

* * *

Four-something. Almost an exact repeat of the previous morning. Vera was not thinking of anything. She walked through deserted streets and courtyards. There were cars everywhere; the earth had been killed by cars, and no living thing could take root in it any more. The asphalt of the

ELENA DOLGOPYAT

children's playground was crumbled and cracked; the grass had been given free rein, and Vera found herself wandering through flaccid grass. Birds sang, or rather spoke, but as if past her hearing, on a different wavelength. The air was brightening, and rare, solitary lights burned in the windows.

She could not remember reaching the station and looking at the train.

Approaching and racing through their tiny station, a speck of dust in the expanse of the world. The wind.

Vera was not aware of any of this at the time, but then she suddenly remembered. The train bobbled to the surface, the wind, the golden circle of light ...

Along the street, at the place where one-storey houses once again stood to the left and right of five-storey houses, a dog came running. The dog tagged along behind Vera, but soon fell back, distracted by something of its own. Vera stopped at their old fence. Time was when her father had kept threatening to replace it, but he never had, and it was not something her mother even thought about; she did not like change. The old silver fence, the picket fence, by which the raspberries and cherry trees had spread effusively, not to mention the stinging nettles. Vera stood behind the bushes and looked at the dark window. There was a flash of light behind the white curtains, stitched way back when by her grandmother, but it went out at once, and the curtains parted. The garden was in shadow.

Vera saw her mother come out onto the steps. She was in her dressing gown, from beneath which a long nightdress peeked out. She put down a bowl of food for the cat, and looked around carefully. At the sky.

Over the earth there are no thick iron walls, no castles; only the air protects us from the harsh rays of space, the fierce heat of the sun, the black breath of the abyss. Such defenceless defence, almost nothing, but it keeps us safe. For a time.

Vera thought none of this; she simply stood, her head empty. As if she could remember nothing of what had happened to her, not yesterday, not the day before; as if she knew nothing about herself and it was easier that way. Her mother went back into the house. Vera could not see what came next, but she knew. Her mother woke Sonia up and made her wash. They had a breakfast of oatmeal. Through the window they could see the garden, and the bushes behind which Vera was standing. Standing like a graven image, her grandmother would say. Breakfast over, mother cleared away the dishes, and put in Sonia's long plait. Sonia purred a song, the words indistinguishable.

The door opened, and they came out.

Mother locked the door. Sonia squatted down and stroked the cat.

They came down the steps and walked along the path. Vera came to and retreated round the corner. She knew their route; she knew they would not turn that way. Her mother was taking Sonia to nursery school, across the road, towards the five-storey house, across the courtyard.

They disappeared from sight, and Vera made her way into the house. She dragged all her clothes off, even her shoes, and shoved them into a bag. She stood under a shower as hot as she could bear. She put on an old T-shirt and jeans and trainers and left the house, taking the bag with her. She did not look in the mirror once. On the way to the bus, she threw the bag in the rubbish container.

She walked to the bus stop. Her phone beeped in her pocket. Vera fished it out as she walked, and turned it off. The bus came rolling up, and Vera ran to keep up with it. She squeezed in and found herself stuck in the tight mass of passengers face to face with The Boar. The loaded bus lumbered unhurriedly on.

They looked past each other. But after perhaps a minute of the journey, The Boar began to cast glances at Vera, then

ELENA DOLGOPYAT

stare at her, breathe her air, take in her scent. He was very close to her.

They turned off the main road onto the country road. The passengers with a view looked out of the window at the field. A fog of smoke with sunlight at its edge. A bridge, a wood, a bend. The barrier up ahead, already lowering, red lights blinking.

The distant fires were burning the air. More patients were brought in. There were already beds in the corridors, and draughts found their way through the open windows and doors, and everywhere smelled of smoke, medicines, bleach. Vera ran to get water at the nearest shop for patients without visitors, scrubbed floors and utensils, handed out medication, took over from the nurse in the treatment room. 'You have a magic touch,' people told her. There was no way she could be idle for a moment that day; she did not want that. The sister in charge, seeing that Vera was not saying no to anything, loaded her with jobs, instructing her to change these sheets, give that patient a wash, feed this one, put up a drip, and Vera changed, washed, fed and put up without getting tired. The sister in charge watched Vera with eyes that were strange, always strange, as if they were addled, and her look disgusted Vera and she avoided it. And she thought that people with that look ought not be allowed anywhere near people who were sick and infirm; the patients were not in a position to turn away when she looked at them and said something with her old, painted mouth.

'Sister can hardly stand you,' Vera's friend said to her in the hospital canteen.

'She's a witch. She can't stand anyone. You watch out.'

A little woman on the cardiology ward asked Vera to place a candle for her, God's servant Olga, and Vera ran to the newly-built chapel near the hospital gate. It was the first time she had been there, and the inside of the chapel smelled like a cellar, and it was just as chilly and dark. A good place to escape the heat. Vera placed a slender ten-ruble candle before the Virgin and Child. In her head she said that it was for Olga's health, and she bowed before an image painted by a local artist who had come in for treatment in the spring, to confirm that he was still unable to work.

Vera went back to the main building and stood by the brick wall in the shade. For the first time that day she stopped. Slowly she smoked a cigarette. The dry grass did not stir, as if it was just waiting for a spark. Vera knocked her ash off neatly, onto the strip of concrete skirting the building.

She stubbed out her cigarette on the grey brick of the wall. She took out her phone, looked at the list of incoming calls, and called Vova. He answered instantly.

'Fine, fine. I turned it off and then forgot to turn it back on.'

She marvelled at the easy serenity of her own voice, and at his confidence, his steadiness.

'Drifted over to Kolya's in the evening. Birthday party. Yes, just to catch up with friends. Dimon came down from Petersburg. He's even more grown up now, deep bass voice. No, everything was fine. There was a ton of grub. Special kind of cakes, not my thing, I'd rather have pasta. I'll get one for you. Just once, so you don't get spoiled. How are you? How's Misha?' (Misha was Vova's partner.) 'Say hi to him, too. A big one. Big Hi. Oh, really? It's raining right now? I envy you. Love you too.'

She lowered her hand, still holding her silenced phone, and stood like that for a long time.

An ambulance pulled up to A & E. A stretcher was hauled out of the back doors. Two orderlies, swearing, heaved a hulking patient onto a trolley. In this heat the patient was wearing woollen socks, the heels neatly darned.

Her shift ended at eight o'clock in the evening. She stayed on for another hour, drinking tea with the girls.

ELENA DOLGOPYAT

She returned home and collapsed onto her bunk without even washing. The sun had not yet set, and was sending out long rays.

Vera woke up in the dead of night.

The windows were wide open. Smoke was hanging motionless in the electric light of the street lamp.

Vera discerned Sonia's party dress on the back of a chair. A small hand on a white sheet. She wanted to be out in the garden, but not as it was now. In autumn, when it was damp and the crows were cawing and a cold wind was blowing. Mother let out a sigh from her place. She said that she had long ago forgotten how to sleep; she never got into a deep sleep, just floated on the surface. She had been saying the same thing for a long time. When she was little, Vera had thought that her mother did not go off into a deep sleep because she was afraid of being smothered. Vera had no time to be afraid.

She thought she should buy sandals and some good quality mascara. Clarins. She thought trivial thoughts, and banished The Boar, Vova, and Kolya from her mind.

She jumped awake again in the dark. True, dawn felt near; the darkness had lost its denseness, its thickness.

Mother was leaning over Vera, holding her hand, and whispering.

'Shh. I've called the ambulance. Shh. They're on their way. If there's anything wrong, if they keep me in, take Sonia to nursery. Give her breakfast. Make oatmeal. Don't give her coffee whatever. She'll ask for it but don't give in. It's all right. It's a fever. It'll go down.'

Mother's fingers were ice-cold.

In the morning, Vera went to her mother's ward first thing. Nadezhda Semyonovna, as everyone there was already calling her, even the older ones, had been cleaning the window in the ward (you'll wait for ever for an orderly to do that). Vera caught her with a bucket of dirty water, carrying it to the door of the ward.

Vera grabbed the bucket.

'Mum, are you out of your mind?'

'I'm taking it gently. Taking it gently.'

'You need to lie down.'

'They'll discharge me tomorrow, you'll see. I feel good, I've had an injection and I feel so good I'm literally flying. There was no need to bring me in here. I'm ashamed of myself.'

No-one had any intention of discharging her. The doctor ordered her strictly to lie down, and if she did walk about, then to do so with care. Said she would be in for a fortnight for sure. Injections, tablets, a machine to monitor the workings of her heart throughout the day. The doctor was grey-haired and authoritative. Mother listened attentively.

She was lucky that a place had been found for her on the ward and not in the corridor. Those in the corridors were the first in line, but mother was fast-tracked because of her connection. She felt awkward when she was out walking in the corridor, but she had not wanted to refuse a favour, make a fuss, and draw extra attention. And anyway, very soon, as was invariably the case, her queue-jumping was forgotten. Within a couple of days, even the corridor-dwellers were calling her Nadezhda Semyonovna, and she was bringing them water on request and teaching them to darn their heels and dictating a recipe for jam as transparent as young honey.

Vera worked twelve hours at a time, two days on, two days off. On top of that, she had been left in charge of the house, with a little sister on her hands who not only had to be fed, washed, put to bed, taken to nursery and fetched home from said nursery, but also had to be jollied along, amused, and comforted.

Vera did not stay late after work; she rushed straight to the bus. Sonia would be standing by the window in the deserted nursery, looking out at the asphalt path. Vera always found her like that, at the window. She willed the bus on, and went into agonies if they suddenly got stuck in a traffic jam on the main road. Who knows what's happened up there. Perhaps there's been an accident. That was what she said to Sonia on the phone. She'd bought Sonia a cheap handset so that they could be in touch.

'We're moving, inching along but moving. The cars' headlights are on. Nothing we can do. It's an accident, for sure. I don't even want to look at what's happened. We're going round. That's it, we're moving normally now. Don't worry.'

The childcare assistant on duty at the nursery yawned occasionally.

Vera would come running in, handing her a hundred rubles or even two hundred when she was really late. The teacher, an old unmarried lady, lived not far from the nursery. They would leave together and walk together for a while, and the teacher would say she was going home to dream. She liked to sleep and dream, and said she wrote her dreams down in a special notebook.

'I even dreamed about you,' she said to Vera.

Perhaps she wanted to recount what Vera was doing in her dream, but Vera did not enquire.

'Good night.'

'I'll see you tomorrow,' replied the teacher.

'What does she spend our money on?' asked Sonia one time.

'Beer,' decided Vera.

'I'd spend it on ice-cream.'

'When I have a day off, you'll have an ice-cream.'

'Chocolate.'

She also needed to read to Sonia and listen to her talk. Along with washing, cleaning, cooking, watering, weeding. Vera was soon so worn out that all she could think about was lying down and closing her eyes. But the weekends were not too bad, a little freer, and Vera even got a taste for it, and caught herself occasionally telling Sonia off just as her mother did, with the same intonation.

'Don't grab me with your dirty hands!'

The moment she realised what she was doing, she would change her tone, and she and her sister would giggle.

They dressed up and walked together all the way to the station. Sonia would wave at the train. They would buy ice-creams and eat them right there on the platform, on the bench. In the distance, the smoke was visible.

They went to visit their mother. She would be waiting for them. Mother was sure Sonia had lost weight. Vera saw that her mother had changed, here where she had company, as if she had left her burdens at home. She spoke to Vera differently, too, treating her as an adult. They became closer.

In the second week of her mother's confinement in hospital, on the Wednesday, the bus got stuck in a traffic jam after Vera's shift. Vera called Sonia.

'Yes but I'm home,' said Sonia happily.

'You what? How? By yourself? I told you, no way!'

'I picked her up.'

'OK,' was all Vera said. 'I'm in a traffic jam.'

Vova. He's there. Well. Yes but that's right, he was supposed to come today. I talked to him yesterday. He was sitting in their house. Perhaps Sonia was showing him her dolls.

Vera looked out of the window. Yaroslavka was at a standstill. And that was fine.

She approached the house without hurrying.

A light was burning in the window.

The cat met her on the steps.

Vera was about to knock when the door was flung wide open, and Vera saw Vova, thin as a rake and sunburned. She suddenly howled, and threw herself on his neck. He embraced her, stroked her head and whispered, 'Whoa, whoa, shhh.'

The cat circled round them. Sonia watched.

They drank strong tea with milk. Vova told them about his journey. Vera didn't understand what he was saying, but smiled, watching him with shining wet eyes.

'I've missed you so much,' she said.

'Me too.'

At that moment, Vera saw the blue dress on the back of the sofa.

'Ah,' explained Vova. 'Ira brought it. She said it was unlucky.'

'I knew that,' said Vera, utterly and completely happy.

BIRTHDAY

I.

She could close her eyes and pretend that today hadn't yet started, that yesterday was still going on and she was twenty-nine and would be forever.

She opened her eyes. The clock showed her that she was six hours and three minutes into the new day. She could, of course, close her eyes again and pretend. But the day was already moving, clearly audible, taking its small steps: tick-tick-tock. Small, precise, and fast. Thirty years had ticked by, no matter how much she might pretend.

Vitya was in a deep sleep, lying on his back. His mouth was slightly open, his expression childish. Ira did not usually wake up this early. She wriggled her hand out from under the covers and wiggled her fingers. She needed a manicure. She needed to go to the hairdresser's. Crop it down to the scalp, perhaps? She wanted to cry. She eased herself carefully out of bed without disturbing Vitya. She took her clothes from the chair and dressed in the kitchen. All the dishes had been washed, which meant that Vitya had washed them late last evening. She had not even heard him. Perhaps she had been already asleep, or reading or chatting on the phone or surfing the internet. She had no recollection of yesterday. She genuinely could not remember. She came out of the kitchen and glanced into the main room. Vitya was snuffling. His large hand lay on the dark blue sheet, wedding ring gleaming on the ring finger.

She stepped out of the front entrance, lit a cigarette, and looked back at their big block. Many of the windows were already lit; it was a weekday, and people were getting ready for work. A neighbour came out, gave the smouldering fire in Ira's fingers a reproachful look, and said hello. The neighbour did not care that Ira was thirty today and that yesterday she had still been twenty-nine; she had no idea how old Ira was, and Ira had no idea how old her neighbour was. What difference did it make? Her neighbour headed for the bus stop, breaking into a run–the bus was coming just at that moment.

Ira remembered that something had disturbed her when she had been looking at the house. She turned round. Of course. She had forgotten to turn off the light in the kitchen. Vitya would grumble. He followed behind her turning off lights and taps and putting out her cigarette butts. He said that if it were not for him she would have burned the house down long ago. He was probably right. Vitya was a sweetheart. He did the laundry when she could not bring herself to do anything and was sitting prostrate in front of the screen not knowing even how to start. Vitya did not reproach her; he just did things. He loved her. Her, not someone beautiful and dreamed up.

In the coffee shop across the street the lights were already on. Were they really opening so early? Inside the little window was a display, a few tables, and a man in black sitting with a tiny cup. She finished her cigarette and headed across the street.

She bought a coffee and settled herself right at the back. The man in the black coat looked at her with old eyes.

It was a very pleasant coffee shop. The music was not thumping out, and the place was bright and cosy. She unbuttoned her anorak and unwound her scarf. She laid her cigarettes out on the table. Smoking was allowed here; there was an ashtray. Ira touched the faceted glass. It was ice-cold. She laid out her cigarettes, but did not light up; she hesitated. She sipped her coffee. It was excellent. Things weren't so bad for a new day in a new decade of life. The waiter behind the counter said to the young woman at the coffee machine, 'I had a dream about a dog today.'

The man in the black coat with the upturned collar got up from his table and headed across the room towards her. *No*, she thought, *not that. I don't want to talk to anyone.*

The man walked over, and grasped the back of an empty chair.

'May I?'

'Sorry, no, I would like to be alone.'

He did not hear what she said. He pulled out the chair and sat down. The table was tiny, and she could see his face right up close. His eyes looked at her with an old man's interest.

'Is everything all right?' he asked.

'Everything is wonderful,' she answered.

He was silent. He stared at her cup, at the steam rising above it.

'I would like–'. She got out the start of the phrase, but he did not let her finish.

'Then why are you so sad?'

'What?'

'You have sad eyes.'

'And you have old eyes!' she blurted out angrily, and immediately regretted her angry words. The man did not take offence. Perhaps he had not even heard her properly; he had selective hearing.

'What's happened?'

'Birthday.'

'Yours?'

'Well, yes.'

'A birthday is wonderful.'

'I don't want to get old.'

'Why not?'

'What a surprising question. Does anyone want to get old? People have mortgaged their souls just to hold on to their youth. Someone grew old instead of them. Someone died instead of them. Doesn't it spook you to watch your own ruination?'

'No.'

'You're lying.'

'I never lie.'

'There's no such thing as a person who never lies.'

'And what age are you attaining?'

'Thirty. Already attained.'

He reached into his pocket and pulled out a broken comb, a plastic lighter, a button, and a little box. Tiny, flat, cardboard, in a mica wrapping. He shoved the comb, the button and the lighter back into his pocket. He put the box on the table, and pushed it towards her cup.

'Happy birthday,' he said, and rose from the table.

Before she had time to object, he was already at the door, already leaving the coffee shop.

Ira touched her cup of coffee. It was still hot. She took a sip.

The box gleamed on the dark brown table top. The coffee machine hummed. The young lad said something, and the young woman burst out laughing. Ira picked up the box carefully, screwing up her short-sighted eyes. She read the inscription in tiny letters. *Take after eating. Possible contraindication during pregnancy: consult a doctor before use. Do not take with alcohol. Use when experiencing an acute reluctance to grow old.*

She tore off the mica wrapper, ripped off the cardboard lid, and saw a single white pill in the box. She sniffed it. The smell of school chalk.

The door opened, and in came a woman with a pale, stern face. She stuck her head into the display, which boasted pastries and croissants and buns and toasties.

'Can I help you?' asked the lad.

The woman did not reply. She went on staring fixedly at the display.

'These buns,' the lad proffered, 'are class. They've got raisins in. Still hot. I've eaten three of them myself.'

'Thank you,' said the woman. 'I don't eat any of that sort of thing. I can't. All I can do is admire. And you need to go easy. Three at once is rather a lot.'

'I have a fast metabolism.'

'You do now. But the time will come when you'll be like me, looking, longing, and unable.'

What the hell! Ira's temper flared. She was angry at herself, at the woman trying to satisfy her hunger with her eyes, at the young lad, who seemed to her too young and therefore too far away from her, at the rolls that were hot and tasty in the morning but stale and fit only for the bin by evening. Most importantly, she was angry at the old man who had left her this white tablet. Perhaps it was poison? She picked up the tablet and clinically put it into her mouth. She kept it in her mouth for a moment, feeling nothing, noticing no taste, and swallowed it. She did not manage to work out what, if anything, it tasted of. There was nothing to worry about. The young lad had a mobile phone; he would call an ambulance if need be.

She finished her coffee, bought some buns to take out with her, and went back home. Vitya had already put on the kettle. He said not a word about the light she had left on; it was her birthday, after all.

'Omelette for breakfast,' he said. The pan was already on the heat.

'I've picked up some buns. Classy, with raisins.'

'May I say Happy Birthday?' he asked carefully. Carefully, because only yesterday she had told him that she did not want to wake up on the day of her thirtieth birthday, she would not even open her eyes, she was not going to mark the day and open presents, she hated all presents in advance, she would throw everything in the bin.

'As you wish.'

'Wash your hands,' he said, setting about beating the eggs.

'They're clean.'

'Did you use the front door handle? Been handling money?'

'You are a pain in the neck.'

When she came out of the bathroom, the omelette was ready, and Vitya was taking the hot pan off the heat.

'Are we going to have a drink?' she asked, sitting down.

'Of course.'

'Oh. Surprise. You usually get angry when I suggest a drink in the morning.'

'Chardonnay. I'll go and get it. I put it to cool. Oh, by the way,' and he took an envelope out of his pocket and handed it to her. 'Happy birthday, sweetheart.'

'How interesting.' She looked at the envelope, but did not pick it up. 'What's in it? A cheque for a thousand euros? A three-month travel card?' She looked at Vitya, but Vitya said nothing. 'What then? I'm actually afraid.'

He smiled, put the envelope on the table beside her plate, and headed towards the fridge. She touched the envelope. There was something firm in there, stiff. He returned with the wine. Ira made no move to touch the envelope again.

He poured the wine into glasses.

'Aren't you interested?' he asked, referring to the envelope.

'I am.'

They toasted her birthday. They ate the omelette, which had already sunk but was delicious. Whatever Vitya cooked turned out tasty. Even though he made everything by eye. Ira occasionally asked if he did his chemistry in the lab by eye as well.

The envelope went on lying there. Ira dripped oil on it, but Vitya did not seem to notice. He started clearing away the table. In the end, just the envelope with its blotch of oil was left on the table top.

Ira suddenly felt her stomach ache, and she remembered the tablet. Poison! Slow-acting but sure; after it you would not age, because what old age was there after death. She was horrified at the thought, and at what she had stupidly done. She rushed to the toilet and stuck two fingers down her throat. Vitya knocked on the door, worried. She came out, her face wet with sweat, and asked him not to knock because his knocking was giving her a headache. Not to knock and not to look at her with those awful eyes. Everything was fine and it was time to go to work; no-one cancelled work for a birthday. She hastily put on her make-up, dressed, and tossed her mobile, keys, and cigarettes into her handbag. She grabbed the envelope from the table and it, too, she tossed into her bag. Vitya followed her into the hallway with a wet, freshly-washed plate in his hands. He kissed her on the lips. She touched her fingers to his cheek.

'When did you have time to shave?' she asked.

She opened the envelope on the trolleybus. The present turned out to be a trip to a warm, faraway sea; there was a publicity picture of it. Vitya had already arranged with her boss for her to take the time off.

A month after the holiday she discovered that she was pregnant. She wanted to have an abortion, and even went to the hospital, but while she was waiting in the queue for the gynaecologist to examine her, she suddenly changed her mind. She had no wish to remain in the company of the other women waiting in the queue for an abortion. They were talking about how the anaesthetic was bad and how much you had to give the anaesthetist to get a good one. One woman was giving instructions to her junior on her mobile, frightening her that she would check tomorrow.

ELENA DOLGOPYAT

Ira had her baby in December. A boy. She could not decide on a name for him. She called him 'My little ray of sunshine', or 'My boy'. Mostly 'My boy'. Vitya waited patiently for her to choose a name. He did not call his son 'My boy'. He said, 'Well, what do you think, son? Let's have a bath'. Ira climbed into the bath with their son and they laughed together, and Vitya smiled and sat on the rim with a terry towel at the ready. The boy slept peacefully. Still, Ira would wake up in the middle of the night and get up and go over to him. His little bed was near theirs.

So passed the thirtieth year of her life.

The boy reached two months, and as she fell asleep on the eve of her thirty-first birthday, Ira promised herself that the next day she would choose a name for him without fail. Pyotr. Or Sergey. Or Dima. Or Mikhail. And she would have to finish her thesis and take the oral, she thought, happily falling asleep, confident that she would finish it and receive her degree.

Vitya was already asleep. He always fell asleep instantly and soundly, and did not hear anything in his sleep. Ira very much wanted the boy to be as like his father as possible, to be just as calm, reliable, kind, and indulgent. Except that Vitya took up an awful lot of room when he was sleeping, sprawling over the entire bed. When we're rich, thought Ira, already asleep, snuggling up next to Vitya, breathing in his scent, we'll buy a new flat with a big bedroom and instal an enormous bed, king sized.

2.

Ira woke up in semi-darkness; the morning had barely begun. She did not feel like getting up. She wanted to close her eyes and pretend that this new year of her life had not yet started, that she was still twenty-nine, that she was still young and carefree, impetuous, smart, ready-tongued, and that men would look at her attentively and become flustered under her mocking gaze. Always, until the day she died. Ira had been at her mother's house recently, looking through the family album, and had seen her mother as a very young woman, twenty years old. For the first time, she had realised that her Mum had once been carefree and impetuous, and that it was only this photograph that could remember her so young; there was not a single person left who could remember her like that. At lunch, Ira had looked at her mother and seen herself in her, what she would be like when she grew old. She did not want it. She so much did not want it.

Ira opened her eyes. The clock showed just after six. She had already been born. Vitya was breathing softly in his sleep. He always, if he was healthy, breathed quietly and evenly in his sleep. Ira cautiously sat up on the bed and saw that her husband's face seemed to have changed during the night. There was some kind of dark stripe on his upper lip. A smudge of dirt? A shadow? She gingerly touched the dark spot with her finger. A moustache! Had it grown overnight? He must have stuck it there on purpose, to scare her, to make her laugh. Ira grabbed the little hairs and went to give them a yank. And froze. The sheet was different. Not dark blue, as it had been yesterday when she had gone to bed, but a grey one with dark stains. And something else had changed. A box of some kind had appeared by their bed. Something strange, on high legs. She looked at this something and could not guess what it was. She let go of the little hairs and slid off the bed. She walked noiselessly in her bare feet over the cold floor to the box. She peeked.

There was a baby sleeping in the box. A strange, unfamiliar child, sprung from who knew where. Suddenly it opened its eyes. Ira let out a shriek of surprise as the baby looked at her and smacked its lips. The baby screwed up its face at her shriek and started to cry. She did not know what to do. She threw herself on Vitya and shook him awake.

Ira refused to go to the doctor. She did not want to leave the house at all. She would not go near the child. Vitya mined his acquaintances for the phone number of a very good psychiatrist, got through to him, and persuaded him to come and give a consultation. The psychiatrist, speaking very softly–with the result that everybody automatically listened carefully and began to speak very softly in response–elicited that a whole year of Ira's life had disappeared from her memory. Ira was shown pictures: her and Vitya at the warm sea, Ira with a growing belly, Ira with her newborn baby boy.

'What's his name?' asked Ira, looking at the picture of the new baby.

Vitya thought briefly and then said, 'Kolya.'

Ira obediently started calling the boy Kolya.

Attempts to restore her memory were unsuccessful. Gradually, however, Ira came to terms with the fact that this was her child. She even felt that he was dear to her, especially as she was feeding him herself: she had milk. Her appetite grew enormously, but she did not put on weight. Vitya enjoyed making her favourite omelette for her, buying smoked sausages and bringing pickled tomatoes and mushrooms from his parents in Voronezh.

Kolya began to sleep badly when his teeth started to come through. Normally a heavy sleeper, Vitya would wake up instantly when the baby cried in the night. He would get up and go to the boy and take him in his arms and walk from the window to the bed and back again, whispering to him, urging him, pointing to the moon outside the window. Kolya would calm down, and Vitya would tuck him back into bed and lie back down next to his wife. Ira mumbled in her sleep that she would get up next time. But she never managed to get up. She began to sleep very soundly, a dead, dreamless sleep that would not let her go.

By the end of the thirty-second year of her life, the boy was already walking and saying separate words. He was patient and stubborn, and did not get bored on his own. He occupied himself banging the lids of pots and ferreting in the table drawers. Vitya patiently and calmly cleared everything up after him, and hid away anything that could stab or cut. Ira was trying to finish her dissertation, sitting in front of the screen with no idea what word to begin her sentence with.

On the morning of her thirty-third birthday, she once again had no memory of the year she had just lived through.

It was as if her memory was unable to absorb anything beyond her first twenty-nine years. A year would go by, and everything was reset to twenty-nine. Vitya, already knowing what was going to happen, would wake up before she did and wait for her to wake up. He would kiss her, and explain who this boy was who was growing up with them. On the eve of her birthday, they always made the bed with a dark blue sheet, so that she would not be spooked by an unfamiliar sheet when she woke up.

It was not just her memory that was unwilling to remember anything beyond the first twenty-nine years. Her whole body was unwilling to remember anything. Her Caesarean scar disappeared. A tooth she had had pulled out turned up in its old place. Ira did not grow old. A year would pass and she would wake up twenty-nine years old again. Her hair did not turn grey. No wrinkles appeared. Her son grew up. Vitya began to go bald and grew a paunch. The whole world grew old, but Ira did not change. The flow of time was carrying the whole world away from her. One day– she knew it would happen–Vitya would die, and even her son would die, and his children would die, and dinosaurs would return to the planet, but she would still be young and she would remember nothing of the past thousand years, because a thousand years would have passed her by.

The evening before her fortieth birthday, Ira told Vitya and Kolya that she wanted to go for a walk before bed.

'It's already late,' fretted Vitya.

'I just want a breath of fresh air.'

'Yeah,' muttered the boy as she disappeared into the hall. 'A breath of cigarette smoke.'

They were playing chess. It was the boy's turn, but he was not thinking about chess. When the door banged shut after his mother, he said, with an adult's bitterness, 'Tomorrow she'll have forgotten us.'

'Think about your move,' his father prompted softly, adding very quietly, 'Tomorrow has not yet come.'

Ira stepped out of the front entrance and lit a cigarette. She knew that in the morning she would forget everything. But why she would, she did not know. She could not remember. Maybe there was no reason at all. She stood there beneath the dark sky. The cigarette smouldered in her fingers. It seemed to her that it was not she who was forgetting. It seemed to her that the universe did not want to remember her. Ira was standing beneath the dark sky, but it was as if she was not actually there. Not there at the entrance, and nowhere in the whole world. A person who did not exist. In the café across the street, the lights were burning in the windows. She could see tables, and the window display. Someone was drinking coffee, raising a white cup to his lips. Ira tossed away her cigarette and headed across the street.

It was quiet in the café; the music was not thumping out. Ira liked that. She bought a coffee and settled herself at a table towards the back. There were very few people there at all. A couple by the window display and an old man in a black coat by the window. He was the man she had seen from across the street, lifting the cup to his lips. The old man glanced at her, put down his cup, and got up and walked across the room straight towards her table. *No*, she thought, *not that. I don't want to talk to anyone.*

The man walked over, and grasped the back of an empty chair.

'May I?'

'Sorry, no, I would like to be alone.'

He did not hear what she said. He pulled out the chair and sat down. The table was tiny, and she could see his face right up close. His eyes looked at her with an old man's interest.

'Is everything all right?' he asked.

'Everything is wonderful,' she answered.

He was silent. He stared at her cup, at the steam rising above it.

'I would like–'. She got out the start of the phrase, but he did not let her finish.

'Then why are you so sad?'

'What?'

'You have sad eyes.'

All this had definitely happened to her before. This café, that white cup, this old man, this conversation.

'I dreamed about a dog,' Ira heard a voice say. That had happened as well. That phrase. That voice.

'Tomorrow I'll forget everything,' she said to the old man.

She started to cry.

The old man reached into his pocket and pulled out a broken comb, a plastic lighter, a button, and a little box. Tiny, flat, cardboard, in a mica wrapping. He shoved the comb, the button and the lighter back into his pocket. He put the box on the table, and pushed it towards her cup.

'A sedative. I recommend it,' he said, and rose from the table.

Before she had time to object, he was already at the door, already leaving the coffee shop.

ELENA DOLGOPYAT

Ira touched her cup of coffee. It was still hot. She picked up the box, bringing it close to her short-sighted eyes. She read the inscription in tiny letters: *Herbal sedative. No contraindications. Exercise care during pregnancy*. She ripped the mica wrapper off the box and tore off the cardboard lid. She saw one single tablet. She sniffed it. The smell of chalk. She popped it into her mouth, chewed it up, and washed it down with coffee. Almost at once, she felt inwardly quieter, more equable. The lad behind the counter yawned.

In the morning her face had aged ten years. And her son, and her husband, and her mother, and everyone she knew, had to get used to her all over again.

She recovered the memory of all her past years. Of course, she remembered them only after a fashion. We all remember our lives only after a fashion.

VASYA

I was watching them through the window. The big basket was glowing, and they were hefting it through the air and tipping it up, pouring out a stream of red-hot lava. I thought lava came from the centre of the earth. One of the other grown-ups had told me that, not Vasya. Vasya was in a boilersuit and gloves, with an eye shield to stop him going blind. The foundry was in an old brick house, next to all the trackside equipment and the depot where the engines sat waiting. The rails the trains still ran along were shiny, but there were others that were neglected and rusting. Carriages stood here and there on the old rails, with people living in them, like on the barges in Paris.

The carriages were a hundred years old, and at one time had been pulled by black steam engines with scarlet stars on their foreheads and coal glowing in their fireboxes, the engines huffing and hissing. I had a whistle: white, heavy, with copper inserts. It sounded exactly like a steam engine, and was a present from a deaf driver who'd retired. Paris has its river and barges; we have tracks and carriages.

I used to steal up to a carriage, lights glowing in some of its windows, and wriggle underneath it to the other side. I could have gone round it, but I was a partisan, so I wriggled under the wagon packed with the enemy's equipment and manpower and waited for the enemy to move on by. If the enemy suddenly stopped, I sat quietly and looked at his legs. A cigarette butt would fall to the ground. Sometimes a cat would appear and look at me without giving me away. On

ELENA DOLGOPYAT

my wrist, a round watch was ticking; I'd been bought it so I knew the time. Time stared at me with its round eye. Lunch at two o'clock. Dinner at seven. Bed at nine.

Men came out of the squat brick building, washed at the stand-pipe, and sat on wooden boxes. They unwrapped and ate their packed lunches of bread, cucumbers, onions, boiled eggs and sausage. They drank milk from bottles or plain water from the stand-pipe or steaming tea from metal flasks. Smoked cigarettes. Vasya would call me over.

'Why aren't you at home?' he'd ask sternly.

One of the men always answered for me. 'Why should she stay home on her own? It's dull on your own.'

One of them gave me a sandwich.

In the evening my mother tore Vasya off a strip: chase her away, she should be having lunch at home, who do you think I made the soup for? You shouldn't be giving a child that dry food.

We lived in a wooden house with an iron roof. In the evenings we watched our black and white television. A white curtain drew across the window, and outside the window stood an apple tree. I could hear it rustling. Vasya was waiting to be called up. Soon he'd be gone.

He had a girl. She promised to wait for him, but in the August they quarrelled. Vasya would come home from work, have dinner, and go out into the garden to smoke. I'd go and sit with him. I could hear the dishes clinking in the house, my mother washing them in the basin.

At the beginning of September, Vasya brought a small casket home from work, the size of my mother's palm, heavy and hot. Vasya said he'd cast it from pig iron, using an ancient mould. The sides of the casket were openwork, the lid and bottom solid. The bottom was totally smooth and the lid bossed. For some reason, the casket never cooled; it remained hot, like a cake fresh from the oven. Vasya brought it home wrapped in newspaper, and the newspaper took up the heat as well. We put the casket on the hearth, and still it did not cool down. The neighbours came in to see and were amazed. The physics teacher from school came and looked at it. We plied him with apples. There was a ton of them that year.

Vasya was to be called up the following spring, when he was eighteen, so he was still at home with us that winter. He brought us coal, and helped Mum put in the second window frame. He made up with his girl, and she came to see the casket too. Vasya said he'd made it for her, but she was afraid to take it, and so it stayed with us. Not in the hearth, once we'd set the heating going. We put it in a chilly closet, where it didn't cool even when it was freezing. The physics teacher told us it maintained a constant temperature. He brought a man from Moscow to visit us; they'd studied together at some point. The man from Moscow looked at the casket, drank tea with us, told the physics teacher about people they both knew, and treated me like a grown-up. The next day he went to the foundry and watched Vasya pouring lava from the basket. He took the casket back to Moscow to examine it. Vasya missed it and asked the physics teacher how it was doing in Moscow. The teacher answered that it was warm. Why it was warm, he didn't say. He didn't know.

Straight after New Year, people came from Moscow and spent a long time talking with Vasya. I was sent off to bed, but I didn't go to sleep, and listened to everything and watched them through a crack in the curtain separating Mum's and my room from the kitchen. In the kitchen there was an oven, a cupboard, a table, Viennese chairs with cushioned seats, and Vasya's couch.

They sat at the table. Mum poured them tea, and they asked Vasya what he'd been thinking about when he was casting the casket, and if anything else like it had ever happened in his life. The research they'd carried out at the institute did nothing to explain it. Cast iron's just cast iron, they said.

'I wasn't thinking anything,' said Vasya. It sounded like he was smiling.

They went out for a smoke in the snowy garden, and my mother took them a rubbish bin for their cigarette butts. They hadn't brought the casket. They'd left it in Moscow for observation.

In the spring Vasya went away to the army, and I scampered off to the physics teacher to ask him how the casket was doing in Moscow. I wrote to Vasya saying that the casket was warm and the mystery unsolved. I imagined him smiling as he read it.

Vasya came back and married his girl. They had little Aleksey, and still the casket did not cool.

A few years later the physics teacher told us it had been broken. A new boss had come to the Moscow Institute, a total fool, and told them to break it up. The bits were no longer warm, and they'd thrown them away.

'Well,' said Vasya. And said no more on the subject.

He and the physics teacher had a smoke and went their separate ways.

After that, my mother made a habit of blaming everything that went wrong on the Fool from Moscow. If he hadn't broken the casket, she said, the Soviet Union wouldn't have fallen apart, Uncle Lyosha wouldn't have taken to drink, there wouldn't have been any terrorist attacks, and we would not have lost Vasya so early.

A JOURNEY

Sergey set off on a journey. He was about twelve. At least that's what I've been told. I don't know any of this first-hand; I'm just passing the story along. Twelve, so 1935. Summer.

He took bread, salt, water in a soldier's flask, and set off.

It was early morning when he made his way from the back step onto the path. By midday he'd reached the slender young rowan. Five paces for his gran, when she wasn't hurrying. Sergey was in even less of a hurry. The speed at which he progressed was pretty much that of the hands of a clock, or a plant ; a plant, after all, does make progress.

It's not that his main aim was to travel slowly. He travelled in detail.

He lay on the ground and examined blades of grass, beetles, cigarette butts, tiny beads of glass. There was so much of everything.

His gran was vexed. 'He's a big boy now,' she said. She put up with it until lunch and then told Sergey to fill the tub with water.

Sergey filled the tub, and his gran sat him down for lunch. He ate obediently, and prepared to set off once more. All over again. After all, over the last few hours, new blades of grass had replaced the old, some of the beetles had scuttled away, others had died, and others still had been born. Sergey observed all of them, from the step to the rowan, right until evening. He even went on into the night, using his torch to light up his discoveries, until his gran chased him to bed with a broom.

In 1941 he went off to the war, and in 1945 he came back.

He sat for a while on the back step, looking at the rowan, then set off to take up a job in the railway workshop. He worked there until his pension, and another five years on top of that.

I remember him as a grey-haired old man with a cigarette. On the back step. In the twilight.

The path. The rowan tree. A red glow. His grandson Nikolay riding his bike.

ABOUT THE AUTHOR

Elena Dolgopyat is from Murom, in the Vladimir region of Russia. She graduated from the Moscow Institute of Railway Engineering (now the Moscow State University of Railway Engineering) in 1986, and worked until 1989 as a programmer at a military facility in the Moscow region. In 1993 she graduated from the Gerasimov Institute of Cinematography, and has worked at the State Central Museum of Cinema in Moscow since 1995.

She was first published in 1993, and has published short stories, novella-length works, and several television serial and film screenplays. Her three short story collections are: 'Rodina' ('Homeland', 2016), which was shortlisted for the 2017 Russian National Bestseller prize; 'Russkoye' ('Russianness', 2018); and 'Chuzhaya Zhizn' (*Someone Else's Life*, 2019), longlisted for the 2020 Yasnaya Polyana prize. The story 'The Facility' from *Someone Else's Life* was runner-up for the 2020 Babel Prize. Her story 'Soobshcheniya s planety' ('Messages from the Planet'), published in the literary journal *Novyy Mir* in 2021, was longlisted for the fifth annual Babel award.

ABOUT THE TRANSLATOR

Richard Coombes has written music, songs and stories of his own, and translates Russian literature (verse, prose, and song lyrics) into English.

Richard's recently published translations include short stories by Elena Dolgopyat and poetry by Lyudmila Knyazeva, Dmitry Vodennikov and Tatiana Voltskaya in a variety of literary journals; poetry for the Second World War in a poetry collection 'Frontovaya Lira' (*Poems from the Front*), nominated for 'Book of the Year 2021' in a category specifically relating to the Second World War; and a variety of poems for the bilingual anthology *Disbelief*, published by Smokestack Books in January 2023. Richard and his colleagues are already working on a follow-up to *Disbelief*. Richard's translations of Pavel Basinsky's documentary-thriller-biography 'Posmotrite na menya' (English title *Liza's Waterfall*) is scheduled to be published in 2023. Richard is currently preparing a translation of Alexey Ivanov's novel 'Pishcheblok' (*The Food Block*).

OLANDA

by Rafał Wojasiński

I've been happy since the morning. Delighted, even. Everything seems so splendidly transient to me. That dust, from which thou art and unto which thou shalt return — it tempts me. And that's why I wander about these roads, these woods, among the nearby houses, from which waft the aromas of fried pork chops, chicken soup, fish, diapers, steamed potatoes for the pigs; I lose my eye-sight, and regain it again. I don't know what life is, Ola, but I'm holding on to it. Thus speaks the narrator of Rafał Wojasiński's novel *Olanda*. Awarded the prestigious Marek Nowakowski Prize for 2019, *Olanda* introduces us to a world we glimpse only through the window of our train, as we hurry from one important city to another: a provincial world of dilapidated farmhouses and sagging apartment blocks, overgrown cemeteries and village drunks; a world seemingly abandoned by God — and yet full of the basic human joy of life itself.

Buy it > www.glagoslav.com

GŁOSY / VOICES

by Jan Polkowski

In December 1970, amid a harsh winter and an even harsher economic situation, the ruling communist regime in Poland chose to drastically raise prices on basic foodstuffs. Just before the Christmas holidays, for example, the price of fish, a staple of the traditional Christmas Eve meal, rose nearly 20%. Frustrated citizens took to the streets to protest, demanding the repeal of the price-hikes. Things took an especially dramatic turn in the northern regions near the Baltic shore — later, the cradle of the Solidarity movement, which would eventually spark the fall of communism in Poland and throughout Central and Eastern Europe — where the government moved against their citizens with the Militia and the Army. Forty-one Poles were murdered by their own government when militiamen and soldiers opened fire with live rounds on the crowds in Gdańsk, Gdynia, Szczecin and Elbląg.

Jan Polkowski's moving poetic cycle *Głosy* [Voices], presented here in its entirety in the English translation of C.S. Kraszewski, is a poetic monument to the dead, their families, and all who were affected by the 'December Events,' as they are sometimes euphemistically referred to.

A BILINGUAL EDITION

Buy it > www.glagoslav.com

- *The Time of Women* by Elena Chizhova
- *Andrei Tarkovsky: A Life on the Cross* by Lyudmila Boyadzhieva
- *Sin* by Zakhar Prilepin
- *Hardly Ever Otherwise* by Maria Matios
- *Khatyn* by Ales Adamovich
- *The Lost Button* by Irene Rozdobudko
- *Christened with Crosses* by Eduard Kochergin
- *The Vital Needs of the Dead* by Igor Sakhnovsky
- *The Sarabande of Sara's Band* by Larysa Denysenko
- *A Poet and Bin Laden* by Hamid Ismailov
- *Zo Gaat Dat in Rusland* (Dutch Edition) by Maria Konjoekova
- *Kobzar* by Taras Shevchenko
- *The Stone Bridge* by Alexander Terekhov
- *Moryak* by Lee Mandel
- *King Stakh's Wild Hunt* by Uladzimir Karatkevich
- *The Hawks of Peace* by Dmitry Rogozin
- *Harlequin's Costume* by Leonid Yuzefovich
- *Depeche Mode* by Serhii Zhadan
- *Groot Slem en Andere Verhalen* (Dutch Edition) by Leonid Andrejev
- *METRO 2033* (Dutch Edition) by Dmitry Glukhovsky
- *METRO 2034* (Dutch Edition) by Dmitry Glukhovsky
- *A Russian Story* by Eugenia Kononenko
- *Herstories, An Anthology of New Ukrainian Women Prose Writers*
- *The Battle of the Sexes Russian Style* by Nadezhda Ptushkina
- *A Book Without Photographs* by Sergey Shargunov
- *Down Among The Fishes* by Natalka Babina
- *disUNITY* by Anatoly Kudryavitsky
- *Sankya* by Zakhar Prilepin
- *Wolf Messing* by Tatiana Lungin
- *Good Stalin* by Victor Erofeyev
- *Solar Plexus* by Rustam Ibragimbekov
- *Don't Call me a Victim!* by Dina Yafasova
- *Poetin* (Dutch Edition) by Chris Hutchins and Alexander Korobko

- *A History of Belarus* by Lubov Bazan
- *Children's Fashion of the Russian Empire* by Alexander Vasiliev
- *Empire of Corruption: The Russian National Pastime* by Vladimir Soloviev
- *Heroes of the 90s: People and Money. The Modern History of Russian Capitalism* by Alexander Solovev, Vladislav Dorofeev and Valeria Bashkirova
- *Fifty Highlights from the Russian Literature* (Dutch Edition) by Maarten Tengbergen
- *Bajesvolk* (Dutch Edition) by Michail Chodorkovsky
- *Dagboek van Keizerin Alexandra* (Dutch Edition)
- *Myths about Russia* by Vladimir Medinskiy
- *Boris Yeltsin: The Decade that Shook the World* by Boris Minaev
- *A Man Of Change: A study of the political life of Boris Yeltsin*
- *Sberbank: The Rebirth of Russia's Financial Giant* by Evgeny Karasyuk
- *To Get Ukraine* by Oleksandr Shyshko
- *Asystole* by Oleg Pavlov
- *Gnedich* by Maria Rybakova
- *Marina Tsvetaeva: The Essential Poetry*
- *Multiple Personalities* by Tatyana Shcherbina
- *The Investigator* by Margarita Khemlin
- *The Exile* by Zinaida Tulub
- *Leo Tolstoy: Flight from Paradise* by Pavel Basinsky
- *Moscow in the 1930* by Natalia Gromova
- *Laurus* (Dutch edition) by Evgenij Vodolazkin
- *Prisoner* by Anna Nemzer
- *The Crime of Chernobyl: The Nuclear Goulag* by Wladimir Tchertkoff
- *Alpine Ballad* by Vasil Bykau
- *The Complete Correspondence of Hryhory Skovoroda*
- *The Tale of Aypi* by Ak Welsapar
- *Selected Poems* by Lydia Grigorieva
- *The Fantastic Worlds of Yuri Vynnychuk*
- *The Garden of Divine Songs and Collected Poetry of Hryhory Skovoroda*
- *Adventures in the Slavic Kitchen: A Book of Essays with Recipes* by Igor Klekh
- *Seven Signs of the Lion* by Michael M. Naydan

- *An English Queen and Stalingrad* by Natalia Kulishenko
- *Point Zero* by Narek Malian
- *Absolute Zero* by Artem Chekh
- *Olanda* by Rafał Wojasiński
- *Robinsons* by Aram Pachyan
- *The Monastery* by Zakhar Prilepin
- *The Selected Poetry of Bohdan Rubchak: Songs of Love, Songs of Death, Songs of the Moon*
- *Mebet* by Alexander Grigorenko
- *The Orchestra* by Vladimir Gonik
- *Everyday Stories* by Mima Mihajlović
- *Slavdom* by Ľudovít Štúr
- *The Code of Civilization* by Vyacheslav Nikonov
- *Where Was the Angel Going?* by Jan Balaban
- *De Zwarte Kip* (Dutch Edition) by Antoni Pogorelski
- *Głosy / Voices* by Jan Polkowski
- *Sergei Tretyakov: A Revolutionary Writer in Stalin's Russia* by Robert Leach
- *Opstand* (Dutch Edition) by Władysław Reymont
- *Dramatic Works* by Cyprian Kamil Norwid
- *Children's First Book of Chess* by Natalie Shevando and Matthew McMillion
- *Precursor* by Vasyl Shevchuk
- *The Vow: A Requiem for the Fifties* by Jiří Kratochvil
- *De Bibliothecaris* (Dutch edition) by Mikhail Jelizarov
- *Subterranean Fire* by Natalka Bilotserkivets
- *Vladimir Vysotsky: Selected Works*
- *Behind the Silk Curtain* by Gulistan Khamzayeva
- *The Village Teacher and Other Stories* by Theodore Odrach
- *Duel* by Borys Antonenko-Davydovych
- *War Poems* by Alexander Korotko
- *Ballads and Romances* by Adam Mickiewicz
- *The Revolt of the Animals* by Wladyslaw Reymont
- *Poems about my Psychiatrist* by Andrzej Kotański
- *Liza's Waterfall: The hidden story of a Russian feminist* by Pavel Basinsky
- *Biography of Sergei Prokofiev* by Igor Vishnevetsky
  More coming . . .

GLAGOSLAV PUBLICATIONS
www.glagoslav.com